DO NO HARM

OTHER BOOKS AND AUDIO BOOKS
BY GREGG LUKE:

The Survivors

DO NO HARM

a novel

GREGG LUKE

Covenant Communications, Inc.

Published by Covenant Communications, Inc.
American Fork, Utah

Printed in Canada
First Printing: January 2008

15 14 13 12 11 10 09 08   10 9 8 7 6 5 4 3 2 1

ISBN 10: 1-59811-506-5
ISBN 13 :978-1-59811-506-2

To my siblings:
C. Lemar Luke, Diane Spransy, Kathi Magner, and Kirk D. Luke
for their love and support in my continuous mindless wanderings.

ACKNOWLEDGMENTS

I would like to thank everyone who gave me encouragement, advice, inspiration, criticism, and the occasional harsh dose of reality in bringing this book to fruition. My sincere gratitude goes out to my wife and primary editor, Julie; my children, Brooke, Erika, and Jacob; and to my many health-profession colleagues whom I greatly admire—in particular Kenny and Todd. While the characters, experimental drugs, and places are fictional, the science, pharmacy procedures, and ornery customer anecdotes are dismayingly accurate.

CHAPTER ONE

NORTHERN CALIFORNIA

The hypodermic needle gleamed with criminal intent under the harsh fluorescent light. Bria Georgopolis strained against the fetters binding her wrists and legs to the cold metal table. A narrow gag cut into the corners of her mouth; moist with her own saliva, the cloth assaulted her tongue with an offensive, coppery mix of wet cotton, blood, and bile.

Inhaling deeply through flared nostrils, Bria fought to suppress an acrid gorge rising from her gut. With her mouth held open by the gag, her throat burned with dryness and her jaw muscles cramped with fatigue. The restraints at her wrists, elbows, and waist cut into her soft flesh, raising angry welts and weeping abrasions. A throbbing in her head pulsed with vengeance, and her eyes were as puffy and bloodshot as a binging alcoholic's.

As she continued to struggle, Bria's vision narrowed with anger and blurred with hatred. And despite the coolness of the small, concrete enclosure, sweat ran from every pore as if she were basking in a steam sauna.

As the light glinted off the hypodermic, Bria tried to concentrate on the person holding the syringe rather than the needle itself. Ignoring as best she could the pain caused by her fetters, she focused on the plump matron holding the hypodermic to the light. The woman wore a full-body biocontainment suit with a large face shield—the kind used when handling bio-hazardous materials. Bria glared at the familiar figure, bitter tears pooling in her eyes. Normally a caring, forgiving person, Bria could not quell the absolute loathing she felt toward the woman. Nor did she want to.

Betty Mumford, the plump syringe-bearer, smiled affectionately. "Please don't fight this, Bria, honey. You don't want the needle to break off in your arm now, do you?" Betty's voice was eerily muted from behind the acrylic face shield.

As much as the gag would allow, Bria uttered an obscenity, but it was lost in the cotton cloth.

"Now don't carry on like that, sweetheart. It's not becoming of a trained professional. Trust me, dear. If your body accepts this vaccine, you will thank me later."

Betty continued to inspect the large hypodermic appreciatively while humming an obscure yet cheerful melody.

A man previously darkened in shadow stepped forward and ripped the sleeve of Bria's blouse, exposing her left shoulder. He too wore a hazmat biocontainment suit. Bria caught only a glimpse of the man through his large face shield. The man smirked maliciously at Bria before he stepped back into shadow.

Scrubbing the injection area with Betadine solution, Betty said, "Gotta be nice and sterile now. Remember your nurse's training, Bria: 'A sterile dab before you jab,' right honey?"

Normally, the musky, astringent smell of povidone-iodine held a curious comfort to Bria, a cathartic promise of health and recovery. Now it stank as if the woman had just swabbed her shoulder with fetid sewer water. Bria shook her head slowly and tried to articulate the words, "Please don't."

Betty paused and frowned playfully. "Now Nurse Georgopolis, you've got to trust me."

Bria remained silent, but continued to plead with her eyes, looking from the evil woman to the syringe while continuing to shake her head.

"What's this? Bria, you of all people shouldn't be afraid of needles."

Betty tapped the syringe casing and put the slightest pressure on the plunger. A single drop of dark fluid oozed from the long hypodermic. The fluorescent light reflected off the droplet, causing an oily rainbow to swim across its anthracite surface. The vaccine was as black as obsidian. It resembled used motor oil or liquid coal tar, only not as viscous. It lacked any appearance of a medicinal product.

If your body accepts this vaccine. If not? For all Bria knew, it was a cartridge filled with liquid death.

"I've been giving injections here since . . ." Again, the woman paused, struggling to remember a date as a whimsical smirk pulled at her face. "Oh fiddlesticks. Never mind when it was. I can't even remember much of yesterday, let alone anything that far back. Still, I'm holding my own better than most my age. Of course, I've never been the stunner you are, Bria. Oh, I admit my caboose is much too wide, and I sport more wrinkles than a handful of raisins, but overall, I'm as healthy as—"

"Just get on with it," a gruff voice commanded from the shadows.

Betty nodded. Depressing Bria's shoulder, she isolated an area between her thumb and index finger, causing the stained, sterile skin to blanch.

Bria closed her eyes and gritted her teeth. The eighteen-gauge needle entered with a vicious bite. A sharp burning immediately flared from the injection site. Scintillating pinpricks crept spider-quick down her arm, across her chest, and up her neck. Her skin squirmed and crawled. Her face beaded with oily perspiration. Her coarse breathing became shallow and quick. Searing spikes of heat burst in her blood vessels as the vaccine spread through her torso and into her belly. Quite rapidly, everything seemed to take on a preternatural clarity. The throbbing in her head began to beat in cadence with her heart. She became acutely aware of every organ system in her body. She could sense the actual exchange of oxygen and carbon dioxide in her alveoli. She swore she could not only feel her cardiac muscles contract and relax, but was aware of the opening and closing of each arterial and ventricular valve. She could even perceive the follicles on her scalp producing nanometers of hair.

Slowly, the hushed, ambient noises in the room drifted into an echo-filled dimension. The large woman's movements slowed—or at least appeared to.

"Hooooww doooo yoouuuu feeeell?" Betty seemed to ask.

Bria shook her head. It felt strangely disassociated from her neck. The burning in her tissues intensified, as if her metabolism had suddenly accelerated a hundredfold. Her vision blurred until everything looked disturbingly amorphous and ghostlike. Her skin continued to crawl as if infested with tiny worms, but she could do little about it. Although unsure she was accomplishing anything, Bria continued to tug against her restraints.

"Doooonnn't ffiiiighhht iiit, Brrriiiiaa," the woman said from some uncharted quadrant, light-years away.

Bria did not intend to comply with Betty's commands; however, within minutes, she found she had lost all muscle control. Her struggles slowed, then ceased. Her body went limp, and her head drooped to one side.

She took one last ragged breath and closed her eyes.

CHAPTER TWO

TEMECULA, CALIFORNIA

It was an odd place to find a "Pharmacy for Sale" ad, even if it was in *American Druggist,* a medical journal written especially for pharmacists. It was almost as if the seller didn't want anyone to see it—or understand it.

Often, the back pages of such journals were crammed with classifieds advertising study guides for quick licensure in any state, the latest in automated pill dispensers, competitive malpractice insurance rates, and guaranteed next-day job placement firms. Wedged between such ads, the announcement of an independent pharmacy for sale was not an uncommon thing to find. But this notice was not located in the magazine's classifieds; nor was it printed in a way to grab the reader's attention. And it was as cryptic in its pitch as it was in its placement.

Pharmacist Paul Randall looked around nervously, as if concerned that his fellow Value-Mart employees might see what he had found— not that a teenage stock boy or a cosmetics associate would have any interest in such a journal in the first place. Paul was the only pharmacist currently in the store—let alone in the break room. He stared at the strange "for sale" notice, wondering if fate had put it there just for him.

Printed at the bottom corner of an article on *Thrombocytopenia in the Cancer Patient,* the brief ad had only two lines.

Be your own boss. Quaint, small-town
atmosphere. Pharmacy sale a must.

No phone number. No contact address. Nothing to indicate where a potential buyer might inquire after the sale, if indeed that was what the bizarre notice advertised.

Paul again glanced around the crowded employee lounge. A dozen or so associates in department-specific vests ate their snacks and lunches, chatted about the latest nasty rumors, shared past ornery-customer anecdotes, and openly berated the latest profoundly idiotic management decisions.

He frowned and smirked, knowing how easily he could add his own disheartening tales to the woeful banter. Three days earlier, Paul had learned that he would no longer be the pharmacy manager, a position he had held at Value-Mart for nearly five years. After a huge drop in stock value due to a scandal involving Value-Mart's CEO and a lingerie model to which he was not married, the company had restructured its administrative pyramid and eliminated all local specialty management. Instead of letting the pharmacy manager make any in-store decisions, a faceless district manager (who wasn't even a pharmacist) now controlled all functions of the business from his office in Milwaukee. It didn't matter that Paul worked some 1,800 miles to the west and that the DM would never set foot inside his pharmacy. Stripped of all of his decision-making power and authority, Paul was now nothing more than a staff worker who still carried all of the responsibility and extra workload of a manager, but no longer received the respect associated with that title— or the year-end bonus. Additionally, the company decided to limit vacation time to one week, regardless of the pharmacist's tenure. As Paul had already accrued two weeks' vacation, he would now summarily lose one. To say he was bitter was an understatement.

"How you doing, Paul?" asked Kathleen Shields, the Women's Wear department head. She was a forty-two-year-old, triple-divorcee who tried too hard to look and act half her age. The fact that she was ten years older than Paul didn't slow her advances toward him. She leaned over the table and flashed Paul a sultry smile of unnaturally white teeth framed by a face tanned to an unnaturally dark tone. Ever since an accident took the life of Paul's wife fourteen months earlier, Kathleen had yet to pass up an opportunity to give him her best *I'm interested* look. Unbeknownst to her, Paul had more interest in a double root canal without Novocain than he did in Kathleen Shields.

"Hanging in there," he said, quickly returning to his journal article.

"Good for you," she said as she slowly unbuttoned and removed her vest. She did have an impressive figure, but Paul had often wondered which plastic surgeon's office regularly received an allotment from her meager Value-Mart check to pay for her upgrades.

As Kathleen rounded the table, her pungent perfume attacked Paul's sinuses with hair-curling force. She wore low-rise jeans and a tight, pink tee that announced, "I ♥ Bad Boys."

Sitting uncomfortably close, she asked, "Whatcha reading?"

Paul pretended to finish a paragraph before answering. "An article on thrombocytopenia."

"Thrombo-*what?*"

"It's a blood disease. It basically means a low platelet count. Causes lots of bruises, bleeding, that sort of stuff."

"Really?"

"Yeah."

"It must be great to be so smart."

Paul looked at his wristwatch. He still had ten minutes remaining on his lunch break, but he knew he would accomplish little with Kathleen drooling over him.

Paul did not have Hollywood looks, but his combination of sandy hair and pale blue eyes regularly turned more than a few female heads. As a health professional, Paul practiced what he preached, and his daily three-mile jog and biweekly visits to the gym kept his six-foot frame toned and trim.

"Well, break's over," he said, standing quickly and taking his sandwich wrapper to the trash bin.

"Good-bye, Paul," Kathleen sang in a voice loud enough for the entire break room to hear.

"Good-bye, Paul," a small group of Garden Center young men crooned, perfectly mimicking Kathleen's singsong tone.

Paul hurriedly exited the room, head ducked and face flushed red.

* * *

Value-Mart was one of the few mega-chain variety stores that allowed their pharmacists to close for lunch—a measly half-hour break in a twelve-hour shift. Still, it was better than nothing. Opening the pharmacy after lunch was always a chaotic experience, but it helped the hours pass quickly.

After the lunch rush ended, Paul placed a call to the 800 number listed on the publication information page of *American Druggist.* After being forwarded twice and placed on hold for fifteen minutes, Paul finally contacted the advertising department, where he listened to a painfully slow, instrumental rendition of the Bee Gees' *Staying Alive* for another six minutes. Just as Paul was about to hang up, a man with a thick East Indian accent answered the phone.

"Yes?"

"Hello. This is Paul Randall. I'm a pharmacist practicing in southern California. I was curious about an ad in this month's *American Druggist* journal."

"Yes?"

"It's the one on page forty-six, at the bottom of the page. It seems to indicate a pharmacy for sale. Could you tell me anything about it?"

"An ad? No, no, all classified ads are on pages eighty-nine to ninety-three."

"Then can you tell me what this is?"

The East Indian voice sighed heavily, indicating what a horrendous interruption this was in his busy day. "What page?"

"Forty-six."

Paul heard the clicking of computer keys rather than the rustling of pages. "Let's see . . . oh yes. That *is* a strange one. The seller indicated exactly where he wanted the ad placed. It says here he insisted it not be put in the classifieds."

"Is he selling his business?"

"It does not say. He gave no identification and paid with a USPS money order. There is simply a forwarding address—a post office box number."

"Isn't that a bit unusual?"

"Yes, but not out of the question. His money order cleared, and the ad was non-offensive, so we decided to print it."

"Interesting."

"Yes, it is."

Paul asked, "Could I get that P.O. Box, please?"

"Certainly."

The man gave Paul the information—a Mailboxes, Etc. outlet in Oakland, California. He then thanked Paul for reading their magazine and asked if he would like a one-year subscription free with the purchase of an additional year. Paul declined and hung up.

That evening, Paul sat at his computer and roughed out a letter, inquiring after the "for sale" notice. A faint glimmer of hope quivered in the pit of his stomach. Perhaps this was an answer to a prayer—the same prayer he had voiced throughout the past fourteen months.

Paul knew he needed a change. For more than a year, he had been hanging onto the hope that his life would turn around, that it would one day make sense again and bring him the joy he once felt when Debbie was alive.

Death was part of life; Paul knew that as well as anyone. Having converted to the LDS Church three months before Debbie's passing, he accepted death as merely a transition, a stepping-stone to a better place. But death at the hands of a drunkard—a man who walked away from the car accident with nothing more than a scratch on his forehead—was wrong, undignified, wasteful, and worse—faith-shaking.

Value-Mart had allowed Paul three days' bereavement, then expected him back in the pharmacy the following business day. Paul tried to take the offensive amount of time in stride. After all, the company really needed him. But he ended up having to take an additional five days without pay to arrange and attend Debbie's funeral.

He had returned to work amidst a chorus of well-wishes and condolences, but the excitement and love of the profession he once felt no longer sated him. Where each day used to bring joy in helping others, Paul no longer found happiness in his career. There was no fulfillment, no reward. Work was a drudgery—forced labor in which he worked without eager anticipation of future goals or heartfelt aspiration for greater accomplishments. He wasn't suicidal by any means, but he felt as if he had nothing to live for, as if all he had achieved before the car accident was a wistful dream-turned-nightmare that continually reminded him of joys he might never again experience in this life.

The members of his ward in Temecula were helpful and kind, offering meals and other courtesies on a continual basis. Paul appreciated the sincerity of their offers, but the Church members could do little to fill the painful vacancy in his heart. After a few months, the suggestion kept arising to start dating again, to find a new companion and get on with life. But as long as he remained in their house, in their town, constantly seeing things that reminded him of Debbie, he found it impossible to move on. It was more than a feeling of remorse or the profound loss of a loved one—of the woman who had become his soul mate. For some reason, Paul felt an insurmountable sense of blame, self-doubt, and guilt. He was alive. Debbie was dead. Nothing could change that.

Yet, deep inside, Paul knew that change had to come. It simply *had* to . . . if he was ever to live again.

CHAPTER THREE

NORTHERN CALIFORNIA

Bria awoke in a daze. She was lying on a cot in a drab, gray-walled room, which seemed to spin, topple, and sway like some ill-conceived amusement park ride. She closed her eyes and tried to master her unstable equilibrium. She felt as if she were literally on the high seas in a small rubber raft. Some deep breathing and aggressive concentration finally helped to quell the cerebral maelstrom in which she found herself. After a time she slowly reopened her eyes.

The tiny recovery room was more than austere in its décor; it was inhospitable. More like a cellblock than a place of healing, the enclosure resembled an isolation chamber in a concentration camp. Bare cement walls formed a room barely eight feet long and six feet wide. A heavy-looking, stainless-steel door stood at the far end of the room. An exterior, aluminum blind covered the small window in the door. A time-yellowed fluorescent light set in the acoustic-tile ceiling illuminated the room with a flat, sour luster. An air vent, a small speaker, and a dark, softball-sized plastic dome were the only other anomalies marring the featureless ceiling.

A state-of-the-art *MED-STATS* monitor kept track of Bria's blood pressure, heart rate, blood-oxygen level, plasma pH, glucose levels, platelet and hematocrit count, and respiratory rate. Instead of beeping in cadence with her pulse, the monitor purred softy with an electronic hum that quietly competed with the incessant drone of the florescent light overhead. The only other sound was Bria's own deep, ragged breathing, which bounced off the cold walls in a scratchy echo. A nasal-gastric tube entered through one of her nostrils and emptied into her stomach, an IV line fed into her left arm, and a catheter drain ran out from under the thin blanket covering her.

Bria tried to sit up—but nothing happened. She drew a sharp, panicked breath as a terrifying realization filled her medically-trained mind. Hot tears blurred her vision. She swallowed hard and tried again to move.

Still nothing.

Bria turned her head, which, thankfully, moved from side to side. But the rest of her body lay dormant, somehow paralyzed from the neck down. She found she could wiggle her fingers and toes a bit, but that was the extent of her dexterity.

A thousand questions assaulted her mind so quickly that no answers could combat the siege. A single tear coursed down one temple and into her ear. Bria bit her lower lip and forced herself to be rational. She was not going to panic. That was not in her nature and she simply wouldn't allow it. She had never been prone to flighty emotions, and she wasn't about to start.

Bria had grown up old.

Her father, a Greek chef from the Old Country, had walked out when Bria was twelve years old. A deadbeat dad from the get-go. Bria's mother referred to the man in terms Bria chose not to repeat. She didn't like that kind of language. Instead, she preferred to call her father a *ghost dad*. You didn't need to see him to know he had been there—at least once. All she remembered about the man was his thick Greek accent, his dark, gloomy eyes, and an occasional beating when he came home drunk. But Bria's American mother was not a perfect parent either. Within a few weeks of Dad's disappearance, Mom had one grungy boyfriend after another spend the night or move in for a week at a time, then leave when Mom's small, biweekly cocktail-waitress check ran out. No matter—there were plenty of bar-hoppers to choose from in downtown Chicago.

Fortunately, their next-door neighbor was a kindly old widow with whom Bria spent countless hours. Almost every afternoon and evening Bria and Mrs. Hoffman could be found talking, reading, and comforting each other. Mrs. Hoffman had introduced young Bria to the wonders of literature and shared with her numerous stories of growing up on a farm in Wisconsin, where the only entertainment she had was hard work and the printed word. Comparing her mother to Mrs. Hoffman was like comparing locusts to hummingbirds, and Bria easily decided which woman she wanted to emulate.

Realizing she basically would have to raise herself, Bria approached her situation with a foresight normally found in people many years older. Where most children ended up as delinquent as their parents, with dead-end jobs or on state welfare, or on the streets selling drugs or themselves, Bria was able to recognize the downhill road that predicated her future and vowed not to follow it.

At Mrs. Hoffman's urging, young Bria spent untold hours in the Chicago Public Library, finding solace, comfort, and friendship in books. She loved Charles Dickens and Rudyard Kipling, C.S. Lewis and Roald Dahl, as well as many early American poets.

A quote by Ralph Waldo Emerson held a particular significance with her: "*The years teach much which the days never knew.*"

Knowing she could not wait for the teachings of hindsight, Bria lived the Latin verse *Carpe Diem.* She seized each day, anticipating how she might remember it ten years later, and then approached that day with firm determination not to waste one second of it. It was a technique she called "fast forwarding."

Keeping her mom sober and earning enough money to avoid being sequestered to foster care was a relentless and often unrewarding job. As soon as she was able, Bria worked random odd jobs to help supplement Mom's sporadic tips and pitiful income.

Near the end of Bria's seventeenth year, Mrs. Hoffman passed away in her sleep. Bria was crushed and spent several days alone in her room using up boxes of Kleenex. The day Bria turned eighteen, she said goodbye to her mother and moved out. It was the best decision of her life.

A full-time job and full-time nursing school kept Bria from the Windy City social scene. She didn't mind. You don't miss what you've never had. Locked in her tiny studio apartment, Bria spent the hours poring over texts, reading classic literature, and listening to classical music. Social playtime was an alien concept to her. While she had many male schoolmates vying for her attention, Bria had little interest in wasting time on romance. Because of her father's poor example, and seeing how shamefully men used her mother, Bria simply did not trust the opposite sex. Several times her mother's current boyfriend took a greater interest in her than in her mother. She quickly learned that it was best not to be at home when Mom had a male guest with her. The lewd glances, the disgusting innuendoes, and the constant battle to avoid being groped were more than Bria could stand.

By what she considered a heartless act of fate, Bria was exceptionally beautiful. People were constantly telling her that she had a perfect figure, that her looks were model-worthy, and that she was visually stunning, and very photogenic. On more than one occasion, classmates referred to Bria as a young Sophia Loren. Her thick, dark, lustrous hair framed a perfectly proportioned face, heavily lidded, almond-shaped eyes of liquid-brown coloring, and a full mouth that naturally formed a playful, yet unintentionally smoldering smile. She was naturally pretty without makeup—with makeup, she was devastating.

But Bria was not wearing makeup now, nor was she smiling.

She had little reason to smile.

She didn't know why she couldn't move. She didn't know where she was. Even worse, she had no idea how she got there. Her memory of the past several days—weeks?—was mysteriously nonexistent.

Bria took several deep breaths and called out, "Hello?"

Surprised by the hoarseness of her voice, she cleared her throat and swallowed. It didn't help. "Hello?" she croaked again.

The ceiling speaker crackled to life. "How you doin', Miss Georgopolis?" It was a young man's voice, clipped with a nasally East Coast accent.

Bria scrutinized the dark dome in the ceiling, wondering if it contained a CCTV camera. It probably did.

"How do I look?" She didn't really care about her appearance—she wanted to confirm she was being observed.

"You're a hot number in my book, Miss Georgopolis."

"Thanks. Where am I?"

"You're bein' taken care of," the young man said. "You thirsty or anything?"

"Terribly. I could use some water."

"I'll send someone right in." The speaker clicked off.

Within seconds, the door opened with a *whoosh* of pressurized air. Someone in a white hazmat suit entered holding a plastic cup and straw. The large face shield revealed a bland, middle-aged woman in a nurse's uniform. She propped Bria's head up with a pillow and helped her sip some water. The cool liquid seared Bria's parched throat. It was painful and refreshing at the same time.

"Thank you," Bria said.

Expressionless, the woman nodded once.

Bria asked, "Why can't I move my arms and legs?"

"We don't know," a man said, entering the room. He was tall, bespectacled, and beak-nosed. He too wore a protective bio-suit. Through his wide face shield, Bria glimpsed a name tag with a radiation exposure chip clipped to his shirt collar. The tag read DR. SMITH.

The doctor waited for the nurse to leave before continuing. His voice, slightly muffled through the plastic shield, was impersonal and detached. "Your paralysis is something we're still trying to figure out."

"Is it permanent?"

"Again, we're not sure. But I personally don't think so. A week ago, you didn't have any sensation in your feet. Now you do, and you can even wiggle your toes."

"My fingers, too," she said, forcing her digits to flex.

"Outstanding," the man said with little enthusiasm.

Bria did not recognize the doctor. He was not one that frequented her place of employment—wherever that was. Panic gripped her chest as she realized her memory lapse was deeper than she initially assumed. Other than accepting a job in California after nursing school, Bria could remember very little—yet she knew she had lived on the West Coast for over three years. She strained to remember. She thought frantically: At first she had worked in Santa Barbara, at the Sampson Clinic. Then she had moved to the Bay Area . . . She recalled having a current job in a hospital of sorts, having a small apartment somewhere, driving an economical car, even having taken a pediatric nursing seminar, a handgun safety class, and a gourmet cooking course . . . but that was it.

Again, she fought wrenching emotions as uncontrollable tears glistened in her eyes. "What am I doing here?" Bria asked after a pause.

"We're observing you for a while. It's standard procedure."

"We?"

The doctor stretched his neck to read something on the monitor. It gave him the appearance of a vulture looming over fresh carrion. He nodded and mumbled to himself before patting Bria on the shoulder with a gloved hand. "You just rest now."

"Wait—please. What's going on here?" she pleaded with an anger-edged voice. "Where am I, and why can't I remember anything?"

"That's nothing that need concern you for now, Miss Georgopolis."

"You've got to be kidding. I'm lying paralyzed in a gloomy observation chamber, hooked to an IV drip, an NG tube, and a catheter, I can't remember how I even got here, you guys come in wearing hazmat suits—and you say I shouldn't be concerned?"

The man tried to put on his best caring-health-professional smile. It looked more sinister than caring. "Yes, but that's actually good news."

A cynical laugh burst from her lips. "And just how is that good news?"

"Well, for one thing, there was a good chance you would die."

CHAPTER FOUR

NORTHERN CALIFORNIA

Five days later, Bria found herself in a room significantly larger but equally devoid of charm. The room consisted of a single window covered by a thick curtain, an extra wide aluminum door, whitewashed walls, and a gray linoleum floor. At least the lighting was brighter and the adjustable bed felt more comfortable. Still hooked to a MED-STATS monitor, an IV drip, and a catheter, Bria had regained movement in her hands, arms, and ankles, but the rest of her body remained paralyzed. Thankfully, they had removed the NG tube.

Bria was sitting up, reading a well-worn paperback—a romance novel with a cover featuring a beautiful, svelte pioneer woman and a raven-haired Native American man whose muscular form looked like chiseled stone. Bold, brush-stroked letters proclaimed the book's title as *Savage Prairie*. Bria had zero interest in such novels, but as there was nothing else to do, she read it anyway.

"Enjoying your book?" a young nurse asked as she entered Bria's room.

Bria chortled. "Not really. There's only so much 'throbbing this' and 'pulsing that' I can take in a day."

"Oh, not me. I love the stuff," the nurse giggled with a slight blush coloring her cheeks. She was not much more than twenty-five years old and stood barely five foot one. She wore her flat brown hair curled out just below her ears in a pixie cut. Her pert nose, close-set eyes, full cheekbones, and large straight teeth gave her an adorable, elfish appearance—she was the kind of person who brightened a room with her effervescence.

"Then *you* should read this," Bria said, indicating the paperback.

"I have. Three times."

"Amazing."

"Well, I bet someone as pretty as you already knows everything there is to know about romance."

"You'd lose that bet," Bria said with little enthusiasm.

The young nurse looked briefly disappointed, then perked up and said, "My name is Nurse Jones, by the way."

"Bria Georgopolis. But you already knew that, right?"

"Yeah, it's on your chart. Would you like some peaches?" Nurse Jones asked while wheeling an adjustable cart to Bria's bedside.

"I guess. Thanks."

As Bria slurped on the puréed fruit, the young nurse set about charting the readout from the monitor and checking the IV line. With an easy smile, she fluffed Bria's pillow and asked, "Do you remember anything new yet?"

Bria sighed heavily. "No. I recall everything from my childhood and from nursing school, and even bits and pieces about my last job . . . but that's where things go fuzzy."

"Well, give it time. The doctors say you're progressing very well."

"Swell. When do I get to find out where I am?"

"You're in a private hospital in northern California," said a serious-looking man as he entered the room. "But that's all I'm allowed to tell you."

Nurse Jones stopped smiling and left the room.

"This room's a bit bleak for a private hospital," Bria commented.

"It's nicer than the containment room you were in earlier, isn't it?"

The man wore a white smock with a stethoscope draped loosely around his neck. He looked about sixty, very professional, with a serious face and silver-gray hair. His demeanor radiated a casual smugness, a condescension that stated he was never to be questioned. Bria felt reflexively defensive as he perused her chart with a scholarly yet disapproving frown. Something about the man's expression, the forced rhythm of his speech, the catching of a breath, told her this doctor was hiding something.

"Why a containment room?" Bria asked.

"You mean you don't know?"

She shook her head.

"We were worried you might be highly contagious."

"Highly contagious with what?"

"An unknown strain of hemolytic virus. You got it from a South American refugee at Mercy Children's Hospital in 'Frisco. Don't you remember?"

Bria struggled against a blank mind. Cloudy snippets of uncertain experiences relating to her job seeped into her memory, yet nothing more about where she worked or how much money she made, or even where she lived.

"I sort of remember the children's hospital . . ."

The man checked her IV bag and grunted softly. "Good. You're an ICU nurse, if that helps you. Highly trained, from what they tell me."

"What happened?"

The man regarded her suspiciously for a moment before answering in a wooden, almost rote tone. "The refugee—a kid about thirteen—came in on a life-flight transport. The Center for Disease Control sent him over from Galveston, Texas. They said he drifted onto shore from the Yucatan or somewhere. Anyway, since Mercy has the West Coast's best children's center, the CDC asked them to take a look at him. You were the nurse on staff when he started bleeding out. They think it's some strain of hemorrhagic Ebola. The virus breaks down the capillary walls of the skin, eyes, lungs—practically every organ. One nasty bugger as viruses go. Apparently, you were covered with this kid's blood when he finally checked out."

"Checked out?"

"Excuse me. When he died. You passed out, and because Mercy thought you might be infected, they transferred you here. Do you recall any of this?"

"No." Bria took a stoic breath before asking, "Am I infected?"

The man shook his head. "We don't think so."

"But you're not sure."

Another shake.

"I notice no one is wearing hazmat suits anymore. That's got to mean something," she pried.

"We're running a lot of tests and are taking every precaution, but we feel you're most likely out of the woods."

Somehow, a tremulous undertone in the man's voice told Bria he was not being completely honest. "Most likely?"

"Yes."

"Thanks for the confidence builder."

The man shrugged. "Speaking of which . . ." He produced a syringe from his coat pocket and uncapped the needle. Bria reflexively shrank back, suddenly terrified but not understanding why.

"What are you going to do?" she trembled.

The doctor smiled as if amused. "I need to get a blood sample— just a couple of CCs, nothing huge."

Only then did Bria realize the syringe was empty. "So you're not going to inject anything into me, right?'"

His condescending amusement increased. "Of course not."

He then swabbed the crook of her elbow and drew 5 CCs of blood from Bria's median cephalic vein. Even with a semi-numb arm, she felt the bite of the needle, bringing to mind a horrible experience . . . not long ago.

"Does this place have a name?" she asked shakily as he performed the phlebotomy.

"Not one you've ever heard, I'm sure. It's called The Pathway of Greater Light Research Center—the PGLRC. We just call it 'Pathway.'"

"Sounds religious."

"Kind of," he said, taping a cotton pad on the puncture site. "Anyway, you get some rest now. If you need anything, just ask."

"How about some decent reading material?" Bria smirked, holding up the paperback.

"I'll see what I can do."

As the man leaned forward to adjust a knob on the monitor, his name tag dangled directly in front of Bria's face, a radiation-level badge with the name DR. SMITH printed on it.

"Thanks, Dr. Smith," Bria said, somewhat confused. This was not the same Dr. Smith she had encountered in the containment chamber. Perhaps the name similarity was merely coincidence.

"Don't mention it," the man replied.

"Before you go, can I ask one more question?"

"Of course."

"How is it my paralysis is fading away? Not that I mind."

"We think it's some kind of Bell's palsy. Some forms of Bell's come from viral infections, like yours. The good news is they're almost always temporary."

"Almost?"

The doctor shrugged again.

"And my memory loss?"

Dr. Smith's eyebrows rose apologetically as he twiddled the end of his tie. "I wish we knew."

"You wish you knew if it was caused by the virus, or if it's temporary?"

"Both."

CHAPTER FIVE

CRESCENT COVE, CALIFORNIA

Built in 1929 as a part of a downtown restoration project, Crescent Cove Pharmacy was distinctly nostalgic in its design. A long, granite-top soda counter lined half of one wall, offering a delightful array of fountain treats from days gone by. A high Craftsman-era ceiling boasted a generous flourish of gilt from lingering Victorian influences. At the back of the drugstore, a raised dispensary hid behind a façade of polished brass, dark oak trim, and frosted glass. The quaint apothecary held nearly all of the pharmaceuticals needed to keep the small town free from ailment and disease.

Paul Randall sat at the soda counter nursing a chocolate fizz. With an unreadable expression, Paul stared at his reflection in the mirror lining the back of the fountain. Seemingly imprisoned behind rows of fluted-glass sundae bowls, banana split boats, and glass and chrome candy jars, he looked like a man trapped in a fragile, crystalline cage. But Paul didn't feel trapped. Quite the opposite, he felt newly liberated, finally free for the first time in a long while.

After receiving a favorable reply to his inquiry about the pharmacy ad, Paul had given Value-Mart a three-week notice, cashed in his remaining stock and profit-sharing reserves, and sold his two-and-a-half-bedroom house in Temecula slightly above market value. Now, with plenty of cash in hand, and a promissory note from a large bank in San Francisco, Paul was chasing a dream, hoping to restart his life.

A few patrons sat on other stools, enjoying sundaes or sodas and exchanging small talk. One or two others shopped in the OTC medicines area. It was not a busy evening.

"You'll find the people here a bit stiff at first, but give it time."

Paul shifted his gaze to the man in the white smock. "In what way?" Paul asked.

Val Mince, the old pharmacist, snorted, then aimlessly focused his attention on the slowly rotating ceiling fans. "Well . . . I bought this place back in '62. Folks were still cordial back then: 'Pleased to meet you,' 'yes sir, yes ma'am,' that sort of thing. Still, it took almost ten years before the town stopped asking where old druggist Bastian had gone. He was the original owner. He still did everything old-school when I came on board—actually rolled his own pills, ground his own herbs with a mortar and pestle, lots of compounding and raw chemicals." Another snort. "Quite frankly, I was surprised he didn't grow his own penicillin."

Paul managed a wry smile.

"Anyway, you might feel like an outsider for a time, but don't let it get you down."

"Thanks, Val."

"Like I said in my letter, I've modernized quite a bit. Everything is HIPAA compliant—State and Federal. Computers are new and run a nice program."

"Foundations?"

"No."

"PDX or ScriptPro?"

"No, it's kind of unique. Some computer geek at UC Berkley sent it over when we took on a contract to do a private hospital's prescriptions a long time ago. We no longer have that contract, but we kept the program. You still have to hand-bill some of the old insurances, but most of the new ones go right through. Brooke can help you with all that—she's a whiz at organization and paperwork. I'll be around for a couple of weeks to help you get acclimated." He leaned forward and softly added, "But don't tell the towns' folk I'm leaving, okay? I'm very serious about that."

"Okay, but . . ."

"Why? I have my reasons. Truth be told, I don't want to make a scene. I've been here a long time and a lot of folks might be upset with my . . . *retirement* plans. I'm not one to make threats, but if you squeal before I leave, the deal's off."

Somewhat confused, Paul merely shrugged. "I can keep a secret."

"Good." Val lowered his voice even more. "Because when I do leave, I won't be coming back. Understand?"

The finality of his added statement left Paul with an uneasy feeling. He shook it off. Probably just new-owner nerves, he reasoned.

"I'll manage," Paul assured the man.

"Yeah," Val chimed, returning to his former jovialness. "You'll do fine. Just remember there's a lot of cans around here with some pretty big worms in them."

Paul chuckled. "Okay."

"This town doesn't take to change real well. Got a lot of history— some best left as history. Everything else is just dandy. You'll notice most everything here is well kept and the town doesn't suffer from small-town decay like so many others do."

"Why's that?"

"The mayor is one shrewd guy. Savvy, too. His name is Harold Bright. Used to be a researcher for the government before becoming a big-time investor. He set up the town savings on a few high-risk port-folios just after he got elected back in '86. That upset the town council something fierce—but only for a while. One of the portfolios was Microsoft the day after it went public. He's been mayor ever since."

"Smart move."

"I'll say. And because of that, all public works are fully funded without taxes. But don't go looking into the nitty-gritty of it. His can of worms is the biggest of all. He likes to stay a private kind of guy, even for a politician—and he knows how to hold a grudge, so don't go rocking the boat."

"I'm not usually a wave-maker," Paul assured him.

"Good. That's always for the best. You seem like a nice kid. I'm not trying to scare you with this info, you know. Just trying to give a colleague a leg up before he pushes off on his own."

Paul took a sip of his frothy soda before speaking again. "Mind if I ask you an awkward question?"

Val smiled. "Go ahead."

"If you were in a selling mood, why did you advertise in such an unusual way? You know, instead of putting your ad in the classifieds of several drug journals."

The smile vanished. "Again, I have my reasons. I guess it was my way of limiting semi-interested buyers so as not to waste my time. Plus, I didn't want to make a big fuss. Like I said, it might upset a few people."

"I see," Paul said. He hesitated briefly before asking his next question. "Not that I'm complaining, but I was also wondering why you're selling this place for a song? Surely, it's worth more—"

Without warning, a glass shattered against the far end of the countertop, startling both pharmacists and the other customers. An unkempt man in a tattered trench coat and three days' growth of stubble on his face tossed a five-dollar bill on the wobbling, glistening shards. "For the suds and the glass," he snarled. The man continued to favor the two druggists with an ill-tempered scowl as he stormed from the drugstore in a blaze of contempt. Slowly, the light chatter in the drugstore resumed, along with a few awkward chuckles.

Paul's eyebrows rose worriedly. "Hopefully he's not a regular."

"I'm afraid so," Val scoffed. "He comes in a once or twice a week for his suds."

"Suds?"

"The pressure vat in the back. I use it to make homemade root beer—real brewer's yeast, desiccated pipsissewa root, sassafras, a touch of malt, raw sugar. Best doggone root beer on the planet, if I do say so myself. Just shy of illegal."

"Fermented?"

"No, but don't tell Bill Fowler that. He's a recovered alcoholic and likes to think he's beating the system."

"Bill Fowler is the glass-breaker?"

Val nodded. "Anytime he gets riled, which is just about always, he feels the need to break something."

"And he always covers the damage?"

Another nod. "Always."

"What set him off this time?"

A shrug. "You, probably. He hates new faces."

"Great. I hope he didn't overhear us."

"Yeah, me too."

"And the recipe for 'suds'?"

"Laminated on the side of the vat. Comes with the building. Everything in here is yours now: files, records, merchandise, hardware, software, nice customers and the ornery ones too—and all the old-school recipes. I don't want any of it. In fact, there are a lot of old boxes and files Bastian left that I've never gone though. Most of it's personal stuff, not business related. Help yourself to the lot."

"Thanks," Paul said, this time with much less sincerity.

"As I said, the important thing is that you don't mention my leaving to any of the towns' folk. We'll just say you're a new druggist come to help me out. I sometimes have a guy from Ukiah come in when I'm not feeling well."

Paul nodded. "Whatever you say, Val."

* * *

Leaving the drugstore with his new set of keys, Paul drove around the downtown section of Crescent Cove. Craftsman-style lampposts cast a pleasant golden hue on the street and sidewalks. Huge sycamores lined Center Street, creating a mottled canopy that seemed in constant motion, and tiny white lights twinkling in the shrubbery at the base of the trees gave the area the ambience of Disneyland's Main Street USA. A large, central park with a whitewashed gazebo and a manicured baseball diamond offered a wonderful place for an afternoon picnic or an evening stroll.

Just beyond town center, side streets randomly crisscrossed east and west in no apparent uniformity, order, or spacing. Residential homes lined the winding streets, with houses standing on one-half to a full acre of land dotted with mature trees. Many had white picket fences surrounding their property. Almost all were clean and well kept. Where most cities possessed linear, gridlike layouts, Paul felt the odd spacing and randomness of the streets added to the town's charm by limiting the ability of developers to build blocky, claustrophobic, copycat subdivisions. Paul drove his Mustang up and down the streets for almost two hours before heading toward the south end of town.

The Sea View Motel sat just off the highway at the edge of Crescent Cove city limits. A rustic, mom-and-pop establishment, the motel boasted twelve ocean-view rooms, eleven of which were vacant. Paul pulled into the empty parking lot, got out of his car, stretched, then walked into the office.

A woman in her late forties sat watching a small TV set in rapt attention. She had multicolored curlers in her hair and a smoldering cigarette dangling from her lips. Paul stood at the counter for two or three minutes while the woman remained glued to her television. An episode of *Cops* blasted from the set. Paul cleared his throat. It did no good—the woman was in a trance.

"See anyone you recognize?" Paul asked loudly.

Snapped from her stupor, the woman regarded Paul with a menacing frown. A large chunk of cigarette ash dropped onto her Hawaiian-print muumuu and continued to smolder. The woman angrily brushed it to the floor. "What'd you say?" she said with a chain-smoker's gravelly voice.

Deciding not to repeat his ill-fated joke, Paul said, "I need a room, please. Preferably a nonsmoking one."

The woman slid a clipboard onto the counter. "Fill this out, sign and date it. It's a twenty-five-buck deposit, pay by the day or week. How many vehicles you got?"

"Just one. A royal blue, '65 Ford Mustang. California plates."

"Lucky you," she said flatly, slapping a room key onto the counter even before Paul finished the paperwork.

The motel room was clean. It was the only positive aspect of the small space. A mismatch of décor led Paul to believe the owners regularly shopped at garage sales and Goodwill thrift stores. Non-paired lamps sat atop non-matched nightstands on either side of the queen-size bed. Two different weaves of carpet of vaguely similar color joined near the center of the room, and impressionistic, semi-religious, velvet-backed pictures adorned the walls in a mix too non-complimentary to be considered eclectic.

Except for a cracked mirror over the sink, the closet-sized bathroom appeared recently upgraded, for which Paul silently thanked heaven. The best thing about the room was its price. At twenty-five bucks a night, one hundred and seventy a week, Paul could afford to take his time looking for permanent lodgings.

* * *

The following day, Paul got ready for an early morning run. Bending over to tie his running shoes, he noticed that each rested on its own shade of carpet. He chuckled at himself for finding so much humor in the situation. He spent ten minutes stretching, another five doing ab crunches, then exited the motel.

Hidden behind the pine- and scrub-covered foothills, the nearly risen sun painted the eastern sky with a brassy pink hue. Opaque mists filled pockets of low ground and much of the shoreline. The cliff-side town of Crescent Cove was just beginning to awaken.

Paul decided against a run on the beach. He didn't want to ruin his shoes. Instead, he chose to follow Shoreline Drive, a scenic byway that was originally part of California's famous Highway 1. Much to the dismay of road trip junkies, sometime back in the fifties the California Department of Transportation decided to reroute the highway to avoid maintaining the excessively treacherous, narrow road through the rugged King Mountain Range of the northern coast. Connecting with Highway 101 ten miles inland, the scenic route weaved through forested hills and open pasture until it rejoined the coastline in Eureka, some eighty miles to the north. From there, one could parallel the coast, following Highway 101 nonstop into Oregon.

Paul did not plan to run that far. He simply wanted a nice perusal of the town's west side that morning before his appointment with Clem Bagley, a local realtor he'd found listed in the phonebook.

Paul began at a slow pace—no more than a jog, really. He wasn't familiar with the terrain and didn't want to overexert himself his first full day in Crescent Cove. He soon discovered how the town got its romantic moniker. Rugged volcanic cliffs dropped steeply to the shore along the length of the town's coastline, allowing for only a few sporadic, narrow strips of sandy beach. A rocky escarpment jutted into the Pacific Ocean to the immediate north, forming an overlook with a vista that stretched for miles. From there, the cliffs gouged eastward a quarter mile in a concave semicircle that ended in a sharp, pointed grotto, then retraced its curve back to the ocean, gradually widening along the way. Apparent from both the air and the ground, the jagged rock cove formed a perfect crescent some hundred feet deep. A small settlement of just over five thousand souls framed the natural crescent. Naming the settlement was a no-brainer.

A small picnic area bordered the northwest side of the crescent, and the town's cemetery lay just north of that. A stone and mortar sign midway along the path declared the venue Crescent Park.

Paul paused at the point of the overlook and deeply inhaled the cool, briny air. A throaty rumble reverberated up from the opening of the misty cove, attesting to the constant battle between rock and wave. Holding onto a safety rail along the path, Paul closed his eyes and let the sound penetrate his soul. He felt truly at ease. Cautiously, he allowed the sorrows of the past to take a backseat to his present adventure—and to his future. A dim flame of happiness flickered in the recesses of his heart. For the past fifteen months, Paul had avoided kindling that fire, fearing it would be unfaithful to the memory of Debbie. Why had she been robbed of life? It didn't seem fair. It wasn't merciful or just.

Justice and mercy were not strange concepts to Paul. His new religion taught him the need for a balance between the two, and the role Jesus Christ played in maintaining that balance. Strangely, thankfully, he did not harbor any animosity toward the drunk who had killed Debbie. It was an accident—a preventable one, to be sure—but an accident nonetheless. The inebriated man was responsible for taking a life but not for murder. Paul knew Debbie would harbor no ill feeling toward the man; therefore, he felt no need to condemn him either. Yet a bitter churning still plagued Paul, burning inside him over the injustice of the event. Not only had Debbie been robbed of life—in many ways, Paul had too.

Paul shook his head and inhaled deeply a second time. Negative thoughts led to negative actions. He wasn't going to let that happen. He wanted a new start so desperately. He was tired of fighting constant depression. The medications his doctor had prescribed seemed only to mask his feelings, not alleviate them. He used to love life. He used to greet each day with excitement and hope. He used to smile without reason and laugh at the hint of humor. Then Debbie was taken from him, and life screeched to a halt.

Paul stretched his arms over his head and forced himself to smile. This was going to be different. Something about this town, this setting, was going to make a difference in his life. He had felt inspired to come here. Life would begin again—he just knew it. Paul began to feel an honest optimism: a flicker of desire, a spark of hope, a tiny flame of happiness. With firm resolve and a faith backed by his belief in a loving God, Paul finally allowed himself to kindle that flame.

And it felt good.

CHAPTER SIX

NORTHERN CALIFORNIA

The mystery surrounding Bria's memory loss baffled her more than her physicians. Although not a hundred percent certain, the doctors suspected a secondary virus. At least that's what they told Bria. She was aware of cases where HIV had caused a short-term memory loss in some patients. She also recalled reading an article where a nasty bug called the cytomegalovirus, which normally infects the retina, causing blindness, had moved into the brain tissue and had rendered the patient amnesiac. Additionally, she had seen CDC reports where the mosquito-borne West Nile virus had caused short-term and long-term memory loss in the remote South American towns of Trinidad and Tobago.

Bria shook her head. She could not remember visiting a mosquito-infested area—ever. Nor could she recall the last time a mosquito had bitten her. Surely, it couldn't be West Nile virus. The diagnosis sounded shaky at best.

Bria aimlessly stirred her Cream of Wheat cereal. She was trying her hardest not to be discouraged. Over the past couple of days, movement had returned to her upper body. Her waist, shoulders, arms, and neck were all functioning within normal parameters. She was glad for that. But her legs still refused to respond to cerebral commands, voluntary or otherwise. Additionally, she was worried that the blank spots in her memory might not ever return.

Being self-sufficient since childhood, Bria hated having to depend on others. Her training was as a giver, not a receiver—a practitioner, not a patient. The paralysis in her legs was one thing, but not having recall of how she became this way was more frustrating than anything she had ever experienced. She felt certain now she had never seen a life-flight-Ebola-infected kid from Texas, nor had her skin ever contacted the blood of any ICU patient. She had never heard of *The Pathway* before. And because Mercy was a children's hospital, they rarely saw CDC-forwarded patients. Too many things did not make sense. Something inside told her the caregivers at Pathway were lying to her. But why? Why would trained health professionals intentionally hide the truth from a patient, especially one who had equal training and knowledge? Unless . . . unless the truth was too horrible to reveal.

A man in a white lab coat entered her room. He was middle-aged and serious, but his manner was much more easygoing than the previous physician's had been. "Good morning, Miss Georgopolis. How are we feeling today?"

Bria grinned. "You've got your pronouns confused."

"Excuse me?"

"Why do health professionals always insist on using 'we' instead of 'you'? It's suggesting they're as sick as the patient."

The doctor guffawed loudly. "Okay. You got me. Good question, though."

He was a plain-looking man but was likeable in his simplicity. His dark hair showed signs of graying at the temples, and fine age-lines crinkled at his eyes when he smiled. His shirt was professionally starched, his slacks creased and pressed, and his tie boasted pictures of Warner Brothers cartoon characters: Daffy Duck, Bugs Bunny, Yosemite Sam, Wile E. Coyote, and the Road Runner. *At least this one seems to possess some human qualities,* she mused.

"Thanks," Bria said. "And I feel fine. Any luck on figuring me out?"

"I'm afraid not. But we haven't given up hope yet, so you shouldn't either. Are you enjoying your mush?"

"*Enjoy* isn't the word that comes to mind."

"Are you kidding? Cream of Wheat is one of my favorites."

Bria slid the bowl forward. "Help yourself."

"Something wrong with it?"

"Raisins. Some fool put raisins in it."

The doctor gasped in mock horror. "That's unconscionable."

"Unforgivable."

"Inexcusable."

"Borders on patient abuse."

The doctor clicked a ballpoint pen and said, "I'll make a note of it and reprimand the kitchen staff right away."

"Thanks," Bria smiled.

The physician winked, then began flipping through a chart he carried with him, humming a tune as he did so. Bria recognized it immediately.

"Bach."

The physician stopped humming. "Excuse me?"

"You're humming Bach: 'Sleepers Awake.'"

"Am I?"

"You didn't know that?"

"No. I just like the tune. Are you an audiophile as well as a nurse, an English professor, and a Cream of Wheat aficionado?"

"I guess. I like classical music, mostly. I assumed you were humming Bach's tune with double meaning."

The doctor raised an eyebrow. "How's that?"

"'Sleepers Awake' . . . amnesia . . ." she hinted.

"Oh. Sorry. I didn't mean to imply anything," the man said in a conciliatory tone.

Bria chuckled. She liked this guy. And she felt he was being honest. Extending her hand, she said, "No harm, no foul. Let me formally introduce myself: I'm Bria Georgopolis."

The physician took her hand in a warm, firm grip. "Doctor Smith. Pleased to meet you."

"Dr. *Smith?*"

"That's right."

"Any relation to the other Dr. Smiths?"

The physician chuckled. "None, whatsoever."

"Coincidence then?"

"Something like that," Dr. Smith said. "Listen, a nurse will be coming for another blood sample in an hour or so."

"Another sample? You guys take a new one twice a day. Why so many?"

"We're measuring the changes in your plasma and CBC. We're also looking for white cell differentiation, variances in chem panels, bacterial and viral markers—that kind of stuff."

"Is my blood changing that quickly?"

"You'd be surprised."

Bria felt the way in which the doctor delivered his last statement sounded almost sinister. Perhaps he was simply teasing. But there was a definite undertone in it that was not there in his other comments.

"Now, you just rest up. We want to begin your therapy sometime this week."

"What therapy is that, may I ask?"

"Something a lover of Bach and raisinless Cream of Wheat will appreciate."

He gave her a platonic wink and left the room. It did not instill the confidence or warmth it was supposed to convey. Instead, for reasons she could not readily dissect, Bria shuddered with trepidation.

CHAPTER SEVEN

CRESCENT COVE, CALIFORNIA

The Kingsford house was Victorian in design. Dripping with time-twisted architectural bric-a-brac, moldering gingerbread trim, and deteriorated clapboard siding, the ancient cedar-roofed two-story fairly screamed, *Norman Bates lives here.*

The front door hinges squealed with hair-raising complaint as Paul Randall and Clem Bagley entered the foyer. Bagley, a balding, overweight man in his late fifties, wore a loud yellow shirt and a regrettable green-and-orange plaid blazer with a large purple-and-gold Coastline Realty patch over the left breast. His dark brown polyester slacks didn't help the combination. Not wanting to allow anything to bias his opinion, Paul chose to ignore Clem's unfortunate ensemble.

The interior of the house was in the same sorry state of repair as the exterior. Off the main foyer, a small greeting parlor stood empty on the left side, a formal living room and fireplace, equally empty, on the right. Cobwebs and dust abounded.

Sharing an entrance with the greeting parlor, and accessed through a door beneath the stairs as well, a cherrywood office sat concealed in dark stillness. Empty bookshelves lined the one wall Paul could see.

With closing papers in hand and an uncapped pen at the ready, Bagley said, "A healthy young man like you oughta be thrilled with such a great fixer-upper. Have you done much construction work, Mr. Randall?"

"No."

The realtor hung on Paul's one-word reply as if it spoke volumes. He coughed. "Oh well. Great place to learn. And there's a couple of good handymen and local contractors I could recommend if you like."

"Sure. Thanks."

Paul reached for a light switch and flipped it up. The foyer chandelier glowed to life. Bagley breathed an audible sigh of relief.

"When was the last time the wiring and plumbing were inspected?" Paul asked.

Bagley quickly leafed through his papers. "Let's see . . . I can't seem to find the latest record in here . . . but . . ." The rotund man's coke-bottle spectacles looked powerful enough to see *though* the ream of paper, let alone the small print on it.

Paul smirked. "*Is* there any record?"

Clearing his suddenly dry throat, Bagley said, "I'm sure I have that information down at the office. I know it was done. I contracted the plumber myself. I shouldn't worry, though. They don't build houses like this anymore. Hardwood everything. We're talking walnut, mahogany, and cherry, not just oak. High ceilings. Cornicing and chair-rail wainscoting throughout, imported French wallpaper, the works. A real Victorian masterpiece."

Taking a few steps into the foyer, Paul stopped at the foot of the steep staircase and peered up into the gloom. Stagnant air hung thick in the tall entrance.

After a cursory glance in the parlor and living room, the two men wandered past the stairs along a narrow hallway to the kitchen. There, old met new in a woeful mismatch of cut-and-paste architecture. A sloppy addition enlarged the space to accommodate modern appliances and long-forgotten, urgent needs.

"Who added this kitchen on?"

"I believe Mrs. Kingsford had it done. Her husband was a radiologist down at some clinic in Marin. She claimed cancer caused his sudden death from doing all them x-rays, so she sued the clinic. Pretty ugly court battle. When she couldn't prove his cancer was job-related, they settled for a fraction of what she was asking. She started renovating this place, but her money went faster than she saw it going. When she got to this kitchen, the money was all but gone, so she hired a couple of boys just outta high school." Bagley looked around in mock appraisal. He smacked one wall with the side of his fist. "The addition's solid enough, but it sure is a Kingsford 'match' that won't light."

He burst out laughing at his play on words. When Paul began opening cupboards and nosing around without joining in the man's hysterics, Bagley gave an awkward harrumph and adjusted his glasses. He capped his pen and swallowed hard, feeling one step closer to losing another buyer.

Forcing a cheesy smile, Bagley asked, "You married, Mr. Randall?"

"No."

"Oh well. I bet a good-looking guy like you is quite the ladies' man. I'd lay even money you never sleep alone, am I right?"

Paul favored the realtor with a disapproving glance. "I'm not that kind of guy. Not that it's any of your business," he continued, "but I'm a widower. I lost my wife about a year and a half ago. And I don't sleep around because I don't believe in doing that. Okay?"

Finally sensing the annoyance in Paul's voice, the realtor nodded and busied himself in his stack of papers. Paul continued to examine the old house.

A single step off the kitchen led to a stoop, which housed the back door and, just opposite, a utility room which held the furnace and water heater. A dank, musty odor seeped from the dark furnace room, testifying to decades of neglect. Outside, an early-evening Pacific fog veiled the backyard in an ever-shifting gloom, giving the open space a claustrophobic feeling.

Moving on, Paul found the upstairs was not much of an improvement from the downstairs, except that it was quite a bit brighter. There were no curtains covering the windows in the large master bedroom and small sitting area. Neither were there any in the bathroom or second and third bedrooms. It was a pleasant change from the gloominess of the downstairs.

By the time they returned to the foyer, Bagley looked ready to cry. Real estate was at an all-time low in northern California, and anytime fresh blood moved into the area, the agents swarmed like ants to a picnic. Paul had asked Clem to show him something with lots of nostalgia, and he certainly found that in the Kingsford house. But something was missing. This house not only looked empty, it *felt* empty.

Life was missing here; Paul believed he could change that. He had always felt that a *house* was merely a structure; a *home* was a symbiotic organism. Without something alive inside, the organism began to suffer and die. The Kingsford house had been vacant for almost four years. It was past dying—it was now decomposing.

Paul retrieved a small notepad from his pocket and scribbled down some numbers. He handed a piece of paper to Bagley. "Here's my offer. I know that's not what you're asking, but there's a lot of work needed here. And since I just bought a business in town, I need to save where I can."

"A business? I wasn't aware of any business for sale," Bagley said, truly curious.

Paul could have kicked himself for forgetting his promise to Val Mince. "Um . . . yeah. I just picked up the keys yesterday. But I'd rather not say which until everything's finalized. I promised to keep it a secret."

After a moment's pause, the realtor staggered back as if punched in the stomach. His face blanched and his eyes bulged in terrified enlightenment. "Wait. You listed your profession as a pharmacist, right? You're taking over Val's pharmacy."

Paul shrugged, not wanting to confirm Clem's discovery.

"But—that's not possible," he said breathlessly, almost to himself.

"Why not?"

"Val can't leave. He just can't."

Realizing his bluff was called, Paul fudged, "I don't know that he is right away. I'll be learning the ropes from him for a long while, so I can't see that it's an issue."

Bagley remained silent, lost, staring at Paul's feet as if they held some answer to his anxious confusion.

"Mr. Bagley?"

Slowly coming out of his trance, Bagley asked, "Does anyone else know about this?"

"I don't know. Probably someone. We'd kind of like to keep it private. Why do you ask?"

"He's gonna die," the realtor said, again more to himself than to Paul.

"Mr. Mince? No, he's just letting me take over. He didn't say anything about being ill."

Still not meeting Paul's eyes, the realtor said, "Oh, I know he's not ill."

Paul was confused—and nervous. Val had clearly stated the sale was off if anyone found out about his leaving. Paul couldn't see how a venture as big as selling a pharmacy could be kept a secret, but as he didn't have any proof to the contrary, he would have to assume no one else knew.

"Listen, Mr. Bagley. I'm thinking Val just wanted to lessen some of the stress of the practice. Having another full-time pharmacist on board would do that. The fact that I want to buy the place doesn't mean he's running away or anything. But it does mean that I have to budget my funds to the penny." Tapping the slip of paper, he asked, "So, is my offer acceptable?"

Bagley shook his head, as if clearing an inner fog. "I'm sorry. Let me clear the offer with the bank. They own the place. Until then you'll be staying . . . ?"

"I'm at the Sea View Motel, south end of town. I wrote my cell number under the offer. Call me when you hear anything, or come to the pharmacy. I'll be working this—"

"Sure," Bagley said, cutting Paul off as he turned and ran to his car. No handshake. No good-bye. No final words of encouragement. As it was nearing six o'clock, Paul felt certain the realtor was not hurrying to the bank.

"Thanks for showing me the house," he said to no one but himself.

* * *

Later that evening, Paul found Clem Bagley at Coastline Realty's small office building at the northern end of Center Street. The marvelous potential of the brick-front office was lost to whoever coordinated its exterior façade and interior decorating. Where one would expect a charming quaintness to prevail, emphasizing a small town, turn-of-the-century rustic blend of Cape Cod and California Gold Rush themes, Coastline Realty instead boasted an unfortunate mismatch of late sixties groove, early seventies funk, and avid deep-sea angler showmanship. After one look at the office, Paul immediately understood why the company had chosen the hideous blazer Clem sported.

Bagley's back was to Paul as he entered. The door struck a large brass cowbell upon opening, further adding to the unappealing ambience of the office. A corkboard display covered one wall of the foyer, an area designed to be plastered with photographs of properties for sale, including single-family homes, undeveloped land, and beach-front condominiums. Surprisingly, there were less than a half dozen such pictures.

Paul knew that up and down the entirety of the Golden State, much of small-town California was regrettably nothing more than fond reminiscences captured in black and white snapshots. With their citizenry emigrating to bigger cities offering higher-paying jobs, or mega stores dominating the financial resilience of independent shops, forcing their premature closure, numerous small towns along the West Coast suffered from negative growth. Other than the occasional high-priced tourist town, many older communities were now either ghost towns or decrepit hamlets—a direct result of a dearth of financial attraction. Consequently, towns the size of Crescent Cove usually had an overabundance of real-estate offerings of every kind. It was all too common to see a mom-and-pop shop gone out of business, a bank foreclosure on a restaurateur's failed endeavor, and scores of empty houses for sale.

Paul wondered if he would see a Polaroid of Crescent Cove Pharmacy, but no such photo existed. Val must really be serious about the secrecy thing. Strangely, there wasn't any listing of *any* business for sale in the small town. Crescent Cove seemed to be an exception to northern California's negative-growth trend. Perhaps it was the financial backing of the mayor that Val had mentioned. Perhaps it was simply a great place to live. For whatever reason, no one was leaving.

"Look, I tell you he *is* leaving," Clem Bagley shouted into the telephone. "Yeah, Val the druggist. Yes, I know he's one of the originals. Of course I know the damage he could cause. Yes, I'm certain—I just talked to the guy who's buying him out."

Paul cleared his throat. "I'm not buying him out. He's selling. There's a difference."

Bagley dropped the phone as he jumped to his feet. Apparently, he didn't hear the cowbell. The man was sweating profusely, as if he had just finished a marathon, or, in his out-of-shape case, a walk around the block. His eyes bulged behind his thick glasses, and the florid ruddiness of his face blanched to a bright pink. With his mouth agape as if silenced in mid-scream, Clem quaked with fright.

"Sorry," Paul smiled. "I didn't mean to startle you."

"What're you doing here?" the realtor snapped.

Paul hesitated. "Trying to buy a house."

A metallic squawking came from the dangling telephone. Clem picked it up, turned his back, and cupped his mouth to hide his voice. He mumbled something into the handset, listened, nodded, mumbled again, grunted, then hung up. He cleared his throat and ran his stubby fingers through his nearly nonexistent hair. He adjusted his tie and then turned around with a cheesy grin stretching from ear to ear.

"Sorry about that, Mr. Randall. You caught me at a bad time."

"Sorry. I can come back later in the week . . ."

"No, no. I'm all yours. How can I help you?"

Paul hesitated again. The whole scene didn't feel right. The realtor was hiding something. And that something not only dealt with Val Mince, but now Paul Randall. Still, Paul wasn't usually given to knee-jerk emotions or superstitious portents. He thought of himself as unsuspecting, forthright, and honest in all things and at all times. Call it naïveté, but Paul expected others to be the same way. If he was the cause of some issue bothering the Coastline realtor, he figured the man would tell him about it. If not, then it really didn't matter.

"The Kingsford house?" Paul offered.

Although seemingly impossible, Bagley's smile widened even more. "Yes, yes, the grand old Victorian on Pierpont Street. They've listed the property on the California Registry of Historical Landmarks. Did you know that?"

"No, I didn't."

"Well, no matter. What's it going to take to get you into that lovely piece of history?"

"My offer stands as is," Paul said, a confused frown creasing his brow. "I just thought something was wrong, you know, the way you ran off like that."

"Something wrong?" Bagley stalled. He was obviously fishing for some way to change the subject.

"Yeah, with me buying the house . . . and Val's pharmacy."

"No, no. Don't be ridiculous. Everything is fine here in beautiful Crescent Cove. A perfect place to raise a family. My wife and kids love the place. Did the wife, God rest her soul, leave you with any kids, Mr. Randall?"

"No."

"Too bad. Kids are the spice of life. Never a dull moment with kids around, I always say. Well, you're young. Plenty of time for that, right?"

"I guess."

"Right you are. Now, I've got your cell number and I know where to find you, so I'll be in touch, okay?"

"Okay. Thanks." Paul paused at the door and turned. "Is everything all right, Mr. Bagley?"

"Yes, yes. I'm just preparing the papers to take to the bank Monday morning. If they accept your offer, you're Crescent Cove's newest homeowner. How's that sound?"

"Fine. Thanks."

Paul left the realty office more confused than when he entered. Clem Bagley was definitely withholding information. Paul knew it would somehow affect him—and not in a good way.

CHAPTER EIGHT

SAN FRANCISCO, CALIFORNIA

Frank Orem was not a son that parents would normally brag about. He wasn't even sure he had parents anymore—he hadn't communicated with them since he was eighteen. While outwardly his high school days seemed typical of any teenager growing up in the Bay Area, they actually concealed the dark reality of a classically dysfunctional home. An alcoholic father and a prescription-drug-addicted mother did nothing to encourage good grades, involvement in sports, or participation in social activities. Frank grew up a misfit, an outcast, a natural rebel. Barely graduating from Pacific High in San Francisco, he immediately joined the Navy for the sign-on bonus alone. Sixteen months later, a dishonorable discharge for repeated drunk and disorderly conduct left Frank roaming the bay-front streets of San Francisco in search of odd jobs, an easy meal, and a quick fix. In a matter of months, he had gone from militarily clean-cut and physically fit to an unkempt, homeless vagrant at whom no one would look twice.

No one except Pathway.

Through certain unofficial connections, Pathway knew of Frank Orem's discharge almost before it happened. They followed his rapid decline with eager yet cautious anticipation, waiting to see what kind of contacts he might make—which turned out to be few. Seeing the young man hit the streets and turn vagrant so quickly, the decision-makers at Pathway knew they had another perfect subject. Now all they had to do was wait for the opportune moment to pick him up.

That moment came at an eatery he frequented.

Hunan Gardens was a reputable Chinese restaurant located in a disreputable part of town. With real estate at a premium, even in the seedy downtown district, the Oriental eatery barely fit on a small, triangular block of property, bordered by two lightly trafficked streets and a dark back alley. Still, even with its unfortunate location and inaccessibility, the food at Hunan Gardens was as authentic and delicious as Chinese food could get. The bay-front restaurant was one of the more popular in San Francisco, even among those found in Chinatown, and it regularly attracted a steady flow of patrons, including Frank Orem.

However, the ex-Navy man never ventured between the ornate, red- and green-lacquered dragons flanking the Hunan's entrance to sample its delicacies. Instead, Frank sat in the shadows near the back-door, next to the restaurant's dumpster, to await whatever scraps found their way into its depths.

A chilling fog had already made landfall as Frank squatted in his shadowy hidey-hole. Being a Sunday night, Hunan Gardens was comfortably busy, and he knew that patience would fill his stomach before the restaurant closed at 11:30 PM. Besides, he wasn't terribly hungry at the moment.

Frank's mind drifted as he watched serpentine tendrils of fog leave the bay to creep along shorefront streets and between buildings. Then a movement caught Frank's eye. A shadow in a shadow. Something had entered the alley in which he crouched. He strained to see what it might be. Stray dogs often visited the backdoors of restaurants, hoping for a scrap of food or a bone on which to gnaw. Frank knew that most dogs were more afraid of him than he was of them. But he also realized a number of curs ran the streets carrying all manner of illness and disease, and that a nip from one could bring about a serious infection or even rabies.

But Frank saw nothing more than a thickening of fog as it crept its way into the alley, covering the asphalt with a gossamer veil. He stood and moved to the other side of the dumpster. He was sure something was there, perhaps hidden behind a buttress of brick wall, a collection of drainage pipes, or a pile of trash.

Just then, the back door to the restaurant opened. Frank squatted back into his deep pocket of shadow. A thin Asian man in black pants, a filthy apron, and a sweat-stained T-shirt stepped onto the back stoop and lit a cigarette. The man exhaled long puffs of smoke as he watched the fog slowly crawl down the alley. Delicious smells wafted from the open door, and Frank's stomach gurgled with need. He heard the chaotic clamor of pots and pans, utensils, and plates; there was an almost musical quality to it.

Suddenly, the man on the stoop froze with the smoldering cigarette poised halfway to his mouth. He was staring toward the end of the alley, the same place where Frank had seen something enter. The man squinted into the gloom. He said something in Cantonese that Frank could not understand. When he got no response, he took one last quick pull on his cigarette and squashed the remainder under foot. Turning to go back inside, he glanced once more down the alley. The man looked scared. He quickly entered the restaurant and pulled the door shut.

Easing from the shadows, Frank decided to leave the alley for better picking grounds. Something wasn't right here, and he wasn't in the mood for mysteries or confrontation. He took two steps in the opposite direction when he heard footfalls echoing behind him. Frank quickened his pace, but so did the footfalls.

He stopped suddenly. His heart was beating, pounding in his frail chest. He mustered his courage and turned slowly. The alley was vacant. The amorphic fog moved as if it were the embodiment of some evil spirit. Frank fought to control his uncontrollable tremors. When he resumed his flight from the alley, he instantly heard the footfalls behind him again, closer, moving quickly. Twenty feet from the end of the alley, Frank turned again. A figure loomed over him—a giant of a man, dressed in a long black trench coat, black gloves, and a black Fedora hat. The light behind the man obscured his face, but Frank sensed it carried an expression of evil. The man seized Frank by his ragged coat and shoved him against the adjacent brick wall.

"Good evening, Frank." His gravelly voice oozed with evil portent.

"Leave me be," Frank whined. "I've got nothing. I am nothing."

"That's precisely why we want you, Frank."

"W—who are you?" Frank stammered in despair.

"I am Surt."

A canister appeared in the large man's gloved hand. A fine mist assaulted Frank's eyes and sinuses. He felt his muscles fail him. His mind drifted into realms unknown.

He went limp and remembered nothing more.

CHAPTER NINE

NORTHERN CALIFORNIA

Young Nurse Jones entered Bria's room carrying a selection of paperbacks: *Lust on the Plains, Savage Springtime, Passion Bay, The Forbidden Yearning of Juliana, Haunted Desires, A Knight in Shining Ecstasy,* and *The Old Man and the Sea.*

"I'll take this one," Bria said, picking out the Hemingway.

Nurse Jones rolled her eyes, sighed with resignation, and softly sang out of the corner of her mouth, "Boring."

Despite the medical assistant's poor taste in literature, Bria liked Nurse Jones. She was young and vivacious, and had an innocence Bria found refreshing. She couldn't help but smile as she watched the young nurse flutter about performing her daily tasks. She was one of those people who constantly seemed to be in motion but never tiring.

As the petite nurse drew a sample of blood, Bria asked, "Do you have a first name, Nurse Jones?"

A hesitant concern flashed across the nurse's face. Her body tensed, and her feet suddenly seemed to bind to the floor as if unexpectedly glued in place. She gently massaged the left side of her neck and spoke softly, "Yes . . . but I'm not allowed to say."

Bria snickered. "Your name is taboo or something?"

The young nurse fidgeted uncomfortably without answering. She snuck a glance directly above Bria's bed then quickly looked away. Bria could not see what she was looking at but sensed it was of great concern to her.

"Is it something dreadful, like Prunella or Beautilda?"

Bria couldn't understand why the nurse was not allowed to divulge personal—albeit insignificant—information, but she intuitively realized it was not an issue to force. At least not at that moment.

"Never mind. If you prefer *Nurse Jones,* I can live with that."

The relief in the young nurse's expression was obvious. She did not possess a very good poker face. Bria read a warning of danger in the nurse's eyes as easily as she read the words of the Hemingway paperback.

For whatever reason, Bria knew most of the staff was withholding information from her—information about her condition, about her past, even about the location of the private hospital in which she convalesced. But if anyone was going to be honest with her, it would be Nurse Jones. Eventually.

As the young nurse finished her blood draw, Bria tried to calm the fidgety girl by striking up a light conversation. During their chat, Bria learned that Nurse Jones had attended school at UCLA College of Nursing, and that Pathway had hired her immediately upon graduation. Having no family on the West Coast, Nurse Jones was somewhat of a loner, a trait with which Bria empathized. Curiously, everything the nurse said rang true to Bria—not only in context, but strangely, in tone. Shyly, the young woman also divulged that she had signed on with the private hospital in hopes of falling in love with a rich, single doctor and raising a family on the West Coast. But this private hospital had not turned out to be what she had expected—in many ways.

"Besides, all the doctors here are too old, and none are very good-looking."

Bria laughed. "The ones that *are* rich and good-looking are usually on their third or fourth wife anyway. You don't want to get tangled up in that, do you?"

The young nurse smiled. "I'd give any romance a whirl if I had the chance. I'd love a night on the town, a candlelit dinner, or a moonlight stroll with any tall, handsome man—preferably a rich one."

"Not me," Bria said, shaking her head. "Give me a good book any day. They're much easier to read than men are—and a lot more interesting."

"Oh I'd take the real deal any day, even if he was hard to read," Nurse Jones said with a pronounced blush coloring her entire face.

Despite her naïveté, Bria couldn't help but like the cheerful young woman.

Bria was being honest about her love of books. She was an information junkie, a character trait formed from hours of study and a love of learning. She found comfort in her understanding of things, solace in her erudition. Yet, although she retained a vast knowledge of many subjects, she never flaunted her intelligence with any measure of condescension. Her knowledge was a personal treasure that she did not share flippantly. Perhaps that was why her current state of health bothered her so much. Her amnesia was a chink in her mental armor, a weakness in her inner realm of security. Try as she might, Bria could not pierce the fog masking her memory of recent events. One would think that an episode as traumatic as contamination from an Ebola-carrying patient would stick in one's brain, to be relived again and again in sleep-robbing nightmares and self-condemning regrets. One thing she *did* recall was a snippet about a needle and some rather unpleasant side effects, but that was the extent of it.

For the umpteenth time, Bria mentally rehearsed the story Dr. Smith had recounted. She couldn't bring to mind a single portion of the actual event, or anything leading up to it. But the more she concentrated the more she could recall other things, as if focusing her mind on any one subject forced the amnesia to dissipate. Presently, she could list her routines and responsibilities at Mercy Children's Hospital and could even remember the names of some of her patients. She knew where she lived, how much money she made, what kind of car she drove, the layout and location of her apartment, just about everything dealing with her life before the "contamination." The event itself and everything afterwards remained a blank.

And that ate at her like a cancer.

A dour-looking nurse entered the room. Speaking to the young assistant, she stated, "Nurse Jones, the administrator would like to see you for a moment."

Anxiety returned to the young nurse's face. She gave Bria a fleeting smile then exited the room with her satchel of romance paperbacks. The dour nurse asked Bria how she felt today.

"I'm fine, thank you."

"Any feeling in your legs yet?"

"No, but my toes are tingling like crazy."

"Good. Anything else?"

Bria lightly touched the left side of her neck. "This spot is really sore, but I don't remember bumping it on anything."

"It's from your encounter with the infected kid," the nurse stated blandly. "Can I get you anything right now?" The questions seemed forced, as if the nurse didn't want to bother helping Bria—or any other patient for that matter.

"Yes, I'm pretty sure I don't need a catheter anymore," Bria stated.

The nurse frowned. "That's for the doctor to decide, not the patient."

Bria bristled. "Look, in case you didn't know, I'm a registered nurse. I've practiced for almost ten years in every setting imaginable. I know when a patient requires catheterization or not. And I'm pretty sure I know when my own bladder is functioning voluntarily or not."

Although seemingly impossible, the nurse grew more dour by the second. Her steely eyes and condescending scowl would intimidate the most confident of physicians. But Bria was granite. The crotchety nurse did not like Bria, and Bria was only too happy to reciprocate the emotion. The two nurses glared at each other in silence for several seconds. Finally, Nurse Crotchety—the title Bria decided best suited the sour woman—backed down, slightly.

"I'll ask the doctor," she said between clenched teeth.

"Thank you, oh so much," Bria said as sweetly as possible.

"Is that all?"

"No. This room is rather drab. I'd sure like to see some sunshine and trees and blue sky. How about opening the curtains over that window?" she indicated with a nod.

"I'm afraid that's not allowed."

"Why?"

"Policy. Anything else?"

"Yes. What is your name, please?" Bria asked.

"Why?"

"I just like to know who I can turn to if I need assistance."

"I'm Nurse Jones."

"Thank you," Bria said, struggling not to sound confused, shocked, or troubled. This was the third or fourth *Nurse Jones* she had met. That clearly wasn't right. And despite her self-assuredness, Bria's continually growing angst loomed over her, inside her, poised for the chance to make her panic.

CHAPTER TEN

NORTHERN CALIFORNIA

Frank Orem was too scared to feel the needle enter his flesh, but the burning caused by the "vaccine" radiating throughout his body brought a sobering realization that something wasn't right.

"Just try and relax, Frank," a metallic voice crackled through a speaker in the ceiling.

The bare cement walls and sour fluorescent lighting held little promise of things pleasant. It reminded Frank of the military prisons in which he'd stayed during his incarceration, court-martial, and dishonorable discharge. It was not a fond remembrance.

"What do you want with me?" Frank asked in little more than a whisper. His voice trembled so much he could barely speak.

The speaker in the ceiling did not respond.

The droning electric hum of the monitor to which he was connected sounded like a swarm of mad hornets in his ears. The walls seemed to close in on him as spasmodic twitches rippled under his skin. Sweat beaded on his forehead and ran into his eyes. His heart pounded fiercely, painfully. Each contraction throbbed in his eardrums to the point that he thought they might rupture.

"What do you want with me?" Frank yelled.

He struggled against the restraints binding him to the metal table. Blistered welts formed at his wrists. His muscles cramped with each movement. His skin continued to crawl as if thousands of voracious worms burrowed and fed just under his flesh.

Frank screamed in agony as the pain intensified. He could feel his scalp tighten as his temples bulged and throbbed in cadence with his heart. His neck and back muscles cramped, causing his head to flex back and his body to arch in a painful contortion. He tried to speak but his tongue had hardened in a spastic knot, preventing any noise beyond a grunt, moan, or scream. Unable to swallow, Frank began to choke on his own saliva. Violent contractions of his rib cage forced flecks of blood-tinged air to burst from his lungs.

"What—are—you—doing—to—me?" Frank forcefully barked each barely intelligible word, no longer able to form a fluid sentence.

"Just relax, Frank," the static-laced voice said.

"I—can't—breathe—" Frank's voice cut short as a massive spasm caused his chest to contract violently. The sound of ribs breaking echoed off the cement walls like gunfire.

The metal door swung open, and a technician in a biocontainment suit entered carrying a hypodermic syringe filled with a thin amber liquid. He went directly to Frank's side and jammed the needle into his shoulder. Being in an advanced state of tetany, Frank's deltoid was rock-hard and allowed only partial penetration of the hypodermic. The thin needle bent and snapped, spraying golden liquid over Frank's arm. The technician paused and looked up at the concealed camera in the ceiling.

"Get another vial," the disembodied voice commanded. "Quickly. We've got to relax his muscles."

The technician hurried from the room and closed the door. Frank lay frozen, held in a state of suspended animation by the severe contraction of every muscle fiber in his body. Bug-eyed, he stared without moving, as if frightened by something so terrifying that his eyelids had peeled back, withdrawing inside his skull, causing his eyes literally to bulge from some internal pressure. Then, slowly, they rotated up into their sockets.

Frank stopped screaming.

The biohazard technician returned to the room with another syringe. He uncapped the needle, then paused. He watched the cardiac flatline register on the MED-STATS monitor. Frank's systolic blood pressure was down to 48mm of mercury and falling. His respiratory rate was zero, his brainwaves nonexistent. The technician capped the hypodermic and left the room.

The fluorescent lights flickered off.

CHAPTER ELEVEN

OAKLAND, CALIFORNIA

The giant called himself Surt. That, of course, was not the name given him at birth, but one he chose later in life. No one knew his real name. Not even Surt.

At six foot ten, 292 pounds, the man was imposing. He had pale blue eyes the color of a summer sky. His square jaw and wide brow looked as solid as carved marble, and his muscular physique could double as a Greek statue of the same substance. When freed from its ponytail, his coarse, blond hair hung just beyond his broad shoulders. All his physical traits bespoke a Scandinavian ancestry. He did not know if he was Danish, Norwegian, Swedish, Finnish, or of another Slavic origin, but since he bore the characteristics attributed to those lineages, he figured he must be descended from the Norse gods themselves. At least that's what he'd been told.

Adopting the name of Odin, the chief among Norse gods, felt too egocentric. The name Thor, the god of war and strength, was overused and much too Hollywood for his tastes. Instead, he chose to call himself Surt, a lesser god, but still one that fit his persona.

Surt was one of the Norse gods of death.

The self-named giant waited patiently by his phone. It was Sunday evening. The center always called him every Sunday evening. He never knew the name of the caller—it was someone different each time. But they were always from the research center where he had met the Light—one of the head scientists there. The Light had sent men to rescue him from the authorities after a botched robbery. Then, after spending a few months being "conditioned" at the center, Surt was given an apartment in the Bay Area and specific instructions to collect people when asked. It was a good life, an easy life. The Light paid for his needs and sometimes his wants. Surt did not know the Light's real name, but that didn't matter. He knew he had to do whatever the Light asked of him. Somehow, he knew his future in the eternities depended on it. He did not understand *how* in a real-world sense, but then, many things didn't make sense to him. Again, that didn't matter. His glorious future was set—all he had to do was obey.

Sitting on a sturdy padded bench, the huge man curled fifty-pound dumbbells. Each arm worked opposite of the other, each rep was slow and methodical. His biceps swelled with the rush of blood, growing to the size of footballs. After a set of nine reps per arm, he would lift both dumbbells over his head in a military press of nine more reps. He would then lock his elbows and slowly lower his extended arms sideways, to a point level with his shoulders. Holding this pose for nine seconds, he would raise his arms back over his head, and repeat the exercise nine times. After the last pause at shoulder level, he would lower his arms to his sides and begin the entire set over again.

Nine was a magic number to him. At the center, he had learned it was the number of worlds at Ragnarok in Norse folklore. The original Surt got his name from a volcanic island off the coast of Iceland. Predestined at some future point, Surt was to lead his hordes against the gods of Ragnarok, setting the nine worlds afire with his terrible blade, reducing everything to ashes. The earth would then sink beneath the waves and rise again, green and renewed for a new age, free of barbarian bickerings between gods and giants. Weaker, lesser mortals would then become subservient to Surt's generals, captains, and warriors, who, in turn, would be subservient to him.

Surt knew if he was patient and followed the orders given him by the Light, this bit of Norse legend would literally come true. *When* and *how* were not his concern. The Light had promised him; therefore, it would happen.

His shoulders and arms burned with forced growth. He chose not to ignore the pain but rather to relish it, bask in it, savor it. The stronger he became, the better he could serve the Light, and the greater a god he would become.

He stood and appraised himself in a mirror. Although his physique was indeed that of a god, his scarred face was regrettably mortal. But he didn't mind. He felt contentment in the memory of the fire. It was his fire—one that took the life of his parents and younger brother. It was a purging fire. A purifying fire.

Years earlier, while hiding in their garage just after midnight, he had poured gasoline in, over, and under his father's cherished Dodge Viper. His dad loved that stupid car more than he loved his wife and sons. His dad had severely beaten him once for simply leaning against the shiny sports car. Anyone who touched it would suffer the consequences—even Surt's mother. He had seen his father viciously backhand his mother for mildly hinting that owning such an extravagance was an economic folly, especially when they could barely afford food and clothing. His mother would then vent her anger on her sons. She would berate and punish Surt for growing out of his clothes too fast—like he had any control over it—and for not taking care of his younger brother when his parents would disappear for days. It made Surt's blood boil just thinking about it.

Young Surt had then struck the match. His plan was to burn the car to get even, then get his brother and run away. Being naïve and unfamiliar with the combustibility of gasoline, he had not anticipated the explosive force with which the distillate ignited. Burning fuel sprayed his face. His hair singed to the scalp. Blindly, he stumbled to the wall, found the door leading outside, and pushed through it. Beating his face and head to extinguish the flames, he fell and buried his face in the dewy grass of their backyard. When he awoke, he was in a hospital with no memory of who he was, only of what he'd done. The house and its occupants had burned to the ground. He missed his little brother, but fate had decided the course of his life. He had destroyed the car—as well as his parents. And that memory always made him smile. From there, he was tossed from one foster home to the next, each asking for his removal a few days later. Finally, Surt lit out on his own, living from day to day as fate allowed until that fate took him to a small town in northern California.

The phone rang. The caller ID displayed a set of numbers. The sequence fit the pattern. Surt picked up the receiver.

"I'm here."

"The Norman conquest . . ." a voice began.

". . . was only the beginning," Surt finished.

The large man then pressed a button, enabling a scrambling device attached to his phone line. Anyone not possessing the right encryption sequencers would hear nothing but static. Having completed the password and filtering, Surt said, "All clear."

After a pause, the voice said, "Frank Orem proved unworthy."

Surt did not respond. Following his training to the letter, he waited for instructions from the voice on the line.

"We have another target: A lesser woman living in San Jose, California. She matches the necessary criteria. Will you collect her?"

Surt knew it was unwise to bring in another mortal so soon. If word of Frank Orem's disappearance had spread throughout the Bay Area, cautions would arise and the police might be extra vigilant. But then, Frank was a homeless vagrant. A nobody. They were all nobodies, foolish mortals whose only redeeming virtue was the life they unknowingly would sacrifice to the Light and His brave scientists at the center.

"As He commands."

"Good." The voice then outlined the details of Surt's next assignment. He did not write anything down. Paper always left a trail. Thanks to his superior mind, Surt was able to memorize the information in real time. The information was good.

The woman was a loner, just like all the rest. She had no family, at least none that cared about her. She had no friends, and no obligations other than a menial job.

A chill burned within the giant. Surt's imagination began to run wild. While his physical build initially attracted women to him, the obscene scarring on his face and neck ultimately turned them away, causing some to gasp in revulsion. He hated that. He hated being the object of disgust, or worse—of pity. Women would never fall in love with him. But that was okay. He didn't love them in return. To him, they were his servants anyway—slaves he could use according to his whims. Although he was never permitted to sate his desires before delivering a subject, the Light had made him many promises. If he was patient, he would eventually become a god—then he could have his pick.

"How old?" Surt asked.
"She's twenty-six."
He smiled.

CHAPTER TWELVE

CRESCENT COVE, CALIFORNIA

On Monday morning, Paul showed up at Crescent Cove Pharmacy at 7:15 AM. The only people seen along Center Street at this hour were garbage collectors and paperboys. No retail shops were open yet. Just three shops down from the pharmacy, Bonnie's Sweets 'n' Treats began serving hot coffee, real potato-flour spudnuts, slow-rise cinnamon rolls, and her famous chocolate zucchini bread at 6 AM. The scent of yeast baking, ground cinnamon, butter-cream glaze, and freshly steeped coffee wafted toward Paul, causing a Pavlovian salivary response. He shook his head to ward off such gluttonous distractions and fished for the keys in his pocket.

Paul unlocked the beveled-glass front door and entered. He immediately went to the dispensary and punched in the alarm code. A timed LED blinked off, a soft beep sounded twice, and an LCD readout flashed ALARM DISABLED. Paul stood and looked around the vacant store appreciatively.

The 1940s ambience of the drugstore appealed to Paul on many levels, most of all because it was now his. He had determined on his first visit that he would not change a thing. He loved the look, the feel, the layout—everything about this throwback from history.

The surprisingly up-to-date pharmaceutical room sat ensconced behind a sliding, frosted-glass partition with a large Rx etched into the glazing. High above the glass, a sizeable faux mortar and pestle protruded from the wall, pinpointing the pharmacy's location. The dispensing area boasted many upgrades one would expect to find in a more modern facility. At either end of a long counter stood two computer keyboards and flat-screen Plasma monitors, each linked to a large central processing tower below the counter. Tablets, capsules, eyedrops and eardrops, injectables, inhalers, and other pharmaceuticals sat alphabetized in three wide bays lined with adjustable web shelving. A refrigerator stood off to one side, filled with insulin, suppositories, and a few odd hormone patches. A shredding machine in the back took care of the disposal requirements of the Health Insurance Portability and Accountability Act and the Personal Health Information Act, and a small office to one side boasted a desk, several reference books, file cabinets, and a Dell personal computer. Additionally, Paul found an accoutrement not normally used in a community pharmacy: a DAW Technologies Laminar Flow Hood—a self-contained, clean-room microenvironment used to make biologically hazardous and ultra-sensitive injectable medications. Paul had used a similar flow hood when interning in a VA hospital during pharmacy school. He had not seen one since. For the life of him, he could not figure out why a small town like Crescent Cove would require one.

Paul shrugged. No matter. In all, it was a tight, well-organized, surprisingly modern operation, and he was delighted to be its newest owner.

Sitting at the desk in the office, Paul again wondered why Val Mince had sold the business to him for such a small sum. Perhaps the man was frustrated with fighting insurance company mandates and feeling scalped with each prescription dispensed. That was a predominate feeling among pharmacists nationwide. Or maybe Val could no longer afford the soaring malpractice premiums necessary to run a pharmacy—even a small one. Or perhaps he simply needed a change.

Again, Paul questioned why Val had not run his "for sale" ad using regular methods, instead of opting for the cryptic note he had stumbled across. The answer Val offered of avoiding unmotivated buyers seemed shaky at best. Whatever the reason, Paul felt excited about the chance to start over, to begin a new chapter in his career and his life, and to become a part of a nostalgic, small-town community.

Paul was sentimental in that way. He often thought of himself as an anachronism, feeling he should have been born in the 1940s instead of the mid '70s. He loved the simplicity and fortitude of the baby-boomer generation, the high moral standards and low crime of the era, and of course, the swing music of the Big Bands. The Andrews Sisters, Glenn Miller, Tommy Dorsey, Benny Goodman; all the greats lived in his mind as not only music legends, but also as people who helped a nation win a world war with inspirational songs and patriotic fervor. Now, owning a pharmacy that had seemingly never aged since those days was a dream come true. The only thing that could complete the dream would be to have Debbie there with him.

Wanting to keep busy so his mind wouldn't wander, Paul went to the twenty-gallon, chilled pressure vat and read the directions for making "suds." It was a simple recipe, one he felt confident he could follow with ease. Val never mentioned who supplied the raw ingredients, but Paul assumed that information would be stored in a binder or computer file somewhere. He'd ask Val when he arrived at 8:30. In the meantime, Paul found the ingredients on a shelf next to the vat, and began mixing his first batch of suds as per the recipe. Before he closed the lid, a flash of what he considered inspiration came to him. Leaving the dispensary to search behind the soda counter, he found a bottle of real vanilla extract. He added three tablespoonfuls to the suds mix, sealed the lid, and turned the machine on. The vanilla might add a richer, creamy flavor to the final product, he guessed.

He then walked around the store, examining the layout, locating products, and simply taking in the turn-of-the-century ambience. This place was perfect. It had everything Paul had ever wanted. He felt comfortable here. He foresaw security, contentment, life anew. And, more importantly, he felt blessed.

Paul returned to the back office, closed the door, and knelt. Bowing his head, he offered a heartfelt prayer of thanks. In spite of the strange behavior of his realtor and the unusual way in which he had purchased Crescent Cove Pharmacy, Paul knew this was where he was supposed to be. He *knew* it. Something had prompted him, led him to this place. The reasons why did not seem important at that moment. A warmth washed over his body and through his soul. His heart swelled with joy. And for the first time in a long time, he felt at peace.

CHAPTER THIRTEEN

CRESCENT COVE, CALIFORNIA

After washing his face in the bathroom, Paul turned on the personal computer in the back office. Waiting for it to boot, he perused some of the texts Val had on his bookshelf: *Facts and Comparisons, USPDI, Pharmacist's Letter, Natural Medicines Compendium Database, California Pharmacy Law,* the Orange Book, *Code of Federal Regulations Handbook*—everything required by law and then some. Stacks of drug journals filled the spaces between the reference manuals. Boxes labeled with prescription numbers and dates lined one wall, awaiting transfer to the attic. Current California law mandated the storing of prescription hardcopies for a minimum of three years. Old signature logs stood next to the hardcopies. Since the advent of electronic signature capture, most pharmacies no longer needed to store reams of paper covered with patient scrawl. Soon, everything would be stored digitally, eliminating the need for so much paper.

The computer beeped. The default wallpaper showed a rich, golden-toned still life of archaic pharmacy paraphernalia, featuring a Bunsen burner heating a test tube bubbling with some mysterious blue liquid, a balance scale with brass counterweights on one side and a pile of sulfurish-looking powder on the other, and a large porcelain apothecary jar labeled *Leeches.*

A row of shortcut icons lined the left side of the screen: Accounts Payable, Accounts Receivable, Rx Inventory, OTC Inventory, Soda Fountain Inventory, Compounding Supplies, Ordering Information, Payroll, Misc. Info., Games. The last icon was a simple box that read

PR. A rather uninformative icon, Paul assumed it meant Public Relations, Prescription References, Pharmacy Roster, or even Public Restrooms. He was about to click on the PR symbol when the bell on the storefront door jingled. He had forgotten to lock the door after entering. Paul looked at his watch: ten minutes after eight. Crescent Cove Pharmacy didn't open until nine. He left the office and walked into the dispensary.

With the aid of an aluminum quad-cane, an elderly woman ambled her way toward the prescription counter. She wore a battered, sun-yellow straw hat with a faded plastic daisy on the front, a time-worn, A-line dress from the '50s, and she carried a black purse that could double as a suitcase.

Perfect, Paul grinned. Just like Gammy Randall—a sweet, kindly grandmother type from the good old days. She probably had a purse full of precious-grandchildren photographs, an atomizer filled with perfume that could pass for insecticide, and a hundred and one hand-written recipes utilizing Campbell's cream of mushroom soup. She looked so sweet and unassuming. Paul knew the woman was techni-cally not supposed to be in the store before it opened, but he didn't want to make a bad first impression. This was his store after all, and he could do whatever he wanted. Shrugging on one of the white smocks he had brought with him, Paul greeted the old woman with a broad smile.

"Good morning, ma'am. How may I help you?"

The old woman's eyes narrowed as she appraised Paul, then raised one eyebrow in a suspicious arch. After a long pause, she hefted her purse on the counter, leaned forward, and snapped, "Are you trying to kill me?"

Paul flinched. "I beg your pardon."

"God didn't raise me to be a fool, and I certainly don't like being treated like one—or having to put up with one."

Paul stammered, "I—I'm not sure what you're talking about, ma'am."

"See what I mean? You young folk like to put on such airs with your fancy words and your book learning. You sit on your high horses and think you're so much better than us simple folk."

"Ma'am, I—"

"When I come in for a medicine I expect to get the right one, not something that's gonna kill me. Just because you're the only pharmacy in town, don't think for a second you can get away with this."

Taking a deep breath, Paul said, "Ma'am, I apologize for being new, but as this is my first day here, I haven't a clue what you're talking about."

A forceful puff of air escaped the old woman's pursed lips. She rolled her eyes and stared off to one side with a perturbed scowl.

Paul continued, "But rest assured, if there's a problem with your prescription, I promise I'll do what I can to fix it."

The old woman's disapproving glare returned to Paul and fixed angrily on him as if he were a literal son of Satan. Finally, she slid her voluminous purse in front of her and opened the brass clasp. Eyeing Paul suspiciously, she scooted the purse out of his reach, turned her back, and leaned in to block his view of what was inside. Retrieving an amber prescription vial, she quickly snapped the purse closed, then turned and slammed the plastic vial on the counter.

"I ordered my purple pills, not these stupid little bluish ones."

Reading the vial, Paul learned that the woman's name was Marvetta Bloomfield. The prescription label read Amitriptyline 75mg, with instructions to take one tablet at bedtime for sleep. He opened the vial and looked inside. Sure enough, it was full of pale blue tablets, each imprinted with the marking M37.

"See? You're trying to kill me."

Paul said, "Let me check the stock bottle. I won't be a moment."

Marvetta huffed again. "I don't have all day, you know."

Paul booted the pharmacy computers and then went to the A's in the alphabetized drug bays. He found a stock bottle of Amitriptyline HCl75 mg, manufactured by Mylan Pharmaceuticals. Paul brought the opened bottle to Mrs. Bloomfield and showed her the label and the contents.

"You see, ma'am? The pills in your vial came from this bottle, and it says right here, 'Amitriptyline 75mg.'"

The woman's scowl deepened as she looked from the bottle to her vial and back again. "That bottle's wrong, then."

Paul blinked. "The stock bottle? No, I'm pretty sure it's labeled correctly."

"Not the label, you ninny, the pills inside. You switched them."

"Excuse me?"

"That bottle's supposed to have purplish pills in it, not them little blue ones."

Paul paused, feeling overwhelmed and somewhat crestfallen. He thought he had left this type of narrow-minded, stone-walled customer back in the big city. Small Town, USA, wasn't supposed to have them too. Still, he smiled congenially. "I think I know what happened."

"Me too. You switched the pills."

"No, I didn't. Just a moment please, and I'll show you."

She loosed another burst of air, this one with enough force that Paul actually felt it waft across his face. It smelled of garlic and buttermilk.

Thanking Lady Luck, Paul found an unopened bottle of the same medicine on the shelf. He brought it out and handed it to Mrs. Bloomfield. "This is a sealed bottle of amitriptyline from the same manufacturer. Please open it."

The old lady grabbed the bottle and held it close to her face to read the fine print. She harrumphed and unscrewed the lid.

"Notice that the safety seal is intact," Paul stated.

She harrumphed again. Peeling the seal away, she looked inside and frowned. Her scowl softened somewhat as she looked at Paul. "I don't understand. They're all blue."

"Yes. That's always been the color of Mylan's 75mg amitriptyline. Notice the tablets even have the same marking, M37. That is exactly what your prescription calls for."

Her scowl hardened again. "Well, they're still the wrong ones. They're supposed to be purplish, almost mauve."

Paul recapped the stock bottles. "I'm guessing you got a different manufacturer last time. It's the same medicine, but each generic house puts out its own shape and color of pill. Rarely do they match. Let me check your records and see which brand you got last time."

Returning to the dispensary, Paul figured out how to pull up her file and noted that Val Mince had stocked Sandoz Pharmaceuticals before he switched to Mylan. He returned to the counter and explained the switch to Mrs. Bloomfield. "Sandoz company makes a mauve-colored amitriptyline. That's what you got the time before."

Marvetta put her fists on her hips in a huff. "Well why in the name of all that's holy didn't you tell me when I picked them up two weeks ago? I haven't taken any because I was afraid you'd screwed up, and I haven't slept a wink the entire time."

Several questions flashed into Paul's mind, the most significant being: *If it was that important to your sleep, why did you wait two weeks to bring it back?*

Instead, Paul said, "I am sorry about the confusion, Mrs. Bloomfield. Whoever dispensed the medicine to you should have told you about the change when you left the pharmacy. I am sorry for not knowing who it was."

"Listen, young man, I don't care who's to blame, just get me the right pills."

Paul sighed. "Ma'am, these *are* the right pills. They just *look* different. However, if you prefer, I can try to order the Sandoz brand in the future."

Marvetta opened her purse, threw the vial of blue tablets in, and snapped it shut.

"Just forget it," she hissed. Then, grabbing her cane and pointing the four-knobbed end at Paul's face, she added, "I remember the days when 'customer service' actually meant something."

And with that, she hobbled out of the store.

* * *

Val Mince was late.

At 8:50, still wearing his white smock, Paul opened the front door for business. A slightly stocky, middle-aged woman stood outside, holding a light blue smock draped over her arm, fishing for something in her purse. She looked like a schoolteacher from the sixties—she had a beehive hairdo, wore a paisley blouse, and had tortoiseshell-framed glasses hanging from a chain around her neck. The woman was curiously surprised to see Paul but wholly unfazed.

"Hi, I'm Phyllis," she said, cheerfully extending her hand.

"Paul Randall."

"You filling in for the day?"

"You could say that."

"Is Val on vacation? He didn't tell me about it."

"I hope not," Paul chuckled, trying to keep his anxieties at bay. Buying a pharmacy was one thing. Learning the computer software and store operation was something altogether different. The former could be accomplished in a day, the latter would take weeks. "I was to meet him here a half hour ago."

"Really? I usually open the place. He doesn't wander in until ten or so."

"You have keys to the pharmacy?"

"Sure do."

"But . . . isn't that illegal?" Paul didn't want to start off on a bad note, but the law was the law, even in a small town.

"Don't worry, Paul. I never dispense any prescriptions until Val checks them."

That didn't matter. Current law stated no one was to be in the pharmacy without a licensed pharmacist present. The store could be open, but not the dispensary. And Paul had noticed there was no lock on the door separating the two areas.

"I see," Paul said, obviously uncomfortable with the situation.

Phyllis smiled and walked past Paul. She had an unassuming manner about her. She was the kind of person who took everything in stride, as if nothing would—or *could*—ever bother her. She went straight to the back room and began flipping on lights. The place lit up like an amusement park. Paul didn't recall noticing so much illumination in the store. Perhaps it was the sudden change from the morning gloom. The ceiling fans slowly began to rotate, and the fluorescent lamps under the fountain flickered to life. Phyllis set her purse in a cubbyhole and primped her bulletproof hair in front of a tiny mirror before returning to the sales floor.

"Have you got the computers up?" she asked as she unlocked a safe and removed a cash register drawer lined with small change.

"Yeah. I had to help a customer before you got here."

"Really? Who?"

"A Mrs. Bloomfield."

Phyllis stopped cold and faced Paul with an impish grin. "How'd *that* go?"

"Is she a regular?"

"Unfortunately."

"Then you can guess."

A warm, sympathetic grimace crossed her face. "I'm sorry about that, Paul. It's no way to start a Monday, I know. Especially your first time here."

"I don't think I did much good. I got the feeling she won't be coming back. I sure hate to lose a customer that way."

Phyllis smiled playfully. "We should be so lucky. No, she'll be back. I promise."

Paul watched as Phyllis moved with clockwork efficiency. She obviously ran the place, and Paul was immediately glad to have her on the payroll, regardless of what her salary was.

"So, how long have you worked here?" Paul asked.

Phyllis filled the napkin dispensers on the marble countertop as she spoke. She was a natural multitasker. "Oh, I'm going on nineteen years now."

"Wow. That's great. You must know everyone in town."

Another playful smile. "Just about. Some I wish I didn't."

Paul shrugged. "Every town has its derelicts."

"Those aren't the ones that bother me."

Phyllis next rolled up the large blinds on the front window displays. Paul felt like a fifth wheel just standing there, but he didn't know what else to do. Val was supposed to walk him through a typical day's routine, introduce him to the employees, and familiarize him with the area prescribers. He checked his watch: 8:58. Hopefully, no customers would require complex pharmacy services until Val showed up.

"You mean you've got some exceptionally nasty customers?" Paul asked, picking up the conversation again.

The nonstop Phyllis began straightening bric-a-brac on a display by the register. "Depends on your point of view, I guess. It's the snobby, rich ones or the all-important local government type I can't stand."

He knew both types. "I see."

Paul wandered back to the pharmacy and opened the sliding frosted-glass partition. Raised sixteen inches from the main floor, the dispensary offered a clear view of the entire shop. He felt humorously omnipotent in his lofty perch; most pharmacies were at floor level nowadays. Still, even with his "tactical" vantage point, Paul was strangely apprehensive about the day. At precisely 9:00, the phone began ringing. Fielding questions and requests for refills, both Paul and Phyllis kept busy the next half hour. After things began to lighten up, Paul experimented with the computer software and faxed off a few refill requests to a local physician. He checked his watch again: 9:51.

"When did you become a tech?" Paul asked.

Phyllis was organizing prescriptions on an adjacent counter, setting them out for Paul to check for accuracy before bagging them. "I haven't really. I do tech work, but I'm not officially licensed."

"After nineteen years, shouldn't you be grandfathered in?"

"I am, but I still have to take the state exam, and I hate taking tests."

Phyllis then left the dispensary and began dusting the front counter. Paul hesitated to ask the next question. He didn't want to "make waves" as Val had warned against. He cleared his throat and chuckled playfully. "Isn't it required by law now?"

He knew very well that it was. Since 1995, nearly all states required pharmacy technicians to hold state and national licenses. He was simply trying to find out how strictly they observed the law in a remote, small-town operation like Crescent Cove Pharmacy.

Phyllis shrugged. "I guess. No one here seems to mind."

Paul opted not to force the issue for now, as with the ownership of keys to the place. He wanted to be accepted before he started resolving issues that had roamed aimlessly in the gray areas of the law for so long no one knew when they had first stepped out of bounds.

"Well, when you do decide to take the exam, I'll help you study for it."

Phyllis stopped dusting and turned to face Paul. She looked truly confused. "Are you planning on being here that long?"

Paul folded his arms across his chest and laughed. "I hope so. I'm the new owner."

Phyllis dropped the feather duster and staggered as if suddenly faint. Her eyes widened in confused fear. "What did you say?" she asked in barely more than a breath.

Paul stopped laughing but continued to smile. "I'm the new owner. Your new boss—but don't worry about that. I'm really a nice guy. I bought the place from Val a couple days ago. Didn't he tell you?"

Not answering, Phyllis placed a hand over her heart and leaned against the counter. Her other hand retrieved a tissue from her smock and dabbed her forehead. Clearly shaken, the woman began taking huge gulps of air with which to calm herself. Paul couldn't understand why she had reacted so drastically to his declaration. Surely she had known about the sale of the pharmacy. Val *must* have told her. Paul could not imagine that Val's warning about keeping the sale a secret also applied to his own staff.

Paul hurried from the dispensary and placed a hand on her shoulder. "Are you all right? Do you need some water or something?"

She shook her head and took a couple more deep breaths. Just as she was going to speak, the bell announced the opening of the front door.

Silhouetted against the glare of the morning sun, a wiry man in a police uniform approached them in a casual stroll. The creaking of his leather gun belt and the faint static hissing from his walkie-talkie echoed through the empty store. With his hat in hand, he stood and appraised Paul for some time before removing his mirrored sunglasses. The badge on his chest read SHERIFF BAKER. He sported a thin, cheesy mustache, and a high-and-tight flattop haircut. His tanned face was terribly pockmarked and blotchy, attesting to a lost battle with severe acne some years past. "Are you Paul Randall?"

"Yes sir," Paul answered.

"I need to ask you some questions about the murder of Val Mince."

Phyllis fainted to the floor.

Paul felt like joining her.

CHAPTER FOURTEEN

CRESCENT COVE, CALIFORNIA

Paul helped Phyllis to a stool at the fountain. She was pale and clammy, but tears had not come because she was still in shock. Paul brought her a glass of water and asked if there was anything else he could do. She shook her head.

The sheriff stood back and watched. He had a cold look about him, a steeliness in his eyes that was judgmental, calculating, almost reptilian. Standing only five foot six, Sheriff Baker was not a tall man, but he was wiry and solid. He had the look of a triathlete or a distance runner, lean almost to the point of sinewy. Although physically small, he carried himself with formidable confidence. One look told you he was not a man to mess with. His gaze was accusatory in nature. His mouth remained frozen in a hard line, seemingly unable to form a smile, as if the acne-scarred flesh of his hollow cheeks would not allow the expression.

The sheriff's leather gun belt creaked softly as he shifted his weight. With arms folded across his chest, Baker watched the goings on with measured scrutiny.

Paul brought Phyllis a couple of pills. She took them without pause.

"Those prescription?" the sheriff asked.

"Just Tylenol," Paul said.

After Phyllis had settled a bit, Paul asked, "Did you say Val was murdered?"

"Coroner thinks it might be suicide. I'm not so sure." He glanced at Phyllis, then back at Paul. "Let's talk outside."

Paul stood with his hand on Phyllis's shoulder. She was still faint, her skin drawn and cold. Not wanting to leave her alone, he asked the sheriff, "Can you give us a minute?"

"No. Let's go, now."

Cold. Uncaring. Ruthless. The aura surrounding the sheriff was one of predatory omniscience, as if he knew everything about everyone and was simply biding his time, waiting for hapless citizens to make a mistake and thus condemn themselves.

"Are you going to be all right?" Paul asked Phyllis.

She nodded. "Sorry."

"Don't apologize. I'm as shocked as you are." He glanced at the sheriff. The lawman had one hand resting on the butt of his .38 Chief's Special. To Phyllis, Paul said, "I'll be right back."

Phyllis nodded again.

Paul followed Sheriff Baker through the store. The officer walked directly to the front door and exited. Paul stopped just beyond the threshold, holding the door open with his body. "How was he killed?" he asked.

The sheriff stopped and turned. Having donned his hat and mirrored sunglasses, his expression didn't show, yet his mood was obvious. The lack of Paul's total obedience visibly perturbed the officer. Baker's patrol car sat parked in front of Bonnie's Sweets 'n' Treats, still idling. Rather than answering his question, Baker said, "Let's go for a ride."

"I can't," Paul said.

With his hand moving back to his gun, the sheriff took a few steps toward Paul. "Say again?"

"Look, I don't mean to be rude, Sheriff, but I can't leave the building. It's the law."

Baker took a few more steps and stood so uncomfortably close that Paul could see his own worried face in the sheriff's sunglasses.

"What law?" Baker spat.

"If a pharmacy is open, a licensed pharmacist must be present at all times. I can't leave."

The sheriff appeared to deliberate over the information, as if determining whether Paul was lying. Baker finally nodded and stepped back a pace. "Inside then."

Paul sat on one of the stools at the soda counter. Sheriff Baker stood in front of him, his legs spread slightly, his body tensed, poised for any eventuality. The man didn't know how to relax. He pulled out a small spiral-bound notebook and a mechanical pencil, moving in quick, staccato bursts, as if powered by mechanical servos wired with too much electricity. Paul glanced around the store. Phyllis had gone to the restroom. Thankfully, only a mom and her two children were in the store.

Thus far, Paul wasn't enjoying his first morning on the job. In fact, the confusion and angst of the past hour had brought his temper to an edge, something that rarely happened.

"Your name is Paul Randall?"

"We've already established that."

Baker looked over the rim of his reflective glasses. It was not a happy look.

Paul sighed. "Yes, I'm Paul Randall."

"How old are you, son?"

Paul found it somewhat amusing—and condescending—that Baker called him *son*. The sheriff could not have been more than four or five years older than he was. "Thirty-two."

"You new in town?"

"Have you seen me here before?"

Paul didn't know why the sheriff brought out such a bad attitude in him, but something about the man filled him with spontaneous acrimony. He had nothing against law officers. He respected and held in high esteem anyone who put his or her life on the line for the public interest. Paul always cooperated with investigators when they questioned him about possible prescription forgeries and drug diversion. He had made friends of several deputies, sheriffs, and CHPs in Temecula. Never did he feel angry or standoffish toward them. So why was he acting this way now? Perhaps it was the manner in which Sheriff Baker presented himself. The man had zero communication skills. All business, no personality. He was menacingly detached, subtly accusatory without making accusation. His body remained rigid, ready to strike, like a rattlesnake waiting to lunge at an unsuspecting passerby.

"How long have you been in town?"

"About three days."

"About?"

"Okay then, three days and two nights."

"Where were you last night?"

"I'm staying at the Sea View Motel."

"Alone?"

"Other than the two dozen trained monkeys I bought from the zoo."

Baker's pencil stood motionless on the writing tablet. He wasn't smiling.

Paul chuckled awkwardly. "Sorry. Yes, I was alone."

"What is your business in Crescent Cove?"

Paul looked at the words "Doctor of Pharmacy" embroidered on his white smock. He felt like saying, *I'm a dog catcher.* Wisely, he chose not to. The sheriff was simply being methodical. *Cut him some slack,* Paul chastened himself.

"I'm a pharmacist. I just bought this place from Mr. Mince last week."

"I wasn't aware it was for sale."

"Apparently nobody was."

"Do you have paperwork on the sale?"

"Of course. It's in the office."

"Paid in full, or do you still owe on it?"

"The payment is being transacted though our respective banks. I don't know if it's completed or not."

Baker's brow rose slowly. "Rather convenient for him to die before the money actually changed hands, isn't it." It was not a question.

Paul gritted his teeth. "I don't appreciate the insinuation, Sheriff. I didn't kill Val Mince. If you're going to continue to accuse me of murder, I want a lawyer present."

"I'm just thinking out loud, son. No need to get your feathers ruffled."

"Fine." It wasn't, but Paul felt he should still try to be helpful.

"Anyone see you at the motel?"

"Other than the receptionist, none that I know of."

"Did you go out to dinner in town?"

"Yeah. To the Oyster."

"Who was your waitress?"

"I don't remember. A young girl, probably nineteen. Kinda cute."

That won another raised eyebrow from the lawman.

"Look, I'm not a stalker either. I just went in for a meal and then went back to the motel."

"You go right to sleep?"

"I read for a while."

"What were you reading?"

Paul folded his arms and clenched his jaw. This was getting ridiculous. "Am I under arrest?"

"No."

"A suspect?"

Again, the sheriff looked over the top of his mirrored sunglasses. Slowly removing his glasses and admiring the reflection in them, he stated coldly, "Until I figure things out, everyone is a suspect."

"Then I should definitely have a lawyer present."

"Why? Do you have something to hide?"

"No."

"Then you won't mind a few more questions, will you." Again, it was a rhetorical statement, not a question.

Paul said, "Whatever."

"If you bought Crescent Cove Pharmacy, I assume you're planning on moving into town."

"Yes. I've made an offer on a property already."

"I see."

Paul hesitated. Baker was still scribbling. "Don't you want to know where?"

"Should I?" the sheriff asked without looking up.

Paul shrugged. "You'll find out anyway. I'm hoping to get the old Kingsford place."

The scribbling stopped. "Really?"

Paul nodded.

"It's got some history."

"So I've heard. I understand she was quite the character."

"That's not what I mean."

Paul was getting tired of these games. "Then what *do* you mean, Sheriff?"

"There was a murder there."

Paul blinked. "Whose?"

"Mrs. Kingsford's."

"Mrs. Kingsford was murdered in that house?"

"Yep."

"I wonder why Clem Bagley didn't mention that?"

The sheriff remained impassive. "Don't know."

"Probably thought I'd withdraw my offer if I knew," Paul reasoned.

"Would you?"

Paul stared silently at the lawman. "Frankly, I don't feel that is any concern of yours."

Baker shrugged.

The doorbell jingled as an elderly couple entered the drugstore. They walked directly to the pharmacy. Phyllis greeted them by name. She still looked faint but managed to smile nonetheless.

"So what happened to Val?" Paul asked.

"You don't know?"

"How could I possi—" Paul stopped short, frustrated for taking the sheriff's bait. "Look, Sheriff Baker, I don't know why you think I had anything to do with Val Mince's murder, if that is truly what happened, but I assure you I know nothing about it. I only got into town three days ago. I responded to an ad Val placed in a drug journal, made him an offer, and he accepted it. The last time I saw him was Friday afternoon. He said something about leaving town soon, but not until he had taught me the ropes here. That's all I know. You can verify that information with a Mr. Fowler. He saw me here Friday, and I believe he might have heard me discussing the sale with Val."

"Bill Fowler?"

"Is there another Mr. Fowler in town?"

The question caused an instant look of irritation on the sheriff's face. *Just fighting fire with fire,* Paul wanted to voice. Phyllis waved to Paul.

"Do you have any more questions? Because I need to get back to work."

"No. But I will."

"Fine. Since I'm the only pharmacist here today, I won't be leaving the store until the pharmacy closes at six. Until then, you know where to find me."

The sheriff slowly put his notepad in his pocket and buttoned the flap. He adjusted his gun belt on his narrow waist and chewed on his lower lip, staring at Paul with expressionless eyes.

Paul nodded sharply. "Good to meet you, Sheriff." He then walked back to greet the customers standing at his dispensary. Phyllis had stepped back into the pharmacy.

The sheriff leaned against the marble counter and watched Paul leave. Because he was out of earshot, he moved to the far end of the counter, closer to the pharmacy, not hiding the fact that he was eavesdropping on Paul's business. It annoyed Paul, but he had better things to do than take issue with it.

"It's nice to see a fresh face in town," the woman was saying, "especially a tall, handsome one. Are you married, Dr. Randall?"

Phyllis had introduced the woman as Beatrice Dare, a retired school administrator. She looked to be in her late sixties. Her husband, Daniel Dare, had just celebrated his seventieth birthday. Both were in good health and still full of life.

"There you go again, Bea. Hittin' on the young ones," Danny jested.

"At least one of us still has blood flowing in their veins," she retorted.

"My blood's circulatin' just fine."

She harrumphed. "The only things circulating in your blood are the six doughnuts you ate this morning for breakfast."

"Hey, I can still cut a rug better than guys half my age, doughnuts and all."

Leaning toward Paul, Beatrice said, "He claims he taught Fred Astaire all his dance moves in *Holiday Inn.*"

Paul did not hide his surprise. "Really?"

"Just read the credits, young man: 'Choreography by Danny Dare.'"

Beatrice put a gentle hand on her husband's arm. "Honey that film came out in 1942. You were born in 1935."

"So?"

"You were a Hollywood choreographer at age seven?" She smirked.

"Why not? Shirley Temple did her first feature film at six."

"Oh, go on," Beatrice flustered. "Dr. Randall, do you know how hard it is to live with a celebrity wannabe?"

Paul laughed. This was a very pleasant change from the morning's affairs. "No, I don't. And please, call me Paul."

"All right, Paul. You have beautiful eyes, by the way."

Danny blew an exasperated puff of air. "There you go again."

"Oh hush now."

Phyllis stepped down from the pharmacy with the Dares' prescriptions. "Here you go, Bea. Will there be anything else?"

Before she could answer, Paul interrupted. "Do you have any questions about your medications, Mrs. Dare?"

Beatrice paused with a look of pleasant shock. "Well, I'll be. You know that is the first time a druggist here has asked me that?"

Paul blinked. "You're kidding."

"I most certainly am not. And we've been buying our medicines here for longer than you've been alive."

"That truly surprises me," Paul admitted. "Federal and State laws mandate that consultation be offered on every prescription dispensed, especially new ones." Paul turned to flash a questioning look at Phyllis.

She shrugged. "Val didn't like to counsel."

Paul shook his head. "That's the first thing we're going to change. Mrs. Dare, if you ever have any questions, you just give me a call, okay? The way I see it, a machine can dispense a prescription. A pharmacist is supposed to dispense drug information."

The older woman reached across the counter and gripped Paul by the wrist. "I'm so glad you're here, Paul. Are you going to be in town very long?"

He flashed a sideways glance at the sheriff, who was still leaning against the counter, blatantly listening in on the private conversation. "Yeah," Paul said defiantly, "I plan on being here a very long time."

CHAPTER FIFTEEN

CRESCENT COVE, CALIFORNIA

Business wise, and with the exception of Mr. and Mrs. Dare, the rest of the morning went as poorly as it had begun. Mondays were usually the busiest day of the week in medical practices, especially pharmacies. Luckily, this one wasn't too hectic. A few customers entered the store and milled about, some buying random OTC items, a few more needing prescriptions filled. In the early afternoon, a young boy spilled his milkshake all over the pharmacy counter and his mother dragged him out of the store without apologizing. Between those moments, Paul spent the time absorbing Kingsford history.

Apparently having nothing better to do, Sheriff Baker leaned against the dispensing counter and, in a less confrontational manner, explained to Paul that Mrs. Kingsford was the victim of a random robbery-turned-murder. The investigative detectives combed the house, top to bottom, and found little evidence of premeditation in the event. The lock on her back door showed indications of being jimmied with simple tools, attesting to a novice forced-entry. They also found evidence of an unorganized ransacking of the house. Not worrying about covering his tracks, the burglar left the safe in the library wide open after removing its contents. The man didn't use gloves of any kind, and his fingerprints covered the house.

The old sheriff had found Mrs. Kingsford crumpled in the doorway of the library, dressed in an authentic silk kimono, lying in a pool of dried blood. According to the county coroner, the cause of death—blunt trauma to both sides of the skull—occurred some eight days prior to the discovery of her body. No weapon was found. "The coroner believed the guy used his bare hands to crush her head," Baker stated without emotion. "Crime scene photos are pretty graphic."

"The only remaining family she had was a daughter who lived somewhere in Connecticut," Phyllis explained, "and a son in Saudi Arabia, working for an oil company. Neither of them bothered coming to the funeral."

"That's not right," Paul said. "Even if they hated her they should still have paid their respects."

"I agree," Phyllis voiced. Sheriff Baker said nothing.

"Was there a will?"

Phyllis looked at Baker and shrugged. The sheriff folded his arms and favored Paul with an accusatory look, as if he were under suspicion for the Kingsford murder too. "Not that we could find. All her money went into remodeling the house. The bank held the deed to the property. There wasn't much else."

"But her husband was a doctor. They must have had some money stashed away."

The sheriff grinned knowingly. "A doctor, a compulsive gambler, and a skirt-chaser. Not much of a role model, you could say."

"That's probably why her kids didn't bother returning," Paul reasoned.

"You know something we don't?" the sheriff asked.

Paul sighed regretfully. "No. It was just a guess, Sheriff."

Sheriff Baker pulled out his notepad and scribbled something in it. The unvoiced implication irritated Paul, but he held his tongue.

"You caught the man, didn't you?" Phyllis asked.

Baker nodded. "He was picked up for some public disturbance in Marin two days before the body was discovered. Still had him in the jail, so matching the fingerprints was a piece of cake."

"Who was it?" Paul asked.

"Why?"

"Just curious, that's all."

"Don't know. He carried no ID, and we couldn't find any record of him through Interstate records, FBI, or Interpol. Big fella, too. Close to 300 pounds and a face that would scare a ghost, all scarred up and misshapen like it had caught fire and someone tried to extinguish it with an ice pick."

You should talk, Paul didn't voice. Instead he asked, "What became of him?"

"Why's that your concern?" the sheriff asked with narrowed eyes.

Paul couldn't believe how insolent the man was. The sheriff examined each comment as if he were sitting on the tribunal board of the Spanish Inquisition. Simply talking to him made Paul feel like he was taking a lie-detector test. He knew it was the officer's job, but there had to be more personable ways to accomplish it. A sheriff was supposed to be a friend to the community, a protector of the citizens. Baker acted more like a pit bull ready to turn on its master.

"It's not," Paul said. "But since I'm considering buying the house, I'd like to know its history."

Baker silently mulled over Paul's words for a moment before answering. "A private mental hospital took charge of him after he was declared incompetent. He's still there as far as I know."

"He should have received the death penalty—should have been fried," Phyllis spat. It shocked Paul to hear such vehemence in her voice. "Ruth Kingsford never hurt anyone."

"No capital punishment in California. And if there was, it'd be lethal injection, not the electric chair," the sheriff corrected.

"Murder involving mental illness is a tough one to call," Paul commented.

Phyllis scowled and snorted. "Mental illness, my big toe. He knew what he was doing."

Paul shrugged. He didn't want to argue the point with his assistant, especially in light of the shock she'd just received and, more importantly, in front of the sheriff.

"Did you recover the stolen goods from the safe?" Paul asked.

Baker shook his head. "The guy claimed the safe was empty."

"All the more reason to fry him."

"Lethal injection," the sheriff corrected again.

"Whatever," Phyllis huffed.

"Wow," Paul chuckled, trying to lighten the tension in the room. "That's not the kind of history I like following."

"So you've done this before?" Baker asked, his pencil and notepad at the ready.

"Done what?"

"Happened to be around to buy a house from someone who was murdered."

Paul sighed again. "No, Sheriff, I haven't. Besides, Clem Bagley told me the house had been sitting empty for four years."

"Yeah. I guess four years is about right," he said. He then consulted his watch and slipped his notepad into his breast pocket. Squaring his hat on his head, Baker turned to leave, then paused. Slowly facing Paul again, he favored him with another condescending glare. "Be warned: I got my eye on this place, Dr. Randall. One twitch, and I close it down."

Paul gawked at the man, dumbfounded. "Are you actually threatening me, Sheriff?"

"It wasn't a threat," he said, tipping his hat. "It's a guarantee."

CHAPTER SIXTEEN

NORTHERN CALIFORNIA

Bria remained leery of everyone. She didn't sense any immediate danger, but a confusing sense of being left in the dark filled her with reticence. The avoided questions, the redundant names . . . Thus far, the only one she felt she could trust was Young Nurse Jones—the romance novel enthusiast.

When the young nurse delivered the evening meal, Bria quietly asked, "What's with the indicators on your name tag?"

"What do you mean?" she responded, barely masking a fearful edge to her voice.

"The radiation indicators you all wear. Is the hospital next to a fission reactor or something?"

"Of course not." The young nurse chuckled. "They measure radon levels, not radiation."

"Radon? Like in the basements of old houses? Why's that a concern in this hospital?"

The young nurse fidgeted. "I—I'm not at liberty to say."

"Oh, come on, Nurse *Jones,* why all the cloak-and-dagger?"

She stiffened. "I don't know what you're talking about."

Even softer, Bria said, "Come on, please. You know exactly what I mean. I know you do." At least she thought so.

In a way she couldn't understand, Bria knew when someone was being truthful or lying. There was a timbre—a strange quavering undertone—in a person's voice that revealed the level of honesty in whatever they said. Bria wasn't positive, but she swore she could detect a fabrication. It was a skill she knew she hadn't possessed before coming to Pathway.

Again the nurse flashed a pensive glance above Bria's bed. "I'm sure I don't."

Bria decided not to push the issue, and instead, tested her newfound ability. "Look, if it's some privacy issue, that's fine with me. I've just never seen a hospital run this way, that's all, have you?"

"No, this place is, um, kind of . . . different," the young nurse hemmed.

"Okay. I can live with that." When Young Nurse Jones visibly relaxed at her comment, Bria continued, "Hey, let's play a game, okay?"

Nurse Jones smiled inquisitively. "What game?"

"I'll ask you two questions. One you answer honestly, the other, make up a lie—but don't tell me which is which. I want to guess, okay?"

The nurse tilted her head to one side. "Okay—as long as it's not about Pathway."

"Fine." Bria thought for a moment. "What is your mother's maiden name, and what is your favorite food?"

Nurse Jones folded her arms and said, "Her maiden name is LaPorte, and my favorite food is pizza."

Gotcha! "LaPorte is true, pizza is false."

The young nurse beamed openly. "That's amazing. How could you tell?"

Incredible. Bria shrugged. "It's just something I'm working on. So tell me, what *is* your favorite food?"

"Fish sticks. I could eat fish sticks for breakfast, lunch, and dinner."

Bria cringed. "Ugh. That answer was true, but I can't say I share your enthusiasm over fish sticks."

"Speaking of food," Nurse Jones said, "are you hungry this evening?"

"A little, I guess."

The young nurse wheeled over a telescoping bed tray. A plastic dinner plate sat atop with a dry pork chop, some waxy green beans, and a spherical scoop of mashed potatoes covered with a yellow goo that supposedly resembled gravy. She stood back, and with an obviously forced smile, said, "Bon appétit."

When Bria stuck her fork in the pork chop, the aluminum handle bowed. She found it impossible to cut any of the beans in two without concerted effort. And when she played with the gravy, it came off as a solid, rubbery cap that retained the domed shape of the potatoes.

Without looking up, Bria mumbled, "Hence the reputation of hospital food."

"I told them you wouldn't like it," the young nurse said, again glancing above Bria's head.

Bria wondered what caused the young nurse's frequent distractions. Earlier, Bria had tried to look above her, tilting her head back and then attempting to twist around, but her partial paralysis prevented her from doing so. Picking up her spoon, she tried to get a reflected image of what the girl kept glancing at, but the convex surface wasn't shiny enough. She set her spoon on the plate and pushed it away. "Do you think I could have some yogurt instead?" Bria asked.

"Is that how you maintain your awesome figure?" the young nurse asked.

"Well, it's not by eating rubber food." Bria grimaced. "Or fish sticks."

"It's not just your figure, Miss Georgopolis. I wish I had your face and hair."

"What are you talking about? I look disgusting."

"Yeah—I wish I looked as bad."

"Nurse Jones, you shouldn't berate yourself like that. I think you're very cute."

"I look like a chipmunk."

"Chipmunks are cute."

"I don't want to be cute. I want men to drool all over me."

Bria shuddered. "There's a picture I could do without. I'm glad I'm not that attractive."

"Oh, you're gorgeous and you know it."

Bria turned her palms up. "Unless you happen to have a mirror, I'll just have to take your word for it, won't I?"

Smiling, the young nurse flitted out of the room and returned a minute later with a small handheld vanity mirror. Bria thanked her and flinched at her reflection.

"Ugh. Why didn't you tell me there was a full moon out?"

Young Nurse Jones burst out laughing. "Miss Georgopolis, you're too funny."

As Bria made a pretense of fixing her hair and pressing against the bags under her eyes, she tilted the mirror to find what distracted the young nurse so often. Just as she suspected, a security camera and microphone mounted directly above her bed caught everything she did and said. If that wasn't an overt intrusion and a direct violation of patient-privacy policies, then it certainly pushed the envelope of decency. Why was the hospital so concerned with her every move? Why was everyone so closed and secretive? What were they trying to hide from her?

"I'm not sure this was a good idea," she said, handing the mirror back to the petite nurse.

"Yeah, right. You look great."

Bria harrumphed. "Mirror, mirror, on the wall, what the heck happened?"

Again, Nurse Jones succumbed to a fit of punctuated giggles and grabbed a tissue to wipe the tears from her eyes. Her high, sharp staccato laugh only added to her chipmunk image.

"That'll be enough, Nurse Jones. Thank you," the pleasant Dr. Smith said from the doorway.

"Yes, Doctor," she said as she gathered her things.

"Thank you, Nurse Jones," Bria said happily. "And get busy storing those acorns for the winter."

With eyes twinkling, Nurse Jones flashed a mock scowl at Bria, briefly stuck out her tongue, and left the room snickering.

Bria smiled at the physician. "I like that one."

"Nurse Jones does have a sweet disposition."

Bria smirked. "*That* Nurse Jones does. The other nurses need some patient-rapport lessons."

"Which one in particular?" the doctor asked.

"Now how am I supposed to tell you that when everyone's name here is the same? It would sure be a lot easier if you guys went by your real names."

"Merely a security precaution, Miss Georgopolis. Nothing more."

"Why?"

He smiled. "I'd tell you . . ."

"But then you'd have to kill me," Bria finished for the doctor. "Come on, you can do better than that, Dr. *Smith*."

"Seriously, it's SOP here. The only thing that need concern you is getting better."

Bria shook her head. "Whatever you say, Doc. But your Standard Operating Procedure leaves a lot to be desired." When the doctor merely shrugged in response, Bria continued. "So . . . what *is* my prognosis?"

Flipping through her chart, Dr. Smith said, "Let's see . . . how are you faring without your catheter?"

"The handheld urinal is a bit awkward, but I manage."

"Good. Got any feeling in your legs yet?"

"Some tingling up to my knees. Not much else."

"Any movement?"

"No."

"That'll change tomorrow," the doctor smiled.

"Such confidence," Bria sighed.

"Thank you. Of course, we'll be doing the movement for you . . ."

Bria favored him with a quizzical expression.

"Physical therapy. But I should warn you, our PTs were trained by the Gestapo. Nothing but whips, chains, and red-hot pokers."

"Sounds like fun."

The doctor's eyebrows rose slightly. A smirk hid just behind his lips.

"Do you really think it'll help?" Bria asked.

"We don't know. But we're pretty confident it won't cause any damage."

"Again, your assurance is underwhelming."

The doctor adopted a disapproving air of censure. Scrawling in her chart, Dr. Smith said, as if speaking to himself, "Not eating her meals . . . arguing with the doctor . . . poor attitude . . ."

"Can you blame me?"

"No. But if it doesn't change we'll be forced to sprinkle salt in your wounds."

Bria held up her hands in surrender. "Okay, okay. I take it all back."

The doctor paused with his pen pressed against his pursed lips, as if evaluating her plea. "All right, then . . . forget the salt. We'll just stick with the whips and chains."

Even though she didn't appreciate his secretiveness, Bria played along. "Bring it on, Doc."

Dr. Smith exited the room, leaving Bria to wonder about the camera and microphone behind her. It wasn't right. In fact, several other things about Pathway were not right. Even though this was a private room, maybe even a private floor, Bria knew she should have heard the bustle typical of a recovery hospital: the constant squeak of rubber-soled shoes against the linoleum floor, pages and PAs interrupting nonstop, calming music overhead, the voices of concerned family members visiting other patients. None of those sensory elements existed at Pathway. The place seemed as quiet as a tomb. It wasn't natural to a hospital setting. It felt disconcerting and somehow very wrong.

Just then, a large woman entered the room. Bria swore she knew her. Or so she thought. Something about the woman struck a familiar chord; she'd had dealings with her before, but Bria could not fix the time or the place. The woman wore a nurse's smock that strained against her matronly bosom and plump girth. A cutesy, blue-eyed-kitten lapel pin and a colorful floral-pattern blouse added to her maternal visage. As expected, her name tag read NURSE JONES.

The woman approached with a broad, warm smile. Sincerity and compassion oozed from her face. If she had been holding a tray of fresh-baked cookies and a glass of milk, it would not have seemed out of place. Strangely, Bria felt her stomach knot.

"I'm so glad to see you feeling well, my dear," the woman sang. "I'm Nurse Jones."

Bria smiled and nodded slowly. Already suspicious of everyone at Pathway, Bria felt a heightened sense of unease in this woman's presence. The undertone in her voice, the forced cheeriness, and the motherly façade reeked of deceit.

The nurse handed Bria a sealed cup of yogurt for which Bria thanked her.

"Any sparks of memory yet, sweetheart?"

"No," Bria said, hesitantly. Something was coming to mind but slowly. Very slowly.

"Too bad, pumpkin. They tell me you were quite the nurse at Mercy Children's. Why didn't you ever go into anything more advanced? Research, for example?"

Bria lowered her eyes. "I love kids. I'd do anything to help a sick child feel better. It's . . . it's a personal thing."

"That's so sweet of you," the big woman gushed. "You must have had a great childhood yourself."

Bria stirred her yogurt aimlessly. "On the contrary, it sucked. My neighbor helped me a lot, but otherwise it was quite dysfunctional. That's why I love children so much. No kid should have to go through what I did. Kids are innocent, and yet so many go through truly awful things. I wish I could do more for them."

"Well, then," Nurse Jones said, patting Bria's leg, "we'll just have to work extra hard to get you better. There are some great times ahead for you, Bria. You're very lucky."

Bria smiled softly, but she was not happy. She did not feel the least bit lucky.

CHAPTER SEVENTEEN

NORTHERN CALIFORNIA

Physical therapy was not as bad as Bria had imagined. After a half hour of assisted stretching, a half hour of weights, and a half hour of electro-stimulation, a large Polynesian therapist moved Bria to a cushioned table where she received an hour-long, full-body massage. Then, already feeling like Jell-O, Bria sat in a whirlpool tub for another half hour, which turned any remaining muscle stiffness to mush. For once, the fact that the man's name badge read DR. SMITH didn't bother her.

"How are you feeling?" the friendly Dr. Smith asked, entering the whirlpool room. Although as a doctor he'd seen more than his share of undressed bodies, Dr. Smith remained behind a movable screen to allow Bria her privacy.

"If I have any bones in my body, they aren't doing much," she sighed.

"Pretty nice, huh?"

"If I had known it would be like this, I would have become infected long ago."

"I don't know that I would recommend that," he said with a laugh. "How did the exercises go?"

"Your PT is amazing. He sure knows how to bend and stretch a body. I had joints I never knew existed."

"The sense of humor is encouraging," Dr. Smith commented.

"Thanks."

"How about the electro-stimulation?"

"Good. I think he actually got the paralyzed muscles twitching and contracting. That's a positive sign, isn't it?"

"You're a nurse—you tell me."

Bria smiled. She closed her eyes and settled farther into the tub. "I believe it shows that my nerve tissue still functions, as does the skeletal muscle. And because I felt tingling during the test, it shows there are no breaks in the relays to my brain. I'm hoping that means full recovery of voluntary movement is imminent."

The doctor cleared his throat. "Well, while I remain optimistic, *imminent* is not the word I'd choose at this stage. How about *probable?*"

Bria tried to deduce the tone of his voice. He was encouraging yet cautious, painfully forthright, yet tactful. More than that, he was honest. "I'll take *probable.* How about my short-term memory?"

"Like the nerves in your legs, I'm hopeful your memory will return in time."

"Good."

"Now, if you'll excuse me, I have other rounds to make."

"Thanks, Doc."

Upon returning to her room, Bria retrieved her paperback and began to read, but her mind could not concentrate on the humanistic prose of Ernest Hemingway. Once again, in spite of the beneficial treatment she received at Pathway, Bria wondered why some of the staff were intentionally withholding information from her.

Rationalizing the concern as part of her amnesia, she chided herself for being so suspicious. What was it with this place? Nothing bad had happened since her arrival. Everyone was helpful—though not always honest. Some of the doctors and nurses lacked personality, but that was true in any hospital. Still, why would she have a monitoring system set up in her room? Why did she not have a telephone or other access to the outside world? Why did the staff go by pseudonyms instead of their real names? And why had there been no contact from Mercy Children's Hospital? Surely they knew of her hospitalization at Pathway. Being fairly new there, she didn't have a lot of friends, but one or two colleagues would have seen fit to send a card or flowers or . . . something.

Once again, the walls began closing in on Bria. She felt cold, isolated, and very much alone. Normally, she found comfort in solitude. It never filled her with the hollow, frightening emptiness it did so many others. But for reasons she could not dissect, things were *wrong* here. At Pathway, she felt more like a prisoner than a patient.

* * *

The following morning, the matronly Nurse Jones entered Bria's room carrying a clipboard and ballpoint pen. Again, she wore the smile that seemed to drip with compassion. To most people, she probably looked like the kind of woman with whom you could trust your newborn son, the keys to your house, a priceless heirloom, and your dog. To Bria, she was the proverbial wolf in sheep's clothing. She still felt she knew the woman; she just did not know how.

"Hello again, my dear. You look very rested this morning." The nurse's forced friendliness was nauseating.

"Thanks. I am."

"That's wonderful. Listen, hon, I need you to sign some papers before breakfast. Are your hands still working okay?"

Bria felt like making a rude gesture to show just how well they worked. Instead, she said casually, "I can still pick the lint from my navel."

The nurse laughed. "You're as sharp as ever, Bria. I like that about you."

"Thanks."

"Sure thing, sweetheart. Now, let's get your signature on these papers, shall we?"

"What are they?"

Leafing carelessly through the sheets attached to her clipboard, Nurse Jones said, "Oh, just some legal mumbo-jumbo. You know, HIPAA stuff, personal information, that kind of thing. We weren't able to get it when you were paralyzed."

She handed the clipboard to Bria with the pages flipped to the signature line at the back. Clicking her pen, she held it to the line, indicating where Bria was to sign.

"Can't I read it first?" Bria asked.

Crestfallen, Nurse Jones forced an I-love-you-anyway smile. "Nurse to nurse, I give you my word you should just sign the papers and forget about it. It's just a confidentiality clause. Nothing to worry your pretty little head over."

"Good. Then you won't mind coming back later after I read it, will you."

Nurse Jones's mouth dropped open. "Excuse me?"

Bria smiled. "I like to take my time with these things."

Recovering her composure, the nurse winked knowingly. "You're still a fighter, kiddo. That's why you're recovering so quickly." When Bria didn't respond, Nurse Jones sighed. "Okay, you win. Read it over thoroughly, but I need to deliver it to administration right away, so I'll just wait here until you're done."

Bria didn't recognize the form, but it looked like a "Release from Fault" disclaimer. The jargon was the worst legal-speak she had ever read, and by the time she was on page three of the five-page document, she was lost. In spite of all her progress, her concentration had not improved. Maintaining her intensity, she continued to read as if she understood everything it said. Bria found nothing unusual other than a silence clause mandating a promise to never reveal anything about Pathway or any of its employees to a potential competitor or to anyone who could forward such information to a competitor. Or something like that. Bria thought it was a bit stringent, but she understood the concern. Many hospitals were now copyrighting unique procedures and treatments, publishing their breakthrough modalities in medical journals to ensure full credit and notoriety— and possible royalty payment.

Shrugging her shoulders, Bria signed the last page. "I don't see what all your fuss was about."

Nurse Jones bristled a bit. "Nor do I," she said, taking the clipboard and turning to leave. As she exited the room, clearly not meaning to be heard, the large woman hissed under her breath, "You never gave me this much trouble before."

Bria's breath caught in her throat. The motherly nurse's words rebounded in her head, bringing to mind a time she'd heard her say them before. *You never gave me this much trouble before.* As if passing through a fog, the mysterious veil cloaking her mind quickly dissolved. Bria instantly remembered the woman—who she was, where she worked, and why she hated her. Spontaneous tears glazed her eyes. Her MED-STATS monitor registered a thirty-beat-per-minute increase in pulse rate, her blood pressure soared, and her breathing became shallow.

The woman's name was not Nurse Jones. Bria knew her as Betty Mumford, the head ICU nurse at Mercy Children's Hospital. As she had suspected earlier, she also knew the woman's outward Mother Hen demeanor was a façade, masking an inner, hideous beast.

Shortly before Bria's "contamination," Nurse Mumford had hired on with Mercy as the head of ICU. Almost immediately, strange things had begun to happen. Nurse Mumford had transferred patients prematurely, supposedly to accommodate newer patients in greater need of intensive care. When such transfers were impossible, a few patients had suddenly died. Although Bria had suspected otherwise, the hospital had ruled the deaths as unfortunate, natural occurrences. Bria suspected Betty Mumford was responsible for the disappearance of at least four teenaged and two preteen patients from Mercy. But there had been no way to prove it. Having produced doctored transfer papers, Mumford had covered her tracks too well. No one at Mercy had known about this dark secret—no one except Bria Georgopolis.

It was all coming back to Bria with unwelcome clarity. Each time Bria had probed into exactly what had happened to a missing patient, Betty Mumford had regaled her about professionalism, then told her to mind her own business and stick to her duties. Bria had even taken her concerns to the hospital director, but he had ended up siding with Nurse Mumford. Finally, after Mumford had put Bria on administrative probation for being belligerent and for breeching patient confidentiality procedures, Bria had known she would have to take her discoveries to the police. But she never got the chance. Later that week, as Bria finished up a night shift, she was accosted by a large man in the basement parking lot. Before she could scream, the man had sprayed her with a nerve agent, rendering her temporarily helpless. She'd passed out without a fight.

When Bria awoke, she was strapped to a metal table in a small isolation room. Betty Mumford was standing next to her, holding a large hypodermic syringe in her plump hand.

CHAPTER EIGHTEEN

SAN JOSE, CALIFORNIA

The young woman managed a small drive-thru hamburger joint. She was a hard worker and very reliable. She had few friends outside of work and never socialized. Perhaps it was because of her rather bland looks—straight, mousy hair, a shapeless nose, no chin, and a sticklike figure. Her one redeeming feature was a pair of vividly blue eyes. Many who did not know her often asked if she wore contact lenses. But no, they were naturally that color. The "you have beautiful eyes" remark, truly meant to be complimentary, always came across as derogatory. Obviously they all thought that a girl as plain-looking as she was needed help beautifying herself, and colored lenses were a natural, easy choice to make.

But April never did anything to make herself attractive. She simply did not see the point. At twenty-six, she was a classic loner. She had no family, she didn't date, and she lived alone with a cat named Hairball.

Pathway considered her perfect.

Hidden behind the severely tinted windows of his black Dodge Ram Mega Cab, Surt waited patiently in line with the late-night burger enthusiasts as they filed past the drive-thru window. He had a verbal description of his latest assignment, a high school photo, and a name, April Blanch. Perhaps her unattractive last name also had something to do with her asocial qualities.

Although a light rain fell that night, Surt opened his window and breathed in the resplendent aroma of grilled hamburger, fried onions and bacon, and simmering grease. He wasn't as overly concerned with health and nutrition as many people these days. With a body he believed to be crafted by the gods, he had a superior constitution, and with that came a superior metabolism, which meant he could eat anything he wanted with little regard to the future. Fast food flowed in his veins but never clogged them. It wouldn't be allowed.

When the teenagers in front of him finished ordering, Surt eased his huge pickup truck forward. The rain plunked hollowly against the roof of the cab and against the shell mounted on the truck bed.

"Welcome to Burger Box. Order when ready," the voice crackled through the tin speaker. It was a lovely voice, even in its distorted, electronic form.

"Three double bacon cheeseburgers, extra onions, a large order of fries, and three large chocolate malts."

"Three double BC burgers, a large fry, and three choco shakes?"

"Malts. Three *large* ones."

"Thank you. Please pull forward."

Even at night, Surt wore large, wraparound sunglasses to hide a portion of his scarred face. When he pulled up to the window, April told him the total for his meal. Because of the rain, she didn't lean out of her kiosk and did not see much of the man driving the Dodge truck. But he saw her, and he knew he had found his mark.

Surt handed over the money. "Keep the change."

Handing a few coins back, April said, "Thank you, sir, but we're not allowed to take tips."

"Too bad," he replied, taking his change and the bag of fragrant bacon cheeseburgers and french fries. The malts came next in a cardboard carrier.

Surt drove to the poorly-lit parking area behind the Burger Box and found a dark spot under a huge globe willow. As he backed in, the feathery tendrils of willow bows caressed his truck lovingly. He lowered his window and shut the engine off. He opened his first cheeseburger and began what he knew would be the first and last meal April would ever serve him. He chewed slowly, savoring each bite as if performing a sacrificial ritual: a bite of burger and a sip of malt to wash it down. Another bite, another sip, occasionally interrupted with one or two greasy, over-salted french fries.

Finishing his first serving, he evaluated the small parking lot. At this late hour, only one car shared the space with him. On the far side of a BFI dumpster sat a small, white Geo Metro. Economical. Good mileage. No frills. Obviously her car.

Chomping into his second burger and sipping at his second malt, Surt planned his "retrieval." He called it a retrieval because that's what Pathway called it. He originally thought of following April home. At one o'clock in the morning and with the rain as a deterrent, there would be little traffic to cause him problems. But it also made it easier for her to see him tailing her. No, retrieving her right here in the parking lot would be much better. He knew a low-budget restaurant of this sort would not spring for security cameras. And the neighboring businesses had closed hours earlier. No witnesses.

Finishing his second cheeseburger and malt, he pulled out a wool-covered strap of Velcro, which he used as a restraint, and a small spray canister of nerve agent.

He checked his watch. Approximately twenty more minutes.

Slowly, meticulously, he opened his third burger.

CHAPTER NINETEEN

NORTHERN CALIFORNIA

April Blanch couldn't breathe. After the contents of the large syringe emptied into her shoulder, she immediately found her chest tightening and her throat narrowing. Tears streamed from her eyes. The small, cement-walled room closed in on her as if she were in a limestone trash compactor. A burning sensation swept through her body, eliciting one muscle spasm after another. Her heart pounded so loudly it echoed off the bare walls.

A large woman wearing what looked like a spacesuit stepped forward. "Just relax, April dear. This is the worst of it, I promise."

April opened her shackled hand like a small child seeking the comfort of a parent. The motherly woman took her hand and caressed it. The young woman stared, doe-like, a slight tremble quivering her lower lip. The woman's thinly gloved hand moved to wipe April's tear-soaked cheek.

"There, there," she consoled as she stroked April's hair with her free hand. "Be strong, kitten. It's not that bad."

Without warning, April turned her face and bit the woman's hand on the meaty bulge, just below the thumb. The thin disposable glove did little to soften the bite. The woman screeched but could not pull her hand free. An animal instinct took over in April as she bore down with all the force her jaws could muster. Her teeth pierced the glove, and the wet, coppery taste of blood filled her mouth. The woman continued to scream as she beat on April's head with her fist.

"Help!" she screeched. "Someone get in here!"

April heard herself growling as if she were a rabid animal. With eyes squinted shut, she bore down even harder, determined to leave an unforgettable mark on her captor. She did not understand what was happening to her or why these people had kidnapped her and brought her to this place. She could not recall having offended anyone, or anyone wanting to exact a vendetta on her. She could not fathom anyone asking for ransom money for her release. She ran a burger joint, for heaven's sake, not an international bank or a multi-billion-dollar conglomerate. She was a nobody, and she knew it.

"Let go, you little monster," the woman screamed. All of her former motherly nature was long gone, leaving a brutal villain in its stead.

April continued to bite. And growl. Blood flowed. The screaming in the small room was intense, and to April, rewarding.

Then April heard a *whoosh* of sealed air escaping as a door opened. Another person wearing a full-body suit entered quickly and injected a syringe full of some other drug into her bloodstream. Almost instantly, she felt her jaw relax and her body go limp.

The big woman left the room whining. The figure in the full-body suit was a man with evil eyes and a beaklike nose.

April tried to smile, but she wasn't sure if her face responded to the mental command. It didn't matter. She knew tomorrow was a day she might not ever see, and strangely, that didn't seem to bother her.

CHAPTER TWENTY

NORTHERN CALIFORNIA

Bria worked extra hard during her next session of physical therapy. Forcing her legs to respond, she ignored any pain she felt and pushed herself to complete muscle failure. Rebuilding muscle tone and nerve response was her only chance of survival. However, when it came time to test her walking skills, Bria would wobble and collapse and claim she still had no balance and little voluntary control. If the staff at Pathway could be deceptive, so could she.

Ever since her recognition of Betty Mumford, Bria limited her questions to immediate concerns and kept most comments to herself. She ate everything they gave her, regardless of how it tasted, and asked for extra portions of foods high in protein. The possibility that Pathway was lacing her meals with strange drugs entered her mind, but she didn't have much choice. She needed the nutrition to regain her strength. It was a chance she had to take.

Six days had passed without the presence of Nurse Betty Mumford. The youthful Nurse Jones came and went, always bubbly and full of life, but never doing more than her regular nursing responsibilities. Bria continued to share small talk and encouraged a friendship with her. The more she learned about the young nurse, the more innocent she found her. She was probably the only one in which Bria could confide at Pathway. Perhaps the one friendly Dr. Smith too, but Bria still wasn't sure. Young Nurse Jones admitted secretly that she didn't like being at Pathway, but she wouldn't say why. She also hinted that Bria should get better as soon as possible—for reasons other than her health.

Instinctively, Bria knew she should trust the young nurse. Especially now that she knew Betty Mumford was there.

Earlier, Bria had decided to assign prefixes to the names of those tending to her care. Luckily, only a few persons were involved. She was certain Pathway had a much larger staff, but apparently, only a handful saw to her convalescence: Bland Doctor Smith (the one who had zero personality), Friendly Doctor Smith, Buff Doctor Smith (her Polynesian physical therapist), Crotchety Nurse Jones, Young Nurse Jones, and Betty Mumford. Bria had seen others milling about, some of whom smiled or offered occasional pleasantries, but few were directly involved with her. Of those she interacted with, only Young Nurse Jones held her complete trust.

"How are you this fine morning?" Friendly Dr. Smith asked, entering her room with a plastic food tray on which sat two covered plates.

Bria sat up and brushed the hair from her face. "Good as new, except for my legs, my memory, and my meals."

Dr. Smith chuckled. "Well, we're working on the first two, so don't give up hope there. The third item I can fix with this—"

Removing the plastic cover off one plate with the panache of a seasoned waiter, Dr. Smith set the tray on Bria's bed stand and wheeled it over her lap. The plate was loaded with three extra-thick slices of French toast dripping with butter and hot maple syrup. To the side of the French toast sat four strips of bacon, a generous pile of hash browns, and a bowl of huge strawberries lightly sprinkled with powdered sugar. Bria couldn't believe her eyes. Her mouth instantly watered and her stomach growled as if saying *thank you* before Bria had a chance to.

"Are you sure this is approved hospital fare?"

"For a recovering patient? Of course not. That's my breakfast." The doctor then pulled the cover from the smaller plate. "This is your breakfast."

The plate contained a single piece of dry toast and a bowl of Cream of Wheat so loaded with raisins it was more black than white. Bria's breath caught in her throat as she stared in disbelief. Dead silence cloaked the room. Time seemed to stand still as she could not take her eyes from the bowl of contaminated hot cereal.

The doctor's serious demeanor didn't last long. He suddenly burst out laughing and doubled over with his hands on both knees.

"I wish—I had—a camera," he gasped through bursts of mirth.

Bria looked at him in total confusion.

The doctor sat on her bed and tried to compose himself while wiping tears from his eyes. "My word, you should see the look on your face."

"I don't understand," she said slowly.

Dr. Smith took the plate containing her meager breakfast and dumped it, plate and all, into a trash can. "I had my breakfast hours ago, Bria." Pointing to the plate of French toast and sugared strawberries he said, "That's your breakfast."

Bria couldn't help but smile. "That's not funny. In fact, it's blatant patient abuse. Where's my lawyer?"

Still pointing at the breakfast plate, Dr. Smith asked, "You're not planning on sharing this with him, are you? If so, then I'd like to try some."

Wrapping her arms defensively around the tray, Bria hissed, "Back away from the French toast and nobody gets hurt."

Dr. Smith patted her knee. "I'm glad to see you in good spirits. That's a big part of healing, you know."

"I'll be even better in about twenty minutes." Perhaps she *could* add Friendly Dr. Smith to her list of confidants after all.

"I'll bet." Dr. Smith chuckled. "Any luck with the memory thing?"

"No. I wish there was. It's like I have this blank spot where my life skips a couple of months. I think I'd have a better chance of orienting everything if I knew what day it was."

After momentarily considering her request, Dr. Smith said, "All right. It's October twenty-fourth. Does that help?"

"Yes, I think so. The last thing I remember was working a graveyard shift at Mercy. I think it was early August."

"And nothing in between?"

"No. Nothing," she lied.

The doctor appraised her thoughtfully. "You sure?"

"Yes."

"Nurse Jones said she feels you remember more than you're letting on."

"Which one?" Bria asked, shoveling a huge portion of syrup-slathered French toast into her mouth.

Dr. Smith chuckled. "Okay, you got me again. Sometimes even I wonder if our hospital pseudonyms are a good idea or not."

"Well, I don't know which nurse you're talking about," Bria lied. "I'm sure the common names confuse the other patients as well."

"I don't think so. In fact, most of our patients don't seem to notice the irregular consistency at all."

"And what other patients are those?" Bria asked innocently.

Dr. Smith regarded her with a wan smile; however, the smile held no obvious answers, and even seemed to hide a few. "I'm not at liberty to say, Miss Georgopolis."

"I haven't seen a soul other than staff the entire time I've been here," Bria continued.

The doctor nodded. "We try to keep things on a more personal level here. Besides, we're still not sure you're a hundred percent recovered, and therefore, safe to interact with the other patients."

Bria plucked a strawberry from the bowl and turned it around slowly, appraising the fruit. "I haven't seen anyone wearing a hazmat suit lately."

"That was more for your protection. For a while you were potentially susceptible to adventitious infections."

Biting the strawberry and savoring its sweetness, she asked, "How's that?"

Dr. Smith cleared his throat and stood up. He glanced at his watch and fiddled with the dial. "Gosh, look at the time. I really need to be going. Hang onto those questions, and I'll try to be back before the day's over to answer them, okay?"

"Okay," Bria said, stirring a puddle of syrup with a piece of bacon. She knew he was avoiding her questions. Why he was so elusive was a mystery she was determined to solve.

CHAPTER TWENTY-ONE

CRESCENT COVE, CALIFORNIA

The rest of the week went a lot better than it had begun. Paul let Phyllis run the store as he did his best to learn the computer system. Luckily, the software was very user-friendly, and Brooke, his twenty-year-old licensed technician, knew the system inside and out. Paul also called the State Board of Pharmacy to fill out the "Change of Ownership" and "Change of Pharmacist in Charge" paperwork required by law. The board asked him to do a complete controlled-substance inventory and mail it to their office in Sacramento. Paul said he'd do it that day, as well as send the necessary fees for everything else.

Val had designed a decent pharmacy workflow, but Paul saw several ways to improve the process. He would make the changes within the month. *It's my place now,* he had to keep reminding himself. To confirm that, Val's bank had Fed-Exed copies of completed fund transfers, proving he had fully paid the first installment as the legal owner of Crescent Cove Pharmacy.

Through small-town gossip channels—which are often faster than high-speed Internet—Phyllis said that a neighbor had found Val dead in his own kitchen. Divorced for eight years, Val Mince had lived alone. He had numerous friends, male and female, but did very little socializing. Val had been the town's pharmacist for a long time and was well liked by everyone. Why someone would kill him was a true whodunit—if indeed it was murder. Some evidence pointed to possible suicide. Either way, Sheriff Baker swore he would solve the mystery of Val's death within a few days.

Both Paul and Phyllis decided not to bring up the tragedy of Val's death with anyone who didn't already know. Neither of them wanted to perpetuate speculative gossip about the bad tidings. When someone persisted, they shared what they knew.

Paul introduced himself to several customers who had prescriptions filled that week. Most seemed happy to meet him. One young mother had a ton of questions that took almost an hour to answer, but because business was slow, Paul didn't mind taking the time. He also met most of the other staff; they were all young kids working random hours on the sales floor or at the soda fountain for some spending money. Paul liked them all. His experiment with suds went over quite well. Everyone raved about it, and by Wednesday evening he had to make a new batch.

Friday evening, the door chime jingled, and in walked Bill Fowler. Paul cringed. He remembered the last meeting all too well. Still, Paul was not one to let anyone intimidate him.

Walking up to the scruffy man from behind the fountain counter, Paul said, "Good evening, Mr. Fowler. How can I help you?"

Bill Fowler appraised Paul through squinted eyes that held nothing but mistrust and guile. He remained silent for a full minute. Standing next to "his" bar stool at the far end of the marble counter, he looked around the store, apparently searching for someone or something.

Paul ventured a guess. "Val is not here today," he offered apologetically.

Bill's head snapped around. "I can see that," he growled.

Paul patted the counter gently. "Take a seat, please. I won't be a moment."

With that, he went to the back and poured a mug of his second batch of suds. It was dark and frothy and smelled wonderful. Bringing it out to Mr. Fowler, Paul said, "This one's on the house."

Bill Fowler held the mug to the light and slowly turned it. He sniffed the aroma and tested the firmness of the foam with the tip of his finger. Looking down the length of his nose, Bill spoke to the mug, saying, "The foam tells all."

"Really?" Paul asked.

Fowler flashed Paul another leery glance, nodded, then sipped the foam, smacking his lips speculatively. A faint smile found its way through the stubble and grime on Bill's face. He took a cautious sip from the frosted mug. The smile broadened.

"What's your name, boy?"

"Paul Randall. I'm the new pharmacist here." Paul thought it wise not to introduce himself as the new owner just yet, even if Bill Fowler was already privy to that information.

"You make this?" Bill asked, indicating the suds.

"My own twist on the original recipe."

Bill drained half of the mug. A resounding belch followed. Paul swore some of the glassware behind him rattled.

"Don't like new faces usually," Bill grumbled. He drained the other half of the mug, leaving a frothy mustache on his upper lip. "I guess you're okay."

"Thanks." Paul almost laughed.

"Pour me another."

Paul refilled the mug, making sure to include plenty of foam.

After taking a long pull from the refill, Bill softly mumbled, "Strange things have been going on here the last few years."

Paul wasn't sure what to make of the cryptic comment. "Strange in what way?"

"A few of the town folk have . . . changed."

"You don't say."

"It's a fact. God's honest truth."

"Changed in what way?" At first Paul thought Bill Fowler was joking. But the serious, almost frightened look in the old man's eyes told him otherwise.

"Actin' strange. Robotlike. Only not artificial."

Paul waited for more, hoping Fowler's tale would become clearer. When Bill went back to his suds without further comment, Paul nodded. "Thanks. I'll keep my eyes open."

"See that you do."

Bill tossed a dollar on the counter and walked to the door. Before exiting, he turned and scanned the store once more to make sure no one was in earshot. "Between you and me," he said quickly, "don't trust any of the town folk, especially the sheriff."

The door chime jingled, and Bill Fowler was gone.

* * *

That evening, Paul Randall stood in the master bedroom of the Kingsford house with a bucket of pine-scented disinfectant, a mop, rubber gloves, and a smile. Cleanup and refurbishing was going to be a long project, perhaps lasting almost a year, but time was on his side, and he didn't mind the work.

The Victorian house still smelled of mold and rot, but Paul had gone over it with a building inspector and found that structurally it was in good repair. Along with an acceptance from the bank, Clem Bagley came through with records that showed an updated electrical overhaul Mrs. Kingsford had contracted, and paperwork showing the installation of a modern gas furnace and an eighty-gallon water heater. Additionally, to lessen the need to tear up the walls a second time, copper piping had replaced the lead waterworks during the same renovation. The confirmation lifted a huge burden of worry from Paul's shoulders. Now all that the old house needed was cosmetic upgrades.

Paul finished cleaning half of the upstairs by midnight. On the floor of the parlor was an air mattress and sleeping bag. Paul's furniture and other belongings were still in storage in Temecula. He wanted his house perfect before moving anything into it. It was simply easier that way.

* * *

The following day was Saturday. Paul told Phyllis he was not coming to work that day. Until he could find some part-time pharmacist help, he would have to keep the dispensary closed on Saturdays. The soda fountain and store would naturally stay open. To make sure he was adhering to California law, Paul had installed locks and a keyed deadbolt on the dispensary door, to which only he possessed keys. Because of his religious convictions, the entire store would not be open for business on Sunday. The announcement of the new hours didn't appear to bother anyone. The whole town seemed to slow to a trickle on the Sabbath.

Saturday morning found Paul running along Cliffside Avenue. The sun had burnt away the ubiquitous fog, leaving a pale blue, cloudless sky to warm the autumn coastline. Paul loved the invigoration jogging brought—the clearing of body, mind, and soul. He saw a few others either walking or jogging. One young couple walked a dog, a gorgeous silver and white Siberian husky with remarkably blue eyes. Paul played with the idea of getting a dog. He could use the companionship. But there was a vast amount of responsibility in owning a dog, and he wondered if he could devote the time necessary to maintain the dog's training and upkeep. Probably not.

Everyone he passed seemed surprised to see him but smiled congenially nonetheless. Paul had learned that Crescent Cove was not a regular tourist town; therefore, new faces were a rarity. With his hair disheveled and his face glistening with sweat, Paul didn't feel like conversing beyond more than a simple wave anyway.

He checked his watch. It was thirty minutes into his run, but he felt surprisingly energetic. He felt he could go on for another hour or more, but knew he was under a time constraint. In spite of having a list of household chores, the likes of which would daunt Mary Poppins, Val Mince's funeral was that evening, and Paul felt obliged to attend.

As Paul jogged down Woodby Lane, the breeze dislodged some golden leaves from the Norway Maples lining that street. Autumn was a favorite time of year for Paul, but it also brought with it painful memories of Debbie. It was mid-October, five years earlier, that they had met. Still, Paul sensed this autumn would be different somehow. Hopefully, in a positive way.

The occupants of the quiet homes along the street were beginning to show signs of life. A few citizens raked leaves or mowed lawns. One older couple sat on their porch, the man reading a morning paper, the woman sipping a hot drink. Paul waved. The woman waved back.

Turning up Pierpont Street, Paul saw Sheriff Baker's patrol car parked in his driveway. He slowed his jog. The officer was not in his car. Paul assumed he was searching the back of the house—for what, he didn't know. Entering his front door, Paul was shocked to see the sheriff standing beside his makeshift bed in the parlor. A stack of papers drooped limp in the officer's hand as he read them.

"What's going on?" Paul asked none too gently.

The sheriff tipped his hat back, and casually placed his hand on his holster. "Just stopping by to see how things are progressing."

Paul stormed up to the sheriff and ripped the papers from his hand. They were the title and closing papers from Redwoods National Bank on the Kingsford property.

"What're you doing in here?"

"I already told you."

"Do you have a search warrant?"

Sheriff Baker snorted, as if Paul's question was pure silliness. "No."

"Then this is trespassing. You'll be hearing from my lawyer soon."

"Now hold on, son," the lawman said in a cautioning tone. "No need to get your feathers ruffled."

"You're on private property, illegally searching through private records—"

"Private records?" Baker scoffed. "They were lying out in the open. Anyone could have read them."

"Anyone inside this house, that is."

"So?"

"Look, Sheriff," Paul said, trying to maintain his rising temper, "while I respect the position of your office, I know my rights. And I know you cannot just traipse into anyone's home on a whim and look around without permission from either the homeowner or a circuit judge."

"So you're an expert on the law as well as drugs?"

Paul clenched his teeth and took several deep breaths. "Get out."

"Say again?"

"You heard me. Get out. You *are* trespassing, and I want you out of my house right now."

Baker stood his ground. He favored Paul with a steady, narrowed glare, one reminiscent of a snake about to strike, a slight smirk playing at the corners of his mouth. Paul moved to the front door and opened it. The sheriff held steady as the smirk slowly grew wider. Finally, he began to walk toward the opening.

Before exiting, he faced up to Paul. The pharmacist was a good six inches taller than the sheriff, but that didn't seem to bother the lawman. "I know everything that goes on in this town, Randall. Anything looks fishy, I investigate. And you, son, smell like old salmon to me."

Not cowing to his accusatory demeanor or his corny simile, Paul said, "Next time, ask permission or get a warrant."

The sheriff tipped his hat and left. Paul slammed the door, barely missing Baker's heel. He almost wished he hadn't missed.

Paul stood with his fists clenched into tight balls. He forced himself to breathe slower and clear his mind. Rash action always seemed to come back and haunt those who succumbed to it. Paul preferred to act, not react.

After pacing between the parlor and living room for a time, Paul went into his library and searched the phone book for an attorney. Finding none listed, he picked up the phone to dial Information. He paused, staring at the handset. If the sheriff was so unscrupulous as to enter his house without permission, what would stop him from installing an illegal wiretap on his telephone?

He hung up the phone and went upstairs to shower, still much angrier than he wanted to be.

Following his shower, Paul moved his makeshift bedroom upstairs to the master suite. A small alcove off the master bedroom provided a sitting area ideal for reading a book or watching the world meander by. Paul plopped on the velvet-cushioned window seat and looked out at the leaden sky. The morning's clear horizon had lasted only a few hours. Paul slid open the single-hung window and deeply inhaled the heavy, moist air. He hoped it would not rain at Val's funeral, but it did not look promising.

Again, Paul wondered why so many strange things were happening lately. This move was supposed to bring closure to his troubles, not add to them. Perhaps he'd been a victim of wishful thinking. Life was never easy. He knew that. But after so much tragedy and grief, he thought the Lord might grant him a little reprieve. Although his church attendance had dwindled somewhat since Debbie's death, he had remained true to his religious convictions. He read his scriptures and said his prayers, obeyed the Word of Wisdom and the law of chastity. He even kept a cashbox full of tithing slips and accompanying checks. This move was to be a fresh start. It was *right* for him; he had felt the Spirit confirm that. He *knew* this was where he was supposed to be. So why all the difficulties? Why was he starting over with even more hardship?

A brisk breeze ruffled Paul's T-shirt, raising goose bumps on his arms. He closed the window and stood. Eyeing the five-sectioned

window seat, he wondered if there was a storage compartment underneath. Starting at one end, Paul tried lifting each section. The center
cushion squeaked loudly as it hinged open. The compartment was
small and empty. Paul was about to close it when he noticed a half-
inch hole bored in one corner of the floor. He stuck his finger in the
hole and pulled. A false floorboard lifted, revealing a secret storage
slot underneath. Inside he found a small plastic-covered badge, about
the size of a playing card. Retrieving it, he found it was a doctor's
identification pass with a magnetic strip running along the bottom
edge. A faded picture laminated in the center of the pass showed a
serious, dour, clearly unhappy man of medicine. The name on the
badge read DR. P. KINGSFORD. Printed under the picture was a clearance level. TOP SECRET, ALL ACCESS, EYES-ONLY INFO. *Too bad the
badge didn't open his eyes to the amount of radiation he absorbed,* Paul
thought as he tossed the pass on a shelf and went downstairs to get a
bottle of water.

The kitchen was mostly a cozy space, despite the remodel, and
very functional. A large window box with three glass shelves jutted
away from the double sink. It would be a perfect place to grow some
herbs or decorative plants. The countertops and island were all a light
shade of faux green marble. The sink and fixtures were stainless steel. A
chrome pot rack hung over the island. The cabinetry was white oak of
Shaker design. Brick-patterned linoleum covered the floor. While
everything looked up-to-date, none of it quite matched, and it
certainly did not add to the authenticity of the elegant old Victorian.

Paul ran some figures through his mind, estimating what it might
cost to bring the kitchen back to the proper period architecture. The
amount was more than he could afford. He shook his head, gathered
his cleaning supplies, and began to scour the kitchen. After two full
hours, Paul moved to the dining area.

The dining room was elegant, even without a table and chairs.
Mahogany trim and paneling adorned the walls, a plush Persian carpet
graced the hardwood floor, and a built-in china cabinet and serving
curio ran floor to ceiling, separating the area from the kitchen. An
authentic leaded-glass Tiffany chandelier hung over the space appro-
priated for the table. It was a bit lush for Paul's simple tastes, but he
liked the feel of the space and could mentally picture a happy family

gathered around a holiday-festooned table, enjoying a Thanksgiving meal.

Paul was just about to tackle the study when his phone rang.

"Hello?"

"Hi. You're the new druggist in town, right?" a panicked female voiced asked.

Paul tensed. Who would know that already? He'd only worked one week at the pharmacy, and, it being a slow week, he had only met a handful of people. He doubted anyone knew his name, let alone where he lived. And he was certain that the phone book had not listed his number yet. Still, the woman sounded distressed, and Paul felt a professional obligation to be honest.

"Yes, but how did you get my number?"

Ignoring his question, the woman breathed a loud sigh of relief and stated, "I hope you don't mind me calling you at home."

"Why would I mind that?" Paul said, trying to keep the sarcasm from his voice.

"Good," she said in a tone that suddenly sounded more angry than relieved. "I have a real problem. I didn't know the pharmacy was closed on Saturday—it never used to be."

"Actually, Saturday hours have always been ten to four." Glancing at his watch, he said, "I currently make the time to be twenty-five after four."

"Really? Well, I need my medicine right away. I haven't had my dose for today, and it was supposed to be taken this morning."

"I'm really sorry, but until I can get more staffing, the pharmacy will be closed on the weekends. However, if you have a true emergency, I'll try to help you."

"Great. I'll meet you there in ten minutes."

"Um—can you give—" Paul didn't get a chance to finish his sentence before the woman hung up. He stared blankly at the handset for a moment, not sure whether to frown or laugh or be rightfully angry.

Still in his Levis, Paul slipped on a button-down shirt and drove to the pharmacy. As he entered through the rear door, he heard some light chatter coming from a few patrons milling about the store and laughter from a few others sitting at the soda counter. He smiled and waved to Jacob Christian, the young man working the soda fountain, then entered a code specific to the dispensary alarm and opened the door.

"I can't believe you're not open," a voice snapped behind him.

A trim, middle-aged woman in an expensive-looking woolen business suit stood with a condescending scowl and an eel-skin purse over one shoulder. A very small dog riding in the purse bared its pointy teeth at Paul. It looked like a miniature toy pinscher or maybe a Chihuahua, but Paul wasn't quite sure. For all he knew it could have been a large rodent. That's what it looked like.

Trying to be civil, Paul chuckled, "Well, as I explained over the phone, I can't be here 24-7, now can I?"

"Oh, I suppose not," the woman said, rolling her eyes. She had a lovely face, one obviously graced by the work of a skilled plastic surgeon, and a contemporary, business-like hairstyle. Her perfectly manicured nails competed for attention with a massive cluster of diamonds on her ring finger. Paul estimated the gem's value equal to that of a small third-world country. The key ring dangling from her purse/dog-carrier overtly boasted a BMW ignition fob. The woman reeked of money and power but otherwise looked very healthy—so Paul wondered what could necessitate an emergency prescription fill: a heart-rhythm pill, a blood pressure medication, an asthma inhaler?

"One moment please." Paul flipped on the computer then returned to the door. "Was your prescription called in ahead of time?"

"No."

"Of course not," Paul said despondently. "What is it you need, ma'am?"

"My phentermine."

Paul froze, the blank look on his face matching the empty feeling in his gut. He was in shock, utterly dumbfounded by the woman standing before him.

"Excuse me?"

"My phentermine. I was supposed to take it at ten o'clock this morning."

"You called me after hours for a diet pill?"

"That's right."

"Not a life-saving heart pill or an anxiety medicine?"

The woman frowned. "If I don't take it soon, I may just need an anxiety pill. Now are you going to get it, or do I have to call my husband?"

Paul stared numbly as if a mat of cobwebs had suddenly clogged his brain. He pinched the bridge of his nose and closed his eyes. He never understood why people felt that resorting to threats would prompt better service. Besides, why would calling her husband make any difference? Taking a calming breath before speaking, Paul said, "I'll get your prescription, ma'am. What is your name?"

"You don't need to know that, young man."

"Yes, actually I do. You see, I can't access your file if I don't know who you are."

"Can't you just give me the pills?"

"No, ma'am, I can't. That would be against the law."

The woman let out a short, exasperated bleat. "I can't believe this. Who's the new manager?"

"He's standing right in front of you." When the woman didn't respond, Paul added, "I'm the manager and the owner, and the only pharmacist presently staffed here. So, if you'd like me to help you, I need to know who you are."

The woman's poreless skin blanched and her perfectly plucked eyebrows knotted. Through gritted teeth she said, "Mrs. Denise Bright."

Paul smiled. "The mayor's wife?"

Denise remained silent.

Paul shrugged. "One moment, please."

Mrs. Bright rolled her eyes a second time and harrumphed. She had the expression down pat.

Paul quickly filled her prescription and dropped the vial in a small sack. Handing Mrs. Bright her diet pills, Paul asked, "Do you have any questions about your medication?"

The woman snatched the sack from his hand. "If I do, I'll ask my doctor."

"Okay," he sighed, not wanting to prolong the transaction any more than necessary. "Please pay up front at the register, and thank you for your business."

Paul felt his cheeks flushing as Mrs. Bright looked him up and down with contempt. With her lavishly-lashed eyes narrowing to little black slits, she hissed, "You don't even look like a pharmacist. The ones I'm used to dress more professionally than blue jeans and an un-ironed shirt." She stuck her nose in the air and spun around so quickly that her small dog almost launched from her purse.

Paul stood in stunned denial for a long time. He then turned off the computer and the dispensary lights and closed the door. On the way out, he checked the vat of suds. It was still half full. Paul fought the temptation to turn off the cooling unit and let the batch ferment, then call Bill Fowler in to have a gripe-fest. He shook his head. Better to simply go home, clean up, and have a bite to eat before the funeral.

CHAPTER TWENTY-TWO

CRESCENT COVE, CALIFORNIA

Although the late afternoon sun had not quite set, an oppressive gloom shrouded the small cemetery. A heavy mist, that at times felt like rain, drizzled constantly as a minister named Sandoval offered a succinct eulogy. Val Mince was a good man, well liked by the community, a friend to all. He would be missed. May he rest in peace. The entire service took just over six minutes.

The cemetery sat on a knoll beyond Crescent Park, overlooking the sea. It was a breathtaking location, offering solitude and a feeling of eternity as one looked out to the endless horizon. An enormous hundred-year-old California Live Oak grew proudly in the center of the cemetery, standing as a sentinel watching over the departed souls of Crescent Cove.

Standing under the massive oak, Paul struggled with his emotions. Painful memories of Debbie's funeral gripped his heart with steel claws. He waited politely until Reverend Sandoval finished, then walked away. Only a few people attended the services, none of whom identified themselves as family. Paul wondered how "well liked" Val had really been. Perhaps the miserable weather kept mourners away. The only ones he recognized were Phyllis, a few pharmacy staff, one or two patients, and Sheriff Baker.

The low rumble of the surf racing up the crescent seemed everywhere, its throaty reverberation dispersing in the thick early evening mists. Paul walked to the end of the path that led to the overlook at the mouth of the deep crescent. Leaning on the safety rail, he gazed out into the ethereal cloak smothering the sea. The steel safety rail and narrow path paralleled the crescent as it wended its way inland. The encroaching mist prevented him from seeing the far end of the path, but he knew it was there.

The scene reminded Paul of Lehi's dream in the Book of Mormon—the narrow path, a mist of darkness, an iron rod, a murky river, a beautiful, eternal tree. All that was missing was a great and spacious building. Paul remembered a public restroom bungalow near the small parking lot at the point of the crescent, but that hardly qualified. And the iron rod didn't lead directly to a fruit-bearing tree. Still, the similarities to Lehi's dream seemed more than coincidental, and Paul let the spiritual nature of the scene soften the sharp pains piercing his heart. Slowly, without forcing it, he let the emotion cleanse him of many past sorrows.

"What a miserable evening," Phyllis said from behind him, causing Paul to flinch. "I'm so sorry. I didn't mean to startle you," she offered. "Are you all right?"

Paul chuckled lightly. "Yeah. It's okay. I just don't do funerals well."

"I didn't realize you knew Val that well."

"I didn't. In fact, I don't know anything about who he was. Why do you suppose there weren't a lot of mourners here?"

Phyllis shrugged. "Val was one of those characters you liked right away but wouldn't think to ask to dinner. He had lots of friendships through the pharmacy, but after his divorce, I don't believe he had much of a social life. He kept mostly to himself, never dated or joined a club. Although he'd never admit it, I think he was very troubled and lonely."

Paul softly scoffed, "Sounds a lot like me."

"You're divorced?"

"A widower."

"Oh. No wonder you don't like funerals. I wish you had told me earlier this week."

"Yeah, well, it's not something I like to spread around."

"I'm so sorry," Phyllis said, gently touching Paul's elbow. "Perhaps that's why he sold the pharmacy to you."

"I don't think he knew about Debbie."

"No, I mean because he saw something of himself in you."

"Oh," Paul said, returning his gaze to the sea. "Didn't he have any other pharmacists interested in the store?"

"No. Like I said, I didn't even know it was for sale until you showed up."

"So why do you suppose he wanted to sell?"

Phyllis hesitated for a moment before answering. "I have my guesses, but I'm not sure you really want to hear them. It's a profitable business, and he'd been here for over ten years."

"I'm not convinced it *was* for sale," the sheriff's voice butted in.

Paul did not know how long the sheriff had been within earshot, but neither he nor Phyllis commented on Baker's statement. The lawman folded his arms and looked directly at Paul as he continued. "There is no record anywhere discussing the sale of the pharmacy. No one at the real estate office has any knowledge of it. In fact, no one seems to know anything about it. Except you, Mr. Randall."

"Why else would I be here?" Paul asked wearily, not wanting to rehash the topic yet again.

"That's the question I'd like to know the answer to."

"I'm sure Paul has documentation on it," Phyllis stepped in. "Val had lots of files lying about. I'll help Paul sort through them, and I'm sure we'll find something."

Baker remained silent, staring at Paul with unmasked accusation. Not realizing his fists had clenched into tight balls, Paul flexed his hands and shoved them into his coat pockets. He was still bitter about the sheriff trespassing in his home, but he had yet to call anyone about it. Fortunately, he had just received the paperwork Baker was seeking. "I have the bank records documenting the transaction back home. I'll try to get a copy to you the first of next week," he said evenly.

"See that you do," Sheriff Baker replied.

Not watching the sheriff leave, Paul leaned over the rail and peered into the abyss of the crescent. The rumbling of the surf soothed him. Leaning far over the rail, he closed his eyes and let the ascending sound envelop him.

"You're not thinking of jumping, are you?"

"No, Phyllis."

"Good. I'd hate to have to train *another* new pharmacist."

Paul chuckled. "Thank you very little."

"Anytime," she said cheerfully.

After a moment of silence, Paul asked, "Has anyone ever been down there?"

"In the cove?" she asked, surprised. "Not intentionally. Years back some young boys tried climbing down at the point, but they got stuck halfway to the bottom, and the county had to fly a Coast Guard helicopter in to pull them out. You can't take a boat in, because the surf is too rough. I don't know why you'd want to anyway. There's nothing down there but jagged rocks, kelp, and a bunch of ugly crabs."

"Crabs? How do you know that?"

"On a clear day you can see them scurrying about. Why do you ask?"

Paul spoke as if talking to the sickle-shaped cove. "Just out of curiosity. You know—because it's there."

Phyllis placed her hand on Paul's shoulder. "Listen Paul. Don't let the sheriff get to you. He's always been a bit of a bully because he was smaller than most of the other boys—always picking fights, acting tough to make up for his size, that kind of thing. As soon as the mystery of Val's death is figured out, he'll calm down."

Paul didn't respond to his assistant. He continued to stare into the crescent as if mesmerized by something. Phyllis patted his shoulder, then turned and walked into the swirling fog.

"I hope so," Paul whispered.

CHAPTER TWENTY-THREE

OAKLAND, CALIFORNIA

It was Sunday night. The phone rang. The numbers matched.

"I'm here."

"The Norman conquest . . ."

". . . was only the beginning." The scarred giant depressed the encryption button. "All clear."

There was a slight pause. "The young woman lasted only two days. We seem to be missing a key factor."

Surt nodded to the phone.

"Lie low for a few weeks. Too many disappearances might arouse suspicion."

"As He commands."

"We will be in contact."

"As He commands."

Surt cradled the phone and stood. He stretched his muscles and looked at the wall clock—6:23 PM. Having been commanded not to go out in public, a childlike pout pulled at his face. He was very hungry, and he craved another bacon cheeseburger from Burger Box. Alas. He knew there was no food in his fridge or cupboards, so he'd have to resort to delivery, which would bring someone to his apartment. That was always a risk. But his advanced metabolism necessitated constant nourishment. He had no choice. He ordered two extra-large Meat Lovers pizzas and two liters of Mountain Dew.

In times of boredom, the large man turned to his weights. Taxing his muscles always refreshed him and reminded him of his immense power. He was beyond mortal; he was invincible. If the Light wished it of him, he could do anything. Be anything.

Taking his time, Surt lay on a sturdy, padded bench and pressed matching hundred-pound dumbbells above his chest, clinking them together. Slowly, he lowered them in a broad arc until his arms, now close to fully extended, stretched out to either side of his torso. Bringing the weights close to his chest again, he pressed them up and repeated the cycle nine times.

The pizza arrived within twenty minutes, and he devoured the meal and drink in half that time. He then returned to his weights. After an hour of various exercises, Surt's body glistened with a fine sheen of sweat. His massive chest was as tight as a drum, and his abs formed uniform mounds that resembled a tray of six hard dinner rolls. Stepping into his shower, he let the steaming water rinse all impurity from him. Shampooing his long hair twice, he then toweled off and stood in front of a foggy mirror. Wiping the steam from the lower three-fourths of the mirror allowed him to mask his face while still examining his body. *Magnificent* was the word that always came to mind. A fortress built for one purpose: to serve the Light.

Surt didn't spend time flexing or posing. Blessed with strength beyond mere mortals, he didn't need to wallow in that fact. Humility was a wonderful characteristic he knew he possessed, one that filled him with welling emotions.

Before getting dressed, Surt went to his refrigerator and removed a zippered bag. Opening it, he retrieved a vial of modified testosterone and a hypodermic syringe. Pathway's doctors had shown him how to use it properly. The "modification" was a secret formula known only to the Light. He had given it to Surt when he was first brought to Pathway. They told him it had saved his life and prepared him to become a god. The giant often wondered if he could survive without it, but he was too afraid to try. *No—not afraid,* he corrected himself. *Obedient. Diligent.* The Light had commanded. He must obey.

Injecting the apportioned amount, Surt dressed in dark clothes and sat in front of his television. No picture formed on the cathode ray tube, as the set was not on. It rarely was. Instead, Surt focused on the blank screen and played out movies in his mind. Similar to free-association, the movies contained no plot, no continuity, no cohesiveness or conflict and resolve. Made from Surt's own memories, they were as real as anything that could have illuminated the screen, were the unit turned on. Vivid pictures and dialogue. Mystery, suspense, and thrills beyond compare filled the emptiness. Explosions, blood, and corruption pushed the action to dizzying speeds. Death, carnage, and mayhem. Recalling things he had done, dreaming of things he wanted to do. The story quickly degenerated and became one of vile, dark, nightmares filled with evil. It always did.

Again, Surt smiled.

CHAPTER TWENTY-FOUR

NORTHERN CALIFORNIA

Bland Doctor Smith held the hypodermic syringe in plain sight, almost as if flaunting it.

Bria cringed. She was not afraid of needles, but her experiences at Pathway made her recoil at the thought of another injection. She remembered her last one, though she had yet to admit that to anyone. And that memory stirred a score of questions she was just now beginning to answer. She had blood drawn on a regular basis, but until now, she had received no injections—except for an IV drip the first few days. Young Nurse Jones stood at the foot of her bed, staring at her own feet, unable to meet Bria's gaze.

"Miss Georgopolis, this is only levofloxicin. It's an antibiotic," the doctor explained in none too gentle a tone.

"I know what levofloxicin is. I just want to know why you're giving it to me."

"You seemed to have contracted a urinary tract infection as a result of catheterization."

"My catheter was removed over a week ago."

"This is a latent infection."

"Then why don't I feel any symptoms?"

"It was detected in your last blood analysis. We want to nip it in the bud, as it were, to prevent more serious complications later on."

Bria stared silently at the doctor for a time. She knew he could be telling the truth. Quite often, staphylococcus infections could grow to septic proportions before they elicited any symptoms. But in this case,

Bria knew the man was lying. The way he forced his sentences and over-emphasized the medical terms told her he was making all this up. Additionally, Young Nurse Jones—who normally overflowed with an excess of personality—now stood uncharacteristically aloof, like a silent specter in a Greek tragedy. That confirmed something was amiss.

"I'd like to see the vial you drew the antibiotic from, please, and the lab report showing my staph count."

The doctor looked clearly offended. "Miss Georgopolis, that is not hospital policy. I'm afraid that cannot be allowed."

Ignoring him, Bria asked, "Nurse Jones, could you show me the antibiotic vial or the report?"

Panic flashed across the young nurse's face. Her eyes snapped from Bria to Dr. Smith, then to the camera above the bed. "I—I'm not allowed into the pharmacy or the lab," she stammered nervously.

"Then how can I be sure you're giving me the proper medicine?" Bria asked the doctor.

Flustered, blatantly snubbed, Dr. Smith stormed from the room, taking the syringe with him. Nurse Jones watched him go, then returned her focus to her feet.

"Nurse Jones," Bria whispered. "What's going on here?"

The young nurse shook her head, not wanting to answer.

"Please, you've got to help me," Bria pled, even softer. She wasn't sure if the microphones could pick up her petition, but she had to take the chance. "You're a good person, and a very good nurse. You truly care about people, I can tell. I know you want to do the right thing."

Nurse Jones looked up. Tears rimmed her eyes. "You need to do what the doctors order," she stated, almost mechanically, and much louder than necessary. Her hand moved to the left side of her neck and gingerly probed the area. Then, much softer, "I can't help you or else . . ." Not finishing her sentence, she turned and quickly fled the room. Her words said little, but her tone confirmed to Bria that Young Nurse Jones was not a willing accomplice at Pathway.

Within a few minutes, Friendly Dr. Smith entered the room. "What's this I hear about a rebellious patient?"

"That would be me," Bria said without a smile.

"What's the matter?"

"I simply want to see the vial the antibiotic came from, that's all."

The doctor sat on the edge of her bed and placed his hand on the mound formed by Bria's knees. "Miss Georgopolis, as a nurse you recognize the importance of the doctor-patient bond of trust. It goes beyond a mutual rapport. It can actually speed healing. You're familiar with these concepts, aren't you?"

"Of course. I'm just a little scared, I guess. First you guys tell me I'm infected with Ebola, then you can't explain my paralysis or memory loss, and worse, why my memory may never come back. Now you say I have a staph infection. Since you're obviously making guesses as to my condition and therapy, I simply want to be more involved. That's fair, isn't it?"

The doctor sighed and scratched an ear. "Yes, I see your point."

"I'm an ICU nurse, so I'm not just quoting stuff I've read in *Cosmopolitan* or *Reader's Digest*. I know what I'm talking about."

Adopting an authoritative expression, Dr. Smith said, "You're absolutely right. I'll talk to the hospital board immediately. It might be bending a few rules, but they've been bent before."

"Can I see the vial then?"

"Of course. By the way, how's your PT coming?"

"Okay. I do all right when I'm helped, but I still need a walker to get around, and even then I feel like a crippled old hag."

The doctor chuckled. "Crippled maybe, but never an old hag. You're much too pretty for that label."

"Thanks."

There was an awkward pause as the doctor twiddled his stethoscope.

Bria cleared her throat. "So . . . the levofloxicin vial?"

"Oh yeah. Give me a minute or two, okay?"

Bria sighed heavily, appreciatively. "Thank you, Dr. Smith."

The doctor left the room whistling a tune Bria didn't recognize. She acted relieved. Inside, she knew the pleasant doctor was as involved in the mysteries of Pathway as everyone else who worked there.

Bria picked up the small mirror Nurse Jones had given her and again played at fixing her hair, but angled the mirror toward the small security camera above her bed. The CCTV was about four inches square and was mounted on a nonmotorized bracket. Even the most technologically illiterate would recognize what it was. Whether it was infrared, low-light sensitive, or simply an audio/video unit, Bria could not tell. But it was obviously put there to monitor her every move. And Bria began to formulate a way to disable it to better her chances of escaping. She had to. Somehow, she knew her life depended on it.

Then something else caught her eye. A small pink scar, about one inch in length, marred the left side of her neck. She was positive she had never had one there before. It was positioned in the concavity between her sternocleidomastoid muscle and her trachea. It was surrounded by a fading yellowish bruise and was slightly tender to the touch. The small blemish did not bother her in terms of cosmetics. In time, it would likely vanish. What bothered her more was how it got there . . . and why.

CHAPTER TWENTY-FIVE

NORTHERN CALIFORNIA

Young Nurse Jones entered Bria's room just after nine o'clock in the evening. Except for a bedside reading lamp, the room was shadowy and dark. A floor-level night-light at the far end of the room offered the only other light in the small space. The nurse looked pale and pensive. Casting a fleeting glance at the camera, she quickly scooted to Bria's side.

"How are you feeling?" she whispered urgently.

Confused by her behavior, Bria whispered back. "Fine."

"Did you let them give you the injection?"

"Yes. Dr. Smith—the nice one—showed me the antibiotic vial."

Nurse Jones looked around then leaned close to Bria's ear. "They switched the labels."

Bria sucked in a gasp of air. "What?"

Outside the room, a light at the end of the hallway flickered on. Footfalls moved in their direction. Nurse Jones went quickly to the door and peeked out. "Oh no."

"What is it?" Bria whispered.

"Nurse Jones is coming. I've got to go."

"Wait. What do you mean they switched labels?"

The young nurse shook her head and put a finger to her lips. The footfalls were nearer. She peeked out again and whimpered.

She ran back to Bria's bedside, clearly in a state of panic. "You've got to help me. If I get caught in here without cause I'll be—"

"What's going on in here?"

Bria quickly slipped a hairbrush into the young girl's hand. Crotchety Nurse Jones entered the room and flicked on the overhead light.

"I—I was . . . I just . . ." the young nurse stumbled.

"I couldn't sleep so I asked Nurse Jones to brush my hair," Bria explained. "My mother used to do that when I couldn't fall asleep, and it always seems to work."

Young Nurse Jones lifted the brush into view and smiled sheepishly. She then began stroking Bria's lustrous hair. Bria closed her eyes and sighed appreciatively. Inwardly, she knew their impromptu act was pitifully weak, but it wasn't totally unbelievable.

The ornery nurse walked over to the bed. She didn't look convinced. "You're not on shift on this floor," she told the young nurse.

"My shift ended at nine. I checked in on Miss Georgopolis, and she asked me to brush her hair. I wish I had hair like this," she said, continually stroking, gaining a foothold in the charade.

"Why not ask for a sleeping pill?" Crotchety Nurse Jones snapped.

Bria frowned. "I hate those things. Even Benadryl leaves me feeling all fogged over in the morning. I'd rather go to sleep this way. Please let her continue."

The temperamental nurse still looked skeptical, but her expression softened somewhat. "Well . . . I suppose for a minute."

"Thank you so much." Bria yawned and stretched luxuriously. "I'm feeling drowsy already."

The young nurse brushed in silence as Bria lay back and closed her eyes. The older Nurse Jones stood with her arms folded, watching. After a moment, Bria stayed the young girl's hand. "That's much better. I think I can drop off now. Thanks."

"Any time." The young nurse smiled.

"Nurse Jones, can I speak with you in the nurses' lounge, please?" Nurse Crotchety said.

Young Nurse Jones nodded as renewed fright tightened her expression. Bria took her hand and squeezed it. "Can I call on you again if I can't fall asleep?"

Happiness briefly filled the young woman's eyes. "Sure thing."

The two nurses left Bria in a darkened room. The young nurse's statement ricocheted in Bria's head like a steelie in a pinball machine. *They switched the labels.* If that was the case, then what had they injected into her bloodstream? So far, she had felt no ill effects.

The unanswered question caused a cold sweat to bead on Bria's forehead. If she did not have trouble going to sleep before, she surely did so now.

* * *

The room swam. Bria closed her eyes and forced her mind to clear. Brilliant colors danced within her eyelids, a glittering of greens, reds, purples, blues, and whites; minute pinpoints of light that were there and then weren't. Bria swore she felt motion. When she opened her eyes, the room continued to swim. She screwed her eyes shut again and concentrated on Hemingway. Having just finished reading *The Old Man and the Sea,* Bria was able to recreate the story in her mind. Images of Spencer Tracy's portrayal filled her head. Although his acting was superb, he wasn't the Santiago she imagined. Her "old man" looked much leaner, weathered, gnarled, accustomed to a life under the punishing effects of a tropical sun. Salty, crusty, wind-blown and nearly toothless, Santiago represented the brutality of life. That's what made his astonishing story so compelling; even in his weakest state, he still beat the odds life threw at him and managed to bring home proof of his conquest.

Bria pictured herself as Santiago, only younger, female . . . and much better looking. She too had insurmountable odds stacked against her—some realized, some still a mystery, but she felt determined to beat them all.

Playing out the Hemingway story in her mind kept her focus off the effects of whatever drug the Pathway doctors had given her. When Santiago finally pulled onto the beach with a beaten boat and an eighteen-foot sailfish, mostly skeleton, Bria chanced to reopen her eyes.

The room had stopped swimming. From the lack of sounds in the hallway, she guessed it was still late at night. Slowly lowering her legs over the side of the bed, she gently rose and leaned against the back wall so the camera could not see her. Thankfully, her equilibrium had returned. In fact, she felt better than normal. She sensed a balance that she had never before felt. It was as if she were a seasoned high-wire performer, blessed with an acuity of poise, stability, and control.

With her back against the wall, Bria squatted into a deep squat and rose again. No wobbling. No straining to stay upright. She repeated the move several times, each time sensing she had somehow gained a faculty she previously had not possessed. Was it something in the injection? Lifting one knee, she squatted again, using only the other leg to perform the maneuver. No problem. She tried the opposite leg and got the same result.

Using the telescoping bed tray as a walker, Bria acted weak and feeble, and shuffled her way to the bathroom—in full view of the camera. She felt confident she could have leapt across the room in two or three bounds, but she did not want to display such ability to those watching her. She needed to keep up her ruse to keep Pathway's staff thinking she was incapacitated and unable to take flight. Escape was her ultimate goal. She had to make her pretend handicap believable. It was a matter of life and death.

Returning from the bathroom, she moved even slower, as if traversing the distance had sapped her reserves of energy. She took a couple of steps and rested, breathing hard. Instead of returning to the bed, she moved over to the curtain and drew it aside. She flinched. Behind the heavy fabric she found—nothing. No window offered a view of the outside world. The curtain was a façade, an aesthetic display that covered a portion of the cement wall only to create the illusion of a window.

Shaking with honest tremors, she returned to her bed and fell into it. Tears she could barely control threatened to spill from her eyes. Her plans for escape had relied on an egress window. Now she was back to square one. Consumed with dread, she pretended to go to sleep.

It was hours before she actually drifted off.

CHAPTER TWENTY-SIX

CRESCENT COVE, CALIFORNIA

Normally Paul spent Sundays in church. The old Temecula Creek chapel on La Paz Avenue housed two English wards and a Spanish branch. Paul was a member of the Temecula Second Ward, but his attendance became sporadic shortly after Debbie's death.

Paul and Debbie had only recently joined The Church of Jesus Christ of Latter-day Saints. Having been referred by their best friends and neighbors, the Levinsons, the Randalls had welcomed the missionaries into their home. Eager to learn what made their friends so uniquely happy, Paul and Debbie soaked up the Church's emphasis on the family and living a healthy lifestyle like a dry sponge. Then came the wonderful message of the Restoration, the extraordinary news of a living prophet, and Paul's favorite, the singular blessing of the Book of Mormon. They accepted the missionaries' challenge and were baptized three weeks later. They were attending temple preparation classes, anxiously making plans for a temple sealing, when tragedy struck.

It still shook Paul's faith to think about it.

When he had been a widower for only four weeks, Paul's concerned member friends began offering the names and phone numbers of eligible single women, both in the Church and out, and started bringing female investigators to church—not out of any interest in sharing the gospel, but solely to introduce them to Paul. He tired of it very quickly.

Paul wanted to stay spiritually fit, and he wondered how he could do it in this town. Crescent Cove boasted two churches: a stately, old

Catholic chapel built of quarried limestone and hand-tooled, redwood beams, and a cedar-sided Presbyterian church with a steep slate roof and gorgeous leaded-glass windows. Neither interested Paul. Although the death of his soul mate had weakened his enthusiasm, Paul still felt that Mormonism was the only true religion. He simply needed time to heal and rebuild his testimony and his relationship with God.

Paul donned a pair of navy Dockers, a white shirt, a subdued topaz tie with maroon *Rx's* angled across it, loafers, and a beige camel-hair sport coat. He found his scriptures in a box still needing emptying, had a quick bowl of breakfast, and got into his Mustang. The morning air was resplendent with the odor of cedar, wet earth, and a tinge of brine. Hazy fog hung close to the ground, but the forecast called for a nice, sunny day with highs in the 60s, so Paul left his umbrella at home. Having no predetermined destination, he headed south along Highway 1.

After about an hour, Paul turned off on a scenic byway and headed inland. The narrow, two-lane road wound its way through rolling foothills blanketed with stands of redwood, eucalyptus, and aspen. Stopping at a rest area, he left the car and hiked along a trail littered with pine needles and yellow and red deciduous leaves. It was a beautiful spot, tranquil and serene. No other people were present. A slight breeze encouraged the pine bows to sway and the aspens to quake. The songs of numerous chickadees and the scampering of chipmunks were the only other sounds. It was as if Paul had the world to himself.

Cresting a rise, Paul seated himself on a jut of volcanic rock and opened his scriptures. He spent the next three hours studying, pondering, and praying. Reading through the Book of Mosiah, Paul reflected on the words of King Benjamin and King Mosiah. As if reading it for the first time, Benjamin's message of helping one's neighbor struck a chord in his soul. He'd always felt he accomplished much of that as a pharmacist, but this went beyond performing his livelihood. It spoke of the kind of service not commonly seen in the world, the kind one did out of the goodness of the heart, with no thought of reward or recognition. Samaritan-like service.

The scriptures also talked about the continual struggle Mosiah had with maintaining a church. The fact that there was an actual body of people serving one another impressed Paul as never before. In spite of the fact that he felt the Spirit whisper utterances of comfort and enlightenment, of cleansing and forgiveness, of restoration and peace, he perceived something was missing. Even though this moment in the hills was one of the most spiritual experiences of his life, he felt a lack of belonging, of fellowship with other Saints. He knew that simply believing in his Heavenly Father and in Jesus Christ was not enough. As in the days of Mosiah, the Lord had organized an actual church body, not just a religion. And for the first time in a long while, Paul longed to be a part of it again.

Rising from his rocky pew, Paul sought out a secluded copse of trees. Although certain he was alone, the added privacy of such a venue would allow him to kneel and vocally raise his voice to his Maker. He soon found a small hollow covered with new grass and surrounded by large ferns. Three enormous redwoods and several large aspens surrounded the tiny cove. Paul entered respectfully, dropped to his knees, and bowed his head. He poured out his soul to God, asking for nothing more than to know he was not alone. He needed direction in his life. He needed to feel a sense of worth. He needed to feel the companionship of the Holy Ghost again. And he needed to feel . . . *needed*. Even before he finished, Paul felt the Spirit fill his heart as he recommitted himself to God's will. He promised to find a local branch of the Church and start attending regularly. He promised to fully live the principles of the gospel and be an example to those around him. And all he asked in return was to know why he'd felt so inspired to come to northern California—particularly to Crescent Cove.

As Paul returned to his car, he knew he had accomplished something wonderful. He sensed he had formed a partnership, and he was actually excited about upholding his half of the contract.

On his way down the foothills, Paul sang along with a collection of the Modernaires' Big Band tunes. He loved the tight harmonies and uplifting lyrics of their music and always felt better with a little Glenn Miller helping him down the road. Since it was Sunday, he figured that something more spiritually oriented would be a better choice, but he didn't have any CDs like that. He made a mental note to find something online when he got home.

Rounding a sharp corner, he passed a road sign he had not noticed on the way up. It read "Pathway to Greater Light Research Center."

Paul considered driving in to check it out, but after consulting his watch, he filed that idea. He still had a mountain of things to do at home before the day was over. So instead, he headed north, singing along with the Modernaires and trying to keep his mind off of his ever-growing lists of temporal and spiritual to-dos.

CHAPTER TWENTY-SEVEN

CRESCENT COVE, CALIFORNIA

After a busy but graciously smooth Monday at the pharmacy, Paul was able to finish cleaning the downstairs of his home that evening. The office turned out to be a pleasant surprise. Cherrywood bookshelves ran floor to ceiling on two walls, a small window with a bench seat let in a soft northern light from the third wall, and built-in file cabinets and a wet bar lined the fourth wall. A worn Berber carpet had covered the hardwood floor. Upon removing the carpet, Paul found the floor pocked and gouged with wear and water damage and decided to re-carpet rather than fix the hardwood. He made a note to find the phone number for a discount flooring company in Eureka the following morning. The bottom portion of one wall of bookshelves ended in a sliding-panel storage area. The empty space looked ideal for storage of games, old electronic equipment, boxes of papers in need of organization, old journals, etc. Paul dusted the area and found a shoe box full of black-and-white photographs. Skimming through the photos, he concluded they belonged to the late Mrs. Kingsford. Faded and timeworn, most showed images of 1940s and '50s vintage cars, various people with period styles of dress and hair, and several snapshots of the old Victorian. Among the pictures were images of what looked like an old Army hospital. One image in particular caught his eye. It was a snapshot of Dr. Kingsford and a dozen white-smocked people standing in front of a sign reading "Pathway to Greater Light Recovery Center." He figured it was the same complex he had passed the day before. Paul shrugged and set the photographs on a shelf, then went upstairs to shower.

* * *

The rest of the week went without a hitch. Brooke showed Paul the unique billing features of the pharmacy's software, and the customer flow was just busy enough to keep him from getting bored. Phyllis delivered to the sheriff's office a copy of the sales agreement Val had drawn up showing the transfer of ownership of Crescent Cove Pharmacy to one Paul Randall of Temecula. Baker wasn't in, but a deputy said he'd make sure the sheriff got it. The deputy also informed Phyllis that the county coroner had labeled Val's death a suicide. The old pharmacist had stuck a knife in the side of his neck. As disturbing and bizarre as that was, Paul hoped the report would end the sheriff's suspicions about him.

* * *

The Monday before Thanksgiving began at a hundred miles per hour. Paul liked to call such times "headless chicken days" because he ran around like a freshly decapitated egg-layer. But such days helped the time pass quickly, and he really did not mind them.

Paul arrived at the pharmacy an hour early and was surprised to find Phyllis waiting in the back office.

"Good morning," she said, sliding a pastry box of Bonnie's sour-cream-glazed orange rolls toward him. "Nothing like a hearty dose of fat, refined flour, and sugar to start the day, I always say. Would you like some coffee to wash it down? I've got a pot brewing."

"No thanks. I don't drink coffee." Having worked with her for nearly three weeks now, he could have sworn he had mentioned the nuances of his religion to her. Perhaps not.

"Ah," she said knowingly. "Can't handle the caffeine, huh?"

"Something like that," Paul answered. He removed his jacket and donned his white smock. After punching in the alarm code, he removed his keys to open the dispensary door.

"You know, if I had a set of those I could have the computer up and running before you get here," Phyllis offered.

He smiled cordially. "Phyllis, it's not that I don't trust you. You seem as honest as the day is long."

"Honest to a fault."

"I'm sure of that. But I'm a stickler for the law, and being a tech, you know a licensed pharmacist is the only one allowed to have keys to the dispensary."

"Val didn't seem to mind."

"I'm not Val."

She laughed good-naturedly. "Okay. I didn't mean to step on a nerve, Paul. You're the boss, and I don't have any problem doing things your way."

"Thanks," he said, entering the dispensary.

Dawna Gardener, a nondescript, middle-aged woman with a flat smile and painfully fake hair color, operated the cash register at the front of the store while Phyllis and Paul worked the pharmacy. Brooke wasn't scheduled until after one. True to every pharmacy practice, at exactly nine o'clock, three of the four phone lines lit up, each demanding to be the first answered. While Phyllis grabbed one line, Paul picked up another and greeted the unknown party on the other end. "Crescent Cove Pharmacy, Pharmacist Paul speaking. How can I help you?"

"I need my formaldehyde refilled," a gruff voice demanded.

Paul paused, certain he had misunderstood. "Your what?"

"My formaldehyde. You know—the little white pill I take."

Apologetically, Paul said, "I don't dispense formaldehyde, sir. Are you sure that's what it's called?"

"Are you calling me a liar?"

"No, of course not." Confused, Paul asked, "Do you have an Rx number I can reference?"

"I doubt it," the old man said.

"Do you have your prescription vial?"

"Well, yeah. It's right here in my hand," the man said, as if stating the obvious.

"The Rx prescription number is that big set of digits just above your name, highlighted in bright yellow, and beginning with an *Rx*," Paul explained the obvious.

"Oh that. It's sixty-one, twenty-five, three."

Paul typed 61253 into the computer and hit ENTER. The name *Bill Fowler* popped onto the screen. Paul rolled his eyes and pinched the bridge of his nose as if quelling a headache in the making. "Oh, good morning, Mr. Fowler. How are you today?"

"I'll be better once you quit goofing around and fill my formaldehyde."

Paul took a deep breath and tried to sound cheerful. "That prescription is your water pill. It's called furosemide. Formaldehyde is used for embalming, and I don't believe you're dead yet."

There was a pause on the other end. Then, "Am I supposed to find that funny?"

The smile left Paul's face. "Apparently not. Sorry."

The line disconnected without further word.

Paul processed the prescription and picked up another line. "Good morning, Crescent Cove Pharmacy, Pharmacist Paul speaking."

A panicked young woman cried into the phone, "Hi. Are you a pharmacist?"

Paul closed his eyes and shook his head. Apparently, the inane questions inherent to pharmacy practice were the same in small towns as well as in big cities. "Yes, I am."

"My daughter just drank the cleaning stuff my father puts his false teeth in. I don't know what to do!" The woman was near hysterics.

Paul grimaced. "What is the cleaner called?"

"I have the box right here. It's called Denture-sheen. I'm afraid she's poisoned herself."

"How much did she drink?"

"Just a couple of gulps, I think. I'm not really sure."

"Does the box list an active ingredient?"

"Let's see . . . oh yes. It says, 'Active ingredient: two percent carbamide peroxide.'"

Paul used his best soothing voice. "I really don't think you have anything to worry about. Your father puts those teeth in his mouth, so I doubt the stuff is toxic, and that's a fairly low dose of peroxide. She might have a stomachache but I don't think it'll come to more than that. If you like, I can give you the number to the Poison Control Center, and you can ask them."

Greatly relieved, the woman sighed, "Okay. Thank you so much."

"My pleasure, ma'am." He gave her the 800-number, then disconnected.

"Paul, there's a doctor on line two calling in a new prescription," Phyllis said.

Paul got a prescription pad and a pen ready. "Hello, this is Pharmacist Paul speaking. How can I help you?"

"Doctor Anderson here. Do you always keep physicians waiting this long?"

"I'm sorry about that, Doctor Anderson. I had a poisoning question on the other line."

"Then your tech should just take down the prescription instead of making me wait. I don't have time to sit listening to canned music."

Paul remained calm. "Only a licensed pharmacist can take a new prescription over the phone, Doctor. It's the law. Now, how can I help you?"

The doctor cursed under his breath, then snapped, "My patient needs azithromycin, 500 milligrams STAT, then 250 milligrams daily for 4 days. Label and dispense name brand only."

Paul scrawled as fast as he could. "You mean a Z-Pak?"

"Yes. And put a couple refills on it."

"And the patient's name?"

"I already gave that to your tech," the physician spat.

"Can I get it again, please, just to be legal?"

"It's Kristen Jensen."

"Birth date?"

"I don't have it."

"Do you know her telephone?"

"Why do you need that?"

Paul's patience was wearing quickly. "As with other common names, I probably have four or five Kristen Jensens in my files. I just want to make sure I give the medicine to the right patient, that's all."

"It's quite simple, son. She'll be the one asking for a prescription from me."

Paul sighed. "Okay. And can I get your first name, please?"

More cursing. "What for?"

"Again, there's probably more than one Dr. Anderson in northern California."

"William Anderson. Doctor William Severance Anderson the Fourth. Do you need my blood type and shoe size too?"

"No, just your DEA number, please."

"Oh for cripe's sake! Zithromax is an antibiotic, son, not a controlled substance. Or don't they teach you that in druggist's school?"

"I am aware of that, sir, but all insurance companies use DEA numbers to identify the prescriber. That's their policy, not mine."

The doctor rattled off his DEA number and then hung up.

"Thank you, Dr. Anderson," Paul said to the dial tone. "And you have a great day, too, sir."

Phyllis smirked at Paul knowingly. "He hung up on you, didn't he?"

Paul nodded. "Charming man. I can't imagine what his bedside manner is like."

"Yes you can, you're just too polite to say."

"I thought days like this didn't happen in small towns," said Paul, slowly shaking his head.

"Welcome to 'drug-free' America," Phyllis said, patting him on the shoulder as she left the dispensary. "Someday, things will be better."

Before Paul could say anything more, two more phone lines lit up.

Phyllis returned smiling. "You take line one, I'll take two."

"Thanks," Paul said with a marked weariness straining his voice. He picked up the handset. "Crescent Cove Pharmacy. Pharmacist Paul speaking."

A voice filled with more happiness than should be legal asked, "Are you tired of your current wireless phone service? Are you fed up with overage minutes and roaming charges? Well, your troubles are now over—"

Paul hung up.

CHAPTER TWENTY-EIGHT

CRESCENT COVE, CALIFORNIA

After having made a good start cleaning the Kingsford place, Paul had contacted the Mayflower Moving and Storage Company in Temecula. The soonest they could deliver his possessions was Wednesday, the day before Thanksgiving. The delivery would include furniture, extra clothing, garage and gardening tools, exercise equipment, several books, a few pieces of art, and a random assortment of kitchen utensils. No major appliances or larger items. He had sold most everything before coming to Crescent Cove in order to avoid a laborious move. He hated moving more than he did a trip to the dentist.

The moving truck didn't show up until half past eight that evening. The movers quickly unloaded everything in Paul's living room, then left. He spent the rest of the evening unpacking and organizing. By 2 AM, the task was only forty percent completed, but he was beat. He was asleep almost before his head hit the pillow.

The following day, not having any invitations to Thanksgiving dinner, Paul was able to finish organizing his possessions by that evening. He sullenly ate a Hungry Man turkey dinner on the large dining room table he had purchased at a local shop.

Sitting at his desk in the study, Paul booted up his PC and reviewed the items he had transferred to a jump-drive from the pharmacy. A list of pharmacy personnel included Phyllis Stevenson, pharmacy technician; Brooke McGregor, certified pharmacy technician; Jacob Christian, sales clerk; Erika Nicholls, sales clerk; and Dawna Gardener, sales clerk.

All personnel manned the soda fountain when necessary. It was actually Jacob's favorite position. It gave the boy a chance to flirt with all the young female clientele. Paul had met each employee and liked them all. Thankfully, he also discovered the name of Kenneth Hoggard, a floating pharmacist from Ukiah who helped out from time to time. In a miscellaneous file, the name Raju Saleh appeared on the list as a computer software specialist.

The next folder contained a list of important town agencies, including the electric company, water conservancy, sewer service, refuse and recycling company, and telephone company. Additionally, Paul found listings for the offices of the mayor and the sheriff, a local medical and dental clinic (which he already knew), and the number to Bonnie's Sweets 'n' Treats.

The final folder contained information on the pharmacy at Pathway to Greater Light Recovery Center. The contact's name was Betty Mumford. Pulling up the file, Paul was surprised to find it empty, as if someone had wiped it clean. He checked the waste basket and recovery files. Still nothing. He shrugged and closed the file.

Phyllis had already called each service and utility company on the list to tell them of Crescent Cove Pharmacy's change of ownership, and to transact any fees for recording the change. According to Phyllis, the whole thing passed without a hitch.

The following Monday, Paul noticed that Phyllis went about her tasks with minimal cheeriness. Normally working with machinelike efficiency, she puttered about the store solemn and melancholy, and refused to meet Paul's eyes. Paul guessed it was lingering anxiety over Val's death.

"Phyllis, if you want to take a few days off, I'll understand," Paul offered. "I'm sure we could call in Brooke to handle the load."

She shook her head. "I'll be fine, but thanks."

"I don't mean to pry, but if there is something besides Val's death that's bothering you, I'd like to help."

She considered him thoughtfully before answering. "Why don't you come to my house for dinner tonight. We really need to discuss some things before you get too stuck in here."

"What do you mean by 'too stuck in'?"

Her eyes misted. She took Paul gently by the wrist and pulled him out of earshot of the sales clerk who was mixing a milkshake at the fountain. "You're a nice man, Paul. I know you've had some sorrows in life that don't seem fair. I just don't want to see any more hardship come your way."

"What hardships?"

She daubed her eyes and said with a forced smile, "Never mind now. Let's get back to work, and I'll tell you tonight. What would you like for dinner?"

Paul did not answer right away. He wasn't thinking of the forthcoming meal; instead, he felt confused by the strange emotions plaguing his technician. Why would she think hardships were coming his way? Did it have to do with the sheriff, or the pharmacy, or . . . what? To the best of his knowledge, he had not done anything illegal or unethical. The only thing he was guilty of was being in an awkward situation not of his making. At least, he didn't think it was of his making. Had his purchase of Crescent Cove Pharmacy driven Val Mince to commit suicide—the straw that broke the camel's back, as it were?

No, that couldn't be it. Val had offered the pharmacy for sale and Paul had accepted. It was as simple as that.

"Paul?"

Snapping from his quandaries, Paul said, "Sorry. I don't really care. I'm sure whatever you make will be delicious."

"Oh, nonsense. You must have some favorite."

Adopting an air of seriousness, he said, "Okay. What are your clam chowder and biscuits like?"

"The stuff of legends." Phyllis smiled.

"Fine. What time?"

"Seven thirty?"

"I'll be there. And thanks."

"Save that for later," she said without humor. "When I'm done telling you what I have to say, you may not be so thankful."

CHAPTER TWENTY-NINE

CRESCENT COVE, CALIFORNIA

The Stevensons' home stood at the end of a residential section of town seated in a wash between two sweeping foothills. Because it was an older neighborhood, each house boasted a yard full of mature trees and landscaping. An ancient brick entry wall flanked both sides of De Fuca Street, a quiet lane named after the 1592 explorer believed to be the first European to see that area of northern California. Timeworn, green patina covered the brass lettering proclaiming the community "Juan De Fuca Valle."

Paul parked on the street next to a fragrant peppertree and walked up to the porch. Mr. Stevenson opened the door before Paul knocked and, shaking his guest's hand, pulled him inside. Paul did a double-take. Something about Mr. Stevenson looked vaguely familiar, but he couldn't place why.

"Call me Cliff," the man beamed. He was a short, balding man with a ready smile and belly fashioned from an excess of wonderful home cooking.

"Thanks, Cliff. I'm Paul. Have we met before?"

"No, I don't think so."

"You look familiar. Have you been down to the pharmacy lately?"

"No, but Phyl probably has a picture of me there somewhere," Cliff chuckled. "I look a lot like Tom Selleck in photos."

"That's got to be it." Paul laughed, removing his jacket. "My word, something smells great."

"Hope you came hungry," Cliff Stevenson grinned. "Phyllis is cooking up a storm."

"I hope she didn't make too much," Paul replied. "I asked her not to go to any trouble."

"Oh, now don't you worry about that. She always likes to put on a feast for our guests. Can't convince her to do otherwise."

"I see," Paul said, following Cliff into the living room.

"What're you drinking?"

"Nothing, thanks. You have a very nice house, Cliff."

"Yeah, it keeps the rain off our heads, but it's draftier than thirty-year-old long johns. I suspect your house has a few drafts too."

Paul laughed. "Actually, Mrs. Kingsford did a pretty good job patching things up before—" He stopped short, not wanting to bring up such a negative subject.

"Before that big guy killed her," Cliff finished for him.

"Yeah."

"Listen, Paul. Phyl and I have lived here since the dawn of time. There's nothing we don't know about, and a few things we wish we didn't know about. I guess that's why she invited you over. She doesn't want you to have any more unpleasant surprises."

"That's right, Paul," Phyllis said from the doorway to the kitchen. "Crescent Cove used to be such a lovely place to raise a family. But . . . I don't know. The last couple of years things have just gotten a little too weird around here."

"What do you mean?" Paul asked.

She shook her head, delaying her answer. "Dinner's ready. Come to the table and we'll talk."

The clam chowder was thick enough to use as spackle; large chunks of clam, potato, and celery lay mired in a sumptuous white sauce. It was the best Paul had ever tasted. In fact, there was so much meat it was more clam than chowder. And Phyllis's layered biscuits were so flaky they resembled puck-sized reams of buttery parchment rather than dinner rolls. Everything was incredibly delicious, and Paul knew why Cliff carried his spare tire with pride.

Their dinner conversation took on many topics but mostly covered the early days of Crescent Cove. To Paul, the town sounded like a perfect mix of a Norman Rockwell painting and a Mark Twain novel. Low crime. No poverty. Just the joy of living from day to day and lots of good, honest, hard work.

"Then, ever since they built that research facility, strange things started happening around here," Phyllis said as she served Paul a third bowl of chowder.

"A research facility?"

"That Pathway place," Cliff explained. "It was a government construction project they built for the Army. Did you know that?"

"Really?"

"Yeah. It's down Highway 1 a piece, hidden up in the mountains. They call it the 'Greater Light Center,' or something like that."

"Yeah, I passed by it the other day." Paul tilted his head. "I thought it was a hospital of sorts."

"Maybe. Top-secret stuff goes on in there. No outsiders are allowed in without security clearance, even today. Everything is done behind closed doors."

"But I saw a computer file from the pharmacy with Pathway listed on an icon," Paul said.

"It's been a while, but we used to send stuff there a lot," Phyllis divulged. "At first Val didn't mind, but later he questioned the kinds of intravenous compounds he made. Dangerous biological stuff, he told me. Stuff he didn't like to make."

"Ah—the laminar flow hood," Paul said, finally deducing why the pharmacy had the Daw Technology unit.

"Yes," Phyllis said. "I don't know why the center didn't just use its own medical services."

"Pathway bought the place from the Army a couple of years after the government abandoned it," Cliff continued.

"I pulled up that file the other day, but it appears to be empty," Paul said. "If we did their compounding, legally, we should still have those records in the pharmacy."

Phyllis shook her head. "They've all disappeared. There's no proof left behind."

"Did Val give them back to Pathway's doctors?"

Phyllis shrugged. "You're right in thinking the place is a hospital of sorts—exactly what kind is the thousand-dollar question. Perhaps they finally got their own pharmacy, too."

"Yeah, that would make sense," Paul agreed, then said, "You hinted that there were other strange happenings outside of Pathway . . ."

"Lots of 'em," Cliff said.

"Like what?"

"Like people disappearing . . . or dying suddenly."

"Murders?"

"Not so as you would suspect. But Phyl and I think they were."

Paul set his spoon into his soup bowl. He no longer had an appetite.

Phyllis continued. "At first, Pathway hired a bunch of townsfolk for civilian jobs. Ever since they moved the highway and connected it to U.S. 101, the town started dying off financially—lots of people out of work and having to go on welfare and such. This was a proud community, Paul. Unlike the rest of the state, people here don't like the idea of the government paying for everything. So when Pathway came along offering regular hours at good pay, it didn't seem to matter what kind of jobs they were."

Cliff nodded. "That's when Harold Bright came to town and became mayor. He started refinancing the town's debts and suggested most of the townsfolk work for Pathway."

"Did you work for them?" Paul asked Cliff.

"Yep. And I saw some things I wish I hadn't. Animal testing of the worst kind. Brutal stuff."

"You're kidding," Paul smirked, sincerely hoping Cliff was pulling his leg.

"No sir. I wish I was. The ASPCA would have a field day if they ever found out."

"Why didn't anyone report them?" Paul wondered.

Tears immediately sprang to Phyllis's eyes. "Some tried," she whispered through a constricted throat. Cliff shifted his stare to his empty bowl, no longer meeting Paul's questioning gaze.

"And . . ." Paul led after a long silence.

"Those are the dead ones," Cliff said quietly.

A few minutes passed in ghostly silence, as if no one wanted to be the first to speak. Then Phyllis got up and began clearing the table.

"Can you prove any of this?" Paul asked hesitantly.

"No. It's all hearsay as far as the law is concerned," Cliff told him.

"But . . . excuse me for asking, but why aren't you dead?"

Mr. Stevenson smiled and winked. "I'm very careful who I talk to about it. When Phyllis said you could be trusted, we both agreed you should know."

"And they still check on us now and then," Phyllis added. "Every once in a while a black SUV parks outside our house for a few hours or so. They think they're being sneaky but it's pretty obvious who they are."

A thousand questions filled Paul's mind. He didn't know where to begin. Or worse, where this all might end. "Do you still work there?"

Cliff scoffed. "Heavens no. After only a few years, all unauthorized personnel were laid off. Civilian contract labor is rarely taken in anymore—and that's only through high-level clearance. I saw a bit of that before I left. The worst part is, anyone who has worked there is sworn to secrecy."

"Or else they die," Paul added.

"Well, that wasn't in the contract word for word, but that's the way it turned out."

"It's not just keeping silent either," Phyllis said. "Anyone who used to work there can't leave Crescent Cove without express permission from Pathway."

"Oh, come on," Paul blurted, unbelieving. "How can they stop someone from just picking up and sneaking out in the middle of the night?"

"Some have tried. But even they end up dead, regardless of where they run off to," Cliff said. "If you ever worked inside the compound, then it's set in stone—even if it's not on paper."

"But how do they know? How can they regulate that?"

"We're not sure," Cliff said, "but we believe the mayor and perhaps a few others in town are still involved—keeping tabs on everyone."

"And Pathway is willing to kill people over animal-testing practices? That seems awfully dramatic—and brutal."

"That's what we never understood. Something else had to be going on in there, but I never saw it."

"We think that Val must have discovered something," Phyllis said. "He went inside a time or two, and I guess that sealed his fate. He must have known the truth for a long time, and it finally got to him. When he tried leaving, they found out, and . . ."

Paul opened his mouth but stopped before asking the obvious. Then quietly, in little more than a whisper, he said, "I hesitate to ask."

"Then don't," Phyllis said, sending a warning scowl in her husband's direction. He nodded in agreement.

"I don't mean to be rude, but I find this all pretty far-fetched. I mean, they would have to monitor postal services, land lines, cell phones, even email messages. And I've seen a few satellite dishes around town that can send email without a land line. How can they do that—and do it without getting caught?" Paul asked.

"That's part of the mystery. It may come down to the ex-Pathway workers being too scared to try." Phyllis paused and shook her head. "You know, most would consider what we've told you senile conjecture, but I know we're right. In any event, I feel we've already said too much for your safety." She again paused as tears welled in her eyes. "That's why it would be best if you got out now."

"You want me to leave?" Paul asked with a forced chuckle.

"No. And yes. I like you, Paul. But I don't want to see you hurt."

Considering everything he'd learned that evening, Paul realized he probably already knew too much. "Am I in any danger?" he asked cautiously.

"No. Not as long as you pretend to know nothing about Pathway," Cliff assured him. "And never go snooping around there."

"*That's* why everyone gets upset when someone talks about leaving town . . ." Paul mused, as a sudden enlightenment answered a dozen questions in his mind.

"Perhaps. It's commonly known that anytime one of the old-timers tries to leave, something prevents it from happening."

"Or they end up dead," Cliff added.

"How many 'old-timers' are left?" Paul asked.

"About a dozen or so. Most of them dear friends," Phyllis said, carrying the last of the serving ware to the kitchen.

After clearing the dishes, the three friends moved back to the table with thick slices of apple pie. Despite its fragrant aroma and mouthwatering appearance, no one was eating the dessert. They all stared silently at the seashell centerpiece on the table. When Paul spoke again, his voice was hushed, as if he were afraid who might overhear. "Is the sheriff in on this?"

"Baker? In cahoots with Pathway?" Cliff asked, a wide smile splitting his face. "Not likely . . . but there's no way to truly tell. He's usually all bark and no bite, that one. He's wily, but if he *has* ever been inside the complex he's doing a great job of keeping it a secret. His dad was the sheriff before him—did you know that?"

"No, I didn't know. Where's his father now?"

Phyllis pushed her slice of pie away from her. "He was one of the first who suspected something illegal was going on. He went to investigate one day. No one's seen him since."

CHAPTER THIRTY

NORTHERN CALIFORNIA

Breakfast consisted of melon slices in light cream, toasted bagels with orange marmalade, a hard-boiled egg, and cranberry juice. Bria ate everything except the cranberry juice. She knew the strong acidic flavor was perfect for masking the foul taste of medicines, with which Pathway had undoubtedly laced the juice. Crotchety Nurse Jones insisted she drink the juice, as it was part of her urinary tract infection treatment. Bria declined, claiming the acidity in cranberry juice hurt the enamel of her teeth. Each claim boasted some truth. Neither nurse was willing to budge.

"Some plain water would be nice," Bria said in the most cordial voice she could summon.

Crotchety Nurse Jones left the room without comment.

Using a walker, Bria shuffled to the bathroom. As there was no shower in the small space, Bria gave herself a quick sponge bath, brushed her hair and teeth, and changed her clothing. The hospital had provided her with fresh underclothing, an assortment of pajama-like pants and shirts, and terrycloth slippers. Feeling refreshed, she returned to her room and sat in a chair while an old orderly changed her bed sheets. It was a fixed routine. She always tried talking with the orderly, but the man remained silent and dutifully performed his chores without comment.

"Thank you," Bria said. The man left the room without returning the pleasantry or making eye contact.

Just as Bria settled into bed, Young Nurse Jones entered, looking nervous and bubbly at the same time. "Good morning, Miss Georgopolis. How're you feeling?"

"I told you before, it's Bria, and I'm fine, thank you."

"I'm so happy to hear that." The young nurse was being overtly open and loud, doing a poor job of subtly masking her anxiety. "I'm here to tell you your PT session has been postponed until three o'clock today."

"Oh?" Bria was truly disappointed.

"So, to pass the time," Young Nurse Jones continued, "I brought you some more reading material."

The young woman was now sweating, yet her hands trembled as if shivering from cold. She studiously avoided looking at the camera and made every movement broad and plain to see.

"Thank you," Bria said, questioning the nurse with her eyes.

Young Nurse Jones shook her head a split second then continued her canned banter. "Now, I know you don't like romance novels much, but I don't have anything else to offer, and this is one of my favorites."

Accepting the paperback, Bria kept eye contact with her nervous friend. "Thank you, Nurse Jones. This'll be fine."

The young nurse daubed her hands on her smock, as if ridding herself of any association with the book. She backed away quickly and fidgeted with her hands while waiting for Bria to look at the novel. The young nurse folded and unfolded her arms, finally sliding her hands into her smock pockets. "Read it cover to cover right away, and then tell me what you think, okay?"

"Sure," Bria said, still very much confused.

Young Nurse Jones scooted from the room in a nervous trot. A few seconds passed before Bria glanced at the paperback in her hands. *Passion Enslaved* was its title. The jacket featured a woman who looked surprisingly like Bria herself, although Bria wouldn't be caught dead wearing the sparse, lurid, Colonial-period clothing the model on the cover wore. Bria scoffed and set the book aside. The young nurse should know better than to bring her such a book. Instead, Bria busied herself with an old *National Geographic* the orderly had left.

* * *

The clock on Bria's bed stand read 2:52 PM. Only a few minutes before they'd come to take her to physical therapy. Bria set her mind to putting on a good act this session. While she wanted to do all she could to get stronger, she needed to appear weak and vulnerable. Precisely at three o'clock, an orderly entered with a wheelchair and helped Bria into it.

"You ready for another torture session, Miss Georgopolis?" the man asked.

"Not really. I'm not one to complain, but I don't feel very strong today," she lied.

"Ah, you'll do fine."

"Thanks for the vote of confidence." She flashed him a radiant smiled. "By the way, I'd rather you just called me Bria." The orderly smiled back as expected, but didn't say any more. "And I can call you . . . ?" she prompted.

"Orderly Jones."

Bria slowly closed her eyes in resignation. "I should have guessed."

Arriving at the physical therapy room, Buff Dr. Smith thanked the orderly and helped Bria onto a table. "How are the legs today?"

"Like soggy spaghetti."

"Oh, come on. The nurses tell me you've mastered the walker pretty well."

"I can get to the bathroom and back, but that's about it."

Testing the range of motion of each leg, PT Smith said, "Well I can't detect anything mechanically wrong with them. And the MRI we took shows normal innervation and solid tendons and bones. By all rights, you should be skipping down the halls instead of coasting in a wheelchair."

"I'll try harder."

The large doctor put on a mischievous grin. "I'm here to see that you do."

Bria tackled her regimen of exercises and therapy with minimal gusto. She actually broke a sweat, but did not reveal just how strong she was. As always, she enjoyed the massage and whirlpool bath, but did little to instill in her trainer any inkling of progress. Still, by the end of the session, she was a limp rag doll, and couldn't walk back to her room even if she had wanted to.

In spite of her relaxed state, Bria could not drop off to sleep. She picked up the paperback Young Nurse Jones had given her and began reading chapter one. After just a few paragraphs, however, she shook her head and closed the book. It amazed her that smut like that actually sold millions of copies each year. She questioned why Young Nurse Jones was so insistent she read the book "cover to cover right away" as she put it. The young woman was more than nervous about it—she had actually been scared.

Bria examined the cover art again and breathed a deep sigh of remorse, trying to delay reading the book. It looked like a typical romance novel, full of syrupy descriptions, suggestive innuendos, fanciful, unrealistic characters, and overstated, nauseating prose. But that was only a guess. Although she had seen countless novels of this sort, Bria had never read one front to back.

"Oh well. There's only one way to find out," she said just under her breath.

* * *

Bria was bleary-eyed by the time she finished the first fifty pages. Shamefully, she had to admit that while the style of writing was not to her liking, the story actually had some merit. The author obviously had done a lot of research, as the novel contained many historical facts Bria knew to be true—if somewhat embellished. Then, turning to page fifty-one, Bria's breath caught short.

Down the length of the page, underlined with a blue pencil, was a series of eight words.

> "If you think I'm going to jeopardize the governorship and change the way I treat my property, you are sadly mistaken." The blaze in Captain Gregory Bordeaux's eyes was like an emperor's funeral pyre: raging, intense, and unquenchable.
>
> Ignoring the danger of contradicting her father, Charity Alexandria Bordeaux spit out her words as if expelling a poison. "They are men and women, not property."

Captain Gregory Bordeaux stepped up to his impudent daughter and stared down at her. His hand gripped the hilt of the dueling sword General Andrew Jackson had personally given him last fall. A voice inside Charity's pretty head cried, *Run for your life!* It was all she could do not to heed that warning.

Bria read the underlined words by themselves. Young Nurse Jones's message was terrifyingly clear.

CHAPTER THIRTY-ONE

NORTHERN CALIFORNIA

Her evening meal held little interest. Bria was sure she could no longer trust anything they fed her. Instead of the spicy cheese enchiladas and refried frijoles placed before her, she opted for a can of Ensure plus Protein. Figuring a factory-sealed can was a good safeguard against tampering, Bria drank the can slowly to make it last. Her reasoning was a queasy stomach, yet it was a heartbreaking excuse; the fragrant, gooey enchiladas smelled dangerously delicious. Believing her complaint of heartburn from Mexican food, the staff at Pathway complied with her wishes. It was the most difficult lie she had ever told.

Bria wasn't sure how much longer she could keep up her ruse. She requested to see Nurse Jones—the young one—to ask her to brush her hair again. In the meantime, Bria leafed through the paperback, skimming the text for marked words. On page 202, she found another set.

> Obediah's dark eyes did little to hide his heart-felt desire; however, he was still very much afraid. "Miss Bordeaux, this be wrong."
>
> Placing her finely manicured fingers on his lips, Charity whispered, "I know, Obe. I know this is wrong. This whole place is wrong, but the love I have for you feels so right." Her voice was strained and husky. "You feel it too. I know you do."
>
> "But—but Massa Gregory. What if he find out?"

"<u>Must</u> my father run every part of my life?" Charity Alexandria Bordeaux exclaimed in a voice that hissed like the rattlesnake Obediah had killed with his bare hands earlier that day to save her life. "I'm eighteen years old. Most girls my age have already had a baby by now. I know you want to <u>run away</u> with me, Obe. Let it be <u>tonight</u>—right now. Please, <u>before it's too late</u>."

I must run away tonight? Bria rubbed her legs. She knew she could walk but wondered how much walking—or running—would be required. There were so many unknowns. She didn't know where Pathway was located. She didn't know the layout of the hospital or the surrounding land. And even if she did get out, what then? She didn't have any clothing other than a flimsy pair of pajamas and some slippers. She had no money, no identification. Nothing.

Skimming through the rest of the novel, Bria found no other hidden messages. She didn't really expect any. What more could be said?

* * *

Just before nine o'clock, Young Nurse Jones entered the room. She immediately picked up the brush and began stroking Bria's hair. "How's your reading coming?"

"Well, I'm very surprised by the storyline."

"Surprised?"

"Yes. Unless I'm mistaken, the author likes to put double meanings into some of her passages," Bria said in a volume the hidden microphone would pick up, but trying to keep her subject matter enigmatic. "I'm halfway finished. I can't wait to *run* through the rest of it."

Nurse Jones nodded slowly. "Good. I hoped you'd like this one."

"Yes, but I'm not sure if I'll read much more tonight. I'm not feeling so good right now."

"Really? What's wrong?"

"I don't know. I feel so weak, like I can't even lift my hands over my head," she said, winking at Nurse Jones. Since her back was to the camera, she knew the expression went unnoticed. "And when I do, it hurts like crazy."

"Do you need a painkiller?"

"I don't like those things, you know that. But in this instance, maybe just one might help me get some sleep, especially tonight."

"I'll ask the floor nurse to bring you a Vicodin. Are you sure that's all you need tonight?"

"Not unless you can personally guide me through dreamland." Bria sighed heavily.

The young nurse chuckled uneasily. "I wish. No, that simply is not possible."

"Too bad. I hope I'll get there on my own. It's strange, but I usually don't dream that often." Understanding sparkled in the nurse's eyes.

"Oh, I dream all the time," Young Nurse Jones said as she continued to brush her patient's hair. "I like the dreams where I ascend up a long flight of stairs, then go through a magical door, and then run through a beautiful field of tall grass."

Excellent. Bria pouted and moaned as if envious of the young nurse's dream. "Sounds like a wonderful place."

"Oh, it is. I'm not much of an athlete, but in that dream I can run forever, day or night."

"Do you follow the setting sun or meet it when it rises?"

"Oh, I always follow it to where it sets on the horizon. It's so beautiful. And the ocean there is so blue."

Bria hugged herself. "I envy you, Nurse Jones. I wish my dreams were as nice."

The young nurse stopped stroking Bria's hair and handed her the brush, giving Bria's hand a tender squeeze before moving to the door. Bria saw tears glistening in the young woman's eyes. "I'll see about that pain pill, okay?"

"Thank you so much, Nurse Jones."

"Sure thing—" her voice cracked with emotion. "And good luck with your dreams."

* * *

Bria placed the pain pill in her cheek and pretended to swallow. Betty Mumford gently tucked the sheets around her body as if swaddling her own child for the night. Stroking her cheek, she whispered,

"You just sleep now, Bria. I knew you'd pull through. I knew it the first time I met you."

Bria sighed low and soft as if already well on her way to dreamland. She listened intently to Nurse Mumford's footfalls moving down the hall. She then spit the pill into her hand and slid it inside her pillowcase. Tonight was not a night for sleeping.

CHAPTER THIRTY-TWO

NORTHERN CALIFORNIA

The clock read 1:54 AM.

Bria had planned on making her escape at two, but the last few minutes had ticked away painfully slowly, so much so that she could not stay in bed any longer.

Opening the paperback novel in which she had received her warnings, Bria silently tore out the marked pages and stuffed them into her pajama pocket. She then smoothed out the rest of the book and placed it on her nightstand.

Slowly pushing her pillows under her covers and rumpling the sheet to mimic the form of her body, Bria slid from the bed as quietly as possible. Standing flush against the wall, she looked at the fake sleeping Bria and smirked. It was a pitiful attempt at an old trick, but it was the best she could do. With any luck, the darkened room would aid her skullduggery.

With her back to the wall, she slumped down and reached for the small trash can with her foot. Sliding the can toward her, she removed the translucent plastic liner and emptied its contents back into the can. Carefully climbing onto the head of her bed, Bria held the liner just under the CCTV box. Taking a few deep breaths, she quickly slid the semitransparent liner over the dome and yanked it tight. She had no idea if the camera would still pick up the nightlight at the far side of the room, but that was her intent. With further luck, the opaque nature of the liner would mask her movements enough for her to slip out of the room undetected.

On her trips to the physical therapy room, she had not noticed any cameras beyond those in her room; therefore, she felt confident she could traverse the hallways undetected.

She climbed down and held her breath, listening. Then, donning her slippers and a beige terrycloth robe she'd taken from the physical therapy room on her last visit, she rolled under the bed to the other side and edged her way to the foot of it. There was only a space of four or five feet to the door—the space in which the camera might see her. Remaining low, Bria rocked back and forth to get her rhythm, then lunged for the open doorway, praying her rapid movement would appear as nothing more than a blur on the masked camera.

Landing with a soft grunt, the highly polished floor offered little friction against the soft terrycloth robe, and Bria slid to the opposite side of the hallway. She remained frozen, splayed out like a helpless animal on an ice floe. She again held her breath and listened to the emptiness of the hallway.

No alarms sounded. No spotlights came on.

Moving much faster now, Bria got to her feet and headed down the hall toward a lighted intersection. Her soft slippers made hushed noises on the linoleum flooring, and she moved down the hall as silently as a feather on a breeze. At the first corner, she crouched to her knees and slowly peeked around the edge. A nurse's station sat midway down the next length of hallway. A nurse she did not recognize concentrated on something Bria could not see—probably paperwork of some kind—under a single bank of fluorescent lights. Bria stretched her neck out a bit further to get a better view of the corridor. Although there were numerous doors within view, she could not see any exit signs along its length. Quickly, she retreated into her hallway and ran to the opposite end, praying Young Nurse Jones's information was correct.

Easing around this corner, Bria breathed a sigh of relief as she saw no nurses' station. The corridor was dark and uninviting, but she ventured into it without pause. Running with surprising balance, Bria suspected her legs had regained more than their original strength. It was as if the influence of "the vaccine," as Betty had called it, had indeed elicited some magical response in her tissues. Even Bria was surprised at her agility. But not having taxed her full endurance for a number of weeks, she wondered how long her newfound strength would last.

Nearing another intersection, Bria slowed her stride and slid to a perfect stop at the edge of the wall. Peering around this corner, she saw another dimly lit corridor, this one lined with doors. An exit sign spilled a soft green glow on the third door on the right. Running toward the exit, Bria paused at the door opposite from it.

The metal door had a small window covered with aluminum blinds. Beside the door, a plaque read: ISOLATION: WARNING—POSSIBLE BIOHAZARD.

The metal blinds clinked and ticked as she parted them for a look inside.

Bria stopped cold. She tried to draw breath but couldn't. Her eyes, wide with horror, revealed a wash of memory she wished had remained forever veiled. She recognized the cold metal table on which she had lain. She remembered the harsh fetters that bound her against her will. With a sudden soreness in her shoulder, she felt the painful jab of the needle, the eerie black vaccine, the horrifying sensations of the liquid traveling rapidly through her body, and the innocent eyes of a malevolent Betty Mumford. It was a nightmare realized; an imagined scene she had to accept as very real. The flashback caused her knees to weaken and her throat to gag. Breath finally came to her in a spasm of anguish, followed by a flood of tears. With sickening assuredness, she confirmed that all her premonitions and suspicions about Pathway were accurate.

Bria tried to pull her eyes from the darkly lit room but could not. Gritting her teeth against the scream pushing from her throat, she closed her eyes, clamped her fists on either side of her head, and slumped to the floor. A high-pitched wheeze of pure anguish escaped her lips. Scorching fury welled within her like magma in a volcano.

After a number of deep, cleansing breaths, Bria steadied herself. *Focus, Bria!* Forcing the images from her mind, she concentrated on the clues she'd received from Young Nurse Jones. Drawing huge, slow gulps of air in an effort to prevent hyperventilation, Bria patiently counted to twenty before opening her eyes and staggering to her feet. Glancing once more into the isolation room, with her fists blanched and trembling, Bria's jaw clenched so tight her teeth hurt. She swore she would exact revenge. When she got out—*if* she got out—she would immediately return with the authorities before anyone else suffered her fate.

As Bria turned to the exit door, a sharp noise sounded at the end of the hall.

The corridor lights flickered on.

CHAPTER THIRTY-THREE

NORTHERN CALIFORNIA

Bria lunged for the exit door. The aluminum push-bar clacked open. It sounded like the report of a .38 revolver. She did not see anyone at the end of the corridor, which meant no one saw her, but she was certain they had heard her.

Beyond the door, the poured-cement landing offered two routes: up or down. Bria found the stairs were surprisingly narrow, allowing no more than two people to walk abreast. The claustrophobic shaft smelled of a stifling mix of damp air and the sharp, acidic-lime scent of old concrete.

Following Young Nurse Jones's "dream," Bria headed up, taking the stairs two at a time. The staircase led to another landing, which offered an exit door and a continued ascent in the opposite direction—a zigzag route, first east to west, then west to east to the next landing. A single incandescent bulb illuminated each landing and cast a fetid white pallor on the next flight of stairs.

Painted on the door was a large location marker. Bria paused, not to catch her breath, but to stare at the marker in disbelief. It read SUBLEVEL 39. Thirty-nine levels below ground? Confused, she wondered why a private hospital would have such an extensive subterranean network of rooms.

Bria shook her head as if to disentangle cerebral cobwebs. Her room was one level below this one. And the stairs there descended even farther. *How far down does this madhouse go?* she asked herself angrily.

Looking up the next flight of stairs, Bria at first worried she might run into someone on subsequent landings while traversing the staircase. But it didn't register as a big concern; she guessed two o'clock in the morning boasted the same activity level at Pathway as it did anywhere else. And she knew her only avenue for escape was up.

Yet forty stories, at approximately fourteen feet per story . . . made 560 vertical feet! That was roughly the height of the Washington Monument.

Bria took a moment to stretch her hamstrings, calves, and thighs. After a few deep breaths, and with buoyed confidence in her newfound strength, she assaulted the stairs with a determined scowl. If only her Polynesian PT could see her now. The man would probably faint.

Arriving at the next landing, she heard the door two stories below clack open. She stopped dead midway up the next flight of stairs. Holding her breath, she listened intently for sounds indicating pursuit. The stairwell remained silent. For one brief moment, she thought she could hear someone breathing, but no footfalls or other sounds of movement echoed up the cement shaft. She remained frozen, unsure whether to continue her ascent or exit through one of the doors. Then—

"Hello?" a female voice called from two flights below.

Bria chose not to answer.

"Is someone in here?"

Silence.

A full minute passed without further communication.

Then, finally, the door closed with a loud click which ricocheted past Bria and dissolved to nothingness above her.

Determined to make it out, Bria knew she had only one option. She continued up.

A crooked smirk pulled at one corner of Bria's mouth as she recalled having once thought the Stair Master machine at Jake's Gym was a fun exercise. The quadriceps in her thighs burned with a needling fire. Her calf muscles bulged painfully as if ready to burst through the skin. Her glutes cramped with every lunge.

Bria staggered and fell hard against the next rise of stairs. Her newfound abilities apparently did not include endurance. Each raw breath felt like inhaling razorblades. Sweat drenched her pajama top and pasted her bangs to her forehead. She forced herself to continue but her efforts were limited to short bursts of energy.

Pausing at the next landing, it took a moment for Bria to focus on the location marker. SUBLEVEL 19. She closed her eyes and leaned against the cold concrete to catch her breath. Her saliva tasted faintly of blood, and she could hear her pulse throbbing in her ears. Looking at her pajama top, she could literally see her heart pounding against her sternum.

"Keep moving," she whispered with each exhalation. "Keep moving. Keep moving. Keep moving. Keep moving."

Concentrating on putting one foot in front of the other, Bria slowly ascended the next ten stories in a rhythmic, measured tempo. Gratefully, her fatigue lessened. Not forcing a rapid pace somehow allowed her breathing to steady and her muscles to stop screaming in revolt.

Finally reaching Sublevel 2, Bria paused again to reorganize her thoughts. She had no idea where she would find herself once she exited the building. She guessed she was near the coast, but how near was impossible to answer. Was the Pathway hospital surrounded by a fence? Was it near a major highway? Was it even a real hospital? Not pausing to answer such unanswerable questions, she took the next set of stairs at a cautious, silent pace.

Reaching her chosen landing, the door's location marker read GROUND LEVEL. The stairs ascended an unknown number of flights beyond, but she was not interested in exploring that part of the hospital.

Depressing the handle with an extremely delicate touch, as if going too fast would trigger an unseen bomb, Bria eased open the ground-level door a fraction of an inch. The hallway was much longer than the ones below ground and much more brightly lit. The place seemed empty, but she knew that was wishful thinking. She exited the stairwell and headed right, taking each step with the caution of a cat on the prowl. Directly adjacent to the stairwell stood an elevator. The LED display indicated the cab was currently at Sublevel 13, and it was rising.

Just then an inexplicable wave of dizziness assaulted Bria. She closed her eyes and pressed her hands against her temples. Nausea surged in her throat, constricting it. Uncontrollably, she slid to the floor. She had pushed herself too hard, she reasoned. Her compromised physique was not conditioned for such a grueling workout. She forced her eyes open. The corridor swayed. *Concentrate!* Both ends of the hallway intersected blind corners. No one was in sight. No noises could be heard. *Take a moment.*

Numbly, Bria watched the elevator continue to climb. Sublevel 8, and still rising. She would never make the end of the hall before the car arrived. *Get moving!*

Forcing herself back on her feet, she stumbled down the hall, passing a door marked NURSES' LOUNGE. Staggering to a stop, she returned to the lounge and pushed on the door latch. It didn't budge. The elevator bell chimed the cab's arrival. Bria put her weight against the lounge door latch and pressed harder. The elevator door opened just as the lounge door gave way.

The room was well lit and lined with tall lockers. Two small tables stood in the middle of the room, and a coffee counter and sink sat nestled under a blind-covered window.

Running to the window, she lifted the horizontal aluminum slats. The dark night sky caused the window to act as a mirror, and Bria jumped at the sight of her own face staring back at her. Catching her breath, she flipped the latch on the sliding window and eased it open. The feather-soft breeze that wafted through the mesh screen was the sweetest-scented fragrance she had ever inhaled. It smelled of grass and dirt, of dew and pine. It smelled like freedom.

Bria located the clips holding the screen in place and slid them out. The screen fell into the night. Just as she was about to climb onto the countertop, rubber-soled shoes squeaked to a halt just outside the lounge door. Letting the blinds close, Bria moved to an open locker.

Suddenly the incapacitating dizziness enveloped her again. She closed her eyes and wedged herself inside the locker. The confined space actually lessened the feeling of imbalance somewhat. Just as she closed the locker, the lounge door opened.

Looking through the vent slats in the tin door, Bria saw a female nurse enter the room and look around. The nurse was scowling, as if suspicious of something. She began walking slowly around the room, staring at the floor as if looking for footprints. Bria wondered if her cloth slippers had left any marks. The woman then stuck her head inside a small bathroom adjoining the lounge. Finding it empty, she resumed her search by looking in the large cabinets under the sink. Bria held her breath, praying the outside breeze would not rattle the blinds covering the open window. Finding the cabinets empty, the nurse began to open the lockers.

Bria felt blindly for the latch securing the locker door. It offered little surface on which to grab hold. She heard the nurse tug noisily on the door three lockers down. It was locked. The next locker opened and closed with a complaining squeak. The nurse then yanked on the locker door next to Bria. It opened and slammed shut.

Grabbing hold of Bria's locker, the nurse paused as a walkie-talkie crackled to life. She fished the unit from her pocket and brought it to her ear.

"Jones here."

"Any sign of her?" a staticky male voice asked.

"I'm not sure, sir," the nurse answered.

"What do you mean?"

"The door to the nurses' lounge was not closed all the way. It usually is."

"Is there any other door leading out of there?"

"No sir, just a bathroom door."

"She probably wanted to steal a uniform or some other clothing—if she even got that far up," the voice reasoned.

"Her implant is registering off the meter. She has to be close."

"Have you used the electromagnetic restrainer?"

"I enable it every five minutes or so."

"Enabling it that often could be dangerous."

"I am aware of that, sir. But since we have no clue where she is, I'm most likely just shooting blanks. Besides, if she were in range, the EMR would have dropped her in plain sight."

"All right. Alert all exits to double check the ID of any nurse leaving the building, then work your way down, checking each level carefully. Sometimes those meters pick up other signals on the same frequency as the implants."

"Yes sir. I double-check each ping."

The nurse pocketed her walkie-talkie and left the lounge.

Breathing a sigh of relief, Bria immediately left the locker and went to the door. Listening intently to the shoes squeak down the hall, she felt safe for the moment. No alarms had sounded, and most of the lights were still out. Apparently, only a few knew of her escape, and they wanted to keep it quiet for the time being. But the news that she carried an incapacitating implant struck a new tone of fear. It couldn't be as simple as something in her clothing. It had to be something . . . inside. Bria quickly felt along her arms, legs, torso, and the parts of her back she could reach. Nothing seemed to indicate an anomaly in her skin. But because she had been unconscious for an undeterminable amount of time, the Pathway doctors could have implanted the device anywhere. Judging from the nurse's conversation, the "disabling" function had a limited range. But the tracking ability of the implant was still in question. Did that mean she could never truly escape? Was it a simple ID chip or an actual location device that any orbiting satellite could pinpoint?

Deciding to cross that bridge later, Bria opened a few lockers as quietly as possible, found a small pair of tennis shoes, and tried them on. Unlike Cinderella's glass slipper, they did not fit with magical perfection. In fact, she could barely get her foot inside. Checking other lockers proved just as fruitless, as many had combination locks securing them. Those that were open offered little in the way of useful items, especially usable clothing. Desperate, she entered the small bathroom adjoining the lounge and found a pair of running shoes. Sitting on the cold, tile floor, Bria slid one on. It fit—not perfectly, but good enough.

With her feet newly shod, Bria crawled onto the counter and eased out of the window. She dropped to the ground and found the window screen in a large azalea just under the sill. Putting the screen back in place, she then ran to the edge of the building. In spite of the disturbing information she had just overheard, Bria's initial success instilled in her an energetic burst of confidence.

When she reached the corner of the building and peered around it, that confidence plummeted like a well-oiled guillotine blade.

CHAPTER THIRTY-FOUR

NORTHERN CALIFORNIA

The hospital, if that's what it was, boasted a chain-link fence, approximately twelve feet high, around its perimeter, with looped razor-wire curling along the top edge. Security lights flooded the fence and adjacent ground with pale illumination that turned the area a dirty yellow-white. Everything else was black or gray. Had the builders erected lofty guard towers on each corner, the place would have been an obvious prison yard.

As she surveyed the compound, Bria's night vision seemed unusually sharp, as if aided by ultra-low-light equipment. Only instead of a monochromatic green hue, the images she saw were slightly colored and sharply defined. Not questioning her newfound ability, she took in the details of the perimeter and grounds in a couple of glances. Assuming the front gate had already received word of her escape, she ran along the dark edge of the hospital to a parking lot bordered by trees. Praying the compound did not have motion-sensing equipment, Bria dashed for the cover of a decorative stand of quaking aspens.

The night air was chill with humid breezes. Clots and wisps of fog scrabbled across the lawn and around trees and cars like frantic spirits fleeing detection. Initially she'd hoped one of the cars in the lot would have keys in the ignition or hidden behind the sun visor, courtesy of Young Nurse Jones. But Bria hesitated checking each car; the parking area was brightly illuminated with mercury vapor lamps. Additionally, she couldn't imagine Pathway not having at least one security camera there. Discarding that plan of action, Bria moved to the edge of the tree cover to seek a second option. She needed to keep moving, both to stay warm and to avoid capture. Also, she was afraid Pathway controllers would trigger another fainting spell at just the wrong moment. She chortled bitterly. Currently, *any* moment was the wrong moment.

As she sat in a pocket of darkness, a smattering of laughter drifted toward her, along with the garbled segments of conversation between two men. The voices hailed from a large warehouse that stood a few yards from the parking lot. Staying low and in as much shadow as possible, Bria dashed to the back of the warehouse. An open service door at the rear allowed her to enter the steel-sided building undetected.

Frowning in confusion, Bria felt she had stepped through a portal which placed her in a location totally alien to a recovery hospital. Moving behind a stack of crates marked FIELD DISPERSION GEAR, she gawked at the amount of high-tech hardware in front of her. A twin-turbo Dauphin helicopter filled the center of the complex, along with a couple of unmarked Mercedes touring sedans, a business-class Hummer, and an electric golf cart. Painted along the tail of the helicopter was a bold insignia from some company Bria did not recognize: GULF SHORE INVESTMENTS.

A few yards to her right, a sign indicated the location of a restroom. The voices were discernable now. Two men sitting at a desk near a large retractable door were comparing the "virtues" of Angelina Jolie versus Christina Aguilera. At least that was Bria's slant on the disgustingly masculine chitchat.

"Hold that thought," one of the men said. "I gotta purge some of this coffee."

"No problemo," the other responded.

As the man came into view, Bria saw he wore a nondescript security guard uniform, a red beret tilted at a jaunty angle, and a holster complete with a large sidearm. He could not have been more than twenty-one years old. Thin, gangly, pimple-faced, the young man sported a frail mustache a stiff breeze could have removed. The guard entered the restroom without seeing Bria.

Easing toward the restroom, making sure to keep out of view of the guard at the desk, Bria followed.

The young man stood facing a urinal, his back toward Bria. "Coffee going right through you too, huh?" he said to the wall in front of him.

Bria stepped up to the man and quickly removed his pistol.

"What the—?"

"Quiet," she demanded, pushing the gun's barrel into the back of the young man's head. "Don't say a word or what little brains you have will be wallpaper."

"Who are you?"

Bria shoved the gun barrel into the base of the security guard's skull, forcing his face into the wall above the urinal. "I mean it."

As much as possible, the young man nodded frantically.

"Finish your business and move to the sink."

The young man complied.

"Wash your hands."

"Huh?" The man asked while trying to get a glimpse of Bria in the mirror above the sink.

"Stop trying to look at me and wash your hands. Or don't they teach you personal hygiene at this hospital?"

"Hospital?"

Bria pushed the gun between the young man's shoulder blades. "Shut up and just do it."

He nodded and quickly washed his hands. Drying them under a wall-mounted towel dryer, Bria asked pointedly, "What's your name?"

"Officer Welker, ma'am." The young man's nervous voice confirmed his willingness to comply with Bria's every command. It was a good thing he'd already relieved himself, or this little adventure might have elicited an identical—although much more embarrassing—response.

"Don't turn around. I need to ask you some questions. If I feel you're lying, I'll shoot you in the leg. And believe me, I can hear a lie every time. Got it?"

"Yes, ma'am," he said, his voice cracking an octave higher than its normal level.

"You got a first name, Welker?"

"It's Bobby."

"Why is an armed security service guarding a recovery hospital, Bobby?"

"A recovery hospital? No, ma'am, this is a research facility."

Bria blinked. "It's not a hospital?"

"No, ma'am. It's a private research center."

A jolt of anger shot through her. Thinking of the illegal, immoral research going on at Pathway, Bria's personal anger spiked to rage. The "patients" deep inside were nothing more than lab rats.

"You don't have any clue what goes on in there, do you, Officer Welker?" Bria barked, not trying to mask the acid tone of her voice.

"No, ma'am. I only guard the vehicles in this building, ma'am." The poor kid was near tears.

Bria paused, then asked, "Does any of it work?"

"Yes, ma'am. It's all in perfect condition."

Grabbing the scruff of his collar, Bria said, "Let's go for a ride."

Immersed in a *Monster Truck* magazine, the second guard did not see the two approach. Bria and Welker came to a halt next to him before he even looked up. Stumbling to his feet, the thirty-something man placed his hand on his holster.

"Just leave it alone," Bria said evenly.

"What's going on here?" the older guard demanded, removing his hand from his sidearm.

"You tell me," Bria said flatly, pushing Welker toward the other man.

"We ain't doin' nothing," the younger man said.

"Nothing?"

"That's what I said. We're just guarding this machinery is all."

"That's right, miss," the older one added. "We're just guards, nothing else."

Bria considered the man's words carefully. She knew they were telling the truth. Angrily, she spat, "You men are being duped."

"How's that?"

"What you are guarding is a throwback from Hitler's day. That research center is performing medical experiments on humans, private citizens taken against their will."

The older guard flashed a quizzical look at Welker. The two men stood silently for a moment before bursting into laughter. "Say what?" the older man asked.

Pointing the gun at him, Bria stated, "I do not like being laughed at."

He promptly shut up.

"What's your name?" she demanded.

A condescending cockiness filled the man's eyes. He stood a good foot taller than Bria and outweighed her by over a hundred pounds. He was not muscular, but he carried himself like a fighter. "I ain't tellin'."

"I'm not playing around here," Bria warned.

"Neither am I. You're obviously not management, so I don't have to tell you squat."

Pointing the gun at Welker's chest, she asked, "What's his name, Bobby?"

The smaller guard paused, unsure of how to respond. Bria stepped closer and pointed the pistol at his right leg. "You're about to lose a kneecap."

"Billings. Sergeant Stan Billings," Welker squeaked.

"Shut up, Bobby," Billings snapped.

Gritting her teeth, Bria didn't try to hide her anger. "I can't believe anyone would want to be involved with this hospital from hell."

"I'm tellin' you it ain't no hospital. Some stuffed shirts from Texas hired out our guard service to watch over the facility along with all this hardware," he said, sweeping his hand toward the vehicles. "But that's all we do. I don't know nothing about no hospital."

"Nice sentence structure, Stanley," Bria said, watching the man intently.

"Huh?"

"Never mind. Don't you men ever go inside the main building?"

"No, ma'am," Bobby answered. "That's a high-clearance area we ain't got no clearance for."

Bria pondered over the information provided by the two guards. Their tone rang true as far as she could tell. As far as they knew they were telling the truth. Additionally, the story seemed too natural to be made up so quickly, especially by two guys who did not appear to have enough intelligence to improvise such a logical explanation on the spot. Follow orders, don't ask questions, collect a paycheck: the perfect security guards for such an operation.

Looking around the room, Bria saw a clear container of plastic zip-ties on a workbench. Keeping Bobby in front of her, Bria asked the sergeant to slowly remove his handgun, hat, and jacket, and then retrieve the can of zip-ties. She had Welker zip-tie Billings to an armchair and put a gag in his mouth. Amazingly, the older man complied with zero resistance. Apparently, he was unwilling to die for corporate America—another indication that he told the truth.

"Can you operate the helicopter?" Bria asked Officer Welker.

"No, ma'am. I got a cousin who used to fly in the Army. Once we—"

"That's nice, Bobby. How about the Hummer?"

"Oh, you bet. Just like drivin' my uncle's SUV, only bigger." Guessing what was on his captor's mind, Welker's body language radiated indecision.

"Climb in, Bobby," she said, shucking on Billings's heavy jacket and raising the collar. "I need a chauffer."

Welker hesitated and flashed Billings a questioning glance. As much as his makeshift handcuffs would allow, the man merely shrugged.

"Now, Officer Welker," Bria demanded. She had the young man open the passenger door then slide over to the driver's seat. After tucking her hair up under the hat, Bria entered, slumped against the door, held the handgun under the jacket, and pretended to be asleep. Using a remote, Welker opened the retracting door and eased the Hummer outside. It had begun to rain, which pleased Bria tremendously. Better to conceal her escape.

"Who's guarding the gate tonight?" she asked.

"Soderquist."

"Friend of yours?"

"Yes, ma'am."

"Is he going to question your driving this thing?"

"Yeah, but he won't do nothing about it. We're always running out for snacks and magazines."

"Isn't that like leaving your post?" Bria wondered.

"Naw. There's a twenty-four-hour mini-mart just down the road a bit. We're there and back in twenty minutes, thirty in this kind of weather. No one seems to care."

"Great." Bria allowed herself the slightest relaxing of her muscles and nerves. "Offer to buy him his favorite. And make it believable. Tell him you got some extra money from somewhere."

"Yes, ma'am."

Driving the short distance to the gate, Bria tried to think ahead to her next move. Not knowing what lay beyond the facility, other than open fields and eventually the ocean, she concentrated on the present. Bobby Welker seemed like a nice kid. She hated the thought of him trying to be a hero, and of what she'd have to do in that situation. She was neither proficient nor comfortable handling firearms. For her own protection, she had taken a beginners' gun-safety course in her early college days, but she didn't really know much beyond what she had gleaned from books and movies. Still, there wasn't much more to operating a gun than to point and shoot.

Pulling to a stop, Welker rolled down his window. Security Guard Soderquist opened an umbrella and leaned toward his friend. "Going for a soda run, Welks?"

"Yeah. You want anything? My treat."

Soderquist smiled crookedly. "Really?"

"Yeah. I got some cash in a letter from my grandma yesterday."

"Cool." The middle-aged guard bent further and looked at Bria, who was snugly wrapped in the shadows of the vehicle.

"Hey, Billings. What's up?"

Bria did not answer. Welker looked at her with panic-filled eyes.

"He asleep?" Soderquist asked Welker.

"Uh—yeah. He's not feeling well."

"Shouldn't one of you be standing watch at the shed?"

"We'll only be a minute. Come on, Larry. I'll buy your favorite."

The guard smiled and pointed a warning finger at Welker. "Okay, but make it quick. I'll hav eto answer for it if you're caught."

"You bet."

Welker rolled up his window and sped out of the complex. "That went well," he said confidently.

Bria waited a minute before rising from the jacket. "Let's hope so."

CHAPTER THIRTY-FIVE

NORTHERN CALIFORNIA

The rain-slick road did little to hinder the Hummer's performance. Although it was noisy in the cab, the heavy machine clung to the road like it had claws. Bria kept her eyes peeled for road signs that would indicate where they were. Occasionally a California highway marker signified a specific mileage point, but that was all.

"What part of California is this?" she asked flatly.

Welker glanced at Bria as if she were insane. "Upper. About 250 miles north of 'Frisco."

"I see."

The heavy night sky offered little in the way of ambient light. The storm continued to soak the ground, but without the pyrotechnics of lightning and only an occasional complaint of thunder. It was a cold night. A sullen night.

The drone of the tires quickly had Bria lapsing into another spell of fatigue. Her eyelids grew heavy, her vision blurred. But it would mean her funeral if she fell asleep.

"So, you from around here?" the young guard asked awkwardly, as if trying to make conversation on a first date.

Bria rolled down her window and let the rain spray her face. It helped. "I'm not sure," she replied honestly.

"What's that mean? You lost or something?"

"Or something."

"Man, that's gotta be tough. Especially for a pretty gal like you, if you don't mind me saying so. You got a name?"

"Just keep your eyes on the road, Officer Welker," Bria said in a monotone.

"Yes, ma'am."

Rounding a wide corner at the base of the hill, the lights of the Mini-Mart diffused through the rain and glowed with soft, muted edges.

"Pull in there," Bria ordered.

"Yes, ma'am."

"Park off to the side."

"You got it."

Coming to a stop, Bobby Welker kept the engine running and both hands on the wheel. At Bria's instruction, he put the Hummer in park and shut off the headlights.

Still holding the gun in one hand, she gently placed her free hand on Welker's thigh and said, "All this excitement's got me starving. Would you get me a doughnut or something, Bobby, and maybe a cup of coffee?"

The young man beamed as if she had just asked him to prom. "You bet."

Bouncing out of the Hummer, Bobby jogged into the Mini-Mart, smiling. Bria leaned out her window, removed the ammunition clips from both guns, and dropped the empty ordinance on the blacktop.

"Good-bye, Officer Welker," Bria said as she scooted to the driver's seat, put the vehicle in reverse, backed out, then sped away, taking the ammo clips with her.

The Hummer proved to be a lot harder to drive than she suspected. Apparently, Welker had logged significant time behind the wheel. Either that or her fatigue was worse than she suspected. She was suddenly unbearably weak.

As she drove into the night, a thousand questions flashed through her tired mind. She could not conclude what Pathway's ultimate goal might be and, more importantly, what they wanted with her. She had no special skills beyond her nurse's training. She was not the heir to a fortune or the daughter of a diplomat. She was a law-abiding citizen, had minimal debts, and as far as she knew, was well-liked by her peers. Obviously, it had something to do with Betty Mumford. How were Mercy and Pathway connected? Bria wondered if it was because she knew about Mumford's evil deeds at the children's hospital. Perhaps Mumford was able to kill two birds with one stone through Bria.

She shook her head. Bria had no real proof that Betty Mumford was responsible for the disappearance of those children at Mercy ICU, just a strong suspicion. That Betty held a personal vendetta against her seemed overly dramatic. Maybe.

Bria pinched the bridge of her nose and closed her eyes for a second or two. Her head pounded, and her eyes stung. She knew she needed some sleep before she would get any answers. She did not want to even think a moment about the implant inside her, and yet she knew that must be a first priority after she got some rest.

The rain thickened as the road intersected with Highway 1. Time blurred as she drove through the night. Following the green highway markers, she soon found herself intersecting U.S. 101, a four-lane complex of two northbound lanes and two southbound lanes separated by a wide culvert. U.S. Highway 101 was a thoroughfare that extended the length of California. Thankfully, the intersection information sign gave Bria a sense of comfort. At least she knew, basically, where she was. To the north lay Humboldt Redwoods State Park, South Fork, Scotia, Eureka, Arcata, and eventually Oregon. To the south were Leggett, Ukiah, Santa Rosa, and San Francisco. Continuing south along Highway 1 lay Crescent Cove and Fort Bragg. Since all her troubles began in the Bay Area, they would most likely be there upon her return. Merging onto the 101, Bria headed north.

At four in the morning, Bria shared the road with practically no one. Occasionally, she'd pass a freight truck on the southbound section of highway, but little traffic presented itself on the cold, wet thoroughfare at that hour.

Bria's eyes felt painfully heavy. Her blurry vision faded to black, and she shook her head forcefully to clear it. A Cal-Trans sign indicated a rest stop just a few miles ahead. Bria forced her eyes wide open and commanded herself to concentrate. The rhythmic thumping of the windshield blades and the excessive warmth pumping out of the heater added to her lethargy and uncontrollable drowsiness.

Finally, the rest stop appeared at the crest of a wooded incline, and Bria pulled the Hummer to a stop at the far end of the small parking lot where it couldn't be seen from the highway. A single sodium-vapor lamp cast a diffused yellow hue over a cinderblock restroom and a historical interest marker. No other cars occupied the lot. She shut off the engine and stretched out across the driver's seat.

* * *

Bria wasn't sure how long she'd been out when the wailing of sirens in the distance awoke her. The rain had lessened to a light drizzle, and the blanching sky hinted at a rising sun, still an hour or so away. She cursed herself for falling asleep in the stolen vehicle. It was careless. Stupid. Searching the dashboard, she saw an overkill of instruments, dials, and switches. It was a no-brainer that the vehicle possessed a GPS location beacon, similar to the other On-Star-equipped cars from GM. Finding the Hummer's location would be as simple as pushing a button. She knew continued use of the Pathway vehicle was suicide. There was also the issue of her implant. The nurse had said something about being able to locate her on a certain frequency and about some kind of restraining ability. What was its range? What were its capabilities? Bria had no way of knowing.

Leaving the Hummer, Bria sought shelter in the public restrooms. Upon entering, she paused and reconsidered. The restrooms would obviously be the first place they'd look for her. The sirens grew louder the longer she paused. She had to keep moving.

Bria found a stone walkway that led to some item of interest through the trees surrounding the rest area. Following the path, she came to an arroyo. The deep swale formed by winter runoff held more rocks than dirt, and she guessed traveling on stone would provide a lesser chance of Pathway tracking her footprints.

The banshee wail of the sirens moaned to silence as several vehicles came to a stop in the rest area behind her. Bria jumped into the arroyo and scampered down the steep embankment to a trickling streambed. *Just don't break a leg,* she warned herself as she moved downstream, away from the encroaching light of dawn and those that pursued her.

CHAPTER THIRTY-SIX

CRESCENT COVE, CALIFORNIA

Paul had wanted to spend one more Sunday at his chapel in the mountains, but the inclement weather persuaded him otherwise. Instead, he drove along Highway 1 until it intersected with U.S 101, then turned north. He still had not found a Latter-day Saint chapel in the area and figured he'd have to drive all the way to Eureka before he'd locate one. He could have simply searched the Internet, but he felt more like taking a drive. Today, he'd see what he could find.

The morning sun was doing its best to burn off the lingering storm clouds. The highway glistened with residual moisture, and dew sparkled from road markers and adjacent vegetation like a thousand tiny prisms. In places where the sun broke though and baked the asphalt, wispy tendrils of steam rose cobralike from the ground.

Paul was listening to a New Age group called *Secret Garden*. The haunting violin melodies were achingly melancholy, making it difficult to avoid a deep sense of sorrow, but Paul loved how the organic tunes stirred his soul. Pondering the ethereal music, which matched the awakening countryside, he drove with a detached perception of the troubles haunting his world.

Paul reflected on the times in the Book of Mormon when spiritual peace reigned supreme, as in the days of King Benjamin and in the first several decades following the visit of Jesus to Bountiful in the land of Zarahemla. What would it be like to live in a Zionistic society where evil was so rare it was almost nonexistent? Moreover, what could he do to make his current situation more akin to those times?

He remembered the missionaries teaching Debbie and him to live "in the world but not of the world." Was that even possible? It must be. So many of their Mormon friends seemed capable of living such an existence. Sure, they had their fair share of hardships and troubles in life, but their faith and commitment to their religion bore them through the tough times. Happiness was omnipresent; sorrow was fleeting. Additionally, the dilemma of living sin-free while surrounded by evil offered a wonderful perspective on why hardships existed simultaneously with joys. There had to be opposition in all things. And many of their LDS friends seemed to grow from hardship rather than let it drag them down.

Paul again admitted to himself that he could not accomplish that level of understanding and faith on his own. He had to find others who believed the same things. And as much as he enjoyed the spiritual oneness with Heavenly Father while in the solitude of the mountains, he recognized the importance of an organized church and the camaraderie of fellow Saints in the gospel. But it was more than a need to *receive* such fellowship; he knew he had to *give* it also. Rather than waiting for others to befriend him, he must first offer friendship to others. Perhaps the Lord was simply waiting for him to take the first step.

As Paul approached an overpass under which flowed a small stream, a movement caught his eye, a flash of color not indigenous to the landscape. More than a scrap of litter, this was an animal-like object that seemed to cower from his approach. As he got closer, it moved behind the guardrail lining the overpass.

It was a person.

Paul pulled onto the shoulder just beyond the overpass. *What are you doing?* he scolded himself. *You have no idea how dangerous that man could be.* In rebuttal, he felt a strong impression to go help anyway. The words of King Benjamin filled his mind: *"And ye will not suffer that the beggar putteth up his petition to you in vain, and turn him out to perish,"* and *"When ye are in the service of your fellow beings, ye are only in the service of your God."* Perhaps this was an opportunity to take that "first step" he had been pondering.

Leaving his Mustang unlocked in case he needed a quick getaway, he walked to the edge of the hollow under the bridge.

"Hello?" When no one responded, he slid down the embankment until he could peer under the trusses. There, cowering in the shadow of a cement buttress, he saw a person with long hair. With his knees drawn up and his forehead resting on them, Paul could not tell how old he was. He was wearing muddy tennis shoes, a filthy, tattered winter jacket, and grimy pajama bottoms. "Hey, buddy. You doing all right?"

Slowly, the person looked up at Paul and—it was a woman. Her face was stained with grime, her hair disheveled. She looked pale, gaunt, and frightened. However, she did not remind Paul of a typical vagrant or homeless woman. She looked out of place, confused.

"Hey there, are you okay?" he asked gently.

The woman stared at him with narrowed, untrusting eyes.

"Do you need help?"

She remained silent. Nervous.

"Look, I'm not some creep you need to be afraid of." He chuckled, trying to strengthen the tissue-thin substance of their rapport. "My name is Paul. I'm a doctor of pharmacy from over in Crescent Cove. If you need a ride or would like me to call the police or an ambulance, I'll be happy to help."

A look of panic filled her eyes. "No police or hospitals. Nowhere public."

"Are you hurt? I've got a first-aid kit in my car."

Tenuously, the apprehension ebbed from the woman as she continued to stare at Paul, judging him. "I'm not hurt. Just cold. And hungry."

"Okay. Come on, I'll take you to someplace warm and get you some food."

"No police, okay?"

Why she was afraid of the authorities Paul could only guess. "Are you in some kind of trouble?"

The woman's face registered a flash of anger. "If you're going to ask a bunch of questions, you'd better just drive on without me."

Elbows cocked, palms forward, Paul held up his hands in mock surrender. "Whoa. Okay. I'm sorry. I'm just trying to help, that's all."

Remaining motionless, the woman scrutinized Paul as if determining his integrity with her eyes. They were beautiful eyes, even with dark circles under them in a face covered with dust and sweat. "I don't trust men," she stated evenly but without accusation.

With hands still raised in surrender, Paul said lightly, "Well, there's not much I can do about my gender, but I'm happy to help if you decide you can pardon my . . . uh . . . *male*-ness."

A fleeting smile slowly found its way through the grime on her face, and she grimaced as she rose to her feet. She brushed off her jacket, smoothed her hair as much as possible, and wiped her face with her sleeve. Walking with a slight limp toward Paul, she extended a dirty hand. "My name is Bria."

Paul took her hand tentatively. "Paul Randall."

"How long have you been a pharmacist?"

"About ten years."

She seemed to be examining his expression as he answered her questions. "Are you a decent man?"

"I like to think so."

She smiled again and nodded with a look of total acceptance. "Pleased to meet you, Paul. Sorry I was so untrusting at first."

Paul's eyebrows rose abruptly. Confused, he asked, "What changed your mind so suddenly?"

She smiled shyly. It was entrancing. "I'm a good judge of character. Besides, anyone who asks me to pardon his 'uh . . . *male*-ness' can't be all bad."

"Thanks . . . I think." He felt cautiously relieved. She certainly didn't seem like an outlaw.

Paul led the way back to his Mustang and opened the passenger door for Bria. She seemed pleased by the gesture. Climbing in the driver's side, Paul buckled his seat belt and merged onto the highway. He turned up the heater and lowered the music. For more than ten minutes, they drove without speaking. The woman kept a vigil through the rear window, as if expecting a tail. Paul chose not to question her about the nervous mannerism. After a time, she settled into the bucket seat and closed her eyes.

"This is beautiful music," she said. "Who is it?"

"They're called *Secret Garden.*"

"A soundtrack from the movie?"

"I don't think so."

"Sounds Celtic."

"Sort of."

"It's beautiful. Could you turn it up, please?"

"Certainly." And he did.

Bria breathed a relaxed sigh. "Thanks."

After a moment's pause, he asked, "So where would you like me to take you?"

Stifling a yawn she said, "Where'd you say you were from?"

"Crescent Cove. A small town off Highway 1, back by the coast."

"That'll do."

At a utility vehicle crossing, Paul turned the Mustang around and headed south. To maximize Bria's comfort, he drove just under the speed limit and as smoothly as possible, but he had trouble keeping his eyes on the road; they kept drifting to the mysterious woman in his passenger seat as a thousand unanswered questions dizzied his mind.

CHAPTER THIRTY-SEVEN

CRESCENT COVE, CALIFORNIA

Paul turned off Highway 101 onto Highway 1 and headed west. Bria had fallen asleep along the way. Following the unforeseen event of collecting his disheveled passenger, and her insistence on not going to the police or even to a hospital, Paul was still a little hesitant to take her to his home.

Nervous portents crowded Paul's mind. The sudden entry of this strange woman into his life seemed bizarre, but somehow . . . right. He felt their meeting was supposed to happen, that he was to help her in some way. Their chance encounter was not really foreordained—that wasn't the appropriate word—but it was the best Paul could come up with to describe his emotions. He *knew* their meeting was not happenstance. *Why* they were to meet was still a mystery. Nevertheless, Paul had learned long ago to trust his feelings, especially when dealing with other people, and he chose to see this venture through.

Pulling off the exit from Highway 1, Paul drove the twenty-mile scenic byway into Crescent Cove. As usual, the town radiated a peaceful tranquility that Sunday afternoon. A slight drizzle had returned, and the sky had darkened to a somber shade of wet slate. Glancing at his passenger, Paul wondered if maybe he should continue driving around, letting the drone of the tires, the steady rhythm of the windshield wipers, and the warmth of the heater continue to grant her some rest.

No. Appraising her bedraggled state, Paul decided what she really needed was a hot shower, some fresh clothes, a painkiller if requested, a good meal, and a real bed.

Pulling into his driveway, Paul let the engine idle as he gazed at the sleeping form next to him. Again, the questions riddled his mind: Who was this woman? What kind of trouble was she in? And what could he do to help?

"Hey," he said gently. "We're here."

Bria did not respond. She remained in a deep sleep.

Turning off the engine, Paul unbuckled his seat belt and exited the Mustang. He ran up to the porch and opened the front door. Returning to the car, he opened the passenger door slowly, making sure Bria didn't fall out as he did so. Squatting, he tenderly shook her shoulder. "Bria. Let's get inside."

Bria groaned a bit but didn't make any effort to comply. The poor woman was utterly exhausted. Taking a chance at offending her, but not having much choice, Paul slid an arm behind her back and one under her knees and lifted her out of the car.

Inside the house, Paul kicked the front door closed and took her upstairs to the guest room. He gently laid her on the sleigh bed and stretched out her legs. Moaning softly, Bria remained unconscious. He then removed her muddy shoes, wet socks, and heavy rain jacket, and pulled a thick, down-filled comforter to her neck. He resisted the urge to brush the hair from her face and kiss her on the forehead.

He flinched—shocked at having such an urge; but he figured it came from tending to a person in need, giving him a temporary Knight in Shining Armor complex. He closed the curtains and tiptoed out of the room, closing the door behind him.

Paul pulled his Mustang into the detached garage, locked it, then entered his house through the kitchen door. After cleaning up a bit, he paced and sat, then paced some more, trying to figure out what to do about the woman in his guest room. He perused a drug journal, which failed to hold his interest. He opened a novel but saw none of the print. He could not stop thinking about the woman upstairs. Paul reflected on why he felt he was meant to help her. *How* was another question that had no obvious answer.

As the hour approached suppertime, Paul decided to make enough hot food for two—in case she awoke before nightfall. The soup was from a can, and the rolls were pop-and-bake, but he didn't think his guest would mind. He ate his portion alone in the kitchen, then carried a tray upstairs. Rapping softly on the door, he awaited an answer. None came. Opening the door a crack, Paul saw Bria curled in a fetal position, facing the window. The slow steady movement of her back confirmed a deep sleep. Figuring she needed rest more than food, he left the tray on a small table beside the bed and exited the room.

In the master suite, Paul sat in the tower alcove and watched the sky go from gray to bruised purple to black. A solid veil of dense vapor choked the sky, showing no form or substance, only a cloak of emptiness. Normally a somber, depressing scene, the subdued ambience filled Paul with a curious warmth and comfort. He had done something right, something life-changing, life-saving. In spite of the bizarre events of the past weeks, he no longer felt that his life was drifting aimlessly. Suddenly, strangely, it all had meaning. And it had everything to do with Bria.

CHAPTER THIRTY-EIGHT

NORTHERN CALIFORNIA

Betty Mumford paced back and forth with a bitter scowl distorting her plump face. Young Nurse Jones sat in a hard-back chair in Mumford's sterile office. The young nurse's eyes were dilated with fright, her palms sweaty with cold perspiration.

"You were pretty chummy with her, weren't you?"

"Sure, I liked her," Nurse Jones said in a tremulous voice. "But she said nothing about running away."

Betty Mumford stopped pacing and seared Nurse Jones with a penetrating glare. "You helped her, didn't you?" It was more of an accusation than a question.

Nurse Jones's hands blanched as she wrung them nervously. "I don't know what you mean." She wasn't much of a liar.

Suddenly adopting her matronly visage, Betty said, "Listen, sweetie. I like you a lot. You know I do, hon. You also know everyone here is fitted with a short-range tracker, so we're going to find her anyway. Just point us in the right direction to help us save time. Do that, and all will be forgiven. You have my word on it, Kimberly."

Tears rimmed the petite nurse's eyes and dripped onto her small hands. The fact that Mumford had used Kim's real name showed some trust, but it wasn't enough to put her at ease. "I don't know where she is. Honest."

"That's probably true. But you can guess where she was headed, can't you? Surely she told you that much."

Kim shook her head.

Without warning, Mumford gripped Kim's jaw and, wrenching it, forced her to make eye contact. A thick, bloodstained bandage wrapped around the heel of Betty's thumb, a wound that evidently caused a great deal of pain. The motherly kindness had vanished. "I'm tired of playing games, you stupid little hussy. So is the director. Either you help us, or *you* get the next injection."

Although seemingly impossible, Nurse Jones's eyes widened even further. "No. Please," she breathed.

"Then tell us!"

Swallowing painfully, Kim whispered, "I think she was headed west."

"Where to?"

"I don't know."

Tightening her grip, Betty hissed, "Why west?"

"I don't know. Honest."

Using her free hand, Mumford slapped Kim twice.

The room spun. The young girl broke into sobs and tried to resist, but the manacles binding her wrists to the chair prevented self-defense.

Slapping her captive a third time, Mumford growled, "I'm on my last nerve here, Kimberly. You tell me what I want to know or you can forget seeing daylight ever again."

"I—don't—know," Kim gasped between sobs. Then, softly, "I . . . I told her to go toward the ocean. That's all."

Betty Mumford stepped back and slid her hands into the pockets of her smock. "Oh dear. That's so unfortunate."

"I'm sorry," Kim said in a thin, whispery voice.

"So am I," Betty said in a concerned tone as she drew a hypodermic syringe from her pocket.

CHAPTER THIRTY-NINE

OAKLAND, CALIFORNIA

The phone rang, surprising the giant. Although it was Sunday, he wasn't expecting a call for a few weeks. Pathway had told him to lay low a while. Reluctantly taking his eyes from the blank television screen, he picked up the handset. "I'm here."

"The Norman conquest . . ."

". . . was only the beginning." He activated the encryption device. "All clear."

"We have a problem."

"I'm listening."

"We need you to collect someone. A woman."

Surt didn't respond. A slight smile played at the corners of his misshapen mouth. A thin, raspy breath escaped the scarred slit.

"We don't know where she is, but we have a proximity. She escaped from the center last night. She's very dangerous to us, to the Light and His scientists. We need your help immediately."

"Is she tagged?"

"Yes, but only with a short-range unit. We never expected her to leave the complex."

"Point me in the right direction. I'll find her."

"Good. Accomplish this, and the Light says your place with the gods is unconditionally guaranteed."

He whimpered a sigh of gratitude, heartfelt, deep, spiritual. Tears formed in the eyes of the giant. For a moment, he could not speak.

"Her name is Bria Georgopolis. She's five foot eight, dark hair and eyes. Trim. Exceptionally pretty. You collected her from Mercy Children's Hospital a few months ago."

"I remember."

"Good. She stole a truck and then abandoned it at a rest stop on U.S. 101, about sixty miles to the north of the complex. We assume she's now on foot. Be cautious but quick. And do not be too visible—especially to the police. There are many in that area who might remember you."

"I'll find her," Surt promised.

"Do that. This woman could bring much hardship to the Light and His cause. You wouldn't want that, would you?"

"No."

"She could hurt Pathway's entire operation."

"Never." He frowned.

"Use any means necessary to bring her back."

"Any means?"

"Yes."

A slight pause. "Alive?"

"If possible."

The smile returned. "As He commands."

CHAPTER FORTY

CRESCENT COVE, CALIFORNIA

Paul awoke to the smell of bacon frying. Forgetting he had a guest, he raced down the stairs in nothing but his pajama bottoms and burst into the kitchen. Bria was dressed in a borrowed bathrobe, freshly showered, with her hair still clinging, and without any makeup. But her easy smile and sparkling eyes made her beautiful just the same.

"Good morning," she said cheerfully. "I hope I didn't wake you."

Paul glanced at the kitchen clock—6:18 AM.

Running his hand through his pillow-skewed hair, he smiled awkwardly. "The smell of bacon could bring me back from the grave, especially when I'm not the one cooking it. Besides, I usually get up around six anyway. I must have forgotten to set my alarm."

"Well, I hope you don't mind me helping myself to your hospitality. I'm usually not this presumptuous."

Rubbing his eyes, he said, "Not at all. Are you feeling better?"

"Better?"

"Yeah. When I found you yesterday, you looked pretty hammered."

"Thanks a lot," she teased.

"That's not what I mean."

She laughed. She seemed fine. Still a bit tired, perhaps, but recovering quickly. "I know. Thank you for your kindness. It was the last thing I expected."

"From me?"

"From anyone."

"Oh." Heading toward the breakfast table, Paul suddenly realized the sparseness of his attire. "I—um. I'd better get dressed. Then we'll talk."

"Okay," she said, as if not experiencing the same embarrassment. "If you show me where the coffeemaker is, I'll brew some up."

Paul stopped in the doorway. "I—I don't drink coffee."

A confused expression played on her face. "You don't drink coffee?"

He hesitated, not sure whether to claim health reasons or admit to his relatively new religious convictions. He found that most people were not sure how to act in front of a Mormon, as if the Latter-day Saint religion was so obscure and alien only monks and extraterrestrials could understand it.

He decided on both. "I'm kind of a health nut, and coffee's loaded with bad stuff. Besides, it's a substance my church doesn't condone drinking."

The quizzical stare remained only a moment. Then, "Okay. I can accept that." And that was it. No probing questions leading to prolonged explanations. No condescending remarks about leading a puritan lifestyle. Just acceptance. Her candid response instilled in Paul a measure of trust he found comforting as well as somewhat disconcerting. He was flattered by her open trust in him, and in spite of the newness of their relationship, he felt strangely comfortable extending the same trust to her.

"Well . . . I'm hopping in the shower. Just help yourself to whatever."

"Thanks, Paul," she said, returning to the frying pan and deftly cracking an egg into it with one hand.

After showering and dressing for work, Paul entered the kitchen and found it sparkling clean and vacant. Bria had not only washed the dishes, including some of his from the night before, but she had scrubbed the counters and mopped the floor. A plate of breakfast sat on the kitchen table.

"Hello?" Paul called out.

"I'm in the library."

Paul retraced his steps and opened the pocket door to the study. Bria, still in his bathrobe, sat on a wingback chair with her feet tucked beside her, reading a book by the light of a brass floor lamp. "Just wanted to say thank you for making breakfast," he said.

"You're weldome," she said, closing the book. "As payment, maybe you can give me a lift after I get back into my things?"

"Um . . . sure. I have to get to work, but I can drop you off wherever."

"Does this town have a Greyhound stop?"

"I don't think so. No Amtrak either. It's kind of out of the way from everything. That's why I like it here."

Bria considered his words for a moment before standing and shelving the book. It was a Steinbeck novel. "I'm sorry to have put you to this much trouble, Paul. You've been very kind and a perfect gentleman throughout."

"Don't mention it. And don't feel you have to run off either."

"But . . . um . . ." Obviously, Bria wasn't sure how to respond.

They stood looking at their feet as an awkward silence stifled the air. Paul wanted to offer her his house while he went to work, but he had no idea who she was or what kind of a person she might be. He sensed he could trust her, but he didn't want to rely on gut feelings alone. Glancing at his watch, he knew he was cutting it close. Remembering she didn't have any clothing other than the sweatshirt, raincoat, and pajamas he had found her in, Paul didn't feel right about simply shoving her out his door. Perhaps he could get her a room at the Sea View Motel. As with the previous day, she would probably refuse a trip to the sheriff's office. And Paul didn't like—or trust—the sheriff anyway.

"Listen," Bria said hesitantly. "I know you don't know me from Eve, and having picked me up on the roadside, you have no idea of the kind of person I am. But if you would trust me just one day, until I get some strength back and can clean my clothes, and perhaps work things out a bit in my mind, I promise I won't be a pain."

Paul looked into her liquid-brown eyes, which broke contact the minute he met her pleading stare. He felt his entire being soften. It wasn't that she was simply gorgeous—which she clearly was. It was more that she knew she could melt a man with a single glance, yet chose not to use her womanly wiles on him. She was in need and was unashamedly honest about it. He knew she could rob him blind the minute he left the house, and yet, he somehow knew she wouldn't.

As if reading his thoughts, she added, "I trusted you and was not disappointed. Now it's your turn to trust me. I promise I won't disappoint you."

Removing a card from his wallet, he said, "Here's my work number. I'm just a mile or so away in town. If you have any questions or urgent needs, call me."

Clearly relieved by his willingness to believe in her, Bria took the proffered card and read it. "You own the pharmacy?"

"Yeah."

Tapping the card against her chin, she spoke as if trying to convince herself, "Isn't it true a number of surveys list pharmacists as the first or second most trusted profession in America?"

Paul shrugged. "I guess."

"Well, I'm a nurse, so we have something in common."

Paul only smiled. He didn't know what to say.

Bria slipped the card into a pocket of the robe and said, "Paul, I give you my word I won't steal anything or damage anything while you're gone. I know the promise of someone you found on the highway doesn't amount to much, but it's all I have."

He nodded. "When I get home, I'd like some answers. Okay?"

"Answers to what?"

"Why you want to avoid the police. Why you didn't want to go to a hospital, or any public place for that matter. Nothing more important than that," he jested, trying to keep the mood light.

Bria smiled, not in a flirtatious way, but Paul felt his knees weaken nonetheless. "That's fair. You know something, Paul? You're a surprising piece of work."

"Is that good?"

"Very."

"Thanks, I guess."

"What time do you get off work?"

"About six or six thirty, usually."

"Great," she said, the scent of freshly washed hair filling his sinuses as she brushed by him. "I'll see you at seven."

She then gracefully vanished up the stairs.

* * *

Bria stood in front of the bathroom mirror staring at her reflection. She had never trusted someone so quickly as she had Paul

Randall. It was totally against her nature and her common sense, especially considering what she had recently endured. But something inexplicable within her assured her Paul was trustworthy beyond question—more so than even her polygraphic hearing divulged. Curiously, the more she allowed herself to indulge that assurance, the better she felt about it. And about him.

Bria knew she would be true to her word and would not take advantage of Paul in his absence. She also knew Paul would respect her privacy and not tell anyone of her presence. Who was this would-be hero, and why did she feel such trust from him? He was pleasantly good-looking, but she knew that was the worst characteristic by which to judge a person. His house was clean and showed no signs of a typical, womanizing, macho bachelor pad. Perhaps it was the way he had treated her and shown a reciprocal trust in her. She felt from Paul stability, loyalty, a safe harbor. And she loved that feeling.

CHAPTER FORTY-ONE

NORTHERN CALIFORNIA

The giant spent half a day at the rest stop sixty miles north of Pathway, off Highway 101. For the first portion of that time, he simply sat in his Ram Mega Cab getting a feel for the flow of traffic that visited the historical marker. He ended up seeing only one car— an old-model station wagon.

Stepping out of the Ram, Surt walked the grounds, looking for signs and clues. This was the last known location of his target, and because of the low rate of visitors, he had high hopes of finding something that would aid in his search. Following a stone path to the historical plaque, he noticed the heavy tread of hiking boots dimpling the dirt on either side. He cursed aloud. The carelessness of a few searchers just might hide the one clue that would lead him to the woman. He pulled out a handheld tracker, turned it on, and slowly pivoted, searching for an electronic signature. The lack of response proved the woman was not in range.

Moving next to the historical plaque, Surt began walking a methodical circle, widening his circumference with each pass. When he was ten feet from the plaque, he noticed a line of shoe treads bearing high arches—the kind of mark running shoes might make. Following the direction the toes pointed, he made his way to the edge of an arroyo some thirty yards behind the marker. Evidence of some disturbance marred the slope of the gulch, and he found impacted earth at its base. More athletic-shoe prints. No hiking-boot treads. Pathway's search crew hadn't even looked down here. Incompetent fools. Mortals.

The rain of the previous evening was light, with little wind. It had not washed away any markings; instead, it seemed to have sealed them as semi-permanent reliefs in the heavy clay soil. A splotch of mud on a rock here, a mashing of bunched grass there; little evidences revealing that the woman had passed this way. She had been careful—or at least tried to be. But Surt knew how to read trail signs. It had been part of his training at Pathway so long ago. An ex-Army ranger was hired to teach him one on one. It was a brief stint, involving only the most rigorous classes in tracking, covert operations, bomb making, survival, and, of course, weaponless killing.

There—a definite shoe print.

The woman *had* come this way. He could almost sense her residual presence. Like a wolf on the hunt, Surt followed the clues, both obvious and subtle, and grew excited from her persistent vibes. He wended his way down the creek bed, wondering if her goal had been the coastline.

After a few miles, he found a collection of her shoe prints under a viaduct of the freeway. Scampering up the incline to the overpass, he had no trouble seeing where the woman had been. Apparently, she had spent a good amount of time here. Searching the area, he frowned. There were other tracks: flat-soled with minimal tread, like penny loafers or some other casual dress shoe. They did not progress to where the woman had sat under the viaduct, but it was clear the two had left together. Had she been awaiting a rendezvous? Did she have an accomplice? No, the giant shook his head. Pathway may have been careless enough to allow her to escape, but the Light knew everything. Surely, He would have known if another person was involved.

Climbing to the roadside, Surt continued to frown. The tracks led to a point where a car had pulled off the highway. A mileage marker indicated this was still a section of U.S. 101. He cursed vehemently, raising his fists to the heavens and accusing the gods of fate of hindering his search. He must find the woman quickly. The Light had requested it. He had said it was urgent.

Scanning the shoulder for any other clues, he at first did not notice a minivan approach from the south. Slowing as it drew near, the driver obviously wanted to lend a Samaritan hand to the man standing alone on the roadside. Surt did not move. He kept his hands to his sides, and his eyes were bitter under a knitted brow. He could see a female passenger watching intently, a sappy, worried expression troubling her face. A gaggle of kids sat wide-eyed behind the man and his wife. As the minivan pulled alongside the giant, the worried expressions turn to looks of horror. Surt heard one of the kids start crying. The woman recoiled, repulsed. The husband floored the accelerator, and the minivan lumbered away, its small engine straining to hurl its oversized burden to speeds higher than its design allowed. With his jaw clenched to the point that his ears rang, Surt resisted the urge to pull out his silencer-equipped .44 and blow out the tires of the retreating minivan. He had trained himself to overcome his anger with other emotions—smugness, superiority, power. Those people were mortal; he was almost a god. His hideous scars were tokens of his ability to rise above mortality. The Light had said so.

His jaw relaxed. He smiled.

Retracing his footsteps, Surt felt troubled by something he was missing. He knew a clue sat waiting to burst forth from the recesses of his mind, a hint as to the whereabouts of the woman. Something he had just seen. Something obvious. Yet there was nothing on the ground, nothing the woman had left behind. Halfway back to the rest stop, the clue flashed brightly in his mind. It wasn't a sure confirmation, but it was a good place to start. A good trail on which to begin his quest. And somehow, Surt knew the woman sat helpless at the end of that trail.

As the horror-filled minivan had lumbered away, Surt unwittingly noticed that the vehicle bore California plates. The license plate frame boasted large, obnoxiously-chromed letters spelling out COASTLINE REALTY. CRESCENT COVE, CALIFORNIA.

Ah, yes, he thought. *I remember. He sent servants to rescue me there. What a fitting place for me to repay the favor. This was meant to be.*

CHAPTER FORTY-TWO

CRESCENT COVE, CALIFORNIA

The day had passed exceptionally slowly. A typical volume of Monday customers flooded the store to have prescriptions filled, with the usual number of insurance problems and customer complaints. Paul concentrated on doing the best he could, trying to remain cheerful, caring, and helpful, but he could not get his mind off the mysterious stranger in his house. Who was she? And why was he willing to put so much trust in her? Yeah, he reasoned, she was pretty, and she seemed honest as well as forthright, but sometimes those were characteristics of the best charlatans—the very people of which he should be extra cautious.

Stapling a receipt to a prescription bag, Paul noticed a man he had not seen before standing at the dispensary counter. He greeted the man, who then handed him a prescription vial without comment. Reading the label, Paul saw that his name was Howard Douglas, that he was on Digitek brand of digoxin for his heart, and that he was out of refills.

"If you'll give me a moment, Mr. Douglas, I'll call your doctor for more refills."

"What for?" the old man snapped.

"For more refills," Paul repeated slower, in case the man was hard of hearing.

Pointing to the vial, Mr. Douglas said, "It's got refills."

Showing him the portion of the label reading, NO REFILLS—DR. MUST AUTHORIZE, Paul explained, "It says right here there are no more refills. But that's okay, I'll be happy to call your doctor right now."

"That's not what it says," Howard snapped.

Paul blinked. It clearly *did* say exactly that.

"My doctor told me I was supposed to take those the rest of my life. They're my heart pills, you know."

"Yes, I realize that—"

"So when it says 'doctor must authorize,' he already has."

"What about the 'no refills' part?" Paul asked, his patience straining.

"That means you can't refill them unless he says it's okay. And he already did."

Taking a deep breath, Paul chuckled lightly. "I see your point, Mr. Douglas. I'm sure your doctor is right. You should be taking these the rest of your life. And I agree. But in California, a prescription is only legitimate as long as it has valid refills, regardless of what your doctor or anyone else says. Nevertheless, it's a simple matter of reauthorizing the prescription with a phone call, which I'll jump on right now."

"And how long will that take, young man?"

"No longer than this conversation has taken," he said, walking into the dispensary to make the call.

Luckily, the doctor's office picked up the call on the second ring. "Dr. Brown's office. How may I help you?"

"Pharmacist Paul calling from Crescent Cove Pharmacy. I need to request a refill for one of your patients, please."

"One moment, please. I'll connect you with one of the nurses."

There was a click, some peppy instrumental music, and a pick-up. An expressionless voice said, "This is Dr. Brown's medical assistant."

"Hi. This is Pharmacist Pa—"

"I am either with a patient or on another line. Please leave a message and I will try to get back with you as soon as possible. Thank you." A click and a beep followed.

Paul gave the necessary information for the refill request, then hung up. Looking out the dispensary window, he saw Mr. Douglas standing hunched over with his hands flat on the counter, a frown on his face, and a steady, perturbed shaking of his head. Paul counted out ten tablets and put them in the vial.

"Mr. Douglas, I notice from your records you only live a few blocks away. Your doctor's office was too busy to take my call—which is not all that unusual on a Monday," Paul said, handing the vial back to his customer. "I put ten Digitek in here for you to get by until they can get back to me with your refills. I won't charge you for these now. We'll make up the difference when you come back for the others."

Howard took the vial and rattled the contents. The frown remained. Paul wasn't so sure it wasn't a paralysis of some kind. "Just how long do you expect these to last?"

"At least ten days," Paul said, trying to sound sincere rather than flippant.

"Is that all you expect me to live?"

Paul again explained the scenario, slowly and with extra volume, hoping this time it would stick. It didn't.

"So I only get ten pills when the doctor said to give me a bottle of a hundred?"

Paul sighed and tried to look pleasant. "Let's look at this logically, okay, Mr. Douglas? If I were to fill your prescription and sell it to you, I'd make money, right?"

"Right."

"So, logically, why would I not fill your prescription?"

Mr. Douglas responded with a baffled, but still perturbed, expression.

"Because it would be illegal," Paul answered for him. "However, I don't want you to go without this important medication, so I'll loan you these pills. Then, when Dr. Brown's office gets back with me, I'll fill the prescription and deliver it to you on my way home from work. Okay?"

"Who?"

"Who what?"

"Who did you say you called?"

"Dr. Todd Brown. The physician printed on the prescription label."

"No wonder you got my refills all screwed up. I haven't gone to Dr. Brown in nearly two years. I go to Dr. Lemar Redd. You need to get your colors straight, young man. Then maybe you'll get the right doctor, too."

Rubbing his eyes, which were suddenly very tired, Paul said, "Take these ten pills for now, Mr. Douglas. I'll contact the right doctor, make sure you have an up-to-date file with his office, and then I'll deliver your refills to your home after work. Okay?"

Clenching his jaw, Howard looked down his bony nose at Paul and snorted. Without another word, he turned and left the store.

"And have a great day," Paul said to no one but himself.

* * *

By day's end, Paul had received confirmation on Howard Douglas's Digitek refills and cleared up a hundred other issues presented to him that day. He bid Phyllis, Brooke, and Dawna good-night and left for the Douglases' house. Dropping off the prescription, Paul met Mrs. Douglas, one of the sweetest senior citizens he had ever encountered. She invited him in for coffee and scones, but he declined. With tear-misted eyes, she took Paul's hand in both of hers and thanked him for showing so much concern for her husband.

"I know he can be cantankerous at times . . ." she began apologetically.

"I hadn't noticed," Paul said with a broad smile. He didn't want to upset the kindly woman.

"Oh, bull. He's meaner than a rattler with a bellyache." She paused as a lump in her throat stopped her from speaking. "But I love him. Always have."

Paul patted her wrist kindly. "I'm used to ornery people, Mrs. Douglas. It's okay, really."

She thanked him once again as he stepped down from the porch.

Arriving home, Paul didn't know what to expect. He closed the garage door and entered through the back door. Although the kitchen was empty, a lingering, delicious smell filled his sinuses and made his mouth water. Moving into the dining room, he found Bria standing behind a chair. A plate of spaghetti sat on the table, along with a small pot of thick, spicy-smelling sauce still bubbling, a plate of toasted bread with garlic spread, a tossed salad, glasses of water, and place settings for two. Even more appealing than the food was Bria herself. She had brushed and styled her hair, pulling it back on either side and securing it with what looked like a twist-tie from a loaf of bread. She was wearing one of Paul's oxford-cloth button-down shirts, and a pair of his sweat pants, with the drawstring pulled tight against her waist. She wore no makeup, but even in the mottled light of the Tiffany lamp, Paul thought she was breathtaking.

"This looks amazing," Paul said, staring at the table fare, as wide-eyed as a kid at Christmastime.

"Hopefully it tastes that way, too. Sorry I had to go with water. I couldn't find any white wine in this house."

Hanging his coat on the back of a chair, Paul said, "I don't drink alcohol either." Then, hurrying to Bria's side, he pulled out her chair.

"Wow, the gentleman thing is real. I thought I was just imagining it. What other mysteries hide behind that boyish face of yours?" Bria teased.

"I was about to ask you the same question—except for the 'boyish face' part."

"Good."

Bria was still smiling as Paul pulled out a chair at an angle from hers, moved his place setting over, and sat down. Placing a napkin in his lap, he then folded his hands in an attitude of prayer. Surprised, but happily following his lead, Bria did the same.

Paul blessed the food and thanked the Lord for helping him aid those in need. Bria softly echoed his amen.

"Now, since this is my house," he began with straightforward seriousness, "I insist you go first. I want nothing but a plateful of honest guts spilled tonight. Okay?"

"I'm afraid I have more than a plateful to spill," Bria said, only half kidding.

"I'll get a bucket then."

She instantly laughed. Her smile would add light to the brightest day at noontime, Paul mused.

Serving her a helping of salad, Paul said, "Really, you don't have to tell me anything if it's deeply personal . . . or if it involves some kind of criminal activity or sacrificing goats at midnight." He smiled hopefully.

"Hey, it's only fair." She chuckled. "And no, it's neither criminal nor sacrificial." Then more seriously, she said, "However, you have to promise me something first."

Pausing with a tong-full of salad poised over his plate, he hesitantly asked, "What?"

"Promise you won't think I'm crazy."

* * *

Paul sat in silence as Bria told him everything, starting from when she first awoke in the isolation chamber. He found much of the story hard to believe—or would have, had he not already received the corroborating information from Cliff and Phyllis Stevenson.

"Do you have any proof of this?"

"Other than my word, no," she said sullenly.

"Is there even a slight possibility you may have contracted an Ebola virus that caused a memory loss like they said? I know it's far-fetched, but you do still have a six- or seven-week memory lapse, right?"

With conciliatory acceptance, she said, "I won't say it's impossible, but it just doesn't fit anything else."

"But why you?" he asked.

"I've asked myself that question a thousand times. My only guess is that they want people with no family or other obvious ties. That way their disappearance won't cause more than a temporary stir."

Nodding, and wanting to lighten the conversation a bit, Paul took another bite of spaghetti. "This is amazing. You made this from stuff I had in the cupboard?"

Bria lowered her eyes. "Yeah. It's nothing much, really."

"Says you. Where'd you learn to cook like this?"

"My dad was a Greek chef—quite good, my mother used to say. I don't remember him much. He left when I was a kid. My mom couldn't boil a pot of water successfully, so I had to learn to cook from a kindly neighbor who sort of took me in. I kind of think, thanks to Dad, cooking's in my blood. It's about the only good thing he left me."

Paul felt ashamed for having dredged up painful memories. "Sorry about that," he said, not meeting her stare.

"Live and learn." She shrugged. "Or my favorite: 'The years teach much which the days never knew.'"

Paul smiled. "Yeats?"

"Emerson. But good guess."

Paul bit into a slice of garlic toast. It wasn't quite the same as toast made from a French loaf, but the flavor—strong, yet not offensive— did more than make up for the thin sandwich bread. After a minute of comfortable silence, Paul asked, "So why did you think I would think you were crazy?"

"Well, the story *is* a little hard to swallow, don't you agree?"

"Yes and no. But I'm not sure what I can do to help you. I'm a pharmacist, not a lawyer or cop."

Bria looked truly disappointed. "You're right." She sighed. "I should probably just go."

Quickly, Paul said, "I don't know that'll solve anything either. But . . . well, I don't feel it's quite proper having you stay here . . . with a bachelor . . ."

"And here I thought you were trustworthy," Bria teased.

"To a fault, actually. No, I was just thinking that people might start to talk . . . you know, a single guy and a single girl under the same roof . . ."

Her grin openly showed her amusement. "Are you really that old-fashioned?"

Paul shrugged and took another bite of garlic bread.

"So then . . . what *are* you going to do with me?"

Paul leaned back, folded his arms, tilted his head to one side, and looked at her with narrowed eyes. "First, let's get you some decent clothes and find you a place to stay."

Her smile vanished. "But . . . I don't have any money," she admitted.

"I do."

"I can't take it, Paul. I don't like charity unless I'm the one giving it."

"Part of being charitable is allowing others the same privilege," Paul said smoothly. "If you deny someone the chance to be charitable, they will not be blessed for following through, and the fault will be yours."

Again, Bria looked pleasantly astonished. "I never thought of it that way."

"Sounds pretty deep, huh?"

She laughed out loud. "Yeah. You're an endless abyss."

After a slight pause, Paul continued. There's only one apartment complex in town, but I'm not sure if there are any vacancies. There are also a couple of tacky motels . . ."

"Tacky beats seedy."

"I wouldn't be too quick to be so generous." Paul chuckled. "And there are a couple of clothing stores to get you outfitted, unless your tastes are more Rodeo Drive."

"Hardly. But I insist on working for my keep. Do you need any help at the pharmacy? I know my meds pretty well."

"Not really. I'm fully staffed at the moment. Besides, if the people at Pathway happen this way, everyone in town would know about the new, pretty assistant I have. I think it's best to keep you out of sight until I get a handle on what's going on."

Bria considered his logic a moment while taking a sip of water. A fragile pall fell over their light banter. She then nodded firmly. "You're right, of course. It's probably a good idea I lie low for a while. Other than you, I don't really trust anyone just yet. And I don't know a single soul in this town."

"I agree with you there, Bria. I'm not sure who in this town to trust myself."

"Really? In what way?"

Standing, he said, "Let's clear these dishes, and I'll tell you what I just learned from one of my techs. It confirms everything you told me. But I'm not sure what to do with her information or yours—especially that part about a traceable implant."

Absently stabbing at a noodle on her plate to avoid eye contact, Bria stated, "My being here is putting you in danger, isn't it?"

Paul placed his hand on her shoulder. "No, not really. I have a sinking feeling I was already in that situation before we met."

* * *

"You mean the whole town knows about Pathway?" Bria gasped.

"I'm not sure, but I think a number of them still suspect something," Paul answered as he placed the last plate in the dishwasher.

"Then why haven't the authorities done anything about it?"

He shrugged. "Not enough evidence, from what the Stevensons told me. The operation is not as big as it used to be. And from what you've said, it seems only a few people in the complex itself know how bad it really is."

Bria stood off to one side, leaning against the counter. Her mood was contemplative, subdued. "I think most of them know, but those that don't like it can't do anything about it."

"Like the girl who helped you escape?"

Bria nodded. "Should we tell the local police what I know?"

"I don't think so," Paul said, shutting the dishwasher door and switching on the unit. "Not just yet, anyway. Without physical proof, it's your word against theirs. Besides, I'm not on the best terms with the sheriff here."

"Why?" Bria asked, unable to hide a curious smile.

Paul suggested they adjourn into the study before continuing the conversation. He rehearsed the highlights of what the Stevensons had told him, then related some of his experiences since moving to Crescent Cove. The more he talked, the more pensive Bria became.

"And the sheriff still believes you had something to do with Val's death?"

"I don't know. He hasn't bothered me in a while, so perhaps not."

"Or perhaps he's just building up steam," Bria guessed.

"That'd be my luck."

"So who can we trust here?" she asked, staring at the floor.

"I'm still trying to figure that one out. I like it here, and I hate the thought of leaving. But if I can't think of a way to resolve this issue, I may have to."

"Would that be so bad? Last I heard, pharmacists are pretty much needed nationwide."

Paul rubbed his weary eyes. "Financially, it would be a disaster. I put everything I had into buying this house and the pharmacy. I have a little left over but not enough to start again. Plus, it's strange, but I *feel* like I should be here."

"In what way?"

Paul hesitated. The only way to describe his promptings was to open his past to this stranger—a past with which he had only recently been able to have closure. It would also necessitate an explanation of his religion. He didn't mind sharing his beliefs, but he didn't feel qualified to teach the gospel. He didn't know much more than the basics. But his testimony was growing stronger every day, and he knew the more he used it, the firmer it would become.

Turning his chair to face Bria, Paul said, "I guess it's time I tell you *my* story. It may sound a bit depressing, but I'm hoping it will have a happy ending."

Bria tucked her legs beside her and folded her arms comfortably. "I'm ready."

Beginning with Debbie and his introduction to the LDS Church, Paul talked about their conversion and then Debbie's tragic death, about how he came to be in Crescent Cove, and everything that had happened since his arrival. He left out most of his deeper, more personal feelings, but he gave enough information that, by the end of his story, Bria's eyes had misted over with sympathetic understanding.

"Wow. And here I thought you had life in the palm of your hand."

"Not hardly, but I'm working on it."

"And being a Mormon helps?"

"I know it sounds cheesy, but it gives purpose to my life in ways I can't describe."

"That's not cheesy in the least," she said softly. "I wish my life had as much direction."

"Perhaps in time . . ."

She shrugged. "Perhaps."

Paul stood and walked to a shelf lined with books. He slid his finger over a few spines but didn't pull out any particular volume. Bria stared blankly at her empty hands, lost in her own thoughts for a time. It was as if neither knew what to say next. Their friendship was tenuous at best, based on terrible events and shocking experiences, but the bond was there nonetheless. And they both realized they needed each other to get through whatever would come next. To what end, was the unanswerable question.

Bria sighed as if in defeat and asked, "So . . . ?"

"So . . . what?" said Paul, returning to his chair.

"So, where do we go from here?"

"I don't really know. But the more I think about it, the more I feel you should stay here—and that no one should know about your being here until I figure things out."

"Until *we* figure things out," she corrected.

Paul smiled. "Okay. We."

"Did you tell anyone at the pharmacy about me?"

"No, thank goodness."

Bria frowned playfully. "I made that good of an impression, huh?"

"It's not that—"

"I know," she said, reaching a hand out to him. "I'm just kidding. Listen, I am very grateful for your willingness to help, but are you sure I won't be a burden, staying here and all?"

"Of course not. Besides, this is a small town. News of a new face gets spread around faster than a winter virus. And if someone *is* looking for you, which I believe is true, then it's best to keep you hidden until things are resolved. The thing that really worries me is the possibility of you being bugged."

"Then I'm more than a burden—I'm a risk," Bria said softly to the floor.

"Perhaps. Perhaps not. But you're welcome to stay here in either case."

"Thank you, Paul. You are an amazing person."

He loved the way she said his name. There was a breathy undertone in her voice, an unintentional, sensuous quality that caused long-dormant emotions to flutter anew in his chest. She wasn't flirting. It was just her way. And Paul felt he could listen to her voice a long time without ever tiring of it.

Glancing her way, Paul noticed Bria's eyebrows rise worriedly. "There are just so many unanswered questions. I hate it—especially the idea that I have an implant somewhere. I checked myself thoroughly, and I can't feel anything abnormal, so I have no idea where it is."

"Well, let's just hope it's like you said—that it's a short-range thing."

"Yeah, let's hope so. But if it's not . . . well, we can't simply sit and wait for something to happen."

"I agree," Paul said without pause.

"Swell. Now at the risk of being redundant, where do we start?"

Paul pondered a few minutes, tapping his fingertips together in a thoughtful way. "Let's try and fill in the blanks. You still have no memory of the time between your job at Mercy and waking up at Pathway, right?"

"None. Believe me, I wish I did."

"Then perhaps we should start at the children's hospital."

Her brow furrowed. "I don't know, Paul. If Betty Mumford still works there, she'll be all over anyone who starts asking questions about me. Plus, what if someone else is involved? From the outside, it's impossible to tell who works for Pathway."

"We'll be all right if we sneak in through the Internet," he said, waiting for the PC to boot. "We'll do some searches and see if Mercy mentions anything about your disappearance. Then we'll have some idea of what they know of your whereabouts."

"Can't they track your searches?"

"Maybe. I'll use an old browser name and keep the searches random."

After Googling "Mercy Children's Hospital," they accessed the archives of a weekly newsletter published by the hospital administrator, and searched just after the date of Bria's last memory. Expecting to find an article about Bria's disappearance, they were shocked to read a headline posted the last week of September.

ICU NURSE'S TRAGIC DEATH MOURNED BY MANY

The article went on to say that Bria Georgopolis had been the victim of a brutal murder. The unknown assailant had beat her so severely it had necessitated a closed-casket funeral. She had been a superb ICU nurse and had been loved by the hospital staff. Lastly, it noted that, though survived by none, she would be missed by all.

"Funny. I don't remember any of that," Bria said with a half-humored smirk. "Except maybe the part about being a superb nurse."

"Well, it does tell us one thing," Paul said. "Someone high up at Mercy knows what's going on, or else they wouldn't have printed this fabricated story. That confirms that we can't go traipsing around there asking questions about you."

Bria's shoulders slumped. "Now what?" she asked, suddenly very tired.

Paul Googled "Pathway." The response listed a number of religious affiliations, an IT recruitment center, and a number of businesses using that moniker. Nothing about a recovery hospital. He tried "Pathway to Greater Light Recovery Center." Again, numerous businesses with hits on specific words, but nothing matching the exact name. Then he punched in "Fort Bragg Research Center." A blurb appeared about an inactive site some thirty miles north of Fort Bragg's main complex. During the Cold War, the Army had conducted secret underground experiments in fields such as bio-weaponry and seismic responses to subterranean pulse generators. The research center, no longer sanctioned or funded by the government, had been purchased by Gulf Shore Investments, and was now inactive.

"Well, we know the 'inactive' part is not true," Bria said with a harsh chortle.

"I noticed the article didn't mention anything about who runs the facility."

Bria nodded. "The security company guarding the place knows the company name but nothing about what goes on inside."

"You're sure about that?"

"Yes, positive," she answered, trying to anticipate the direction of Paul's thoughts.

"And you feel a lot of the nurses and others in the complex might not be one hundred percent committed to what's going on in there?"

"I don't know. No one ever fully opened up to me. It may have been commitment through coercion—especially with Young Nurse Jones."

"But they had a large staff, right?"

Again she shrugged. "I assume so. I only knew a dozen or so, but I saw a lot more. Could be hundreds. I really can't say."

"Good. That'll make it easier for me to blend in, won't it?"

Bria's eyes widened in fear. "Paul, no. I can't let you go in there. It's too dangerous."

"Look. Judging from what the Stevensons told me, my pharmacy is probably under surveillance anyway. If whoever is behind all this has something in mind for me, this will simply speed things up a bit."

"But to what end?"

He gave a lopsided smile. "Won't know until I get there."

"*We* get there," she corrected again.

"No. They definitely know who you are. This one I'll have to do solo."

"You can't do it, Paul. You'll be risking your life."

The look on Paul's face acknowledged the truthfulness of her statement. But his eyes softened with an acceptance of the inevitable. "Listen, I can't see any other way to get the information we need. From what the Stevensons said, the place probably still uses contract help now and then, so I'm not too worried about being a new face there. If I can gather some physical evidence of what's truly going on, then it'll help get the authorities involved. And besides, didn't you say your nurse friend there might be in serious trouble?"

"If they know she helped me escape, she's probably dead."

"Then we have no choice. The only other thing I can think of is to take you to a hospital and have them x-ray you for that implant device. It's obvious it had to come from *somewhere,* and that could get the authorities on our side."

Bria shook her head. "What if they're secretly involved too? They could trigger the device, and I'd be dead in an instant. Then there'd be no evidence to shut that place down or rescue Nurse Jones."

"Then I guess it's up to me to gather more evidence." He paused and knelt beside her chair. "Don't worry, I've never been one to blindly rush into things—except for maybe picking up pretty strangers on the highway."

Paul noticed a twinkle of appreciation sparkle in her eyes. She tried to hide it by randomly smoothing an eyebrow. "But . . . how will you get in?"

He smiled like the Cheshire Cat. "I already have an idea."

CHAPTER FORTY-THREE

CRESCENT COVE, CALIFORNIA

Tuesday evening, Paul searched the temporary help listing in Val's computer file, called stand-in pharmacist Kenny Hoggard in Ukiah, and asked if he could cover the pharmacy a few days. Kenny said he happened to have a couple days off and would be happy to help Thursday and Friday. He then asked how Val was doing.

"You haven't heard, then?" Paul asked.

"Heard what?"

"Val is dead. They think it was suicide, but not everyone has ruled out murder either."

There was a long pause on the line. Then, "That's terrible news."

"Sorry to be the one to deliver it," Paul sighed.

"Hey, it's gotta be done. So, you taking over then?"

"Yeah. I bought the place a few days before he died."

"Interesting timing."

"Yeah, the sheriff thinks so too."

"Baker? Is he still around?" Kenny asked in an annoyed tone.

"Constantly."

Kenny laughed. "Hey, hang in there, Paul. You sound like an okay guy. I'm sure if you ride out the transition, everything will end up all right."

"Thanks."

"Sure thing. You've got a sweet pharmacy. Good staff, too. Just let me know what changes you've made, if any."

Paul told him he had installed a lock box in which he kept the appropriate keys to the dispensary. He then told him the combination to the lock box and the alarm code and thanked him again.

Turning to Bria, Paul said, "All set. Now, tomorrow's Wednesday. That gives us one day to perfect a plan. Here's what I have in mind . . ."

* * *

Bria told Paul everything she remembered about the layout of Pathway and the characteristics of the staff. Her main concern was helping Young Nurse Jones, if she needed help, and finding some kind of physical proof of unlawful drug testing. He was not to try to shut the place down or personally confront any of the staff. Just gather evidence.

The following day, Paul went to work as usual. Phyllis went along with his decision not to discuss what he'd learned and seemed content in performing her regular tasks. That evening, Bill Fowler came in for a glass of suds and gave the fountain attendant the usual guff. Paul chanced a wave at him, and he returned a friendly nod. *Progress.*

Just before Paul left, a young woman came up to the pharmacy and asked for him by name. She said she was the mother who called a while back about her daughter swallowing the denture cleaner.

"I can't thank you enough," she said in a heartfelt tone. "You were so kind over the phone and you didn't treat me like I'm an idiot—the way my husband did. I just had to thank you in person."

"You're not an idiot, and it was my pleasure, ma'am. Is your daughter all right now?"

"She's back to coloring the walls, tormenting her sister, and spilling her milk, so yeah, she's quite normal."

Paul laughed. "That's good to hear . . . I think."

The young woman shook Paul's hand, thanked him again, and left.

Paul returned home that evening to another home-cooked meal. "You're going to spoil me," he cautioned Bria.

"That's the idea," she beamed.

That evening, Paul and Bria slumped over his computer with one of Paul's credit cards in hand. They logged onto the JC Penney web page and ordered Bria a bunch of clothes, then had them next-day shipped. It cost a small fortune, but Paul didn't mind. Bria gave him a big hug as thanks and held on for a moment longer when he tried to pull away. He presented her with an extra toothbrush he had brought home from the pharmacy and a few other articles she had requested.

That night, Paul knelt by his bedside and thanked the Lord for the chance to make a difference in Bria's life. He prayed for guidance, safety, and success in their plans. He then petitioned Heavenly Father for her protection, because he cared about her. He stopped abruptly, expecting pangs of guilt to fill his heart. Instead, he was surprised when a warm peace permeated his body. Returning to his petition, he also asked that he could understand all the confusing emotions troubling his soul. His relationship with Bria, though barely started, felt so natural, so correct.

Paul got up from his knees and sat on the edge of his bed, staring into the darkness. *What relationship?* he scoffed inwardly. *You picked her up on a barren stretch of road, for heaven's sake. You know almost nothing about her, and she so little about you. Are you insane?*

But he had to admit that this was different. Every time he had gone on a date after Debbie's death, he had felt awkward, shameful, like he was cheating on his deceased wife. It was all he could do to imagine holding another woman's hand, let alone enter into any kind of romantic foray. But with Bria, he felt comfortable, open, relaxed. He could trust her with his feelings, maybe with his soul someday. He thanked the Lord again for her appearance in his life, for whatever reason and for how ever long is was to be, once again asked for direction, and then crawled into bed.

* * *

The following day went smoothly at the pharmacy. When Paul returned home, Bria sat in front of the computer with a curious expression souring her face.

"Hi, honey, I'm home," Paul jested.

"Hi, Paul. Come here, will you? What's this supposed to mean?" she asked, pointing at the screen.

Bria had booted the pharmacy records Paul had transferred to his home PC. The self-explanatory icons lined a toolbar on the left of the screen, and the header "Dr. Paul Randall" labeled the top.

"Where'd you find this?" he asked, kneeling beside her.

"It was the icon labeled 'PR,'" she explained.

"PR. I never opened that one." He chuckled. "Pretty dumb of me not to recognize my own initials, huh?"

Bria didn't answer. On the screen was a letter to Paul from Val Mince. It was not a cheery welcome note.

> Paul,
>
> If you are reading this, then I am dead. I can assure you it was not suicide, although they may make it look that way.
>
> I will not write much because I fear they may be hacking into my files.
>
> If things begin to seem strange to you, just ignore them. Go on with your life and do not delve into any mysteries that may intrigue you. Like I said, there's a lot of worm cans in this town you don't want to open. If, however, at any time you feel your life is in jeopardy, then look in Galen's vessel.
>
> Good luck.
>
> Val

"Well, the worms are already out," Bria said. "And I supplied the can opener."

"Nonsense," Paul countered. "I already told you I was involved before you got here."

Bria smiled as if she were about to cry. She leaned over and kissed him on the cheek. "Thanks, Paul."

He rested his hand on her knee and said, "We're in this one together."

She patted his hand and left hers on top, interlacing her fingers between his. "What is Galen's vessel—a ship of some kind?"

Paul's eyebrows knit in concentration. "I'm not sure. Galen was the first doctor to compile a book of medical recipes, mostly herbs and such. He was a Greek who lived around AD 130. He's known as the Father of Pharmacy."

"Did he build boats, too?"

"I don't think so," Paul said, still lost in concentration. "But if Val left some evidence of Pathway's misdeeds, we've got to find it."

Bria squeezed his hand. "Does that mean you don't have to go in there and snoop around?"

Paul sensed that she honestly feared for his life. But things were moving too quickly now. Val's cryptic message would have to wait. "I'm afraid not. I don't think we've got the time to decipher what he meant. And who's to say we'll find any *evidence* against Pathway in 'Galen's vessel'? His note only said 'if you feel like your life is in jeopardy.' On the other hand, we *do* know they're going to be looking for you, and your friend in there may still be in serious trouble. Besides, I'm not so sure I'm out of the woods with the sheriff, either." He broke their handhold and stood, a pained look worrying his eyes. "I've got a bad feeling about delaying this whole mess. We need to close this can of worms before it gets any worse."

CHAPTER FORTY-FOUR

NORTHERN CALIFORNIA

Admitting to herself that her dreams of falling in love with a handsome young doctor were now shattered, Kim "Jones" went about her duties sullen and withdrawn. Knowing she was under disciplinary observation, nothing appealed to her, not even her romance novels. She used to think one mistake would potentially mean the loss of her job. Now, she knew it could mean her life.

At first she had had no idea what Pathway's true purpose was, and she had decided that her uncomfortable feelings were simply due to the newness of everything. Soon each day brought new evidence of the insidious nature of the hospital: the way Pathway isolated patients from each other, the clandestine practice of using false names, the secretive way in which they hid all patient records and histories, the inaccessibility to the pharmacy and labs, the unlabeled medications.

The day she arrived at Pathway, Kim was asked to sign a nondisclosure contract with the company. It seemed a bit excessive, even suspicious, but she did so anyway without reading the fine print, which ended up being an agreement to carry an identification chip subcutaneously—merely as a security measure, they assured her. It did require a minor operation to implant, but it was performed under local anesthesia and completed in less than two hours. What she didn't realize was that in addition to the ID chip, a radio-wave-sensitive, microfiber constriction mesh was secured around her left carotid artery. When issued a specific electronic frequency, the carbon-titanium sleeve would close around her artery, cutting off the blood supply to her brain. Everyone at Pathway was fitted with such a device—employees and patients alike. Kim later found out that the constriction mesh could render its carrier unconscious with only a few seconds of electro-magnetic induction. When triggered at high intensity for more than 60 seconds, it would completely close off the artery, severely restricting the brain's oxygen supply, which could ultimately kill the carrier in a massive, mechanical stroke.

Kim had seen it happen. A fellow nurse decided she wanted to leave Pathway without permission. She was found dead the next morning from brain hypoxia. Pathway coroners filed an autopsy report determining that the nurse had had a congenital defect that resulted in a stroke-like blockage of the left carotid, which caused her death. Kim knew better. Everyone at Pathway knew better. But none were brave enough to do anything about it. After all, what could they do that would not lead to death?

The one limitation in the system was that the mesh only reacted to a pulse of radically high-powered, electromagnetic radio waves. Such a pulse required a significant power source, which meant the implant only worked within a few yards of the transmitter. But it was a limitation no one at Pathway wanted to put to the test.

Kim gently fingered the tiny scar on her neck. She had assumed there would be some initial questioning from Pathway concerning Bria's escape, but that it would blow over in a few days. Now, after the incessant harassing from Betty Mumford, numerous physical threats issued and inflicted, and having all her free-time liberties revoked, she knew the only way for her to survive was to escape as Bria had.

She then slid her hand to the injection site in her shoulder. Not knowing what Mumford had given her, Kim suspected the worst. From the constant fog in her head and a total lack of energy, she suspected it was some kind of long-acting hypnotic. She mostly feared that it might be one of the "new drugs."

Throughout her first six months, she had overheard a few doctors discuss breakthrough compounds Pathway had developed, many of which were mind-altering substances. Kim had never commented on the topic, feeling it best that no one knew what she knew. Research hospitals often worked with drug companies to develop beneficial medicines. But Pathway's drugs were anything but beneficial.

Shortly thereafter she had snuck into the morgue and glanced at the charts of the deceased. Each read the same: "Compound X3 caused such and such, leading to death; Compound Y69 . . . Compound Z8 . . ." The charts also indicated that each patient had been reasonably healthy *before* the initiation of therapy. So why would they need the drugs— especially experimental ones? She realized with sickening clarity that 'experimental' was the key word. But by then it was too late.

Just thinking about it caused her forehead to bead with oily perspiration and her heart to pound with fear. *Exactly what have they injected in me? Will the outcome be the same as with the patients I saw in the morgue?*

Obviously they now considered her one of their test subjects. If they had wanted to kill her, they simply would have enabled the implant. Kim knew the answers about the experimental drugs lay in the research files stored ten floors up.

The forty-story underground complex was actually a narrow, self-contained city. The lower eight levels housed the secret hospital and patient chambers. A multi-million-dollar research lab and experimentation facility filled the next twelve floors. The ten above those accommodated staff apartments, a recreation area, a small theater, and an even smaller cafeteria. Huge banks of mechanical and environmental machinery occupied the next five levels, including heating and air conditioning; water and waste management; and electrical, communications, and computer services. The next three were strictly storage units. The uppermost two levels housed another hospital of sorts, this one filled with several empty beds and unused recovery services. It was a façade, a showplace for inquisitive inspectors and government agents. A 24-hour guard station saw to escorting such visitors to elevators that only went to the first ten levels. Special identification and passkeys were required to use the regular elevators. Without a passkey, no one could enter. Or exit.

Kim knew that very few people ever left the facility without upper managerial permission. Because of the severe questioning she had endured, she guessed she would never be able to leave—alive. But it had also revealed that, somehow, Bria *had* escaped. And that realization made her happy.

CHAPTER FORTY-FIVE

NORTHERN CALIFORNIA

Friday morning, Paul drove to Leggett, where U.S. 101 intersected with Highway 1, and rented a nondescript, white Ford sedan from a Hertz store. From there, he drove to the rest stop Bria had described. Finding it empty, he parked and replaced the license plates reading HERTZ CAR RENTAL with official-looking government plates he had printed on glossy card stock at home. From a distance, they looked sufficiently official.

The guard station at Pathway boasted a pair of metal barricade poles with red and yellow caution-striping. Paul handed the guard in the kiosk a medical badge. Earlier, Paul had retrieved the ID he'd found in the master bedroom window box, and had spliced his picture on top of Dr. Kingsford's.

"What is the nature of your visit, Dr. Kingsford?" the young man asked.

From behind his dark glasses, Paul gave the kid an annoyed scowl. "A medical emergency."

The young man nodded. "Excuse me one moment while I clear this, please."

"Look, buddy, I said *emergency,* not *social visit,*" Paul snapped. "As you can see from my badge, I'm a radiologist. My clearance is top-level. They're having problems with their MRI scanner—it may be leaking radiation. It's urgent I get in and see what the damage is before we have another Chernobyl on our hands."

"But sir—"

"We're talking full nuclear meltdown here. You want that on your employment record?"

The guard blanched. "Yes sir. I mean, n—no sir. Head right on in, sir." He depressed a button, which raised the striped poles.

Paul sped directly to the main building's entrance and parked, grateful that the young guard had no knowledge of magnetic resonance imaging—and its lack of radioactive properties. Paul was wearing a pair of khaki slacks, a starched white shirt, and a dark blue tie. Bria had said most of the doctors dressed similarly, and Paul hoped his attire would blend in. Shrugging on a white smock and draping a stethoscope around his neck, he stormed into the complex and approached the guard at the main desk.

"I'm Dr. Kingsford. I need to access the elevators to the research area," Paul said casually. "Pathway's research area."

The guard looked like a block of marble: a square jaw, a buzzed flat top, hard, steely eyes, broad shoulders, no neck. His name badge read OFFICER STONE. It fit.

Handing the ID back to Paul, he pointed down the hall. "Second set of elevators, around the corner to your right, sir."

Paul nodded curtly and marched stiffly down the hall as if he had a specific purpose.

A polished aluminum panel next to the elevator boasted only a thin passkey slot. No up or down call buttons of any kind. Inserting Dr. Kingsford's ID card, magnetic strip first, a chime dinged softly, and a green arrow above the doors indicated the cab was now ascending. *Incredible.* Paul breathed a silent prayer of thanks, grateful that the key still worked. Soon, a second chime sounded and the cab doors opened.

Once inside, a selection panel to the right detailed each level per venue. Paul was pleased to see forty-two lower levels indicated—just as Bria said there might be. He pushed the button MARKED RESEARCH LIBRARY AND LOUNGE.

The descent took forever. No music played in the small cubicle. The only sound was the buzz of electrical servos and the slight *whoosh* of an A/C unit. When the doors opened, Paul stepped into a brightly lit hallway. A woman in a nurse's uniform walked past, busily reading a chart. She didn't even acknowledge him. He waited a moment, then followed the nurse. Passing a few other nurses and one orderly, Paul managed to smile congenially but not so much as to invite conversation. Most simply returned his smile, but a few stopped and stared, not recognizing the new face in their midst.

Rounding a corner, Paul didn't have to go far before he found the lounge. Entering, he grabbed a medical journal from a rack and sat at a table facing the door. One other person occupied the room, a large Polynesian man wearing a white smock and sitting in front of a tray of pastries.

"How you doing?" the man asked Paul after swallowing an enormous bite of a bear claw.

"Fine, thanks. Just taking a break from the old folks."

A quizzical smile formed on the large man's face. "What sector you working in?"

Paul hesitated, not knowing what truly went on in the depths of the Pathway complex. "Radiology. Doing bone density scans on geriatrics." He gave a bitter laugh. "Same old stuff, different day. All I do is listen to stories about their dysfunctional grandchildren and discuss their latest bowel problems. Not really what I had in mind in med school, you know what I mean?"

The big man laughed. "I hear you, bro. I'm PT myself."

Paul shivered. "Ugh. You have to fondle saggy flesh a lot more than I do, then."

"Not really," the Polynesian said. "Most of my test subjects are younger folk. Some old timers, but not many."

"Lucky you," Paul said, opening his magazine. The words *test subjects* struck a nervous chord in his chest. He thought a PT would refer to his charges as *patients.*

The big man stood and walked over. Extending his beefy hand, he said, "Pete Tua'tueleku."

Taking the proffered hand, Paul said, "You mean 'Dr. Smith,' right?"

He laughed again. "Only to the subjects."

"I'm Dr. Paul Kingsford 'Smith.' Pleased to meet you."

Polynesian Dr. Smith looked at his watch and groaned. "Free time goes too quickly. Gotta go bend some more bones. Good to meet you, Paul. Be seeing you around."

"See ya," Paul said, watching the big man leave. It was hard to believe someone as friendly as that could be involved in something as sinister as Pathway. Perhaps he wasn't a willing accomplice. Perhaps he was a Jekyll-and-Hyde type of character. In either case, he wasn't the person Paul was hoping to find. His plan was to keep a low profile until his contact found him. Bria had assured him it wouldn't take long.

It didn't.

Entering the lounge with an inquisitive, searching glance, Young Nurse Jones's eyes focused on the youthful, sandy-haired doctor sitting alone at a table. She glided over and placed her hand on a chair across from Paul. "Mind if I join you?"

Not looking up from his journal, Paul said, "Sure."

Kim quickly dropped into the chair, pulled a paperback from her smock pocket, and began flipping the pages randomly—and quite noisily. Ignoring her, Paul continued to read. She then began humming a happy-go-lucky tune, somewhat forced and very off-key. Paul turned a page and continued reading. The nurse next began lightly tapping her fingernails on the tabletop. Paul suppressed a smile and looked over the edge of his magazine. Kim stopped humming and flashed him an adorable combination of prominent cheekbones, large teeth, and an impish nose. *The chipmunk,* Paul thought. *That's got to be her.*

"Can I help you?" Paul asked in a non-communicative tone.

"I bet you can," Kim replied flirtatiously.

Playing his part, Paul acted confused. "Excuse me?"

Instantly, Kim moved to the chair next to Paul and placed her hands very close to his. This might be her one chance to escape. If she could just get this new guy to ask her out, she might able to convince Mumford to let her go for just one evening . . .

Kim took a quick breath, then in rapid-fire succession, she spouted, "My name's Kim. I'm a nurse here. It's so nice to see a new face, especially a cute one. I work on the recovery and observation levels. I've been here almost a year. I like movies and romance novels and long walks and candlelight dinners, and just about anything in the right company. I went to school in LA at—"

"Whoa, slow down a bit," Paul said with his hands up, palms forward. *Yep, this is the one, all right.* "I'm Dr. Paul Kingsford."

Extending his hand, Paul intentionally knocked her book off the table—making it look like an accident. He waited for Kim to bend down to retrieve the paperback and then knelt to join her. He placed his hand on top of hers and quickly whispered, "Bria sent me."

Kim drew a sharp breath. Her eyes registered extreme fear, and Paul felt her skin suddenly grow cold and clammy under his hand. "What?" she gasped.

Urgently, he said, "I need your help. Bria needs your help."

Kim looked around the empty room nervously. "Where is she? How did you get in here?" she whispered.

Paul remained on his knees, as did Kim, partially hidden under the table. "She's safe. How I got here's not important. We need your help to gather some information."

"What information?"

Putting his mouth to her ear, he said, "Anything that will help us expose this place. Anything that will shut it down."

"But . . . that's impossible," she said hesitantly.

"Why?"

"That information is kept locked up, and nothing leaves this place without permission, including the staff."

"I'm not planning on actually taking it from the building."

She leaned back and stared at him, bewildered and scared. "Then what good would just seeing it do?"

"Let me worry about that. Can you help me? Bria said you were her only friend in this place. She said you gave her clues in a romance novel with which to escape. She said no one knows about that but you and her."

Kim considered his words very carefully. She was still scared and shaking, but her eyes revealed a commitment to help. Standing, she slipped her book into her pocket and smoothed out her uniform. Paul rose and brushed off his pants. "Sorry about knocking your book off the table," he said lightly.

"It's an old copy. Don't even worry about it," she said just as lightly. "Are you about done with your break, Dr. Smith?"

"Uh, yeah, sure."

"What department do you work in again?"

Paul hesitated. Kim smiled.

"Um, radiology . . ." Paul said tentatively.

"Good. That's right on the way to my station. You can walk me there." Taking the lead, Kim opened the lounge door.

"Thanks," Paul said, more nervous than he cared to admit.

Exiting the lounge, they moved quickly down the hall. Kim walked briskly but not so much as to look strange. Even so, Paul had to lengthen his stride to keep up. The girl continually shot glances at Paul along the way. Occasionally, as they passed a staff member, Kim would say hello, but she did not bother to introduce Paul to anyone.

As they stopped at an elevator and pushed the call button, Kim began talking about a movie she had seen at the complex's small theater the other night, some romantic comedy starring Hillary Duff. She had loved it. Paul was certain he wouldn't have.

The elevator door opened, and an old orderly stepped out. Entering, Kim pushed the button for a specific floor. Just before the doors closed, a hand shot in and tapped the safety stop, causing the doors to reopen. A tall, dignified-looking man in a business suit entered, followed by a stocky, motherly nurse.

Paul heard Kim draw a quick gasp. At first, he didn't know who these people were, but he immediately sensed that their sudden appearance was not a good thing. The man looked strangely familiar, but Paul could not put a name with the face. A quick glance at the woman's name tag identified her as Nurse Jones. From Bria's apt description, Paul knew it was Betty Mumford.

CHAPTER FORTY-SIX

CRESCENT COVE, CALIFORNIA

Bria spent the day trying to keep her mind busy. She knew Paul was in danger. She knew it was mostly her fault—although he would say otherwise. There was something extraordinary about this man.

Pondering over a bowl of vegetable soup and a half-eaten grilled cheese sandwich, Bria reveled in feelings long dormant, emotions sequestered away by mistrust and bad experiences. A curious excitement tingled inside her every time she thought about Paul. Denying the feelings was unsuccessful. Dissecting them led to unanswerable questions. Rationalizing them ended in dead-end paths. Each time she thought of how generous and trusting he had been, a reciprocal trust welled within her—one that confused her with its*rightness.* The emotions were strange and unrecognizable, but only because of a lack of experience. Somehow, she knew opening herself to those feelings was now a safe thing to try. And oh, how she wanted to try. Paul was a good man, inside as well as out—there was no questioning that.

Returning to the kitchen, Bria cleared her dishes, then headed upstairs to take a shower. She needed to keep moving to escape those irrational—although curiously welcome—emotions.

While toweling off, she heard the doorbell ring. Wrapping herself in the towel, she moved to the master bedroom and parted the wood-slat blinds just enough to peek outside. Since the Victorian's large veranda covered the porch, she could not see who was at the door. But she didn't have to. The late afternoon sun gave enough light to show a patrol car sitting in the driveway, its engine still purring. The decal on the driver's door read CRESCENT COVE SHERIFF. The doorbell rang a second time. Moving catlike to the banister overlooking the stairwell, Bria crouched low and saw a backlit, muted shape through the beveled glass on one side of the door. The person was attempting to look in. Bria could make out the shape of an octagonal hat and a dark gun belt. It had to be Sheriff Baker, the lawman Paul had mentioned. Thankful she had not switched on any lights, Bria felt confident she remained unseen at the odd angle and in murky shadow. The doorbell rang a third time, followed by knuckles rapping on the glass pane. A cold shiver eeled down her spine. Paul had said Baker was not a bad guy, but he was certainly not to be trusted. Besides, Bria was certain Pathway had already issued an APB on her, labeling her as a dangerous criminal or an emotionally unstable escaped patient. If the sheriff found her, her life was forfeit.

The front door's brass knob rattled as the man tried to turn it. A suffocating panic gripped Bria's throat. Irrationally fearing that the sheriff had clairvoyance enough to see into the dark, she remained frozen in place.

"Randall, open up. It's the sheriff," a voice called from outside. More pounding followed. The knob rattled again. Thankfully, it remained locked. "I know you're in there, Randall. I heard you." Bria's knees began to quiver as the cool of the evening air pricked at her damp skin. The doorbell rang in a staccato barrage of nerve-twisting blasts. Gooseflesh covered her arms and legs.

The sheriff used a string of verbiage not becoming of a law officer and rapped his nightstick against the window. Bria expected to hear the shattering of glass at any moment. "Randall! Don't make me bust this door down."

Bria looked around in terror. More sharp pounding filled the dark entrance hall. Finally breaking from her immobility, she moved quickly to the master bedroom closet and entered but left the door slightly ajar. "This is so stupid," she muttered to herself, yet it did little to loosen the acidic knot in her stomach. Forcing herself to breathe slowly and deeply, she closed her eyes and concentrated on listening to the sheriff continue his tirade.

Finally, after a few more minutes of listening to threats and swearing, Bria heard the sheriff enter his patrol car and back out of the driveway. The gunning of the engine and squealing tires faded quickly as the car sped away.

Bria wasn't sure how much time she spent in the closet struggling to calm herself, but when she eased from the closet, she saw the afternoon had progressed well toward evening. She brushed her hair, hung up her towel, dressed quickly in her room, then returned to Paul's master bedroom. She simply felt safer there. But with nerves still poised to spontaneously discharge, Bria truly wished Paul had some alcohol in the house. Moving to the edge of the bed, she slumped down hard and buried her face in her hands. She felt like crying out of helpless frustration, but she didn't want to let herself be so flighty. Paul would not have reacted this way. She wondered how he maintained such inner serenity and calm. Was it something in his nature, or perhaps the way his parents had raised him? Or was it his religion? Whichever the reason, Bria felt comforted just being in his room, under his roof.

Glancing at his nightstand, she noticed a small book next to a reading lamp. Holding the text to the last light of evening, she read, "The Book of Mormon: Another Testament of Jesus Christ."

Turning the book a few times in her hand, her curiosity grew by the second. She took it to her room across the hall, clicked on her nightstand lamp, and then quickly clicked it back off. Even though her curtains were drawn, she inwardly scolded herself. *Idiot! No lights.*

Still, she felt a compulsion to open the small text and read from it. She couldn't explain her feelings, but it was more than random curiosity. Something told her she could learn a lot about Paul from the book. She knew it was a religious work of sorts, a kind of second Bible to the Mormon people, but that was about it. She ran her fingers across the embossed cover. It was obviously a Christian text from its title, andshe felt it might simply be a collection of rules by which to live. But she couldn't know that for sure unless she read it.

Returning to her closet, Bria shut the door and clicked on the overhead light. It was a small space, but since she didn't have many clothes inside, it didn't feel claustrophobic. Slumping to the floor, Bria opened the book to the middle and began to skim the pages.

The text read like the New Testament. The names were new to her, but she found herself immediately comfortable with them. The story was not one with which she was familiar—it sounded more like actual narrative than metaphorical parable. She read for almost an hour—if only to get her mind on something else—before her legs began to cramp.

Just as she stood, the phone rang, startling Bria. Exiting the closet, she saw that the caller ID registered the Stevensons' household. She knew the Stevensons were friends of Paul's and could be trusted, but she hesitated picking up the line. Paul had suggested they keep Bria's presence a secret until they could gather more evidence. He said he had not mentioned her to any of his pharmacy staff. She decided that was good advice to follow.

But the phone continued to ring.

Phyllis was Paul's number-one technician. She and her husband had openly revealed the sordid truth about Pathway to him. Maybe they had remembered something else about the complex of which Paul should be aware. Perhaps they knew why the sheriff had come that evening. It was probably a very important phone call.

Bria picked up the handset and cautiously said, "Hello?"

No one responded on the other end.

She waited in silence. She could hear breathing, deep and raspy.

"Hello?" she repeated.

A short burst of air sounded in the receiver, as if the party on the other end gave a brief chuckle of gladness.

Then the line disconnected.

Bria stared at the phone as a new fear crept into her heart. She set the handset into the cradle, her mind racing with questions she couldn't answer. A dull pain began to sharpen at the base of her skull. Irrational tears misted her eyes. She knew she was in trouble—so much so, she almost wished the sheriff would return.

* * *

On the other end of the line, the scarred giant smiled at the phone with an effluence of pure evil. He had first driven to the mayor's house but found no one home. He then remembered the name of Cliff Stevenson, one of the original workers at Pathway. The Light had requested Surt memorize the list . . . just in case.

Although the Stevensons initially would not comply, Surt knew the gods had led him there. He was to use these people to find the girl. With the backing of deity, the giant knew his unique means of extracting information could be very persuasive.

Cliff Stevenson sat at the kitchen table with his hands pressed flatly against its cold surface. Phyllis Stevenson sat beside him, her hands duct-taped to her chair. She stared blankly at the barren tabletop, hating herself for having just put Paul in imminent danger. But she didn't have a choice. At the threat of having her husband murdered before her eyes, Phyllis told the giant she suspected someone might be staying with Paul in the old Kingsford house. He had taken home several items from the store that were particular to a woman's preference.

She despised herself for having shared this.

Surt silently appraised his two captives with the look of a judge, jury, and executioner combined. He then removed a pair of black leather gloves and, continuing to grin, slowly stretched them on.

Phyllis began to cry.

CHAPTER FORTY-SEVEN

NORTHERN CALIFORNIA

"Hello, Kim," Betty said dryly.

"Hi." Kim's voice was strained.

The man in the business suit stepped to the back of the small elevator without speaking. Paul kept his eyes on the illuminated numerals sequentially indicating each floor they passed.

"I don't believe we've met," Betty said, stepping around Kim and tilting her head to catch Paul's eye.

"Dr. Kingsford—or Dr. Smith, whichever you prefer." Paul tried to sound detached and somewhat irritated.

"Your name sounds vaguely familiar. Are you new here?"

"Sort of. I work mostly on the outside. I haven't been down here for a while."

Paul knew to keep his fabrications short and open-ended. Trying to improvise too much detail would lead to inaccuracy and disaster.

"I see," Betty said, casting a quick glance at the man behind her.

The businessman cleared his throat and stepped forward. "Dr. Kingsford, did you say? Seems like it's been a while since I heard that name. How long have you worked here?"

Paul briefly looked the man over before returning his gaze to the elevator readout. "More off than on for about five years. And you?"

The businessman guffawed. "I helped with the purchase of this place from the Army—that's how long I've been here."

Kim stood rigid, her eyes wide and staring straight ahead, her pallor like death. "And exactly what is the nature of your visit today, Dr. Kingsford?" the man asked.

Paul scowled. "Is that really any of your business?"

The suit raised his eyebrows. "Listen, chum, even though I don't come here often, I still say what goes on down here. You obviously don't know who I am. Suffice it to say I'm from HQ; I drop in only when certain issues come up."

"Me too," Paul stated, still not facing the man. "I'm checking out a bug in the MRI scanner."

"What's the problem with it?"

Paul shrugged. "I won't know until I take a look, now will I?"

Paul could hear Kim's breath come in short, quick bursts. From the corner of his eye he saw Mumford again exchange glances with the businessman. Paul could only guess what their expressions read. It was too late anyway. He couldn't back down now.

Even though Bria had warned Paul about Betty Mumford, he didn't know the extent of her involvement at Pathway.

"Paul Kingsford . . . Paul Kingsford," Betty mused, tipping her head to one side and chewing on a knuckle, as if that helped her concentration. "I know I've heard that name before . . ." Then, turning to the businessman, "Harold, didn't we used to have a Dr. Kingsford working in radiology here before?"

"I'll have to look into that," the man said flatly.

Betty's eyebrows furrowed deeply. "That name just sounds so familiar . . ." Her voice trailed off as she continued to ponder the borrowed name.

A soft ding announced their arrival at the predetermined floor, and the elevator gently heaved to a stop. As the doors slid open, Betty asked, "What are *you* doing on this floor, Nurse Jones?"

"I, um . . . I'm running an errand for Dr. Smith," she said hesitantly.

Paul exited and turned left. He hated leaving Kim in such a tenuous situation, but he knew suspicions would increase if he waited for her. As Kim stepped out of the car, he heard Betty say, "Remember our appointment tomorrow morning, Kim. This session's very important."

"Yes, ma'am," Kim said, lowering her eyes vacantly.

The elevator door closed, and Kim slumped against the far wall, barely keeping her feet under her. Paul rushed to her side.

"Are you okay?" he asked, taking her shoulders in both hands.

Kim nodded and drew a choppy breath. Instantly, tears flooded her eyes, and she fell into his chest. They stood in silence for a moment, her arms clinging desperately to Paul, his hand gently patting her back. Then, in a voice just above a whisper, she said, "If I go to that appointment, I'm dead."

* * *

A large glass door secured the Records Room. The place looked deserted. That surprised Paul. He assumed such potentially damaging information would be under constant guard. Perhaps there was an internal surveillance system of some kind. Or perhaps Pathway knew anyone this far down would already have clearance enough to be criminally involved. He glanced around then tried the door. It was locked. A slot over the handle resembled the one on the elevator. Inserting his ID badge, the door clicked and opened.

"Where'd you get that?" Kim asked.

"A friend," Paul said bluntly.

The room resembled a small library, with rows of open file cabinets encircling a long desk with reading lamps.

"Where do we start?" Paul whispered to Kim.

"What do you need?"

Paul shrugged. "Let's start with Bria."

"Over here," she said, leading to a section marked alphanumerically. Moving a few feet down the aisle, Kim pointed to a set of numbers reading 2007.09.17:37.46.N.122.26.W.

"What's that mean?" he asked, indicating the numbers.

"Year, month, day, latitude and longitude."

"Of what?"

"Collection data."

"*Collection* meaning . . . ?"

Kim folded her arms as if to protect herself. "Patients. Test subjects. Whatever you want to call them. The numbers indicate when and where they retrieved the test patient." Then softer, "Where they were *collected*." She mumbled the words as if ashamed of them.

"I see," Paul said without accusation. "Are you sure this is Bria's file?"

"Yes."

"How do you know? I noticed you don't have a passkey."

"I used to help out in here all the time. Only now I always have to have someone with me."

Removing the folder from the shelf, she handed it to Paul. He opened it and began reading as quickly as he could. The facts filled him with a noxious chill: personal history, likeliness of acquisition, possible repercussions of disappearance, next of kin, general health, likelihood of positive test results. The next section held information on initial testing and reaction to a particular test drug, this one labeled SB-470—a structurally enhanced form of acetylcholine, one of the major chemical neurotransmitters in the brain. The last page listed stats on her progress, both physical and mental, and her potential for future testing.

Near the bottom of that page, a handwritten entry in red ink listed Bria Georgopolis as "escaped." Below that, someone's sloppy scrawl ordered,

CODE RED. Time-sensitive. Immediate capture imperative. Return to PW at all costs—alive if possible, but not necessary.

Paul placed Bria's folder under a desk lamp and removed his camera phone from an inside pocket. He had Kim hold the pages open as he clicked one shot after another.

"How many pictures does that hold?" Kim asked quickly, as if each second counted against them.

"Not enough," Paul said.

Finishing Bria's file, they shelved it and moved to another section. "Just grab any file," Paul ordered. "We'll snap some of the basics off it, and then we'll need a few pics from the very beginning of this nightmare."

After fifteen minutes of hasty photography, Paul's phone beeped a CARD FULL warning. They returned all the files and stepped back to make sure the place looked as if they had never been there. Moving to the door, he asked, "Does this complex have a back door?"

"Funny. No, just an elevator and a stairwell."

"Bria said you told her to take the stairs. Is that safer?"

"It was when no one was expecting her to run." The look of dread began to worry her face again. "If Nurse Mumford has spread word about your being here, I'm not sure how you'll get out."

"How *we'll* get out. I'm taking you with me."

The worried look on Kim's face turned to one of white fear. She shook her head slowly as her hand involuntarily covered the left side of her neck. "I can't," she whispered.

Confused, Paul asked, "Why not?"

"They're watching my every move. And then there's the . . . the implant."

"Implant? You have one too? Bria thought only the patients had them."

Kim shook her head and glanced around as if verifying no one was within earshot. "Everyone here has them, employees and most patients. It's the only way the bigwigs can be sure this place stays secret."

"What kind of implant?"

Kim explained the small but deadly device to Paul. He blew a low whistle and ran a hand through his hair. "What's the range on them?"

"I'm not sure."

"Bria heard a nurse mentioning a specific frequency and a limited range or something."

"Yeah, I know the person with the transmitter has to be fairly close to activate the implant."

Paul paused, as if afraid to ask the next question. "How close?"

Tears brimmed and fell from her eyes. "I've seen it kill a person who was about thirty yards away."

He checked his watch. It was just after 11 PM. "Then we'd better move quickly and get you farther away than that." He opened the door and peered out. The hallway was clear. Taking Kim's hand he said, "Let's go."

Together they ran to the elevator and depressed the call button. In only a few seconds, the cab arrived. They simultaneously held their breath as the doors opened. The cab was empty. Entering, Paul looked up. The ceiling had a fluorescent light fixture, an air duct for air conditioning and heat, and a small access door. At six feet tall, he could barely reach the latch, but he could not push it open.

Crouching, he said, "Hop on my back."

Kim clambered on and, after a few heaves, was able to push open the latch. "You want me to crawl up?"

"No," he said, shifting her off his back. "You'll have to trust me on this one. Get down on your hands and knees, okay?"

When Kim gave him a look, Paul quickly explained that he wanted to climb on her back and hoist himself into the space above the cab. He would then reach down, grab Kim by the wrists, and haul her up. "You can't weigh more than a hundred pounds, and I am pretty strong," he stated without bravado.

"I can tell," she said with a smile.

Kim groaned slightly as Paul used her as a step stool. Completing the first part of the maneuver, Paul stuck his face back into the cab. As he did so, his cell phone fell from his pocket, smacked the sill, and dropped into the cab. Luckily, Kim caught it before it hit the floor. She tossed it back to him.

"Thanks. Just a minute," he said, disappearing into the blackness of the elevator shaft. After a pause, he called into the cab. "Push the top two buttons, for ground level and the first sublevel."

Kim did so, and the elevator began to rise very quickly. Paul looked up into the blackness, searching for any kind of light. Darkness enveloped the shaft. The sensation of rising toward freedom filled Paul with a soothing weightlessness. He closed his eyes and relished the breeze caused by the cab's motion.

"Paul," Kim called from below.

Wiping his hands on his pants, he knelt before the access door and reached inside. Kim raised her hands but couldn't reach his. "You'll have to jump," he called.

"Okay," she called back. Bending her knees, she prepared to leap upward. "On three, okay?"

"No problem," he answered, leaning farther into the space.

"One . . . two . . ."

The elevator chime announced its arrival at a hailed floor—one Kim had not cued—still several floors below ground. Kim's head jerked up; her eyes widened, seeking Paul's help. The cab heaved to a stop, causing Paul to lose his balance. He caught himself just before falling, but the sudden movement again caused his cell phone to drop from his pocket into the elevator cab. It landed on Kim's sneaker before clattering to the floor. Kim moved to retrieve it.

"Leave it," Paul urged softly. "Jump!"

Kim crouched.

The elevator door opened.

CHAPTER FORTY-EIGHT

CRESCENT COVE, CALIFORNIA

The strange phone call plagued Bria's mind with evil portents. She wandered through the house making sure all the lights were turned off. She already knew they were, but it made her feel better to double-check. She then returned to the alcove in the master bedroom and seated herself in the little tower. Nervously, she watched the dark street through a slit in the blinds. Her heart pounded fiercely. Her mind raced illogically, uncontrollably.

The street below sat in gloomy stillness, disturbed only by an occasional dry leaf skittering across the driveway on a breath of wind. Waiting, listening, Bria felt her muscles twitch at every little sound. Even after a hundred years of weathering, the old Victorian still groaned and creaked sporadically as it continued to settle more comfortably on its foundation. In the distance, a swirling fog began to creep inland from the black ocean.

Suddenly, Bria flinched. A disturbingly loud snap caused her to leap from the bench. Her eyes darted around the dark room, searching.

Silence followed.

Then a low humming outside brought her attention back to the window. A car approached quickly from the north. Bria watched intently as the vehicle passed through the yellow haze of the streetlight. It was an old Chrysler minivan, with faded paint and a section of cardboard taped over one of the rear panels. The van slowed as it approached the corner on which the house stood, paused at the intersection, and then continued down the side street. Bria closed her eyes and blew out a slow, shaky breath.

"You're acting so flighty," she growled at herself. "Think of an escape plan or something."

She forced herself from the window and paced around the room. Just then, a muffled thump sounded from the floor below her. Frowning, she paused and listened intently. There was a faint scratching, a rattling, and another thump. Frantically looking around the room, she tiptoed across the hallway to her bedroom and entered the closet. The muffled noises ceased for a moment. Bria closed the closet door to a crack.

There—she heard a third muffled thump, and then the creaking made by the back door slowly opening. There was a pause, then the door squeaked closed. Sticking her head out of the closet, she heard footsteps, measured and stealthy. Someone was walking through the house. It couldn't be Paul. He would have called out her name. This was someone else—an intruder, someone uninvited. The footfalls continued to press heavily on the hardwood floor.

Just as Bria mustered the courage to leave the closet, the footfalls began sounding up the stairs. Looking desperately around the dark closet, Bria found nothing more than a couple of shirts, a light jacket, a few empty hangers, and a footstool.

Don't panic!

The footfalls stopped at the top of the stairs. Harsh breathing, deep and ragged, crept along the hallway and into her room. She heard a thick, noisy intake of air, as if someone was filling his or her lungs. A slow, steady release followed, full of pleasure and affirmation.

Bria's own breath caught in her dry throat. Trying vainly to remain calm, she found herself hyperventilating in rapid bursts.

Then—

"Mmmm." It was a man's voice. Low, husky, laced with vile longing. "I can smell fresh soap and steam. Just out of the shower, are we?"

Bria backed into the corner of the tiny cubicle, her eyes wide with fright. *Paul, where are you?*

CHAPTER FORTY-NINE

NORTHERN CALIFORNIA

The divided door disappeared on either side of the cab's frame. Betty Mumford scowled at Kim from outside the elevator. She immediately noticed the cell phone on the floor and gasped. "Cell phones are forbidden in here, young lady. You know that."

Kim nodded.

Paul had closed the access door just as the elevator had opened, but he could still see through the vented air ducts into the cab.

"Well?" Mumford snapped, picking up the slim phone.

"Yes, ma'am," Kim whispered.

Betty held the phone to Kim's face. "Where did you get this?"

"I . . . it was . . . I just . . ."

Paul heard a vicious slap. Kim yelped in pain.

"Don't you dare lie to me, missy," Betty warned. "You're in deep trouble already. Lying will only make it worse."

Kim stifled a sob. "I'm sorry, Nurse Jones. I know I shouldn't have brought it down—"

Another slap stopped her cold. "Stupid girl. Only a bumble-head like you would do this. Cell phones don't even work this far underground."

"I know—" Another slap. Kim was crying openly now.

"I don't know why they hired such a twit in the first place," Betty growled, as if complaining to the admissions board. "Always more interested in her worthless novels instead of concentrating on the project at hand. Never grasped the true spirit of Pathway. Never been part of the team." Then, again directing her venom toward the young nurse, Betty snapped, "Who were you going to call anyway? A boyfriend? The police?"

"I—I don't know," Kim stuttered, then gasped, "Please! Don't hit me again."

There was a pause before Paul heard Mumford speak. "You're right. A slap is nothing compared to what's going to happen."

"No," Kim said hoarsely.

"Oh yes. And unless you tell me what's going on with this phone, I'm going to see that you get the worst of it." She pulled a small black remote from her pocket and thumbed the tiny switches menacingly.

Kim sobbed. "No. Please . . ."

"Let's go."

Paul heard the elevator doors reopen and Betty Mumford lead Kim out of the cab. The chirping of rubber-soled shoes mixed with Kim's weakening protests faded down the corridor. Paul opened the access door and jumped into the cab before the doors closed.

He heard Mumford continue to berate the young nurse.

Paul stepped out of the elevator and saw the backs of Kim and Betty. They were some thirty feet down the corridor. He yelled, "Hey, Mumford!"

Both women flinched. Nurse Mumford looked shocked, stunned.

"Run, Kim!" Paul cried. "Now!"

Seeing her momentary advantage, the young nurse slammed her heel on top of Nurse Mumford's foot and at the same time ripped the small remote from her hand. The large woman screeched in pain as Kim ran toward the elevator. Paul repeatedly pushed the "close doors" button in the elevator while holding the safety stop. The doors struggled against his contradictory commands. When Kim reached the elevator, Paul yanked her inside. Along with numerous profanities, Betty screamed for help. The doors closed. Paul pressed the ground-floor button, then the next two buttons down. The elevator lurched upward.

Clinging to Paul's frame, Kim was sobbing, trembling uncontrollably. He shushed her tenderly. "Is that what controls your implant?" he asked, indicating the black remote.

Kim nodded, then drew a quick breath and let out a prolonged, pitiful moan.

"What's wrong?" Paul asked. "Isn't that the right one?"

Still struggling to speak through her sobs, Kim said, "It's—the right—remote. But—but Betty—still has—your camera phone."

CHAPTER FIFTY

CRESCENT COVE, CALIFORNIA

On her knees, backed against the closet wall, Bria's hand slid across a metal grate. A closer examination revealed a decorative grill-work to a 20-by-30-inch air intake, the kind that drew fresh air into the furnace from a remote part of the house. Fortunately, snaps had been used to secure it in place rather than screws. Using her fingernails, she pried the metal covering from its frame. She couldn't see into the shaft more than a few inches, but it looked just wide enough for her needs.

"Where are you, my sweet?" the man said playfully, as if beginning a simple game of hide-and-seek from the top of the stairs.

From the sound of his voice, Bria guessed that the man had first moved to the bathroom to search it out. Leaving that room, he paused again at the stair head. "Mmmm, you *did* get nice and clean for the great and magnificent Surt. How thoughtful. How touching. How . . . stimulating."

As quietly as possible, Bria slid her feet into the air duct. It went back about two feet before angling down ninety degrees. It was a tight turn, but she was able to squeeze and bend until her entire frame was inside; her torso in the intake, her waist and legs dangling down the vertical shaft. She reached out and pulled the metal covering back into place. Seating it in its frame, she gave a slight tug to secure it firmly with a soft metallic *pop*. To Bria, it sounded like cannon fire. Unfortunately, only two of the four snaps latched. Keeping her fingers laced through the decorative grillwork, she dared not let go, lest the whole thing fall out and make a second incriminating noise.

"There you are," the man said, moving from the stairs to the bedroom. Entering, he cooed lustily. "Still playing hard to get? I like that."

The man searched the room, looking under Paul's bed and behind a highboy and a large curio. As he approached the closet, Bria held onto the grillwork by the tips of her fingers, terrified to let go. The giant yanked open the door, which caused a *whoosh* of air to waft over her clammy skin.

Bria heard the man's hand scrape against the closet wall, searching. She gritted her teeth and released the grillwork just as the light flicked on. Thankfully, the grillwork stayed in place.

The man entered and slid the few articles of clothing on hangers back and forth. He toed the footstool thoughtfully. Then, stepping back, he looked up. There was an attic entrance in the closet ceiling.

"This gets more fun by the second," he mused openly. "Such a resourceful girl. Worthy of my talents, that's for certain."

The big man easily reached the pull-string that opened the access door. A small ladder slid down halfway into the closet. Grabbing the rungs, he kicked the footstool aside, causing it to slam into the decorative grillwork. Bria gasped as it fell noisily to the floor.

The giant tilted his head to look at the dislodged metal grillwork. He bent further, trying to look inside the dark airshaft. He then dropped to one knee and reached a hand into the blackness of the vent.

Bria cringed and held her breath. She saw the man's thick fingers creep toward her face. They stopped inches from her nose. The fingers slowly probed back and forth. Just as she felt she could hold her breath no longer, the hand withdrew and the man returned his attention to the black and inviting attic entrance.

"Ready or not, here I come," he sang in a voice dripping with ill intent.

Bria saw his feet disappear as he clambered into the attic. She heard the rafters complain against his weight as he moved away from the opening. When she was confident he was well inside, she scrambled from the air duct, closed the attic door, and ran from the bedroom.

A muffled "What the—" sounded from the space above her.

Bria had just reached the bottom of the stairs when she heard the man crash through the attic access. He landed with a grunt and a vile curse amid what sounded like a shower of plaster and lath. She sprinted to the front door, opened it, and bolted into the thickening fog of the night.

CHAPTER FIFTY-ONE

NORTHERN CALIFORNIA

"Why did you push the first three floors?" Kim asked, struggling to be stoic.

"You said there are only a few people on the night shift, right?"

"Yeah, but it only takes one to communicate with the ground level."

"I'm not worried about the ground-level staff," Paul said, still watching the numbers decrease. It wasn't nearly fast enough.

Confused, Kim asked, "Why not?"

Paul wiped the sweat that had formed on his brow. "For one thing, you have the remote to your implant."

"*One* of the remotes. Every senior staffer carries one, and their frequencies are adjustable."

"Fine. But that's one less they now have. Plus, Bria said when she escaped, she questioned a few security guards outside, and not one of them seemed to know what went on here. She felt they were telling the truth, and I agree. Apparently, Pathway hires a national security company—instead of using their own people—to look less suspicious, less clandestine. There may be a few government people involved on the outside, but only a few. Most of the guards up there don't have a clue what goes on below ground."

"Okay. So why aren't we going to the ground-level floor?"

"I'm assuming everything is controlled below ground. I think we'll be lucky to make the ground floor before they shut down this elevator. I'm hoping we can at least reach the third sublevel before that happens. Besides, if they do warn the main floor, they'll be expecting us to exit the elevator, not the stairs."

Paul checked his watch—12:10 AM. "It's just after midnight," he told his frightened companion.

Kim drew a choking breath but couldn't stop trembling. With her nerves shot and her endurance frazzled, she found it impossible to remain composed.

Paul put his arm around her. "It's okay, Kim. We'll be fine."

Just then, the elevator screeched to a halt. The LED floor indicator read SUBLEVEL 14.

"Uh-oh." Paul pushed the "open doors" button.

Nothing happened.

A brief moment passed. Then, a small red light began flashing above the control panel in sequence with a loud, ear-piercing alarm.

Kim trembled, looking hopeless.

Paul cupped her face, smiled, and winked. "Time to be strong."

The young nurse's expression registered anything but strength. "I don't think I can."

He grabbed her shoulders firmly. "Think about one of the heroines in those novels you love. Are they all brainless, flighty wimps?"

She shook her head.

"Of course not. They're strong-willed women who set their minds on getting what they want. Now, do you want to escape or stay here?"

"I want out," she answered softly.

"Then let's go." And with that, he had Kim get down on all fours, stood on her back, and heaved himself through the access door in the elevator. He braced his legs firmly and reached back inside. Kim took a hesitant jump but couldn't reach Paul's hands.

"How badly do you want to get out?" he asked forcefully.

Kim angrily wiped the tears from her face, gritted her teeth, and jumped with all her might. They caught each other by the wrists, and Paul pulled her into the space above the cab.

The thirteenth-floor elevator door was only two feet above the roof of the cab. Grabbing the seam, Paul pulled the safety doors apart. The hallway beyond was dark and still. Exiting the elevator shaft, they went directly to the stairwell and began their ascent. Because of his daily exercise regimen, Paul had no trouble setting a steady pace upward. Kim, however, panted heavily, doing her best to keep up. In way of assistance, he took her hand and literally pulled her up the stairs.

Each time they passed a landing and exit, they could hear the continued wail of the alarm through the door, signaling an emergency—in this case, their escape. Within a few minutes, they reached the ground-level exit. Pausing to catch his breath, Paul put his ear to the door and listened intently. Kim leaned against the wall with her hands on her knees, gasping for air. The alarm either had stopped blaring or, for some other reason, was not sounding on the ground floor. Paul assumed the latter, reasoning that Pathway would want to keep all emergencies to themselves.

Easing the door open, he recognized the brightly lit hallway of the entrance area. Leaving the stairwell, Paul led Kim to the corner adjacent to the main entrance. He whispered his plans in her ear, making sure she knew exactly what to do and why.

"We don't have much time. They'll be up here any minute."

"Okay," she said, swallowing hard. "I can do this."

He gave her a big hug, knowing it would boost her confidence greatly. "Good girl."

Returning to the stairwell, Paul opened the door wide, then slammed it shut. The harsh noise ricocheted quickly down the hall. Kim took off running. She turned the corner and bolted for the entrance. The square-shouldered, no-necked guard was already on his feet. Ignoring him, she ran directly toward the glass doors.

Then Paul rounded the corner at full speed. "Stop her!" he yelled to the guard.

The guard, recognizing Paul, leapt in front of Kim with surprising agility. With one arm, he hoisted her petite body into the air while her legs continued to churn. Kim beat on his broad shoulders and back with balled fists. It was like marshmallows striking an anvil. She started screaming, commanding the guard to put her down. The man ignored her requests.

With a frown creasing his brow, Paul jogged up to the guard. "Calm down, Nurse Jones," he ordered.

Kim settled only slightly.

"Do you want another injection?"

Slowly, she stopped struggling.

"What's going on here, Doc?" the guard asked.

Paul took a couple of deep breaths. His eyes narrowed at the guard, as if considering whether or not he could confide in the man. "It's somewhat confidential, but . . . I'm sure I can trust you."

The man gave a curt nod.

"We caught this nurse pilfering in the narcotics cabinet—again. She's hooked on amphetamines. That's why she's so hyper. We've had her under observation for some time now and are trying to rehabilitate her on site. It'd be bad press having one of our own people sent to a detox center or the county jail, if you know what I mean."

The guard set Kim on the floor while still maintaining his viselike grip. "That makes sense, Doc. I used to be in the Marines, and we had stuff like that happening all the time. What happens on base stays on base."

"Exactly," Paul said with a knowing grin.

"I'm not addicted to nothing, you big ape," Kim hissed, playing the part.

"You want me to take her back down for ya?" the guard asked.

Paul thought for a moment. "You got any handcuffs or restraints?" he asked the big man.

"You bet, sir," he answered as he reached for a pair of handcuffs kept inside a pouch on his gun belt. He whipped them out and slapped them on Kim's wrists with expert speed and accuracy.

"Ouch, these hurt," Kim whined. Scowling at Paul, she continued, "What's next? Whips and chains? Maybe a red-hot poker? You sick, twisted jerk."

Paul almost smiled. "Now, Nurse Jones. We've already had our talk about manners, haven't we."

"Bite me," she snapped.

Paul rubbed his temples as if quelling a bad headache. Then he said, "Officer Stone, if you'll trust me with the key to those cuffs, I'd like to take this patient—"

"I'm not one of your patients," Kim snapped.

"You are now," Paul said calmly. "We have a second facility down in Marin better suited for this kind of . . . situation."

"You got it, Doc. I've got another pair in the desk anyway," the big man said, happily handing Paul the key.

"Jarhead," Kim hissed at the guard.

"The few, the proud," the soldier affirmed.

"Thanks," Paul said as he led Kim through the glass doors and to his rental car with fake government plates.

After helping Kim into the passenger seat, Paul secured himself behind the steering wheel. "Halfway there," he said softly. "I'm gonna leave those on for a while, okay?"

The young nurse nodded, nervously twisting the handcuffs. She was pale, and her skin gleamed with a fresh film of perspiration.

Driving to the gate, Paul left his brights on to obscure the reading of his fake license plates. He flashed his badge, grumbled something through a partially opened window, and pointed at the security bars. The guard nodded and raised the gate.

At the base of the hill, Paul pulled over and unlocked Kim's handcuffs. The young woman was silent, staring straight ahead as if in a trance. Paul chose not to speak or ask questions. Kim was in shock, obviously fearing for her life, and needed time to acclimate to freedom.

Paul drove speedily to the Hertz car rental in Leggett. Neither of them spoke during the drive; each was lost in a jumble of personal thoughts and worries. Pulling next to his Mustang, Paul put the sedan in park but didn't switch off the engine. The rental lot was dark, the business being closed until morning. Paul turned to face the young nurse. "Kim, I need you to be strong again."

She nodded, quietly wringing her wrists where the cuffs had chafed.

Paul tenderly took her jaw and turned her face toward his. "I mean it, Kim. I need you to be strong. Bria needs you to be strong. This is only the beginning of the battle, remember?"

She nodded again.

"Kim?"

"Yes, I know," she snapped. Then, much softer, "Everything's happened so fast, I'm still in sort of a daze, all right?"

Paul reached over, tenderly squeezed her shoulder, and wiped a lingering tear from her cheek. "I'm sorry. You're doing great. Where'd you learn to act like that?" he asked, referencing their recent escape.

"I was just quoting lines out of my favorite novels."

Paul chortled. "Excellent. Now look, here's what has to happen next. Are you listening?"

"Yes."

Removing the remote from his pocket, Paul said, "If any one of these can trigger anyone's implant—and there's no telling how many transmitters there are—then we'll have to find a way to remove the implant."

Tears again glistened in Kim's red eyes. "That would require major surgery."

Paul thought for a moment. "Can the signal be blocked?"

Kim shrugged.

"Well, let's concentrate on exposing Pathway first. Hopefully, we can get the authorities involved in time."

Kim whimpered plaintively, "In time to stop them from killing me?"

"Honestly, yes. And Bria. But I promise I won't rest until you're both safe, okay?"

Kim suppressed a sob and nodded quickly.

Reaching deeper into his pants pocket, Paul pulled out a small electronic SD chip, about one-half inch square. "Here's the memory chip from my cell phone."

Kim's eyes widened in disbelief. "You're kidding."

"I took it out when I first got on top of the elevator. My stupid phone kept falling out of my pocket, and I didn't want the chip to get damaged." An admiring smile spread across Kim's face. "I want you to take my Mustang and drive to Fort Bragg down the coast on Highway 1. Do you know how to find it?"

"Yes, but why your car?"

"Because they'll be looking for *this* car," he said, indicating the rental. "You're more likely to make it without being stopped if you're driving a car they don't recognize."

Kim nodded but looked frightened again. Paul pressed the SD chip into her palm, then folded her fingers over it and gave her hand a reassuring squeeze.

"Take this chip and give it to the commanding officer, whoever he is. Tell him it's vital information on a cover-up at the Pathway complex. They may not know anything about it, but I'm not sure who else I can trust—including the local police. Besides, the Army might know a bit more about the layout of the complex since Pathway bought it from them."

"You don't think maybe the Army's involved, too?" she asked.

"No, I doubt it. If they were, it'd probably be controlled at the Pentagon level anyway, which would mean we're in over our heads. I prefer to remain more optimistic."

"What if they don't want to get involved?"

"I'm taking a chance on the top dog being a straight arrow enough to at least start an investigation."

"Taking a chance with my life, you mean," she reminded him.

He nodded. "Yes, Kim. But then I took a chance getting you out, and you took a chance helping Bria escape. If our luck holds out, this'll be the last big chance any of us has to take."

Sliding the SD chip into her breast pocket, she asked, "What're you going to do next?"

"They'll be looking for this car. I'm going to try and make it back to Crescent Cove to get Bria before they stop me. From there . . . I really don't know." Removing a card from his wallet, he wrote down several numbers. "Call me when you get there."

Kim started to giggle. It was a refreshing sound.

"What's so funny?" Paul asked.

"You put down your cell number. A lot of good that'll do me."

Paul chuckled too. "Oh yeah. Don't bother calling that one."

Walking Kim to the Mustang, Paul handed her the keys. He then bent quickly and gave her an encouraging kiss on the cheek. "Go get 'em."

With keys in hand, she grabbed Paul's shoulders, tiptoed up, and kissed him lightly on the lips. She sighed openly, wistfully, and said, "Go get Bria."

* * *

The night was deeply still and overcast. Paul switched on the radio. He then switched it off. Listening to the drone of the tires on the wet highway, time lost all bearing as he considered what would follow. The fact that Kim had perhaps the only piece of evidence against Pathway gnawed at him like an ulcer. Well, maybe not the only piece. There was also "Galen's vessel"—whatever Val had meant by that.

Uncertain that he had done the right thing, Paul drove faster toward his little town.

Right or wrong, only time would tell.

CHAPTER FIFTY-TWO

CRESCENT COVE, CALIFORNIA

Ultra-dense fog penetrated Bria's T-shirt and jeans. The cold bit at her with thousands of needle-sharp teeth, causing her to shiver uncontrollably. She knew little about this town, only its name and that it was peopled with some strange characters—none of which she could trust. She had no money, no identification, and the only protective clothing she possessed was back in Paul's Victorian along with a murderous stranger who called himself Surt.

Of course, she only assumed Surt was murderous, but she didn't need more than that assumption to spur her into flight. Paul had given her explicit instructions not to trust anyone, even the police. That made everyone in the small town a potential accomplice to the scientists at Pathway. And yet, she needed help. She needed to find adequate clothing and a place to hide. She needed to find answers and closure. She needed solace, security, belonging. In short, she needed Paul.

Running along fence lines and hedgerows, Bria was totally lost as to orientations of the compass. The fog impeded any celestial clues such as moon and stars, and the street signs gave no indication of north, south, east, or west—they were only obscure Spanish names and the taxonomy of indigenous trees and shrubs.

The occasional barking of a dog kept her moving as much as the cold night mists. Movement kept her warm, if only slightly. She followed one street after another, never sure in which direction she headed, but always staying well away from sidewalks and open spaces.

Within minutes, the deep rumble of a car's engine idling toward her sent her diving into a large lilac bush. Even though the shrub was semi-dormant this time of year, the lingering fragrance of its characteristic purple blossoms teased her sinuses and gave her an unexpected measure of calm. But it was a fleeting calm. The throaty sound of the powerful engine came from a black-and-white patrol car. It was the sheriff. A roof-mounted spotlight searched each side of the street, bringing illumination brighter than daylight to random pockets of shadow. Twice, the intense beam brushed past her, each time causing Bria to draw a reflexive intake of air. She could not see the man inside, but she knew it was Baker. From what Paul had told her, she knew he was not trustworthy.

Struggling to keep motionless, willing the shivering of her hypothermic frame into stillness, she gritted her chattering teeth to the point that her ears rang.

The patrol car cruised slowly by, its powerful spotlight continuing to highlight random sections of the sleeping residential neighborhood. Reaching a corner, the vehicle turned and faded into obscurity.

The cross street bordered a ravine choked with huge eucalyptus trees and Indian laurels. Finding an old hiking trail, Bria skidded down the incline to the base of the ravine and began inching her way amongst the fragrant trees. Her footfalls made little sound on the moistened leaves littering the narrow dirt trail. A few yards down, the street above boasted a sodium-vapor lamp, which cast a ghostly yellow luminescence that barely penetrated the dense fog. As she glanced toward the lamp, a strange shape caught her eye: something on the trunk of an ash tree that seemed unnatural to its form. Drawing closer, she found it was a fourteen-inch section of two-by-four lumber nailed to the trunk. Looking up, she saw several more two-by-fours leading to a dark object nestled in the branches some fifteen feet higher. It was a tree fort—the kind she had read about in childhood adventure novels. Wiping her moist hands on her damp pants to little effect, she began climbing the makeshift ladder, hoping the young architect had made his hidey-hole strong enough for an adult. Reaching the top, she found an unobscured opening in a hodge-podge of faux paneling, two-by-fours, and plywood. But it was reasonably roomy, and it felt sturdy enough to support a whole group of boys.

Bria climbed inside and waited for her eyes to adjust to the increased darkness. When they did, she found the walls papered with personalities from teen and pop-culture magazines: Orlando Bloom, Justin Timberlake, Ashton Kutcher, and other young male celebrities. Bria could not suppress a smile. This was a *girl's* hideout. Evidently, the influence of women's equality was alive and well in Small Town, USA.

With the shifting, cold mists held at bay, and a modicum of security wrought by the small hideout, Bria allowed herself to relax—a little. She was bone-weary and felt the beginnings of a vicious headache building behind her eyes. This awkwardly constructed tree fort was now her sanctuary, her place of refuge and retreat.

As the minutes passed, Bria grew more relaxed. Her frazzled nerves ceased to crawl, her staccato respiration steadied. Yet instead of simply curling up to wait out the night, she found herself on her knees, with her hands clasped tightly in her lap. She heard her voice whispering the words of a desperate prayer. Having never been affiliated with a church, she didn't really know how to pray, yet she was openly communicating with God. Was it something she had learned from her mother? Doubtful. Mrs. Hoffman? Perhaps. In her heart, she knew the answer lay in the stranger who had become an instant friend, confidant, and savior. In a matter of days, Paul Randall had shown her the powerful influence of his religion by doing nothing more than offering his friendship and help.

Rudely, the snapping of a branch yanked her from her reverie. Bria peered over the edge of the tree fort. The giant stood at the base of the huge laurel, smiling up at the makeshift fort. In spite of her fervent prayer, her temporary sanctuary was now a prison—perhaps even a death trap.

"Rapunzel, Rapunzel, let down your hair," the scarred man sneered. The moist ground had made it all too easy for him to follow the woman's footprints to this ravine.

When Bria did not respond, the man began climbing up to the fort. Upon reaching the entrance, he saw Bria cowering in a corner. Once again, the gods were with him.

As Surt made the awkward climb over the edge, Bria suddenly lunged from the corner and shoved his shoulders back. The giant struggled for balance. Bria swung her leg around and kicked him in the chest. He grunted and fell from the tree fort, landing hard on his back. A painful explosion of air burst from his lungs, followed by a string of expletives.

Before Bria could begin to climb down, Surt was on his way back up. This time, her attack was blocked with a powerful arm. She scrambled backward. The huge man gripped her ankle and yanked her out of the fort, letting her fall helplessly to the ground. She landed face first, knocking the breath from her lungs. She rolled over and tried to sit up. Her vision swam as the man leapt from the two-by-four ladder and landed, straddling her. With one hand he picked her up by the throat and lifted her off the ground. Bria struck, flailed, and struggled to regain her breath. It wouldn't come. Her mind quickly faded to blackness.

CHAPTER FIFTY-THREE

CRESCENT COVE, CALIFORNIA

Paul drove into Crescent Cove around 3:30 AM. Thick fog moved along the streets like a churning mass of alien life. Few business lights penetrated the gloom. Heading into the residential section, he drove slowly, warily looking for anything out of the norm. Although near exhaustion, his nerves were on edge, making every movement, every shadow, something to vie for his attention. Turning up Pierpont Street, he passed a parked vehicle he could not recall ever seeing on his street before, let alone in his neighborhood. It was a huge, black Dodge Mega Cab, with a windowless shell on the back. Pulling into his driveway, he immediately noticed the front door to his house standing open.

Panic seized his heart. Bria would not be so careless. Something was wrong.

Leaving the rental car idling, Paul ran into the house and called Bria's name. The house remained silent. He ran upstairs and found a mess of shattered lath and plaster in the guestroom closet. The footprints of a large man marred the plaster dust. Bria's footprints were not among the debris. Creating a mental scenario was easy, but it was not a pleasant picture. Going down the stairs two at a time, he flew through the open front door to his rental car.

With both the driver's and passenger's windows rolled down, Paul drove faster than was safe through the milky-hued streets. The humid cold pelted his face and kept him alert. He squealed tires around every corner. His eyes searched intently for any sign of movement, anything that did not look right. The town lay dormant, as if held in catatonic hibernation.

Stupid! How could he be so stupid as to leave Bria alone while he went off to play hero? If anything happened to her, he'd never forgive himself.

An inner prompting compelled him to head back home. He drove like a madman, taking risks in the dense fog he wouldn't normally dream of taking, relying on his memory of streets, corners, and obstacles to guide him in the cloaking mists. *Slow down,* an inner voice told him. Paul had learned long ago to trust his feelings, to listen the promptings of the still, small voice in his heart. That same voice had led him to the Church, to Crescent Cove, and possibly even to Bria. He knew he should follow its promptings now.

Just before turning onto his street, Paul turned off his headlights and coasted to a stop. The sounds of a strained voice filtered through the suspended, watery veil. It was Bria's voice, struggling, fighting, desperate.

Leaving his car, Paul jogged quietly toward his house. A movement ebbed its way through a thinning in the fog, then disappeared. He ran toward it. A large man—a giant of a man—was struggling with a smaller person. *Bria.* Her strained gasps and grunts proved that fight was still in her, but she was no match for the behemoth who held her captive. She screamed, or tried to—the fatigue clear in her strained, weak voice. The man growled in reply. An interior light came on as the man raised the rear panel of the Ram's shell and lowered the tailgate, illuminating the scene with eerie refractions of light. But it was enough light for Paul to see everything. The giant tossed Bria into the back, an area that appeared to be adapted as a cage of sorts. She landed with a sickening thud. Paul continued to move toward the confrontation. The dense, swirling fog helped to mask his footfalls and movement.

"If you continue to scream, I'll gladly break your jaw," the man growled, his voice as coarse as sandpaper.

Bria threw back some obscenity that was lost in the fog. She was still fighting.

As the giant angrily closed the panels, Paul flew shoulder-first into the small of his back, nailing him in the kidneys. It was a hit worthy of any NFL tackle. The big man grunted sharply as he slammed into the truck. Finding himself at the man's feet, Paul grabbed his ankles and heaved backward as he stood. The giant dropped quickly, smacking his chin on the bumper with a nauseating *crack*. Paul stood for a moment with legs spread and arms cocked. But the big man lay motionless on the ground. Not waiting for further confirmation of his brief victory, Paul opened the rear panels—and barely missed being clocked by Bria's snapping foot.

"Bria, it's me," he cried.

A gasp of air sounded from the enclosure.

"Hurry out, before he wakes up," he urged, offering his hand to help her.

Bria fairly leapt from the pickup bed into Paul's arms. The two staggered back, almost losing their footing. She clung to him as if her life depended on it. Paul wrapped his arms around her and held her tight. She was crying. He tenderly consoled her. She shivered from fear and elation, breathlessly repeating his name again and again. He stroked her damp hair and kissed the top of her head.

"Don't ever leave me again," she whispered urgently.

"I won't. Ever," he promised.

Her pleas turned whispery, tremulous. Paul gently shushed her, stroking her hair.

At their feet, the giant groaned, waking.

CHAPTER FIFTY-FOUR

CRESCENT COVE, CALIFORNIA

With an arm around her waist, Paul helped Bria to his rental car. She was very weak and stumbled frequently. Glancing back, Paul saw the giant struggle to his feet and rub his swollen jaw. The glow of a nearby streetlamp allowed Paul to glimpse the hideousness of the man's scarred face.

Being far enough away not to give chase on foot, and appearing quite groggy, the large man wobbled toward the driver's door of his Dodge Ram. He wiped the blood from his lacerated chin, climbed in, and started the powerful engine.

Paul quickly helped Bria into the Ford sedan. Jumping behind the steering wheel, he struggled to slide the key into the ignition. His hands would not stop trembling. Stomping the accelerator to the floor, he turned the key. The small engine sputtered and whined but wouldn't turn over. A squealing of tires sounded behind them as Surt whipped his large truck around in a tight circle.

"You're flooding it," Bria said desperately.

Paul removed his foot from the pedal and paused. The Ram's engine roared behind them. Paul tried the ignition again. Wide-eyed, Bria sat with her knees drawn to her chest, her breathing suddenly shallow and dry. The sedan's engine turned a few times, then caught. Roaring like a T-Rex, the Ram leapt over a curb, blasted through a small picket fence, through a triangle of flowerbed, and slammed into the rear corner of the Ford. Bria let out a harsh chirp as the sedan spun around 180 degrees. Paul floored the accelerator, and the rental car screeched away from the curb, dragging its dislodged bumper behind it.

Paul had no idea which direction to go—other than away from the large pickup truck. But the four-cylinder Ford was no match for the powerful truck. Paul's only tactic was to keep turning sharp corners and angling through narrow alleys. In such a small town, however, his options proved minimal. Further hindered by the clotting fog, Paul was forced to blindly guess his way through the streets. Along several lengthy straightaways, Surt overtook the sedan and rammed the back of it with bone-jarring force.

"I can't outrun this guy," Paul growled in frustration.

"Look out!" Bria yelled just before the Ram's bumper again wrinkled the trunk of the Ford, this time with a full-on collision.

The small car lurched forward, the tail end skipped out of control, and the car shot over a curb and into the city's town square. The Ford's rear bumper flew off to one side, taking out a park bench along the way. Paul managed to get the car under control and headed across the baseball diamond as the Ram overshot them and screeched to a halt.

Making a U-turn in the street and gunning the truck to full speed, Surt hopped the curb and drove into the park. Huge clods of turf sprayed into the air as his knobby tires struggled to gain purchase. Being nearer the coast, the disorienting fog thickened considerably, reducing visibility to a few feet. Quickly gaining momentum, Surt yanked the steering wheel to one side to avoid a cement light post— and barreled right through the park's white gazebo, sending shards of wood through the air as if a bomb had detonated inside the structure.

Some distance ahead, Paul glanced at his instrument panel. The gas gauge read one-third full, and was dropping quickly. A moment later it read one-quarter tank. "Oh great," Paul grumbled. "The gas tank must have ruptured when he rammed us."

Cursing silently, Paul drove at a slower pace, peering into the fog with hopeless intensity. The sedan began to cough and sputter. Deciding to get off the road and hide, he turned the rental car into the Crescent Park parking lot, near the point of the cove. Just then, the sedan's engine died, and Paul coasted the vehicle to the far side of the restroom bungalow. Leaving the sedan, Paul took Bria's hand, and together they ran along the path into the security of the ultra-dense fog.

The rumbling of the surf rising from the crescent did little to mask the roar of the Dodge Ram as it peeled into the parking lot and screeched to a stop beside the Ford. The blinding glare of the headlights penetrated the fog, looking like two malevolent eyes peering from the depths of hell. Paul and Bria cast a furtive glance at the orbs. Cold fog bit at Bria's exposed arms and through her thin clothing. Flecks of salt spray landed on her face and hands, causing her to wince. Then a large figure stepped between the disembodied headlights. The huge man looked even bigger in the fog-distorted backlighting.

"Let's go," Paul said quietly, encouraging Bria forward.

"Where to?" she asked.

Looking around, he whispered, "I wish I knew."

* * *

Surt followed the faint footprints left on the moist blacktop. Two sets. He was angry, more at himself than at those he pursued. He had allowed a lesser man to get the best of him. He was a near god. This other man was nothing.

As he made his way forward, a figure slowly emerged from the shifting fog. It was the man, standing with his legs slightly spread, his arms locked straight forward at shoulder level, his head tilted slightly to one side looking down the length of his arm. A shooter's stance.

"Stop where you are or I'll blow your head off," the man said evenly.

Surt slowed but didn't stop. He could not see a gun in the man's hand, but there was something there, roughly the right size and shape.

"Who are you?" the man asked.

Surt did not answer. He took a few more slowing steps and stopped twenty feet from the stranger. Both men were in silhouette. Surt felt for his gun, then realized it was back in his truck, as was the spray can of nerve agent he used on his "collections." No matter.

A few walkway lights gave enough illumination for Surt to see the man was in good physical shape, about 30-something, and that he looked scared. But then, everyone was afraid of him.

"I asked who you are," the man repeated.

Smiling crookedly, the giant replied, "I'm your worst nightmare."

"Oh, please," the man said, somewhere between a scoff and a chuckle. "Can't you come up with anything better than that?"

Surt took two more steps forward. The man repositioned his gun, firming his stance. "That's close enough." And it was.

The glow cast from a lamppost showed Surt's horribly scarred face and long blond hair, but his eyes remained hidden in shadowy sockets.

In a low voice, the man asked, "Who are you?"

The giant smiled. "I am Surt."

"Surt? What kind of a stupid name is that?"

The smile vanished. "You'll say my name with more respect when we're through," the giant said. "If you're able to speak," he added malevolently. He then took another step.

"I'm not kidding," the man warned.

Another step.

"Stop right there."

Surt squinted into the thinning fog. There was no glint reflecting off the steel of the gun. No indication that the man held a weapon at all. He took another step.

Suddenly, the man threw his weapon at Surt. The giant's reflexes were amazingly fast. He caught the object, held it to his face, and cursed. It was simply a small stick. With a growl that matched the rumbling crescent to his left, he threw the stick toward the abyss and watched it quickly dissolve into the fog.

Looking up, Surt cursed again. The man had vanished, using the fog as a cloak. But if the mortal could use it to his advantage, so could a near god. Surt leapt into the darkness along the side of the asphalt trail and crept quickly toward the man's last location. Moving like the fog itself, he made a narrow arc, always keeping his eyes open for any unusual movement. He crouched low, knowing the insignificant man would be looking for a giant.

A dark object materialized as he neared it. A shrub, probably a Manzanita, about five feet high, with the same diameter. Too thin and branchy for good cover. Another shape stood closer to the path, nearer the rim of the cliff. Surt crouched lower and edged toward it. It was a drinking fountain set in a four-foot stone obelisk. The walkway lights behind the fountain cast a dim shadow toward him. But something wasn't right. The shadow wasn't uniform; it didn't match the contours of the obelisk. A dark lump protruded on the far side. Someone crouched on the other side, using the stone bubbler as a hiding place. The man? Or perhaps the woman? He did not know where she had vanished to during this brief bit of fun.

Surt rose, took three lengthy strides, and reached over the edge of the fountain. His hands latched onto a crop of hair. A scream sounded as he yanked upward. The gods were still with him, smiling on him as usual, welcoming him as one of their own.

It was the woman.

CHAPTER FIFTY-FIVE

CRESCENT COVE, CALIFORNIA

Bria screamed and lashed out. It did no good. Again with one hand, Surt clamped her throat like a vise, lifted her off the ground, and silenced her cries. Within minutes, the lack of oxygen caused her struggles to cease. She blacked out.

Tossing her over his shoulder, Surt headed toward his truck. He made it about twenty feet when a movement to his left caused him to pause. The fog ebbed and swirled, white on white, giving the illusion of ocean currents in midair. The sconces along the path set the ethereal substance aglow, adding shadow and depth to its motion. Perhaps that was what he saw. He knew the man was close, but he couldn't see or hear him. As Surt didn't fear anyone, a cocky smile played at the corners of his twisted mouth.

Surt continued on, keeping an eye toward the park on his left. The man was out there, somewhere. And he was unarmed. He was no match for a Norse god.

* * *

As the giant moved closer, Paul held a stout stick firmly cocked like a baseball player at bat. The piece of wood he had found was about the same size as a Louisville Slugger. A six-foot-high historical marker, made of local stone mortised with cement, provided Paul's hiding place. It stood halfway along the path, just to the right, overlooking the crescent. Fortunately, it was wide enough to conceal his body; unfortunately, it stood directly below a lamppost. He would have preferred to strike in the dark.

Driven by a desire to remain focused, Paul fought to control his trembling. The ocean roared below. Every two or three minutes an exceptionally large breaker would race up the cove, sounding like a runaway freight train and shaking the ground above like a small earthquake.

Surt slowly materialized in the churning haze. He had Bria slumped over one shoulder. Paul had to make his strike precise. He guessed he'd have only one chance. Crouching in as much shadow as he could find, Paul's body tensed like a tightly wound spring. His knuckles blanched white. He said a quick, silent prayer.

As the giant walked by slowly, Bria's body obscured the man's vision, temporarily concealing Paul and his weapon. Instantly, Paul leapt from behind the monument, took a step to better position himself, and swung with all his might. The bat narrowly missed Bria's dangling hand and struck Surt in the small of the back. The big man let out a surprised grunt as his knees wobbled. But he didn't go down. Paul wound up and hit him again in the same place. Surt staggered but held on. A chilling cry issued from deep in the giant's throat as he turned around. Paul wound up a third time and brought the stick down on the great man's head. The perfectly aimed hit cracked with a sickening wetness. The thick piece of wood snapped in two. Pain, mixed with confusion and anger, distorted Surt's already disfigured face.

His legs weakened, and he stumbled into the guardrail. As his eyes rolled back, his grip loosened and his knees buckled. Collapsing sideways, he dropped Bria over the safety rail.

Paul had seen the man's knees quiver. Anticipating the direction of Surt's fall, he leapt toward the guardrail. Diving headfirst underneath, he caught Bria's hand in both of his as she disappeared over the rim. Locking his feet around a support pole, Paul's stomach scraped harshly against the coarse volcanic rock forming the lip of the precipice. The weight of Bria hanging over the edge added pressure to his belly, causing the stone to cut deeply into Paul's flesh. Years of salt-spray buildup stung the wound like a thousand hornets. Paul cried out in pain and frustration. The wet fog and wisps of spray coated Bria's wrist with a slick layer of moisture. Paul felt his grip slipping.

Bria, who was still unconscious, hung limply from Paul's hands, her body scraping against the sharp rocks of the cliff. Below her, the black void released spectral vapors of spray into the mute light, accompanied by the guttural roar of the surf.

Paul could not see the bottom, but it loomed beneath them like the hungry jaws of death. He tried to pull Bria higher, but he didn't have the strength to overcome the awkward angle. He yelled at Bria to wake up. He couldn't save her by himself. She needed to reach up and grab hold. He called out again, screaming above the tumult of the raging surf. Paul felt her wrist slip another half inch from his grasp.

Slowly, Bria shook her head and opened her eyes. In a panic, she screamed, seeing nothing below her but a terrible emptiness. Paul then saw her look up, absolutely terrified. She reached up to grab Paul's wrist, then struggled to get a foothold on the irregular surface of the cliff. After a few vain attempts, her toes found a grip on the coarse stone, and with her free hand she latched onto a pocket of rock.

"You got it?" Paul yelled.

"Yes!" she hollered back.

"You sure?"

"Just let go and find something to lower down!"

Reluctantly, Paul released his grip on her bruised wrist. She grabbed onto another pocket and pressed her body to the volcanic stone face as if she were a part of it. Paul had started to use his hands to crab-walk back onto the ledge, when he felt his feet yanked from the support rail. Suddenly, he was dangling in midair over the vacuous chasm.

Surt held Paul firmly by his ankles, but his immense strength was rapidly taxed by the smaller man's weight. It did not matter. He didn't plan on holding him long. He then heard someone calling out for him to stop. A useless plea—his mind was made up. Besides, he wanted the girl. This man was inconsequential.

Bria screamed and held a hand out to Paul. She could hear the giant laughing deeply, brutally. Paul whipped around, trying to reach her outstretched hand. Their fingers brushed each other's. Surt yelled something, his voice as resonant as the deep rumbling from the cove.

Blood coursed down his scarred face. His eyes glowed like a jungle cat's, eerily reflecting the lamppost's muted yellow light.

Panic-born fear glazed Bria's eyes. She repositioned her grip on the face of the rock and reached out further to Paul. He twisted again, reached. Their fingertips locked. Surt cried out a second time—something about deity.

A sharp report fractured the murky night—Bria thought it was a large wave buffeting the rocks below. The giant's voice caught sharply in mid-cry. His grip faltered. Bria glanced up at the blood-soaked face. Surt's expression registered shock, disbelief. Another report rang out. Both Paul and Bria recognized the sound. It was a gunshot! Surt winced in pain. A third shot shattered the thick atmosphere. The giant let go and slumped over the railing. Paul plummeted toward Bria. They grasped hands. Bria's arm acted like a lever, and Paul swung into the jagged cliff, slamming against it with brutal force. It knocked some of the wind from him, yet he was able to grab onto enough of the rough surface to keep from falling into the chasm.

As Surt flipped loosely over the railing, he cried out. It sounded like a mournful, questioning plea rather than a cry of panic, surprise, or pain. He clawed pitifully at the stony surface as he slid hopelessly past Bria. Then, one of his lacerated hands latched onto a sharp jut directly adjacent to Paul's right foot. He looked up and met Paul's hard stare. The giant hissed at the meddling mortal, but Paul looked as if he didn't care. Roaring with hatred, Surt swung his free hand up, trying to grab ahold of Paul's ankle. The pain in his back was intense, but he tried to ignore it. With any luck, the gods would still be with him.

This time they weren't.

Without pausing, Paul placed his shoe atop Surt's fingers and pressed down hard. The porous, volcanic jut snapped cleanly from the face of the cliff. The scarred giant tumbled into the churning blackness.

As Paul and Bria turned from the abyss toward the rim, a face peered over the edge of the railing, searching. The person wore an octagonal hat. He clicked on a powerful flashlight and located Bria, with Paul just below her.

"Hold on, you two," the sheriff called out. "Help is on the way."

The fog thickened, Paul could barely see the glow from the lamppost above. He clung tenaciously to the volcanic stone, praying Bria also had a firm hold on the cliff. He closed his eyes and tried to think of pleasant things, taking his mind off the fact that he was likely seconds from death. He could almost hear Bria calling out to him. Assurances filled her desperate voice, but he could not understand a single word. The ocean rumbled below them like an angry beast. It had fed on one soul, but it wanted more.

Paul's fingers ached and his legs quivered. He didn't know how much longer he could hold on. The passage of time blurred before a nylon rope dangled past him. Looking up, he saw a man rappelling toward Bria. The rescuer wrapped a bolo around her, which hoisted her to the rim. The man then lowered himself farther, stopping beside Paul. He fed another rope under Paul's shoulders and across his chest, secured it, and then yelled for him to let go of the cliff.

Paul took a deep breath and obeyed. He dropped a few inches before the rope cinched his armpits, then he felt himself slowly hauled to the rim of the crescent.

CHAPTER FIFTY-SIX

CRESCENT COVE, CALIFORNIA

In his office, Sheriff Baker offered Bria and Paul cups of steaming coffee.

"Thanks, Sheriff," Paul said, "but I don't drink coffee."

"I think I'll pass, too," added Bria.

The sheriff regarded the two bedraggled people with a curious stare. "It'll help warm you up."

"Thanks anyway," they said simultaneously.

The sheriff raised a questioning eyebrow at the two survivors. They sat close together, nestled under a large blanket. Two deputies stood off to one side, quietly winding up repelling gear and rope.

"How about some hot chocolate?" Paul asked, shivering deeper into the blanket.

"You may want to send someone over to the Stevensons' place, Sheriff," Bria said though chattering teeth. "I think they might be in trouble. Surt called me from their house."

"I already have," Baker assured them. "They were strapped to chairs with duct tape. Mr. Stevenson is in really bad shape. He may not make it. Mrs. Stevenson is in shock. She was beaten up a bit, but she'll survive. You care to revise your story about this evening, Mr. Randall?"

Paul stared blankly at Baker. Then said, "You care to back off a little bit? Bria and I were almost killed an hour ago—obviously by the same guy who assaulted the Stevensons."

The sheriff didn't flinch. "Just doing my job, son."

"Look, tell the hospital to check Cliff's left carotid artery. There's a small device in there. I don't know if it was triggered, but it shows what Pathway did to its people."

"And just how the Sam Hill would you know that, Mr. Randall?"

Paul hesitated. He knew this information might push Bria over the edge. She knew she also carried an implant. Undoubtedly, she would deduce hers was identical to Cliff's. "I'd like to call a lawyer before I say any more," Paul said—for multiple reasons.

The sheriff harrumphed and chewed on his lower lip while he continued to stare at his charges. A deputy brought two cups of hot chocolate to Bria and Paul. They cradled the Styrofoam cups as if they were sacred goblets. Sipping, they felt the hot liquid trickle down their throats and settle into empty stomachs. It was ambrosia.

"Did your men find Surt yet?" Paul asked after a few moments of silence, hoping to change the focus from himself.

"No. It's too dark and foggy," said Baker. "We'll call in the Coast Guard tomorrow after the fog clears. I doubt it'll do any good. The current down there is rough and unpredictable. With luck, we'll find a body, but I wouldn't count on it. He took three of my slugs in the back. I'm sure that guy's fish bait by now."

"How did you know where to find us?" Bria asked.

"My deputy notified me of several calls complaining about reckless kids cruising the streets in the middle of the night. I went to investigate and found that Dodge Ram parked next to your house," he said to Paul. His eyes softened somewhat and behind them was a glimmer of friendliness. "I called in the plates and found it was registered to the Pathway complex. I knew that wasn't good, so I began patrolling the area. Not much later, I saw the same truck chasing a small white sedan—yours, I presume—and tried to head him off. I finally found the two vehicles at the crescent. As soon as I got out, I heard some screaming. I called in backup, then went looking." He frowned. "I recognized Surt immediately. I ordered him to put his hands up, but he was intent on holding something over the edge of the crescent." The lawman fidgeted briefly, averting his eyes. "If I had known that something was you, Mr. Randall, I wouldn't have shot him. The darkness and fog obscured everything. Sorry."

"If you hadn't shot him, I would be at the bottom of the cliff instead of here," Paul said in acceptance.

"Yeah. Anyway, like I said, I put three slugs in him before he went down—no pun intended. I didn't know you were down there either, Miss Georgopolis," he said to Bria.

"You couldn't have," she replied, also in acceptance. "You don't even know who I am."

"I know who you *were*," he stated, the reptilian aura resurfacing. "I ran your name through Interpol. You're supposed to be dead."

"Surprise," Bria responded without humor.

The sheriff folded his arms and regarded the two with an equal amount of skepticism and concern. "You care to go over that story with me once again, and this time, include what you know about the Stevensons?"

"Not really," Paul said, clearly annoyed with the sheriff's persistence. They had already explained everything on the way back from Crescent Park. "Not right now, anyway. First, we need to contact Fort Bragg to see if Kim made it, then go back to the Pathway complex. I guarantee if we don't get to there right away, they won't be around in the morning."

"I already got CHPs heading up there right now. No one will leave without us knowing it."

"They have a helicopter," Bria warned.

Sheriff Baker turned to a deputy. "Pass that on to Bragg immediately. See if they can send an Apache or some other combat copter up there. STAT."

The deputy nodded and picked up a desk phone. Baker then said to Paul, "You up for taking a ride?"

"Sure," he replied in a weary but committed tone.

"Me too," Bria added.

Paul immediately shook his head and took her hands in his. "No, Bria, it's too dangerous. Until that implant is removed, I don't want you near that place."

"But I can identify those—"

"That doesn't matter," he interrupted. "Once we get in there, I have a feeling we'll uncover more than enough incriminating evidence to shut that place down."

A deputy stepped forward. "The Army's on its way. ETA about two hours, they said."

The disappointment on Bria's face tore at Paul's heart. But there was a trace of anger and betrayal too. "I'm going, Paul. We'll just have to figure some way to make me blend in so they won't trigger the implant," Bria said defiantly. "I *have* to go back there. Don't you see?"

"Bria. It could kill you," Paul stated desperately.

"This is my decision, Paul. I know it's foolish, but if I don't personally see that place shut down, it'll haunt me the rest of my life. I've got to end this."

Paul turned to the sheriff with a questioning look. Baker stared at Bria a moment before answering. "Fine by me. An on-site ID is always helpful. Besides, I like a gal who's not afraid to get back on the horse."

"But your implant?" Paul persisted.

"It'll be worth the risk. Please, Paul."

After a moment's reflection Paul asked, "You're sure? Because I sure don't like it."

"Positive. Now let's stop wasting time and get up there."

Paul could tell that Bria was deeply terrified, but that she was dead set in her resolve. He stood and kissed her forehead. Then, jerking his head toward the door, he said to Baker, "Let's ride."

CHAPTER FIFTY-SEVEN

PATHWAY COMPLEX

The guard at the gate blanched when he saw the convoy of military trucks converging on the Pathway Research Complex. Insignias, warrants, and rifles were presented, and access was immediately granted. Within minutes, the research center was swarming with military personnel. The Dauphin helicopter was secured, as were the other guards and vehicles in the garage.

After hearing Bria's story and seeing the proof on Paul's phone chip, Major J. D. Dickson, the commanding officer, had decided to treat the event as a hostage situation. As with other potentially volatile circumstances, the plan was to attack quickly and neutralize any attempt of the Pathway staff to eliminate evidence, including the hostage-patients. In addition to giving a detailed diagram of the complex, Kim had described exactly what the implant transmitters looked like, and each soldier was ordered to confiscate all transmitters as a first priority. If anyone was seen trying to activate one, they were to be shot.

Standing behind a phalanx of fifty assault personnel, Bria felt her stomach churn with trepidation. She still wore sweats and a T-shirt, but the Army had provided a thick jacket to keep her warm. Regardless of that, her knees trembled as if she were freezing to death. The thought of her implant being triggered was foremost in her mind. The Army had agreed to let her accompany them to help identify those in charge, but that allowance stopped at ground level. They adamantly refused to let her go below into the "combat zone." At first Bria was angry as well as scared, but Paul finally convinced her of the logic behind the decision. She could point out individuals as they passed by in handcuffs.

Paul used Kingsford's passkey to call the elevator. Major Dickson suggested a few men ride the elevator to sublevel one, then return up the stairs to let the others in. Only hand signals were to be used. No talking. No noise. The group was to reassemble on the floor just above the mechanical room, then, using Kim's diagram, infiltrate the complex in a uniform, single sweep.

Watching the soldiers file stealthily into the bowels of the complex, Bria felt a cold line of nervous perspiration trickle down her spine. She paced about the entry foyer, willing herself to remain calm. Paul stood with an ear to the elevator doors, listening for sounds of the Army's return. As Bria wandered down an adjacent hall, she saw a door marked FIRST AID. Entering, she rummaged through the cabinets and drawers looking for additional evidence with which to convict Pathway.

* * *

Betty Mumford was gathering up her personal files and cramming them into a large box. One of the many doctors Smith stood in her doorway with a remorseful, lost look haunting his eyes. "You think that'll do any good?"

"I don't know, Richard, but I'm not taking any chances. We got a few people out looking for Bria and Kim right now. They might catch them, they might not. But if either of them took any evidence with them, we're all sunk. I, for one, am getting out of here until this all blows over. Call it a spontaneous vacation."

The doctor shrugged. "What about the patients?"

She stopped and wiped her glistening brow. "Do you think I care? I'm here as an administrative nurse, not one of Harold's researchers. You all are the doctors—you take care of them. I couldn't tell you the first thing about what you're shooting into them, and I don't want to know. Everyone knows I don't carry an implant, so I could care less if this place blows wide open. In twenty minutes, I'm going to be headed for the Bahamas."

The doctor shrugged again and turned to leave. He paused, then turned again to face the plump nurse. "Oh Betty," he sang. "It looks like there's someone here to see you off."

Betty Mumford slammed a stack of papers into her box and rounded her desk. Nearing the door, she spat, "What is it this time—" Her words cut short as she looked past the doctor and into the barrel of an army assault rifle.

"Lie down face-first on the floor, ma'am, arms out to your sides. You too, Doc," the soldier stated evenly. "Move slowly, please. I have authorization to shoot you if necessary, and I'm guessing you don't want to be shot."

The doctor lowered himself to the floor. Mumford crumpled. Once she was down beside him, the doctor whispered, "Have a nice vacation."

* * *

Thanks to Kim's thorough information, every section of the underground research lab was uniformly infiltrated and secured. The Army found nineteen other patients in private rooms or isolation chambers, all in various states of health, and six bodies in the morgue. All Pathway personnel were rounded up and handcuffed.

In less than an hour, the prisoners began filing one at a time through the complex's main entrance past Paul and Bria. Very few of the staff looked them in the eyes. Bria would occasionally point to someone and nod. That individual would then be marked with an X on the shoulder with a black permanent marker.

When Betty Mumford appeared, Bria began trembling with anger. "Stop right there," she said through clenched teeth. Taking a moment to compose herself, she continued, "This one's especially guilty."

As a young soldier was about to mark Betty's arm, Bria said, "Please, let me do that."

The soldier escorting Mumford glanced at Major Dickson, who nodded in return. Bria walked briskly up to the large woman and, without hesitation, removed a hypodermic syringe from her pocket and rammed it into Betty's shoulder. Betty screeched in shock and pain as Bria began depressing the plunger. Immediately, two soldiers leapt forward, yanked Bria away, and pinned her arms to her sides. The half-empty hypodermic clattered to the floor. Bria didn't fight back, but her scowl remained fixed on the shackled nurse. Betty's eyes bulged in sheer terror as a clear liquid slowly dripped from the syringe at her feet.

"What did you inject in me?" Betty demanded.

Bria just smiled maliciously.

"Tell me this instant, you little tramp!" the large nurse screamed, flicking drops of spittle from her lips.

"It's a special vaccine I call 'payback,'" Bria said with a crooked smile.

"Take her away," Major Dickson ordered the soldier escorting Mumford.

"Yes sir." The man immediately complied.

On the way out, Betty continued to shriek, demanding to know what she had been injected with. Her voice turned shrill and panicked as she disappeared into the darkness of the night.

Major Dickson walked up to within inches of Bria and looked at her sternly. "That was a very foolish thing to do, Miss Georgopolis. I'm afraid this could fall under 'inhumane treatment of a prisoner.'"

Bria scoffed. "After seeing what they were doing to people down there, you call *me* inhumane?"

"It's simply the way things are done. I don't like it any more than you do, ma'am." He waved away the two soldiers who were holding Bria. "Now, I really need to know what was in that syringe."

Bria pulled a vial from her pocket and handed it to the major. "It's just normal saline. It won't do anything except worry her to death—even though she deserves much worse."

Major Dickson's stern look didn't waver. "Where did you get it?" he demanded.

Bria pointed down the hall to the first aid station.

Major Dickson sighed. "We will, of course, have to test the remaining solution to verify that it is only saline. And I suggest you look into getting a lawyer, just in case."

Bria nodded, yet her expression was anything but contrite. Whatever the outcome, she felt amazingly vindicated.

The major then turned to Paul. "Dr. Randall, I am giving you a civilian order to take this young lady to a hospital and get her and yourself taken care of. We'll have the police give you an escort, but

Bria is not to leave your sight under any circumstances. When we need you, we'll be in touch. Is that clear?"

"Yes, sir," Paul said through a wide smile.

CHAPTER FIFTY-EIGHT

EUREKA, CALIFORNIA

Redwoods State Hospital was a small but modern medical arts facility seated on the bay-view foothills of midtown Eureka. The staff was well trained and friendly. As per request, the hospital allowed Bria and Paul to share a room. The county sheriff's office had a deputy stay outside the room in addition to one from Crescent Cove. Because of the potential ramifications of their story, it was a justifiable precaution.

* * *

When Paul awoke the following morning, he expected to see a haggard, weary, near-death-experience survivor. Instead, Bria looked quite beautiful—even with morning-hair, a severely bruised neck, and sleep-puffed eyes. "Morning," he whispered, as he sat on the edge of her bed.

"Morning," she answered with a happy grimace.

"You okay?"

"Never better. Any word on Pathway?" she asked.

"Yeah. Sheriff Baker came by later last night after you were asleep. He said that thanks to you, they really cleaned up."

"Thanks to *us*."

Paul shrugged.

"Were there many other patients?"

"Not many."

"Any kids?" she asked with a suddenly dry throat.

"No, thank heavens." He smiled.

Bria closed her eyes and sighed gratefully. "Good."

A respectful knock sounded at the door.

"Come in," Bria and Paul said together.

Sheriff Baker entered with a smirk playing at the corners of his mouth. "I have a guest with me," he said.

Bria sat up and fussed with her hair a bit. A trim Army lieutenant, dressed in full uniform, entered the room. He was in his late twenties, tall, and pleasantly handsome. He removed his hat and gave Bria a sharp, courteous half-bow, then went to Paul and shook his hand.

"I'm Lieutenant Prescott," the man said with a smile. "I saw you yesterday at the complex, but I don't think we actually met."

"Things were happening pretty fast."

"Yes sir, they were. I can't thank you enough, sir, for sending your messenger when you did."

At first, Paul was confused. Sleep still fogged his brain. Then Kim walked in the room and stood suspiciously close to Lieutenant Prescott. The young officer did not try to move away, though he did look somewhat embarrassed by the informality. They clearly liked each other's company. "Hi, Paul. Good to see you again, Bria." Kim grinned.

Bria gasped as she recognized Young Nurse Jones. "Nurse Jones? What are you doing here?"

"I came to see you and Paul. He's a great guy, Bria. You're very lucky." Bria blushed at the inference but didn't try to hide it. "Oh, and my name is Kim." Then, to Paul, "I went straight to Fort Bragg like you said. I didn't know anyone, but when I got to the front gate, Lieutenant Prescott was standing right there, checking on the guards. I told him everything and handed him the memory chip, and he just took it from there. Isn't he amazing?"

"The best of the best, I'm sure," Paul said. "Are they going to hold you responsible, too?"

"I don't know. I have to go back to Fort Bragg for several more interviews. Honestly, that scares me to death, but this terrific officer assures me it'll all turn out fine. He's been so wonderfully helpful," she said, gently touching the lieutenant's arm. The dreamy look in her eyes was almost comical, but Paul was more than happy for her.

Paul rubbed his temples. "I'm glad it worked out. We weren't so sure the government wasn't involved as well," he said tentatively.

"Not a chance, sir," Lieutenant Prescott shot back. "An investment group purchased the property from the government back in the early '70s. Once they had ownership, we could no longer get in without a ton of legal hoop-jumping. Besides, there really was no need to. But the press will have a field day just knowing it *used* to be a government operation, so we are more than willing to help shut them down. With any luck, we can do it without any fanfare. And with Kim's affidavit, and yours, Miss Georgopolis, we shouldn't have any trouble exposing everything."

"What about those affiliated with Pathway outside of the complex?" Paul asked.

The officer's confidence fell slightly. "We're hoping to find that information once we hack their computer files. The ones we've opened thus far are pretty complex: encrypted, white-washed, trap-doors and such."

"So there's no way to know who's secretly involved," Bria said.

"We won't know for a while. There may be several others, there may be just one. You know, the silent partner type—someone who could benefit financially from such an operation but wishes to remain anonymous in case something goes wrong."

"Financially, how?" Bria asked.

"Despite laws prohibiting it, black-market biological and chemical agents are constantly popping up worldwide. It's a billion-dollar business."

"And if we don't find who's behind all this, they will get away scot-free," the sheriff hissed.

Bria sat up straighter. "What about the citizens of Crescent Cove still involved with Pathway? Do we have any idea who they are?"

"I might," Paul said.

The sheriff stepped forward. "Say again?"

"I may have all the information you're looking for."

"And how's that?"

"It's in Galen's vessel," Paul answered.

"Who?"

"Galen's vessel. Val Mince left me a note we just found a couple days ago. In it he said to look in Galen's vessel if I ever felt like my life was in jeopardy. I'm still not sure what that means, but it may have the answers you're looking for."

CHAPTER FIFTY-NINE

CRESCENT COVE, CALIFORNIA

The following day, the hospital released Paul and Bria. Their cuts and bruises were non-threatening and would heal quickly. Bria still felt weak, and though she fought the idea, Paul insisted she let him push her in a wheelchair to the hospital entrance. As Bria signed some paperwork, Paul wandered the foyer wondering what Val had meant by "Galen's vessel." It had to have something to do with pharmacy . . . but what? The amount of concentration he gave it was causing a headache to build behind his temples. Just past the admissions desk sat the hospital outpatient pharmacy. As Bria walked slowly toward him, Paul noticed a large plastic mortar and pestle positioned above the pharmacy door. It was almost identical to the one in Paul's pharmacy, except this one had the name *Galen* embossed on the bowl. Seeing it, a light sparked in Paul's mind. *Of course!* A pestle is a sturdy grinding bowl, or *vessel.* Val had left a perfect clue for Paul, as only a pharmacist would be able to connect the dots.

Arriving in Crescent Cove, Paul immediately went to the pharmacy with Bria and Sheriff Baker in tow. The two men used an extension ladder to look inside the faux mortar over his dispensary. And there it was: a small Ziploc bag with a high-load Lexar SD chip within. The chip contained several files, including the names of everyone in Crescent Cove ever affiliated with Pathway. Most of those listed had died or disappeared. Of those remaining, only Clem Bagley, Cliff Stevenson, two of the town's council members, and a few others still lived there. Even more revealing was that Mayor Harold Bright was on the list. In fact, Mayor Bright was further identified as the disgruntled ex-military researcher who had been dishonorably discharged for his alleged ties with foreign drug trafficking. To retain some anonymity at Pathway, the mayor went by the pseudonym of *the Light.* Since he was not found at Pathway during the siege, an immediate APB was issued on Harold Bright.

Much to Paul's surprise, Sheriff Baker was not on the list, but the lawman was only too happy to help round up those that were. The local arrests made the cover of the area newspapers, but somehow missed the attention of the national media. It was just as well. The small town of Crescent Cove did not vie for such attention. They wanted to remain a quaint community—unmolested by paparazzi, the overly curious, and the devastating effects of negative publicity.

Further downloading showed that the SD chip also contained records of the bizarre drugs manufactured in the pharmacy for Pathway and a list of financial links between Pathway and the multi-billion-dollar firm of Gulf Shore Investments. The Texas company claimed to be a support group only, and that they had no idea what went on at Pathway. It was later determined they had ties to militant groups in Northern Ireland and Turkey and had been selling them biological agents developed at Pathway.

* * *

The carotid artery implants were examined by a renowned vascular surgeon in Sacramento. The surgical removal was delicate, very risky, but doable. Everyone, including those guilty of the heinous crimes at Pathway, had their implant removed.

Bria submitted to numerous blood tests in an effort to determine what she had been "vaccinated" with. Pathway's documents simply listed the substance as SB-470. The chemical proved to be a bio-enhanced form of acetylcholine, one that not only prevented plaque buildup in the capillaries of the brain but also enhanced circulation to little-used areas of the cerebral cortex, including ocular and auditory faculties. Pathway's goal was to develop extra-perceptual abilities in common individuals. The chemical could not be tested on animals because of the inability to ascertain efficacy. With Bria, they had apparently almost struck gold.

As far as Bria could tell there were no ill effects from her ordeal, other than a lack of endurance. Bria's doctors reasoned that the new oxygenated pathways created in her cerebral capillaries were what caused her temporary amnesia and paralysis. Until her brain tissue had acclimated to the increased amount of oxygen and unusual chemicals, it had restricted blood flow to other areas of her head and body. Also noted in Pathway's charts were a number of patients who failed the same vaccination. It was determined that their particular vascular construct did not tolerate the new chemical. So why had Bria's? That was what Pathway wanted to find out.

Other researchers, too. When news of Bria's acceptance and unexpected reaction to the chemical was somehow leaked to the public, BioCraft, a biopharmaceutical company out of Thousand Oaks, California, offered her an obscene amount of money to continue the research—under legal parameters, of course. She summarily rejected their offer.

The other patients rescued from Pathway were transferred under pseudonyms and high security to various hospitals around the country. All were individuals with no family, no social ties. Most of them showed promise of recovery.

EPILOGUE

CRESCENT COVE, CALIFORNIA

The next few months were a blur of making it from one day to the next for both Paul and Bria. With numerous mysteries cleared up, the entire ordeal was still a jumble in their minds.

Paul had come to Crescent Cove to start a new life. Now it was Bria's turn. She had no desire to return to Marin or her old job at Mercy Children's Hospital. For the first time ever, her life included a man, possible romance, and a new career—working for a local family practitioner. Paul insisted she get an apartment so they could continue their courtship under proper auspices. He was so old-fashioned—Bria loved it. She loved everything about him. She also wanted to learn more about his religion, but there was no rush there. That was okay with Paul too. They had plenty of time.

* * *

Sitting in front of a cheery fire in his living room, with a cup of herbal tea in hand, Paul opened up to Bria regarding his deepest feelings about Debbie, about his conversion, and about his promptings to move to Crescent Cove. She, in turn, revealed her life's story in a depth that was shocking even to her.

"I'd like to think you were part of the reason the Lord wanted me here," Paul said.

"I'd like that too."

"But I still need time to heal," he said hesitantly. "I hope you're patient."

"And I hope you're patient with me as far as Mormonism is concerned."

"No pressure."

"Nor from me."

"Do you think this will work?"

Bria smiled as if amused and mystified at the same time. "It's strange, Paul, but somehow I *know* this will work."

Paul hesitated. "And the chemical in your bloodstream?"

She shrugged. "Not much anyone can do about that. Pathway never developed antidotes for their vaccines. But it *is* very nice having an ear for when someone is lying or not."

"Well, I hope that's all it does to you. I guess we'll find out down the road."

"Yeah, I guess we'll never know for sure what'll happen down *that* road."

He set his tea down and turned to her. "Bria, there's one thing you *can* be assured of," Paul said, cupping her face gently in both hands. "You won't travel that road alone."

"*We* won't travel it alone."

He kissed her tenderly. "*We* won't do anything alone. I promise."

About the Author

Gregg R. Luke was born in Bakersfield, California, but spent the majority of his childhood in Santa Barbara. He served an LDS mission in Wisconsin, then pursued his education in natural sciences at the University of California Santa Barbara and Brigham Young University. He completed his schooling at the University of Utah College of Pharmacy. His biggest loves are his family, the gospel, and science. His hobbies include reading, singing, and writing—which he has pursued since childhood. He currently practices pharmacy in Logan, Utah.